falling for gypsy
SWEET PEA RIDGE BOOK ONE

AMORA BLAKE

Cover Design by Lorissa Padilla Designs

Editing & Interior Formatting by Sarah Fraps Editorial Services

ISBN 979-8-218-45226-1 (paperback)

Visit the author's website at www.amorablake.com.

For all the beautiful people out there who feel undeserving.
You are enough.

lacey

"She ain't worth much o' nothin', but I reckon she'd be fittin' if ya cleaned 'er up a bit," the old man says. Brown juice wells up in his mouth from the wad of tobacco in his jaw, and he spits a streak of it onto the ground. Still yet, some dribbles down out of the corner of his mouth, and I stop myself from gagging as it disappears into his unkempt beard. "What's a lil' thing like you doin' lookin' fer a camper, anyways?" the old man asks, startling me out of the debate taking place in my head.

I turn back to him. He's eyeing my slender frame warily, and I'm not sure what he's thinking as he silently judges me. My long brown hair is pulled up in a messy bun, and I'm overly aware of my freckled complexion that I didn't bother trying to cover with makeup like I usually do. As he stares into my hazel eyes, I pray he can't see the anxiety pulsing through my veins.

"Are ya sure the ole man wouldn't rather be doin' the lookin' himself?"

Chills slide down my spine at the mention of a man in my life. No, I'm overreacting. He has no idea who I am. I open my mouth to speak, but nothing comes out. I clear my throat and try again.

"No, no man. I'm gonna be one of those travel bloggers," I lie. "You know, that travels around to all the different places and then writes about it."

The cold chills are replaced by fire sweeping over my skin, leaving me flushed. Hopefully, the light is too dim in the barn for him to see the evidence of my lie. Either way, he just grunts at me in reply and scratches his bearded chin with dirt-packed fingernails.

He slings open the door of the old camper. It clangs when it hits against the side of the camper, making me jump. The old man grunts as he steps aside, giving me access. My heart is beating hard, like it might pop right out of my chest. Wiping my sweaty palms on the sides of my pants, I take a deep breath to calm my nerves before stepping inside, flashlight in hand.

The camper's interior is dark and musty in the deteriorating evening sunlight. I shine the flashlight around, taking careful steps in case the floor is rotting away. There isn't much to see. He's right. It isn't worth much, but I can't pay much. I was only able to scrape together a few thousand dollars in the short time I had, and I need to make the most of it.

I step into the tiny kitchen and shine the flashlight over the stove, using two fingers to pull open the oven door whose hinges creak in protest. The stove and oven look decrepit, but the old man claims they still work. The brown remnants of food that have been spilled and burned onto them will have to be chiseled away before I'll be able to find out, though.

A tiny sink sits next to the stove, along with a countertop nearly as small. I spin around cautiously to the wooden bench and table that fill the greater area of the space. He says the small table can be folded away, but it will clearly need the help of some WD-40. Not wanting to inhale all of the dust and grime floating around in the air, I take another breath—this one shallower—and step deeper into the camper.

The flashlight in my hand illuminates the room on my right. It's a bathroom. Boxes of junk are stacked up over the toilet and in the shower. I move forward to the back of the camper, and my knees meet a wood platform where a mattress is supposed to go. Dusty shelving runs down one wall for a limited amount of storage.

Slowly making my way back out, my eyes bounce around to catch anything I may have missed my first time through. The grime inside this camper is unsettling. It'll be a challenge, mentally, overcoming the filth, even if I manage to scrub it all away, but I don't have any other options.

I can do this.

I have to make this work.

The old man continues studying me, his thumbs now hooked in the straps of his overalls. I look over the camper again. He's waiting for me to make a decision. Honestly, this will have to do. I haven't found anything else in my price range. I don't have much money saved up, and heaven knows, I can't wait any longer to save more. The seconds tick by. I need to leave town now.

"How much did you say?" I ask him as we step out of the barn.

"Oh, nothin' less 'en $2,000, I don't guess."

He's rubbing the back of his neck with one of his dirty hands, the other hand still looped in the strap of his overalls. He spits again into the grass, only feet away from us.

"It needs a lot of work. Barely livable as it is. I could probably find the likes of her down the road for $500."

"Ah, shoot. She's worth more 'en $500! Hell . . . I could get $500 down at the scrapyard!"

"Hardly! Anyway, $1,500 is all I've got."

I shrug at him and wait. I can see the wheels turning in his head. His pursed lips make it evident he doesn't like the way this conversation is going. After a few beats of silence, I turn and walk toward my truck.

"A'ight! A'ight! $1,500 and we call it a night," the man huffs.

I pull a big wad of cash out of the back pocket of my light-washed jeans and hand it over to him, leaving the additional $500 in my other pocket. I'm grateful I was able to talk him down on the price. Every bit helps.

"Darn young'uns don't know the value a nothin' these days . . ." he mutters under his breath as he counts out the money.

The last several months I've stowed away portions of my tips from each shift in an envelope, which was stuffed under the tracks of the bottom drawer in my dresser where he wouldn't find it.

"Y'even know how to hook up to yer pickup?" the man asks me, stuffing the wad of cash in the chest pocket of his bibbed overalls.

Shaking my head, I divert my eyes. I'm sure he thinks I'm helpless. I look helpless as I stand here nervously chewing my bottom lip. How embarrassing.

"I didn't reckon ya would. Don't know what business a lil' thang like you's got travelin' in a camper by 'erself, no ways. Well, go 'head. Back 'er up here, and I'll tell ya when."

I slide into the driver's seat of my old Chevy pickup and grip the wheel tightly with both hands, my knuckles turning white.

I've got this.

The engine revs to life when I turn the key over in the ignition. Twisting my body, with my right arm resting over the back of the bench seat for added leverage, I steer the truck in reverse while watching out the back windshield.

The taste of freedom entices a smile from me.

The clock on the dash reads 7:16. At this rate, I'll be long gone by daybreak, and he'll have no idea where I am. I climb out of the cab and join the old man at the rear of my truck.

"You said yer gonna be livin' in it?" the man asks me while showing me how to hook up the camper. "Where ya headed?"

I don't want to tell him.

I don't want to leave any more of a trail behind me than necessary, just in case someone comes asking around.

"On up the road, I suppose."

The old man grunts at me. He gives me a once-over, probably sizing up my chances of surviving on my own. Okay, I admit it. The odds aren't exactly looking in my favor at the moment. But he doesn't know my story. He doesn't know what staying would mean for me.

"Well, thanks, I guess," I say.

I give him a timid wave and slide back into the cab of my pickup, grateful to have that exchange over with. Pulling down on the gear shifter, I put the truck into drive. I've never pulled anything behind my truck, and I nervously chew on my lip again as I slowly take my foot off the brake and press the accelerator. My truck grumbles at the added weight but pulls down the tree-lined road.

I look back at the old man in my side mirror just in time to see him, standing in the same spot, spitting again without aiming this time. He turns and disappears behind the dark foliage of the trees as he walks back in the direction of his fading, rusted single-wide trailer.

I pull onto the two-lane highway, only a few miles from the old man's place. My pickup roars with the extra weight of the camper. Grumbling less once I get up to speed, the truck carries me away from my hometown nestled in the Appalachian Mountains.

I'm not sure where I'm headed, but I can't stay here. Simply existing makes people famous in a small town. There isn't room to breathe without someone having something to say about it. Even if I told my story, despite him being the one in the wrong, people are still going to take sides. I'd be shamed and treated with hostility, and I still wouldn't be safe. The only way to get away from him is to get away from that town.

My grandparents raised me. They're dead now, and I don't

have any other family. I have no reason to stay. Nothing is tying me to that town anymore.

The moon has replaced the sun now, as though the universe is trying to cover for me as I make my escape. It has an eerie reddish glow—a blood moon. I laugh because it couldn't be more appropriate.

Tired of letting him occupy my thoughts, I begin making a mental list of the things I need to buy. The camper needs some serious cleaning, not to mention a mattress for the bed and a stock of some dishes and food. Hopefully, with a touch of love and elbow grease, I'll be able to make a suitable home for myself. I don't know if this is gonna be my home for the next couple of months or the next couple of years.

I drive through the night and into the next day, the need to put miles between us the impetus to keep going. The familiar hills and trees of the Appalachians slowly give way, flattening out to open fields and clear views for miles as I cross into Kansas and up through the endless cornfields of Nebraska where a farmer, planting his field with the help of his young son, gives me pause. It's a simple yet wholesome scene that belongs on a wall somewhere, and I momentarily consider pulling off the road to sketch it. The urge disappears as quickly as it came, though, as I remember the threat that may be trailing behind me.

Does he know I'm gone yet? How long will I have to stay on the run? Will he try to find me? His words seldom suggested that he cares about me anymore. His actions only confirm his hostility and hatred.

I'm done settling.

I'm done being a victim.

I'm done giving him power over me.

jacob

Snapping on a pair of gloves, I enter the corral of sick goats. I'm about to examine them for suspected sore mouth virus, which can be transferable to humans. Goats haven't exactly been a favorite species of mine since my last vet conference. Catching sore mouth from one would only solidify my newfound disdain for them.

My contempt for the animal began about six months ago, when I walked down from my room at the annual veterinary conference I attend every year for my required continuing education. I wasn't sure what that day's beginning session was on because I had spilled water on my itinerary the night before. When I'd tried to unfold the dried program, the paper tore, leaving only the word *goat* for the first session. I walked into a deserted auditorium where a lady at the front of the room was setting out packets. She told me the first session was being held on the front lawn, so I headed outside.

It didn't surprise me to see goats when I stepped out the door. I figured they had a live demonstration planned for us, so it made sense to hold the session outside. Glancing around at the other attendants, confusion overtook me. Everyone was wearing athletic gear. I shifted on my feet, and a slight discomfort swept over me as I realized I'd overdressed for whatever we were about to do.

A small woman in matching neon leggings and sports bra walked to the front of the group and stood by a tub of rolled-up mats. The crowd of attendees naturally turned and gave her their attention.

"Welcome, everybody, we are going to go ahead and get started. If you will, come grab yourself a mat, and find a spot out on the lawn. Once everyone has a mat, I'll lead us into our first pose."

What?

I followed along and grabbed a mat, trusting the process and mistakenly chose a spot at the front. It wasn't until everyone had a mat that it hit me. *Yoga.* They had us doing fucking yoga at a veterinary convention.

"Let's start off in child's pose. Come to the back of your mat, spread your knees wide, and have your big toes touch," Yoga Woman said.

I stood there and looked around at everyone following her instructions to get into position. When I twisted forward again, Yoga Woman was standing at the head of my mat.

"You can kick your boots off and set them to the side," she said.

"I'm sorry, I don't think I'm supposed to be here," I told her.

"Are you an attendee of the vet conference happening here this weekend?"

"Yes."

"You're in the right spot, then. Take your boots off."

I looked around again at the people down on their knees with goats meandering around them. A couple of them were looking back at me expectantly. I reluctantly gave in and removed my boots, but I wasn't happy about it.

"Good," Yoga Woman said. "Foreheads to the mat, now."

A goat hopped up onto my back, and I cursed under my

breath, missing the next couple of instructions Yoga Woman gave.

"Left leg straight back and reach forward with your right hand."

The goat wobbled around on my back as I focused on holding the damn pose. Why the hell did I comply with this bullshit anyway? A *tap . . . tap . . . tap* pulled me from my thoughts, and I looked down in the direction of the noise to find little balls of shit falling from above me onto my mat. Yup. I got shit on by a fucking goat. Wasn't that par for the course in my life? Everybody shitting on Jacob.

The rest of the day passed in continuing education sessions, which was what I actually went to the conference for. Not fucking goat yoga. I swear, the things people come up with these days.

At the end of our sessions, we were dismissed for a buffet dinner and a meet and mingle. I don't care much for the mingling these days, but it's good to make connections. You never know when they may come in handy. I headed to the open bar for a whiskey, hoping it would lighten my mood. Just when I thought it was starting to help, her laughter rang in my ears.

Damn, I loved her laugh.

I spun around and was immediately assaulted by my not-so-distant past. She stood there in a tight black dress, hanging on *his* arm—the arm of the man she cheated on me with. She hadn't noticed me yet; at least, she didn't look my way. They were talking to another man seated at the table they were standing next to. I watched them, frozen, and heard her tell the man at the table that they were living together now.

Only a month had passed since she'd last slept in my bed, and she was already sleeping in another man's bed. Even though it had been my decision to break off our engagement, seeing her like that on another man's arm made our breakup hit me like it hadn't hit me yet, slamming me down into reality. My world wasn't mine anymore, and the last still-whole part of me crumbled away. I shoved my whiskey into the hand of an unsuspecting passerby and left the conference.

Staying busy with work has been the one thing I can rely on to keep my head straight. Maybe the goats weren't the worst part of that conference after all, I decide as I take hold of the first goat, ready to get this appointment over with, and inspect her mouth. Immediately, I find the telltale sign of sore mouth—her mouth and muzzle are covered in sores and scabs. I move on, checking each of the goats that have been sectioned off.

"Not much to do for it," I tell the old farmer. "Just make sure to keep the sick goats separate from the healthy goats, and check the healthy ones regularly for symptoms. It should run its course in about a month. If any of the lesions start looking infected, rub them with some iodine."

I sanitize my hands and get back in my truck. Damn goats. I could go the rest of my life without laying eyes on another one, and I wouldn't lose any sleep over it.

lacey

The hum and honking of traffic gradually grows louder, accompanied by the crashing of grocery carts as they're being gathered in the parking lot I stopped to rest in. Gradually, I begin to come to. My mind, still groggy from my nap, is slow to process my surroundings. It's darker in the camper than it was when I laid down. Quite darker. I try to stretch out the soreness from my body and sit up, not having the mental capacity yet to make my body stand. The watch on my wrist shows I slept for six hours.

I force my body up, trying to shake off the last remnants of sleep. I hadn't meant to sleep so long. Sure, the chances of being found at this point are slim, but I want as many miles behind me as possible before I slow down.

Trying to get my bearings, I stumble a little as I walk to the front of the camper to lock it up and then slide into the cab of my truck. I grab my fully charged phone purchased only this afternoon and load the minutes onto it. He made me get rid of my cellphone long ago, his excuse being that the landline hanging on the kitchen wall was sufficient, though he was never wild about those long-distance charges from me talking to my best friend, Jalynn. It wasn't long before it became easier to stop calling her than to set him off and give him one more thing to explode over.

Just the same, I don't have to look up Jalynn's number, despite the months that have passed since I've talked to her. I know it by heart. As the phone rings, I look at the clock on the dash. It's only about seven o'clock her time.

"Hello?" Jalynn's familiar voice replaces the ringing.

"Jalynn! This is Lacey."

"Lacey? Hmmm, I don't think I know a Lacey."

"Jay—"

"I'm teasing, but gosh, Lacey, it's been ages since we've talked. Where have you been? Have you found a wedding dress yet? I talked to Lizzy the other day. You remember Lizzy who moved to Florida in high school? She said she was back in town visiting her aunt Irma, and she heard you and Ben finally set a wedding date! I'm telling you what, it's not right that I've been having to get all of my information about my best friend from third parties, instead of straight from the source. I've missed talking to you."

"I've missed talking to you, too! And about the wedding"— I pause to take in a deep breath—"it's off. I bought a camper instead."

"What? You bought a camper? For heaven's sake, what are you talking about? And what does that have to do with your wedding? I'm so confused. Have you lost your mind?"

"Maybe. Or maybe I'm trying to keep from losing it."

"Lacey, what's going on? Why haven't you returned any of my phone calls? Are you mad at me for something? You running from the law?" Jalynn asks with a fabricated chuckle, but I can tell she isn't totally sure that's too off base.

"Jay, you know my dumpster-fire-starting days began and ended with you," I joke, referencing an unfortunate event from years ago. Thankfully, a case of beer was enough to get old Harold Thompson to turn a blind eye, and the culprit was never apprehended. "I'm not running from the law. And I'm not mad at you, either. Look, it's a long story, but it ends with me and Ben not getting married."

Jalynn listens as I give her the CliffsNotes version of the last twenty-four hours of events, but I don't tell her the worst of it. I can't speak the words. She'll be on my side as always, but she tried over and over again to get me to leave, and I chose every time to stay. I can't complain to her about getting what I deserved.

"So let me get this straight. You snuck off in the middle of the night, pulling some hunk-of-junk camper that you bought with your wedding dress money with that old hunk-of-junk pickup your granddaddy left you. You don't have any clue where you are going, what you are doing, or even anything else in between?"

"Yup. That's pretty much the gist of it."

"Bless your heart. Girl, this isn't going to work. You have indeed gone mad."

"What do you mean?" I ask defensively. She is supposed to be my person. She, out of everyone, should be the one to have my back. I've finally left, just like she told me to do for years. "I couldn't stay with him. Not like that. You know I couldn't have."

"I know that. I'm not saying you shouldn't have left. In fact, I'm proud of you for leaving him. I'm just saying you're gonna have to put down roots somewhere. At least long enough to earn some money from time to time so you can support yourself."

Silence fills the line.

"Why didn't you call me?" Jalynn asks with an unusual sadness replacing her typically joyful tone. She quickly slips out of it and answers her own question. "Probably because you knew I'd tell you to buy a plane ticket to come see me instead of spending your money on an old camper."

"I don't know where to go," I admit. "I was too busy

thinking about leaving to think about where I would go once I finally got away."

"Oh, honey, that part's easy. You're going to figure out where you are, and you're going to turn that rolling junk heap in whatever direction necessary to roll it on up here to Montana. Our town's not all that much bigger, but it's nothing like back home in the holler. You can put that thing somewhere and call it home until you find a job and can afford to get a real place. Or just sell it all to the first dummy to take the bait and catch a flight up here. You can stay with us as long as you need. We have plenty of space. Not that you would know since you let that plane ticket I bought you go to waste instead of coming to see me after we got settled in up here. But George finally got our spare bedroom cleaned out, and we painted it and fixed it up real smart. You'll love it."

"I can't come there, Jay. Of all the places I go, I can't come there. You know that will be the first place he looks."

"Assuming he looks at all," Jalynn says with a judgmental tone, though I know it isn't directed at me. "So what's the plan? How can I help?"

"I don't know. I'm in South Dakota now, not far from the border. Maybe I'll start by seeing what the Dakotas have to offer. What do you think?"

"I think you are absolutely bonkers."

"Maybe. But it's good for the soul to do stupid shit every now and again."

I CHASE the last cold ravioli around the can with my fork. It doesn't want to come off the side. Finally, I coax it off and carefully balance it on the fork from the can to my mouth, trying not to drop it on myself and leave a big stain on my shirt. It's not the most satisfying lunch I've ever eaten, but it will do.

Like Jalynn said yesterday on the phone, I need to come up

with a plan. I can't afford to float around endlessly, and I'm going to run out of money sooner than later, especially if I don't find a place to park my old gas guzzler.

I stare out at the buttes here in South Dakota. They sure are beautiful. This doesn't seem like a bad place to land. At the same time, it doesn't hold anything for me. Nowhere does anymore.

Maybe I was too quick to leave, to walk away from so many years with him.

Things would be better if he quit drinking. Alcohol was his way of dealing with the pain, and I should've done more—been more—for him. I should've tried harder to help him quit. I was selfish. Weak. If I'd been a better girlfriend, he would've been better, too. This wasn't all on him. I played my own part in it.

My teeth chew at the skin on my bottom lip as I drift away from the buttes ahead of me and back to a couple of days ago when I left him.

The front door slammed shut, rattling the house. I pushed my bedroom curtains ever so slightly to the side, exposing enough of a sliver of the window for me to see him stomp down the wobbly wooden steps of our small deck. Too anxious over what was to come to sit still, I rubbed my free hand up and down the jean fabric on my thigh. Acid burned at my throat, rising from my churning stomach, and I thought for a moment that I might vomit. I needed to see him go, though. When I saw him climb into his old beater car, I let the curtains close again and forced my lungs to suck in a deep breath of air to steel my nerves.

Maybe I should wait. Maybe I was moving too quickly. Surely he didn't mean it. He wouldn't. Would he? This was my chance, though. I needed to make the most of it.

The gravel outside crunched and popped as he pulled away, and a sadness washed over me. I would never get the closure of an actual goodbye. I shared years of my life with him, and just like that, it was over. Warm tears ran down my cheeks as I mourned both the good and the bad I'd had with him. I wiped my damp cheeks dry again and tried to blink away the remaining tears blurring my sight. No, I couldn't wait any longer. It had to be now. I pushed myself off the wall and grabbed my suitcases from under the bed, filling them quickly with my clothes and things I couldn't bear to leave behind. It would have to do. This was my chance to get away.

My phone buzzes in my pocket, bringing me back to the present and alerting me to a phone call. I slide it out and look at the screen. I don't know why I bother looking to see who it is. Only one person has my number: Jalynn.

"Lacey," Jalynn says when I answer, "I know you already said no to Montana, but I'm calling you to tell you that's a mistake, honey."

"Jay—"

"Now listen to me. I thought this through last night. Ben still has control over you as long as you are making your decisions based on him. Don't give him that power. We can help you but only if you let us. Don't let him win this."

"What if he finds me, Jay?"

"What if he does? What's he going to do, anyway? You're not a piece of property, Lacey. He can't just come in here and take you away against your will. And I'll be damned if he is going to lay a finger on you. You're safe here."

The buzz of traffic rushing by fills the line while I mull over what she said.

"What if I do come up there? What then?"

"You start over. You can make a life here just as well as anywhere else. Maybe even better since you already know me and George. Plus, we'd love to have you close by again. If you want, I can get a job interview lined up for you. I just talked to Mrs. Jones today down at our local flower shop. She needs full-time help. I think it would be perfect for you."

"I don't know . . ." I pick at the loose threads hanging from a rip in my jeans.

"You trust me, don't you?"

"Of course I do."

"Then give it a try. If you get up here and decide it was a bad idea, I'll help you figure out where to go next."

I sit silently, holding the phone to my ear. It's time to make a decision.

"Come on, now. Tell me you're on your way," Jalynn says.

I want to say yes. I want to go to Jalynn and be with my bestie again, but I don't know what to do. Is that the right choice? Or did I give up on him too soon? Maybe I'm better off going home. There'll be no denying I left if I go back. I'll surely have to face the consequences of leaving, but maybe it's not too late for us. Maybe I can help him get better. My feelings were hurt when I found out about his affair. My judgment may have been clouded when I decided to leave. I remember the first time I told him I was leaving, and the memory washes over me, over-taking my senses.

"You're nothing but a big bully, Ben!" I yelled at him. "I'm sick of taking your crap, and I'm not doing it anymore. You can't hold me here."

Ben pushed me back down into my chair and leaned down in my face.

"You're not leaving," he said firmly.

"Get off me!" I pushed him away. He stumbled backward, and I stood from my chair and started grabbing up my suitcases. He rushed back toward me after finding his footing and wrapped his arms around my waist, pulling me tightly against him.

"The only way you're leaving here is in a pine box," he spit out into my ear.

My blood ran cold as the threat echoed in my mind, and when he released me, I fell onto my knees. My fingernails dug into the fibers of the carpet as I held on to the last minute shred of hope I had left.

"Lacey!" Jalynn's voice booms through the speaker of the phone, pulling me out of my head. "Tell me you'll come to Montana."

I inhale deeply, still feeling the ice course through me from my memories.

No, I already have the answer.

I know what I need to do.

"Okay," I finally concede. "I'll come. But for the record, I'm keeping my camper."

CHAPTER FOUR

The gravel of Jalynn's driveway crunches loudly under the tires of my truck as I pull up to the little gray ranch-style house. Blue skies hang over the flat, open land. A barbed wire fence runs through the field on the right, and a single shade tree looms above the house from the backyard. As I climb out of the truck the front door of the house is flung open and Jalynn comes barreling off the porch and into my arms.

"You made it!" Jalynn says too loudly in my ear as she squeezes me.

I squeeze her back and rock us back and forth, unable to contain the joy exuding from me over our overdue reunion.

"It's been too long!" I remark, still not letting go. "It's beautiful out here, by the way. No wonder you deserted me."

"You're here now, and that's all that matters!" Jalynn says. She pulls back and looks me over as if she can't believe I'm actually here. "We'll figure out what to do with your camper later. I want you to stay here with us for now."

"I couldn't—" I say as Jalynn pulls me by a clasped hand toward the house.

"Oh, Lacey, it's still so cold out at night. You will freeze in that old camper. It's not reasonable up here this time of year," Jalynn says over her shoulder to me.

"I kinda like being in the camper. It's cozy. And it does have a heater. All I need is a good place to park it and to find myself a job."

"Speaking of jobs," Jalynn says, "I got that job interview lined up for this afternoon like you asked me to. After you get freshened up, we can head into town."

"You're the best! Thank you for setting that up. It'll make me feel so much better once I know I have a job."

"I'm sure. And this one will be perfect for you. I'm just glad that I happen to know the owner and knew that she was looking for help. You're gonna love her floral shop. I swear, this job was meant for you. It's almost as though the universe knew you were coming," Jalynn says, her free hand waving animatedly as she talks.

Finally, she lets my hand loose to open the front door. I step inside, seeing my friend's home for the first time.

"It does sound like a nice idea. I wouldn't mind a change from waitressing, either," I agree, my eyes scanning over the living room, the inviting essence of the place pulling me in. The house isn't large or fancy, but I notice the peace that washes through me. It's a home built with love. I follow Jalynn through the open living room to the kitchen, where she pulls open the fridge door and offers me a bottle of water. It's just a cold bottle of water from the fridge, but it's also one more reminder of how differently our lives have played out so far. "Where's George?"

"He's out on the ranch somewhere. He'll be back in time for dinner," Jalynn says, pulling a skillet of corn bread out of the oven. "I've got a stew cooking as we speak. He was pretty excited when I told him you were coming to stay for a while."

"It's gonna feel an awful lot like old times," I say, following Jalynn when she heads down the hallway from the kitchen.

"Like old times for a while at least . . . until the baby's born," Jalynn says with a sly grin, stopping at an open door and motioning for me to look inside.

"No way! You're pregnant?"

"We just found out. You're the first to know. We're waiting to announce it, so you'll have to keep it a secret for now."

"I'm so happy for you guys!" I say, wrapping Jalynn tightly in a hug. We walk into the room she's already started redecorating for a nursery. The walls are painted in a soft neutral beige, and a crib still in the box and a pile of new nursery décor sit in a corner, clearly the start of a boho-themed nursery.

"Thanks. I'm so glad you're going to be here for it," Jalynn says and motions to the neatly folded towel sitting on the foot of the full-size bed in the room. "Here's a towel. You can get cleaned up, and I'll just be waiting out in the living room for you when you're all done," Jalynn says, flipping on the light in the bathroom, then heading back down the hall.

I COMB the tangles out of my hair and switch on the blow dryer after the much-needed shower. Once I have my hair done and makeup on, hopefully I'll feel ready to interview for a new job. Nervous butterflies are already fluttering around, doing fancy fighter jet tricks in my stomach. I hope this interview ends up being everything Jalynn suggests it will be and that I do get the job.

Waitressing isn't bad, and I've always made decent tips, but I've been waitressing since high school. It would be nice to finally have a change, especially a full-time job without late-night hours.

I pull clothes out of my suitcase, searching for a suitable outfit. I'm not sure how formal this interview is supposed to be, and that makes it more difficult to decide what to wear. After several minutes of debate, I finally settle on a brightly colored, knee-length floral dress with a gathered waistline and blush pink flats. I inspect my outfit again and wander down the hall in search of Jalynn. She's in the kitchen checking the stew.

"Are you ready to go?" Jalynn asks, looking up from the crockpot.

"As ready as I'm gonna be, I guess. I don't have a résumé. Think I need one?"

"Eh." Jalynn waves off my concern. "I'm as good as some fancy résumé with Mrs. Jones. You'll be fine."

Jalynn picks up her purse and keys and motions for me to follow her.

"I'll drive," she says.

I climb into the passenger seat of Jalynn's SUV and buckle my seatbelt. It feels like old times again. Jalynn was almost always the driver when we went somewhere together. Once the car is started, I get to work fulfilling the unspoken yet dire responsibility of the shotgun rider . . . I handle the music.

We ride with the windows rolled down, belting out the words to our favorite songs since high school. In this moment, I don't care if my hair is wind-blown and tangled for my interview. I know I should, but I can't put off this cruise down memory lane. It's too good to postpone. Reba leads into the chorus of "You Lie," and my mind drifts back to North Carolina.

Our voices belt out, together with Reba McEntire's voice ringing through the speakers of Jalynn's coupe. Ben and I had another fight, so Jalynn and I grabbed some snacks from the gas station and hit the backroads to help me get out of my head. Our childhood wasn't one filled with movie theaters and bowling alleys. We didn't have any of that in our town. We were left up to our own devices to entertain ourselves, which frankly was probably the cause of a lot of the trouble we found ourselves in.

"Where does this road go?" Jalynn asked me, pointing to the road up ahead.

"I have no clue. Let's find out," I said with a shrug.

Jalynn whipped the car down the unknown road. I pulled my hair up into a ponytail, tired of it whipping against my face as the wind blew into the car but enjoying the fresh air too much to roll up the window. The sun shined down, kissing my arm that hung out the car window as we cruised down the road.

"Jay . . ."

"Yeah?"

"I've got to pee."

Jalynn pulled up the gravel driveway of a tiny white country church. We both got out of the car to stretch our legs. Jalynn meandered over to the graveyard to read the headstones while I looped around the back of the church, looking for a good spot to pop a squat.

I glanced around me again to make sure the coast was clear. Satisfied with the location I'd scouted, I dropped my drawers. Mid-stream, a buzzing began to circle my head. Followed by another and another.

"Ouch!" Burning pain radiated from a sharp pinch on my left ass cheek.

Bees.

I pinched off the draining of my bladder and took off running around the church, trying to pull up my pants as I ran, hooting and hollering for Jalynn to get back to the car. She was already starting the car back up when I swung around the front corner of the church and went barreling full speed for the passenger seat.

"Go! Go! Go!" I yelled, only halfway in the vehicle.

Jalynn didn't ask any questions. She laid her lead foot down on the gas pedal and slung gravel behind us as we fishtailed out of the driveway and back onto the road.

"Look over there." Jalynn points out through the windshield, bringing me back to Montana. "You don't see that very often back home, huh?"

We pass a herd of buffalo grazing in an open field. The Montana landscape is beautiful, and I admire the view on our way into town. Broad fields roll out, one after the other, separated by fences meant to subdue the livestock. Astounding mountains stand supreme as the backdrop to this breathtaking view.

"Gosh, I'm sorry, Lacey," Jalynn says moments later, keeping her eyes fixed on the road ahead of us.

"Sorry for what?" I ask, bewildered by her random outburst.

I turn to look at Jalynn, searching her face and finding it riddled with guilt.

"I'm such a dreadful friend. I should have realized what was going on. How did a miss what a nasty piece of work Ben is? When y'all finally broke up, I shouldn't have let you go back to him. It's no wonder you didn't confide in me. There you were, dealing with all of that, and I was too wrapped up in myself, marrying George, and running away to Montana. I should have noticed. If I hadn't been so selfish, maybe I would have seen the signs and been able to help you—"

"Jay, stop. Don't do this. It's not your fault. Honestly, it was no secret how much you hated Ben. You'd been trying to get me to break up with him since we graduated high school. There's nothing more you could've done. You were there for me every time I needed you."

"Yeah, but . . ." Jalynn paused momentarily, struggling to form the words. "He hurt you. I thought he was just a colossal ass, but he was hurting you. And I had no idea."

"No, he was a colossal ass. And you didn't miss anything." Jalynn glances over at me and quickly returns her eyes to the road. "He . . . he hit me for the first time a couple months ago. He's always been a manipulative shithead with a horrible temper, but . . . you didn't miss anything. And you're here for me now."

Jalynn reaches over and grabs my hand in hers, squeezing it tightly. I squeeze her hand in return, then pull away, reaching to turn the volume on the radio back up. I change the song to another old favorite of ours, officially ending the conversation.

After about twenty minutes, we roll up to a four-way stop that appears to be at the center of town. The cutest park and town square, like one from the movies, sits to the right of us, with a bakery and coffee shop next to it. Jalynn turns left, putting the church with a tall white steeple and beautiful stained-glass windows on the corner lot to our left and a little diner on the corner lot to our right now. We pass a hair salon next to the church, and Jalynn pulls up in front of a shop that looks like it's straight out of a storybook. Underneath the blue- and white-striped awning, pink climbing roses form an arch over the front door of the shop. Stands holding buckets of fresh bouquets sit out on the sidewalk, and a chalkboard sign advertises the special of the day.

Frankly, the whole town is picturesque, but the flower shop is the icing on the cake. I have a feeling I'm going to be very happy here. I've always dreamed of traveling to new places. That dream is finally coming true.

The jingle of little bells announces our arrival as we walk in the door of the flower shop. Inside, a display of bright, beautiful flowers and shiny ribbons decorates the room. A white wicker loveseat, coffee table, and two matching chairs sit off to the left of the room with books and magazines of flowers spread out for browsing. On the wall behind the register hangs delicate floral prints in distressed white frames.

"Hello, Jalynn, dear," a bright-eyed woman welcomes us as she enters the front of the store from a door next to the checkout counter.

Her graying brown hair is pulled up in a French twist on the back of her head. A few curly flyaway strands hang loose on the sides of her face. She wears a green apron over her blue jeans and a soft yellow blouse.

"Hi, Mrs. Jones. Your shop looks as splendid as ever. No one would believe you're short on help . . . Speaking of which, this is my friend Lacey that I was telling you about. She just got here this afternoon and is anxious to get to work somewhere."

"Hello, Lacey," Mrs. Jones says, coming around the counter and reaching out to shake my hand. "Welcome to our little town. Jalynn has given you quite the recommendation!"

"You probably know how she's inclined to exaggerate, but I do need a job, and I've always dreamed of working in a shop like yours."

I take Mrs. Jones's offered hand and firmly shake it, hoping if I try hard enough to fake being calm and gathered, my nerves will follow suit.

"Why don't we have a seat over here"—Mrs. Jones motions to the wicker furniture off to the side—"and have a chat?"

"While you do that," Jalynn interjects, "I'm gonna run down to the post office real quick. I'll be back in a jiff."

Jalynn scurries out the door and the bells jingle, dismissing her. I follow Mrs. Jones to the wicker set and take a seat on one of the chairs as she sits on the loveseat. Mrs. Jones begins telling me about the position she has available. I try to focus on what she's saying, but my nerves keep dancing around, making it difficult to absorb her words.

I did catch enough to know that if given the position, I'd primarily hold the responsibility of working the front of the shop. I'd take orders and payments from customers and handle the nightly bank deposits. If time permits, Mrs. Jones might use me in the back, making arrangements to fill the orders we take and preparing stock that needs to be delivered to the other location in the city.

Mrs. Jones switches gears and starts asking me an array of questions about my background. I answer her as politely as possible without getting into too many dirty details. It strikes me as odd that her questions are more general, like she is trying to get to know me rather than gather my work experience.

"I don't believe Jalynn exaggerated at all in her description of you, Lacey," Mrs. Jones says. She stands up, indicating that our chat is now over. "I think we could get along just fine. How long do you need to get settled in before you start work?"

"You mean, you're offering me the job?" I ask, following her lead and standing, too.

"Dear, the job is yours. Frankly, it was yours when Jalynn called me. I just wanted to meet you more as a formality than anything," Mrs. Jones says with a genuine smile. "I know Jalynn to be a pretty good judge of character."

"Thank you! I can start as soon as tomorrow if you'd like."

"Then tomorrow it is. We open at ten. I'd like you here about thirty minutes early to help me get everything set up and ready for the day."

"Great! Thank you so much." I shake Mrs. Jones's hand again and make my exit before I can do something to screw it up.

Life isn't supposed to go this smoothly. It never has. It's almost as though I've slipped into another dimension or onto a movie set where dreams come true. If this is typical of life in Montana, I'm here for it.

I glance up and down the street, unsure of which direction Jalynn went. Across the street is a feed store and a doctor's office, then the diner on the corner. Deciding to head right, I turn toward the town square. I make the mistake of looking through the window of the hair salon as I walk by and see several sets of eyes watching me. Quickly, I look away and quicken my step to hurry out of their line of sight. I may be the pretty new toy in town, but I'd prefer to make it longer than a day before I make the town gossip mill. Without slowing down, I walk by the church and step down into the road to cross over to the town square.

A flash of red from the middle of the intersection catches in my peripheral vision. Realization hits, and instead of getting out of the way, my feet turn to stone. I throw my hands up between me and my assailant to brace myself for impact, as though that will actually make any difference. The red mass jolts to a stop about five feet away from me, and I turn to face it head-on. I stare into the cab of the red pickup truck. Electricity pulses through my body as my gaze meets the eyes of a very attractive man.

His T-shirt pulls tight over his muscular chest, and the sleeves bunch ever so slightly over his biceps. His sharp jaw wears a dark stubble that matches the hair mostly hidden by the gray, worn baseball cap he wears.

He reciprocates my stare, and I wonder if he is feeling it, too. He could've killed me if he'd run me over with his truck, but I don't even care in this moment. My stomach is doing somersaults, and tingles run down my spine. My limbs feel detached from my body. He's as still as I am, just looking at me. Maybe he's also as entranced as I am.

My breath catches with anticipation when finally he makes a move. Releasing his previously white-knuckled grip on the steering wheel, his hand drifts over and—

Really?

His truck horn blares at me, startling me out of my reverie.

What an ass.

With all of the grace of the Southern belle I am, I wipe my face clean of the annoyance he sprouted in me and replace it with a sweet smile. Without skipping a beat, I flip him off and walk away, finally making it to the town square. His truck revs as he speeds down the road, but I don't give him the satisfaction of turning around to look at him again. I keep walking until I can no longer hear the roar of his truck.

"Lacey!"

My name is called out from the other side of the street, across from the bakery, where Jalynn's SUV sits in front of the post office, which is next to the library. I jaywalk across the street, this time pausing to check for traffic before crossing.

"Did you see that?" I ask Jalynn, still reeling from the close call I just had moments ago in the street.

"See what?" Jalynn asks, carrying a stack of mail in her hand.

"That truck! He nearly turned me into roadkill, and then he honked at me like it was my fault! The nerve . . ."

"I must have missed it. Are you okay?"

"Yeah, I'm fine. Just shook up."

"How did the interview go?" Jalynn asks.

"I owe you! I start tomorrow."

"I knew you could get that job! It's perfect for you. And you are going to love Mrs. Jones. She's a sweetheart and a half." Jalynn hugs me with excitement.

"I can hardly take any credit. It was all you. She even said she'd already decided to give me the job before she even met me," I say, heading to the passenger side of her car.

"Well, I don't care how you got the job. You're gonna do great. Let's hurry home. George should be home soon, and I know he's excited to see you."

We climb back into Jalynn's SUV and head to her house.

Sure enough, George's white pickup is next to my camper. Jalynn parks behind George's truck. We hurry inside and find a freshly showered George leaning over the crockpot in the kitchen, picking at the stew.

"Aha! I caught you red-handed!" Jalynn calls out, pointing a finger at him.

George throws up his hands and steps backward away from the crockpot, feigned guilt covering his face.

"I can't help it. You're starving me, woman."

Jalynn and I giggle. George drops his hands and walks toward me, a grin stretched across his face. Without hesitation, he wraps his arms around me, tottering us from side to side. His touch catches me off guard at first, throwing up warning bells, but I remind myself that it's George, and the sirens slowly begin to quiet.

"And how are you, little Lacey? We've missed you."

"The Three Stooges reunited at last," I say, breaking free from him, my nerves still rattled.

Having reunited with my friends and with the start of a new job in the morning, fresh hope springs up inside of me. Life is finally looking up.

AFTER DINNER IS EATEN and cleaned up, and a few hours of catching up with my besties, I finally get ready for bed. Exhaustion snuck up on me, and I can't wait to slide under the covers.

I forgot how good it felt being with these two. I wash the makeup off my face and change into pajamas. Jalynn wouldn't let up till I finally agreed to stay with them tonight. It's just for one night, though. Tomorrow, I'm gonna claim a spot for my camper and get settled in.

Jalynn has always been the worrier between the two of us. She's always reminded me of a mother hen, where the people she cares about most are her little chicks to protect and watch over. I know she's especially worried about me right now, but I also know that I can't go from depending on Ben to depending on Jalynn. It's time for me to have faith in myself and prove to myself that I can do this.

Under the covers, I curl up on my side, feeling more satisfied and content than I have in years. I don't think I could wipe this smile off my face if I tried. I fall asleep while the happy memories of home swirl in my head.

I slid into a desk near the middle of the classroom as Jalynn plopped down in an empty seat next to me. Excited chatter filled the room. A gray-haired teacher stood in the front of the classroom writing her name on the chalkboard.

"I can't believe we're juniors this year!" Jalynn squealed next to me. "This is gonna be our best year yet! I can feel it." Jalynn leaned across her desk and lowered her voice to a whisper. She wore a mischievous grin on her face. "And don't look

now, but guess who is sitting across the room, drooling over
you . . ."

My body stiffened at the suggestion of someone watching me.
The hope of it being my crush from last year popped into my head.
I leaned in toward Jalynn to further discuss the urgent matter.

"Who? Where? Who is it?"

"Benjamin Tolley!" Jalynn practically purred his name.

"Don't tease me like that, Jay!" The heat of a blush spread
across my cheeks at the mention of my crush's name.

"I'm not teasing you, honey. Count to five, then look to your
left, and see for yourself."

"One . . ." I counted silently, reminding myself to breathe as I
continued. "Two . . . three . . . four . . . five!"

I casually scanned the classroom to my left till my eyes locked
with Ben's. He grinned, slouched back in his seat with his legs
extended forward, and gave me a wink. My skin burned as a
blush spread over my face again. I mustered up the courage to give
him a little wave, then turned back to Jalynn.

"Told you!" Jalynn sang as the teacher closed the door and
called the students to attention with roll call.

At the end of class, Jalynn was chattering about how we
should spend the rest of the afternoon while we packed up our
books to leave. I turned to slide out of my desk to find a pair of
boots standing next to me. My eyes slid up the figure looming over
me. Ben.

"Hey, Lacey," Ben said with a nod.

"Hey, Ben."

I stood and slung my backpack over my shoulder, but I didn't
walk away.

"How was your summer?" he asked me and shoved his hands
deep into the pockets of his jeans.

"It was good. Yours?"

"Uh, yeah. It was good, too."

"Cool."

"Cool."

Gah, we were so awkward.

"Well, I guess I'll see you tomorrow," Ben said and started to turn away.

"Ben," Jalynn interjected, "we were just talking about heading down to the river for a bit. You wanna come?"

"Sure." Ben perked back up.

"Good. Lacey can ride with you. My car's already full," Jalynn said and nudged me.

"Oh. Okay. That's perfect."

CHAPTER FIVE

I storm out of the hardware store, not even bothering to make the purchases I came for. I need to get out of here. My strides lengthen in my effort to escape the *click . . . click . . . click* of high heels following behind me.

"Jacob, wait."

I spin around to confront my pursuer, clenching and unclenching my fists at my sides, frustration and anger vying to escape.

"How did you even find me, Ashley? Did you track my location on your phone?"

"I might have glanced at it," she admits, "but you wouldn't answer my calls."

"There's a reason for that. I didn't want to talk to you, damn it." I turn again and close the remaining gap between me and my pickup.

"You'll have to talk to me about this eventually," Ashley calls after me as I climb inside and put the truck into gear.

"Don't fucking count on it."

I hit the gas too abruptly, and the truck lurches forward. I swing it around now and unintentionally squeal the tires as I pull out onto the road. I can't be near her. After three years with that woman, even three minutes is three minutes too long.

I make a rolling stop at the intersection while turning off the location on my cellphone, because I don't need this woman following me to my next appointment. I haven't raised my eyes back up to the road when I'm already hitting the gas pedal.

Shit!

My phone goes flying as both of my hands grab hold of the steering wheel, and I slam on the brakes, my balls in my throat. I was too busy looking at my phone to see the woman in front of me step out into the road. My truck skids to a stop, mere feet away from her. If I'd been hauling a trailer, this story would've ended differently.

When she turns and faces my truck, I watch the fear melt off her face as she overtakes me with a Medusa-like power, and I just sit here staring back into those big eyes. Who is this woman, and where did she come from? My mouth goes dry and goose-bumps break out on my arms.

I'm not sure how much time passes, but finally, I come to again and remember I was in the middle of fleeing from my ex. The rage is gone, but a nervous anticipation replaces it. Is she going to move out of the way?

I let go of the steering wheel and give the horn a light push. The honk startles her, but she promptly recovers and smiles at me. She is stunning.

And now she's flipping me the bird.

Okay. I deserve that.

She steps out of the way, and I speed down the road, watching her till she disappears from my mirrors. Shaking the image of her out of my head, I plow down the road, away from town. The last thing I need is another woman on my mind.

THE FOLLOWING EVENING, after several taps on the front door, I make my way over to open it and let Ashley inside. I've been avoiding her for three days now, and unfortunately, she doesn't seem to be getting the hint. Her determination finally wore me down, and I agreed to talk to her.

Ashley saunters through the door with a bottle of wine in one hand and drags the fingertips of her other hand across my chest as she walks by me, a sultry smile on her lips. She's wearing one of those little dresses she always wears . . . the ones that effortlessly bring every part of me to attention. Without a word, she heads to the kitchen and pulls two wineglasses out of the cupboard as if this is still her kitchen, too. I follow behind her and put one of the glasses away, keeping her from pouring me some of her shitty wine.

Instead, I pull out a lowball glass and pour myself some of the Gentleman Jack on the counter. I know she's annoyed by it, but I don't care. She can drink her wine, and I'll drink my whiskey neat.

Her footsteps follow me into the living room where I sit down on one of the chairs. I lean back and take a sip. Ashley sets the open bottle of wine on the coffee table and sits down on the couch, crossing her long legs. She swirls the glass of wine in her hand as though she's some sort of wine connoisseur. I shouldn't care, but it pisses me the fuck off.

"Why are you back here? We broke up seven months ago, and last I heard, you've been living with him for the last six," I finally ask, breaking the silence.

"I want to be with you, Jacob," Ashley says, scooting forward in her seat and setting her glass of wine down. "I was only staying with him because I had nowhere else to go. He was a friend with a spare bedroom. That's all." Ashley wrings her hands, sitting atop her crossed knees. "We should have never broken up. I promise you it's not what you thought it was." She pauses briefly, waiting for me to tell her I forgive her, no doubt. When I don't, she continues. "You overreacted, and I never got a chance to tell you what actually happened." She stares across the coffee table at me, her round eyes full of regret.

"Ashley, I came home early from my camping trip and found you sending pictures of yourself in skimpy lingerie to another man. What do you mean it's not what I thought it was?" I speak with slow, controlled words.

My anger begins to flair again, and suddenly, it's too warm in here.

"Oh, please. The pictures didn't actually show anything," Ashley says nonchalantly, waving me off and grabbing her glass to take another sip of wine.

"That doesn't make it okay!" I shift forward in my seat, dip my head into my hands, and wipe away the beads of sweat that have formed on my forehead.

"He was just a friend. I was trying to make a special photo album for you for our wedding, and I was getting his opinion on a few pictures. It was totally innocent."

Ashley refills her glass of wine.

"Were you going to put his dick pics in the album, too? Because you should know by now, that's not what gets my motor running."

I dump the rest of the Jack from my glass down my throat and plop the empty glass down too hard on the coffee table. The loud snap of glass meeting wood bursts through the room, startling Ashley momentarily.

"Please. The only penis on my phone belongs to you," Ashley says, sitting up straighter.

"The hell it does!" I stand, unable to sit still any longer, and pace the room. "I've never in my life sent anyone a picture of my dick," I spit out.

"Jacob—"

"How can I trust you anymore?"

"You're just going to have to decide you want to. You have to decide if what we had is important enough to you. If you ever loved me like you claimed, that should be an easy decision."

Ashley leans back in her seat, one arm folded over her middle, the other bent at the elbow, still swirling her glass of wine. I turn to face her.

"I loved you more than anything else in this fucking world. You know that."

Turning away from her again, my fingers link behind my head, and I focus on my breathing. I don't want her here. The tap of Ashley's glass being set on the coffee table signals her change in position, and without any other warning, her arms wrap around me, and her cheek presses into my shoulder.

"Give me the chance to prove myself to you, then. Just one chance. I don't want to lose what we had together."

Ashley kisses my shoulder, then tugs gently at my arm, trying to turn me to her. I shrug her off of me but turn to face her so there's no question about the words I'm about to speak.

"I don't want you here. Get out."

"Jacob, please—" Her hands clasp at her chest.

"I can't do this, Ashley. Even if I could get past what you did, I don't see how I could ever trust you again."

"Just tell me you'll think about it. Please." She steps toward me again but doesn't reach out for me this time.

I can see tears filling her eyes, and despite it all, an avalanche of guilt piles up in my chest. Fuck. This is all her doing. She has caused me so much pain, and yet, a few tears from her leaves me feeling like somehow I'm the bad guy.

"I'll think about it. Now go," I say, running a hand though my hair.

Ashley leaves without a fight, and I collapse on the couch once she's gone. With my head resting back on the cushions, I link my fingers over my eyes and exhale the stress of the evening. I search my memory for the woman I fell in love with, because frankly, I'm having a hard time remembering what I loved about her. People probably thought the want-to-be socialite was out of my league, and I'd be inclined to agree. The only reason she was looking for a job when she applied for the position at my clinic was because her father said she had to be working to have access to her trust fund.

Honestly, I think it was the glitz and glam around her that initially caught my interest. It wasn't about money, though. It was about something new and different. Most of the women in town are girls I've known since before any of us hit puberty. I dated a handful of them over the years, but when Ashley came to town, she was new and exciting. She didn't usually go out on calls with me, but we worked in close quarters at the office. It's not surprising that I would fall in love with the beautiful woman I spent more time with than anyone else.

Maybe I wasn't seeing the real Ashley, but soon, I was mesmerized by her. It was her laugh, and the way she commandeered the attention of every room she walked into, and even the way her nose crinkled up when she smelled manure on me. She was captivating.

In no time, I packaged up my heart, tied a bow around it, and handed it over to her. I didn't care what people were saying. She was my world. She was the woman that would nurture my future children and grow old with me. She was the one that I was going to have it all with.

And then she wasn't.

CHAPTER SIX

Struggling with the hitch, I try to unhook the camper from my truck. Today is my first day of work, and I can't be rolling up with a camper. I don't need to waste the gas, either. Eventually, I get the stubborn hitch unhooked. I climb into my truck, trying to ignore the butterflies that seem to have claimed my stomach as their new home.

As I was getting dressed this morning, I started to worry about whether Jalynn exaggerated my experience to Mrs. Jones. Maybe that's why she didn't ask me a bunch of questions about my previous work history. Surely Jalynn wouldn't have embellished my work experience, would she?

I knew things were going too smoothly. I'm gonna ruin all of this on my very first day, and it's gonna turn into a giant disaster like the rest of my life. Jalynn is gonna be disappointed in me, Mrs. Jones will probably tell the whole town I lied to get a job, and nobody in this town will want to hire me. I should've stuck to what I know and tried for a job waitressing at the diner.

With my seatbelt buckled and key in the ignition, I twist the key forward. Nothing happens. The butterflies turn to nausea. I take a deep breath, counting to five as I draw in the air and exhale the same way, hoping to steady my nerves, then I turn the key again, praying the truck will start. This time it sputters to life.

I pull out of the driveway while trying to think positive thoughts, hoping they will help calm me. Everything is gonna be fine. I'll go in there, catch on to everything Mrs. Jones teaches me, and she isn't gonna have any regrets about hiring me.

Feeling more confident, I pick up speed. The truck engine revs a little and starts to sputter, but it keeps driving down the road. That's something at least.

"That can't be a good sign, though," I say out loud as I scan over the gauges on the broad, dusty dashboard. Nothing looks out of whack, best that I can tell. "Please, Jesus, keep this truck running."

I make my way into town without any more incidents and pull into a parking spot to the side of the storefront. I glance down the row of businesses on Main Street and absorb the beauty of this little town. Climbing out of my truck, I inhale deeply, full of hope and excitement to start this new chapter of my life, despite being somewhat scared.

Peeking through the glass, I knock on the locked door. Mrs. Jones comes out from behind the counter and lets me in.

"Good morning, dear. You're just in time to help me put the bouquets out front and change the special on the sidewalk sign. How's your penmanship?" Mrs. Jones asks, a stick of chalk in her hand.

"Um . . . legible?"

"Good enough for me. Put ferns on the board, buy one get one at half price," she says, handing the chalk over to me. "But first, let me show you around."

I trail behind Mrs. Jones into the back of the store.

"Here's the cooler," she says, opening the large walk-in cooler door so that I can see inside. "This is where all of the fresh-cut flowers are kept. These tables over here are our work-station for making arrangements and such. As you see, we have vases and ribbons on the shelves below the tables. You'll find more vases and supplies over there in that closet." Mrs. Jones points at the door labeled "storage."

She leads me out an exterior door in the back that opens to a brick patio. On the patio sits a small painted wrought iron table set. Against the brick wall of the store, there's a long wooden workbench with pots, tools, and bags of soil on the shelf underneath. The patio leads to three greenhouses lined up behind the store. Mrs. Jones walks me through each greenhouse, explaining the routines and procedures for care of the greenhouse plants.

"You have a wonderful setup here," I say as we walk back into the store. "For a town this small, though, it must be full of romantics."

Mrs. Jones laughs.

"You might be surprised. Actually, I own another shop in Bozeman. My daughter runs that one. We ship a lot of our flowers out there, and that's where the bulk of our sales are. Space is cheaper here, though. It just works out well for us this way."

"How many kids do you have?" I ask, wiping down the chalkboard.

"Four. A thirty-two-year-old and thirty-year-old, both married and moved away, and twenty-eight-year-old twins. One lives here in town still, and the other is the daughter I was just telling you about who runs my shop over in the city."

"You were busy!" I say, glancing up from writing the special on the chalkboard. "Four kids in four years! That must have been a challenge."

"It was, but it was also well worth it. How about you? Do you have a significant other you're hoping to have kids with one day?" Mrs. Jones asks while tying a bow from the ribbon on the worktable.

"I'm newly out of a long-term relationship. If I do meet someone, though, I like to think I'll have a few kids one day."

"What happened with your boyfriend? Why did you break up?"

I hesitate and debate my wording.

"It just wasn't what it was supposed to be," I finally say, wiping chalk from my hands.

"Ah. It happens. Well, let's get to work. You can start with this list. Let me know if you have any questions."

Grateful Mrs. Jones didn't press for more information, I look over the list she handed me and take the chalkboard outside to the sidewalk.

ON THE DRIVE back to Jalynn's house, I replay my day. I'm tired, but I'm happy with how my first day went. Jalynn was right about Mrs. Jones. She's terrific. She has a natural, motherly, nurturing way about her. I can't remember much about my parents, but I like to think my mother was something like Mrs. Jones.

If I'd grown up with a mother like her, I bet my life would have played out quite differently. My grandparents were great, of course. They loved me, and they did the best they could by me. It just wasn't the same as being raised and loved by a mom and dad.

I pull into the driveway and discover I'm the only one here. Jalynn and George must both still be working. Without getting out of the truck, I pick up my phone and dial George's number.

"Hey, George. Sorry to bother you while you're hard at work, but I was wondering if you had any ideas of where I can park my camper."

"We don't mind it where it is," George replies. I can hear the cattle and horses in the background. Unfamiliar male voices drift through the line as well. "Put them in the barn. I'll check on it in a minute . . ." George says to someone else. Maybe I should wait till he's home to have this discussion, but then again, the commotion on his end is likely to work in my favor.

"I appreciate the hospitality, but I need my own space. I need a place to park it that I can call home." I trace a finger around the steering wheel of my truck.

"You're sure that's what you want to do?" he asks, too distracted by his work to put up a fight.

"Yes."

"Okay. I'm almost done here. I've got the perfect spot in mind. I'll lead you down there when I get home."

I gather up my stuff from inside and hook the camper back up to the truck, finishing up as George pulls into the driveway and asks me if I'm ready to go. I hop in my truck and follow him down the road. We drive about a quarter of a mile, and George pulls off the road into a small grove of trees.

George gets out of his truck and directs me while I back the camper onto the lot. It takes me a few tries, but he's patient while I figure it out. I climb out of the truck and look around. It's pretty here. The trees give it some privacy. I can hear the gurgle of a creek close by. It appears to be only about twenty yards from my camper. A firepit sits off to the side of the clearing.

"We're still on your damn blasted property, aren't we?" I ask and roll my eyes at him.

"I mean, one might say we own it. Others might argue that the ranch owns it." George gives me a nervous shrug, "Look, just accept this, please. For me." His palms are stretched out in front of him in a pleading manner. "I'm never going to hear the end of it from Jalynn as it is. At least this way you're close enough to us if something happens or you need something—"

"I'm *not* gonna need anything," I say, interrupting him.

"I know, but it will ease Jalynn's mind. She's worried about you being by yourself in this camper. Do me a solid here, Lacey. My wife is pregnant and hormonal, and she will be stressed out of her mind if you are any further away. Plus, you have a place to hook up to electricity here, and it's rent free."

"Fine."

I roll my eyes at him again just to be dramatic. Truthfully, I like the fact that they will be so close. I'm just too stubborn to admit it. After all, they are my people.

After George leaves, I get right to work, unhooking the truck again and getting the camper settled. Electricity is definitely a bonus I didn't really think about needing.

I unpack the groceries I picked up on my way home from work and organize the cupboards. Though the place isn't magazine worthy by any means, my stop for décor and staples once I arrived in Montana has given the camper a personal touch. I replaced all of the old curtains with new ones, put some plush blankets and pillows in the back for bedding, and added some textures and a pop of color with pillows for the bench.

The stovetop has already been scrubbed clean, but I have yet to test it. I turn the knob to high. The burner lights, turning a bright orange. It works! I unbox the pans I purchased, wash them, and put them away.

Despite the heat being on, there's a slight chill inside the camper. I pull out a sweatshirt, slip it on, and get to work chopping vegetables to go in a soup for dinner.

I eat my soup and wash up my dishes, putting the leftovers in the fridge. Sitting on my makeshift couch, also known as a wooden bench with throw pillows on it, I look around, unsure of what to do next. I mentally note that I need to run to the hardware store to pick up some paint tomorrow. The place still needs some sprucing up, but I've got nothing but time these days. I'm not much of a TV watcher, so even if I had one, which I don't, I would still have entirely too much time to sit and think. That has always been the perfect storm for me to come up with something stupid to do.

A sudden banging on my door pulls me away from my mental to-do list. I glance at the clock. George held Jalynn off longer than I expected. I get up and push open the door. A red-faced Jalynn climbs into the camper without waiting for an invitation.

"What the heck are you thinking, Lacey? This is no place for you to live, especially when there's a perfectly good house just down the road for you to live in. It's not safe out here by yourself! You're likely to freeze to death in your sleep. And what about the wild animals?" Jalynn's hands rest impatiently on her hips.

"I'm gonna be just fine, *Mom.* I know how to take care of myself. I have heat and air conditioning, and thanks to George, I even have lights. Plus, I'm hardly worried about some little critters coming to visit."

"You might not be worried about the little ones, but what about the bears? Or mountain lions?"

"Jay . . . I need my own space. I appreciate you looking out for me, but this is a little ridiculous."

"Come back to the house with me, and join us for dinner."

"I already ate." I fold my arms stubbornly across my chest, holding eye contact with Jalynn.

Her anger has dissolved by this point, and she's fueled instead by the stubbornness we were both blessed with. She narrows her eyes at me, trying to decipher if I'm bluffing.

"What did you eat?"

"I made soup."

"Cold from a can, I presume," Jalynn says accusingly.

She knows me well, but this time, I actually made my own from scratch. Of all the things Grammy succeeded at with me, teaching me how to find my way around the kitchen was not one of them. I would've starved in college if it wasn't for Jalynn.

"You see that thing behind you? It's called a stove. You see that box over there?" I motion to the mini-fridge. "Open it up. My leftovers are there. Give them a try and tell me again that I'm eating cold soup from a can."

Jalynn doesn't budge. A few seconds tick by. Finally, she

reaches into the fridge and pulls out the leftover soup without moving from her spot. I hand her a spoon, and she pops the lid open and takes a bite. I watch as her face scrunches up. She turns to the sink and spits it out, then puts the lid back on the bowl and places it back in the fridge.

"What do you think?" I ask, even though I already know what she's going to say. "As good as store bought?"

"Please . . ." It's Jalynn who rolls her eyes this time. "Add food poisoning to the list of things that are liable to go wrong for you out here. You might not starve to death, but you're not going to stay healthy eating your cooking. Sell the stupid camper, Lace. You don't need it. I'll even feed you dinner every night. You can have *real* food."

Jalynn isn't gonna give up, but she has lost her steam entirely. Now she's just giving me friendly fire. I've always made my lack of skills in the kitchen fair game for joking about, because frankly, I've never cared about it being a weakness for me.

"Tempting offer, but no. I'm staying put."

"In all seriousness, though, is this truly what you want, or are you just afraid of imposing? Because you know you'd never be imposing, right?" Jalynn asks me, suddenly earnest.

"I know, Jay. Truly, though, I need to do this my way. I need to know I can."

"Fine," Jalynn replies. "Stay here. However, you have to come over at least a couple of nights a week for dinner. I'll cook. You can come whichever nights fit your busy social calendar best. Which means I'll be seeing you frequently."

"Yes, ma'am," I say in the same sarcastic tone she is using with me.

"And now that you're settled, I expect you to make an effort to get a social life. No sense in locking yourself up in this thing any more than necessary. This is like something out of a horror film." Jalynn turns and inspects the door. "You can lock the door from the inside, right?"

"Yes. In all seriousness, you don't have to worry. I'll be perfectly safe here," I say, trying to reassure her. I know beneath the sarcasm she is genuinely concerned about me.

"Okay, well, George said I had to hurry back. We haven't eaten dinner yet, and he's getting impatient. Plus, I need to pee, and if I don't hurry back to the bathroom I might wet myself."

"Do you want to use my bathroom?" I hook a thumb toward the back of the camper.

"Uh, no. I've got a perfectly good toilet just a couple minutes away. Call me tomorrow."

Jalynn winks at me, then steps down and out of the camper. She shakes her head on her way back to her car.

"You're an awful lot of trouble, you know it?" Jalynn hollers at me.

"One of the many things we have in common," I yell back and giggle, closing the door behind me.

I lock the door and tap my fingers on the kitchen counter, trying to decide what to do with myself. Remembering some books I brought with me, I head for the back of the camper to choose one off the shelf above my bed. A few chapters in, the couple's meet-cute in the story leaves me dwelling on Ben and how happy we were in the beginning. I can remember the excitement I felt when he finally asked me out.

I tossed my jean shorts to the side and slid on my faded blue jean skirt. Inspecting myself in the mirror, I pulled the capped sleeves of my pale yellow shirt further off my shoulders and I turned to examine myself again. Ben should show up any minute to pick me up for our first date. Jalynn did me a solid by inviting him to the river with us last week.

I jumped at the sound of the doorbell and hurried over to the window to peer down at the driveway. Sure enough, Ben's pickup was behind Grammy's car. I slid on my flip-flops while simultaneously dousing myself in my favorite body spray, glossed my lips one final time, then grabbed my purse and quickly made my way downstairs. Ben was standing in the living room with Grammy, looking uncomfortable.

"You two kids have fun and behave yourselves," Grammy said, seeing us out the door.

Later that night, holding hands at the front door and not wanting the evening to end, Ben slowly leaned down toward me and kissed me. I could taste the smoke from his last cigarette on his breath, but I didn't mind. I smiled up at him when he pulled away. I rose up on my toes and kissed him again. When the porch light began to flicker, I pulled away and said goodnight and slid in through the front door.

My phone buzzes next to me, and suddenly, I'm back in my camper, alone. It's a text message from Billy, my old boss. Billy is the only one who knew I was leaving. When I made it to Montana, I sent him a text to let him know I was settled. I open the text, not sure what to expect.

Billy: Ben came by today. He's been all around town asking a bunch of questions. Said he talked to some old man in Warbler's Hollow that sold you a camper.

Me: Does he know where I am?

Billy: I don't think so.

Billy: I'll keep you posted.

lacey

After a month in Montana, the camper is really starting to feel like home. I pass the time with little projects. Everything is painted now. A pale, muted yellow claims the walls inside the camper, with bright accent colors on the cabinets and furniture. My color choices and the blend of textiles I've scattered around might be wild, but it's my own little gypsy wagon. My camper is my place of peace and retreat, not that I have anything here I feel the need to escape from.

The exterior of the camper is now a bright and cheerful teal. With assistance from George—okay, a lot of assistance—I now have a wood deck along the front of the camper. A bench and a few pieces of cut logs are positioned around the firepit for seating, but my favorite place is the hammock hanging between two large trees down by the creek.

"Have you heard anything from he-who-shall-not-be-named since you left?" Jalynn randomly asks me, bringing me out of my thoughts.

I glance across the picnic table on Jalynn's expansive back porch where we sit and sip on lemonade while George cooks steaks for us on the grill.

"No. But then again, he probably doesn't know how to find

me or contact me. I hope." I skim my finger down the side of my glass, leaving a trail through the condensation. I don't mention the texts I've received from Billy. He's continued to update me weekly on any gossip around town concerning me or Ben. Billy said Ben has been asking around, but Billy was pretty sure he didn't know anything else. I hope he's right.

"You did the right thing. I hate what he did being the reason you moved out here and got away, but I'm glad you did it before you tied the knot."

"Yeah . . ." I trail off. Being back with Jalynn and George has been like a breath of fresh air, but it gets hard, too. Being here, I've been reminded that George is one of the good ones. I love watching him dote over Jalynn, and even still, a sweet, gentle love radiates from both of them. If only I could have that, too, it might be worth giving love another shot. My mind returns to thoughts of the past.

"It's such a hot day. This water feels amazing!" I said, wading into the river in my underwear. Ben wrapped his arms around my middle and pulled me down on top of him below the water. Sputtering, I resurfaced. "Benjamin! I told you not to do that. Grammy's gonna see my makeup all smeared and my hair all wet and know we were back out here. You know how mad she got when Mrs. Moore told her she'd seen us swimming half-naked out here, and I got a long lecture from her about pretty is as pretty does."

"Oh, screw that old hag," Ben said.

"Benjamin!" I pushed him away angrily.

"Mrs. Moore. She's the old hag, not Grammy," Ben insisted. He, like all of my friends, called my grandmother Grammy, too. She was the type of grandmother who took all the kids under her wing, related or not.

"You'd better not be talking like that about Grammy," I warned him. "I won't stand for it."

I folded my arms across my chest. Ben made his way back over to me, waist-deep in the water, and wrapped his arms around me. He kissed me, pressing hard against my mouth. I slid my arms up around his neck and pulled him down closer. The strong current of the river caused us to sway a bit, and I broke off the kiss.

"Come here," Ben said, still holding my hand and leading me out of the river.

We returned to our blanket, spread out on the riverbank on the tall, soft grass. Ben tossed our discarded clothes aside, pulling me down onto the blanket with him. He kissed me again, letting his hands wander over my slick skin.

"Ben . . ." I whispered, stopping him.

"Come on, Lacey, I've waited two months. I don't know if I can wait any longer. Don't you love me?" Ben chided.

"You know I do. I'm just not ready."

"Do I?" Ben rolled over onto his back, his hands behind his head.

"Don't do this, Ben. Please."

"I just don't understand how you aren't ready if you do love me. The more I feel for you, the more I want to show you. Don't you want to show me how you feel about me?"

"I want to, Ben, I swear I do. But Grammy—"

"Don't play the Grammy-made-me-promise card again," Ben interrupted. "This isn't about Grammy. This is about me and you and the way we feel about each other. I love you, Lacey. I want to show you how I feel about you. You're the only girl for me, but I just don't know if I can go on like this any longer."

"What are you saying? You aren't breaking up with me, are you?" I sat up, looking down at Ben, afraid to hear his answer.

"I need to be in a relationship with a woman who knows how she feels about me and isn't afraid to show it. I don't want to break up with you, but you're going to force my hand if I have to wait any longer."

"Don't say that, Ben. I know how I feel about you. I love you."

"Then show me."

Steady patting on my arm pulls me back, and I give Jalynn

my full attention. I catch a worried glance between her and George.

"Are you good?" Jalynn asks. "You look like you've seen a ghost."

"Yeah, sorry. Just got swept away there for a minute," I say and take a drink to wash away the bile climbing my throat at the thought of my first time. He may not have forced himself on me, but I was young and naïve. He told me what love was, and I accepted his definition. Instead of looking back at the occasion with fondness or humor like most people, my memory of it is filled with regret and pain. I wish it had been different.

"I've got to grab our plates. The steaks are almost ready," George says. He kisses the top of Jalynn's head before going inside.

"Y'all are so cute with each other," I say. "I wish I could have that one day."

"Of course you can!" Jalynn insists, her brow furrowing at the suggestion that I can't.

"I don't know. I don't think it happens for people like me."

"People like you? What's that supposed to mean? Just because Ben was an asshole doesn't mean you don't deserve more. You do know that, right?"

"I don't know," I whisper, letting Ben fill my thoughts again.

"You know what you need?" Jalynn asks. "You need to go on a date. With a decent guy. You need to see for yourself that Ben is the exception, not the rule."

I let the idea settle for a moment as I consider what she said. Do I deserve more? I don't know. What I do know is that I want more. I want to experience what it's like to be cherished and loved unconditionally. One day, I hoped to have a family. A happy family. To be the mom that kisses away scrapes, bakes cookies, and never runs out of hugs. But that's not me, is it? Ben definitely isn't the dad that comes home cheerful from work, greets the family with hugs and kisses, and passes a football in the yard with the kids. It just wasn't us.

"Something casual maybe," I agree, after a moment of contemplation, daring to hope that I could have more than Ben offered me. "I was with Ben for so long, he's all I really know. I'm not sure I'd know how to go on a date with anyone else."

"It'd be fun for you," Jalynn says. "You hardly know what it's like to date. You spent nearly half of your life committed to that jerk, and what time you weren't, you were focusing on school for a change."

"You're right. I'd have to meet someone first, though. I'm not doing any of that internet dating stuff," I say, shaking my head.

"Oh, we can help you meet people," Jalynn excitedly offers, clapping her hands, and I know her excitement stems from finally finding something she can do to help me.

"MADDIE, there's a phone call for you. It sounds urgent," I tell Mrs. Jones, poking my head into the back of the store where she is busy making arrangements. She insisted I start calling her by her first name. "I can finish this one up for you if you'd like."

"Thank you, dear."

Maddie heads to the phone at the front checkout, and I take her place at the workbench to finish the arrangement.

"I've got to run, dear," Maddie says, reappearing just moments later. "My mother had a fall, and I've got to go help her."

"Oh no! Is she okay?"

"She's fine. It wasn't a bad fall. I'm not worried, but the home likes for a family member to be present while the doctor looks her over. She does this every once in a while."

"What about the shipment to the city? Want me to take it after closing up?" I ask.

"No, that won't be necessary. I'll send someone over to take it. You just do your usual thing, and I'll see you in the morning."

After fishing her keys out from her purse, Maddie hooks the strap over her shoulder and heads for the door.

"Okay. If you need anything, let me know," I call after her.

A couple of hours pass, and the jingle over the front door alerts me that someone's here. I head back to the front of the store to tend to the customer. Though I've never met the man, I recognize him instantly. It's the man who nearly ran me over in his pickup truck on my first day in town.

He looks like he's just stepped off a ranch with his messy clothes and muddy boots. He still wears a couple of days' worth of stubble on his face. His frame is slender but strong, the muscles in his arms defined. My eyes follow his strong, sinewy muscles up his arms, but my imagination takes over at his sleeves, imagining how the muscles must stretch across his body under his shirt.

Stop drooling, I scold myself. Get a grip! This man nearly turned you into roadkill.

What can I say? I'm a sucker for the rough country boy-type. And trouble. That makes him a double whammy. Definitely something I don't need. It still doesn't mean I need to gawk at him, though.

"What can I do for you?" I choke out in what I hope sounds like a pleasant voice, and I give him a friendly smile.

"I'm here to take the truck over to the city for Maddie," he says gruffly.

If he recognizes me, he doesn't show it. And he doesn't seem to be in any better of a mood than he was when he blared his truck horn in my face. Maybe he takes a minute to warm up to new people, and then he turns into a big teddy bear. It's more likely, though, that he's an entitled prick.

Just my type.

I roll my eyes at myself. Despite everything, I can't deny I'm attracted to the man.

"Oh, okay. I'll help you load the truck."

I turn from the counter to lead him into the back room where the shipment waits to be loaded while contemplating the situation in front of me. If I'm going to do this, going to try for something better than I had with Ben, I'm going to have to step way outside of my comfort zone. This man may not be on a roster of candidates I should consider, but there wouldn't be any harm in trying to flirt with this tower of handsome masculinity, right? Heaven knows, I need the practice. I slide my sweaty palms into my pockets, conflicted. My body wants to be close to him, but my mind is screaming at me to run away.

"I don't need your help. I know my way around," he says sharply and brushes past me.

I bristle, and yet, tingles explode through my body from his touch.

"Excuse me"—I chase after him, close on his heels as he enters the cooler—"but you can't come strutting in here, putting on airs like you own the place. Where do you get off? I haven't done anything but offer to help. Anyway, how do I know that Maddie sent you?"

I was right. He's an entitled prick.

The man turns abruptly on his heels with an arrangement in his hands. Not expecting his quick change in direction, my momentum keeps me going straight for him, and we collide, knocking the arrangement out of his hands. It crashes to the floor, pieces of the glass vase shooting off in every direction. We both freeze, eyeing the broken mess on the floor between us.

"Yeah. Some help you are. If you'd be so kind as to step aside, I'd like to get this done."

The man grabs two more arrangements and sidesteps me to get out the door. I crouch down and begin picking up the larger pieces of the mess we made, then take a broom to the floor. By the time he has the truck loaded, I have the mess cleaned up and a new arrangement prepared to replace the broken one.

"You have yourself a nice day, now," I say in an overly sweet voice with a stiff smile as I shove the new arrangement into his hands.

He barely even looks at me when he takes the arrangement and heads back to the door. My blood boils.

"Asshole," I mutter to myself, louder than I intend.

He stops in his tracks. Realizing my mistake, I suck in a breath and will myself invisible. With no more than a slight cock of his head, the man continues out the door and leaves.

True to her word, Jalynn finds me a date. A blind date. I hate blind dates. Knowing that, and knowing I still have no life outside of work, Jalynn sets the date up before telling me about it.

"This first one is undoubtedly going to be hard," Jalynn says over the phone as she breaks the news about my impending date. I groan. "But that's why I think this is gonna be a perfect date for you to dip your toes back in the dating pool, so to speak."

"Why?" I ask with a sigh, remembering I did ask her for this. It's not her fault I was feeling more . . . brave?—or desperate, more likely—when I originally agreed to this.

"He's really sweet, Lace. Maybe too sweet, if that's even possible. And he's going to take you to an orchestra performance, so you won't have to make much conversation. Like I said, easy first date."

I browse through my wardrobe, trying to decide on an outfit. What do people wear to orchestra performances, anyway?

Eventually, I settle on a knee-length black dress with a scalloped hem and white embroidery. I slide into black high heels and check in the mirror to make sure I haven't missed anything.

My date taps on the door, and I step out onto the deck and lock up. I turn back to him just in time to catch him taking a step back and checking me out from head to toe and back up again.

"Wow, you are beautiful!" he says, shaking his head in admiration.

He may be cute, but this is awkward. Hopefully, he's just nervous.

"Thanks." I offer him a fake smile. "I'm Lacey. You must be Kevin."

I stretch a mildly trembling hand out toward him.

"Wow, just beautiful."

What has Jalynn gotten me into?

He takes my hand in his, and rather than a quick handshake like I expected, he lifts it and plants a wet kiss on the back of my hand. I swiftly reclaim my hand and realize I probably should've insisted on meeting him in town, rather than letting him pick me up. I realize how unqualified I am to make decisions like this after growing up in a town of less than two thousand people. Stranger danger isn't really a thing back home. Then again, Jalynn knows him, and she wouldn't send a serial killer to my doorstep.

The drive to Bozeman is quiet, and aside from Kevin's inability to keep his eyes on the road rather than on me, it's uneventful. I sit awkwardly in the passenger seat, pretending not to notice as he steals glances at me. His attention is making me so uncomfortable I stare out my window, watching the fence posts roll by until I can't handle it anymore.

"So how do you know Jalynn and George?" I ask, trying to ease some of the discomfort.

He doesn't respond.

"Kevin . . ." I say more loudly.

"Oh, what? Sorry. The porch light was on, but no one was home. What were you saying?"

What have I got myself into?

We finally make it to the venue for the orchestra, and I follow Kevin inside to our seats. The lights dim, signaling that the orchestra is about to begin, which may be the best part about the whole evening. The dark auditorium keeps the ogling to a minimum. Regardless, I subtly cling to the opposite side of my chair and slide my hands under my thighs to reduce the threat of him trying to hold my hand. I'm barely into this date and could already use a break.

My stomach rolls as the lighting in the room slowly returns to its full brightness, signifying that the event is officially over. I'm not ready for more strained conversation with this man. We rise from our seats and begin the walk out to his truck.

"The orchestra was great," I say, trying to politely cut our date short. "But I'm pretty tired. Would you mind taking me home?"

"But I haven't taken you to dinner yet. I was really looking forward to taking you to a nice restaurant," he replies.

"Oh." Suddenly, I don't know what to do. Will he be angry if I say no? "Okay."

It's just dinner. I can make it through a dinner.

He assures me on our drive to the restaurant that I should order whatever I want from the menu and insists that I choose something substantial, like a steak. I suffer through his rant about women who don't eat enough, and I can't help but think maybe he's the appetite suppressant his other dates seem to be afflicted with.

The hostess seats us in a booth, and I read over the menu, debating which choice will get me out of here the quickest without another lecture.

"I need to go to the little boy's room," Kevin says, standing. "Don't go anywhere while I'm gone."

He's only a few steps away when he stops in his tracks and backpedals to our table again.

"Seriously, though," he says, "please don't leave. Promise?"

"Uh . . . I promise."

Is this guy for real right now? This evening cannot end fast enough.

I make sure to have my order ready when he gets back, not wanting to delay the ending of our evening any longer than necessary. Kevin returns and we put our orders in with the waitress and make awkward conversation until our food comes. His eyes constantly bore into me, leaving me feeling uncomfortable and trapped. I focus on eating my food and wish I could click my heels together like Dorothy and wake up back home.

I thought the best part of the date was the lights dimming at the orchestra. That was a premature assumption. The best part of the evening was shutting the door in Kevin's face when I finally got back home. I unzip my dress and laugh to myself about the way he tried his best to delay me stepping inside the camper, undoubtedly hoping for a goodnight kiss. Much to his dismay, however, it was wasted effort, because Chinese water torture couldn't have convinced me to kiss that man goodnight. I couldn't be happier to have that one over with.

Pulling out my cell phone, I dial Jalynn. I put the phone on speaker and toss it on my bed.

"You're dead to me!" I say, laughing, when she answers. I pull on a T-shirt and pick up the phone, carrying it into the bathroom with me so I can brush my teeth.

"Why?" she asks.

"Do you even know this Kevin guy? Please tell me he's not the best you think I can do."

"Was it bad?" Jalynn asks with surprise in her voice.

"Was it bad?" I repeat. "Oh, let me tell you . . ."

Spitting the toothpaste into the sink first, I replay the evening for Jalynn who cackles on the other end of the line.

Though she hasn't offered me an explanation yet, I'm quickly able to determine she had no idea what she'd set me up for this evening.

"I'm so sorry!" Jalynn giggles through the phone, but I know her apology is sincere. "I had no idea he would be that awkward."

"Oh, Jay . . . you owe me for this one."

"Why didn't you tell him to take you back home? Or call me and ask for a rescue?"

"I tried. But he was set on going to dinner," I say, taking a seat on the edge of my bed.

"What do you mean you tried?" Jalynn asks. The humor is suddenly gone from her voice.

"I asked him to take me home after the orchestra. He was set on having dinner, though."

"Why did you agree on dinner if you didn't want to?"

"Well, I didn't want to put him out. He was really insistent on it, so I just thought it was best to go along with what he wanted."

A brief silence hangs in the air.

"Lacey, you do understand, don't you, that you don't have to say yes to everything your date suggests?"

"I just thought—"

"No." Jalynn's voice is growing more insistent. "It's okay for you to say no. You don't have to do anything you don't want to do. And if it's awkward, or the guy gives you a hard time, you call me. You are entitled to make your own decisions. Promise me you'll remember that."

"Okay," I say, biting at the skin on my lip.

She's right. I know she's right. I just don't know that I can be that person.

"We're hosting a barbecue next week. That would be a perfect opportunity for you to get to know some more people in town," Jalynn offers.

"I'll have to check my busy schedule before I can commit," I joke. "But that sounds like fun."

If tonight's date is any indication of what the dating world has to offer me, though, I'm better off staying single. I plug in my phone after telling Jalynn goodnight and settle on my bed, waiting for sleep to find me.

THE WEEK DRIFTS by slowly and uneventfully. I stay busy working at the flower shop every day and join Jalynn and George for dinner a couple of nights. Much to Jalynn's dismay, I decline her invitation to be the third wheel on her date with George on Friday night.

Saturday morning, the ringing of my cell phone stirs me awake. I stumble out of bed in search of it. Where did I leave it? And why is it ringing so early? I follow the sound to the bench, where I dig in the pillows until they produce my phone. It's Jalynn, of course.

"What?" I yawn and collapse on the bench.

"Did I wake you? It's nine in the morning, Lacey. Is everything okay? I've never known you to sleep this late. Did you go out last night after all? Did you meet someone?" Jalynn rattles off questions quicker than my groggy brain can follow.

"What? Nine? In the morning? How *did* I sleep so late?"

"That's what I just asked you. Sheesh, I've about forgotten what it feels like to sleep in. They say I'm not supposed to have trouble sleeping till later on in the pregnancy, but I swear this baby has already changed life as I knew it. But tell me, is everything good with you?"

"Ugh, I feel like I was rode hard and put up wet."

"Were you out somewhere? Did you meet someone? *Were* you rode hard and put up wet? Come on, don't hold out on me now."

I can almost hear her eyebrows waggling on the other end of the phone.

"No. But I wish I was," I say with a chuckle. I move back to settle on my bed. "I haven't been sleeping very well, and I think it's catching up to me. But surely that's not what you were calling me about."

"Hold up, why haven't you been sleeping well? Is it the nightmares again?"

"Yeah, but it's okay. I'm fine."

"Lace . . ."

"No really," I insist. "Moving on . . ."

There is silence on the line as Jalynn no doubt debates whether she should let me push the conversation forward or not.

"I was calling you about tonight. You're coming, right? To the barbecue?"

"I don't know if I feel up to socializing with a bunch of strangers today," I say, setting the stage to tell her I'm not coming. "That date you set me up with last weekend was painful. I'm not sure I'm cut out for this dating thing after all. Plus, I have some projects to finish up on the camper."

"No. No, you can't back out of coming. My asking was a polite formality. I will drag you over here by my teeth if I have to. You have to come! You're my best friend, and I want you here. Please come, Lace."

I let out a dramatic sigh. I've not only already promised to attend, but I encouraged her to host a barbecue in the first place. It would be pretty shitty of me not to go.

"Fine. Lord willing and the creek don't rise, I'll make an appearance. I can't promise I'll stay the whole time, though. What time?"

"Yay! I knew I could count on you. The party starts at six. Don't be late!"

I hang up the phone and grab a blanket, wrapping it around

me and lazily trudging outside to the hammock. I settle myself in the hammock to continue resting.

Once I've stored up some energy and found a degree of motivation, I spend the latter part of my day cleaning the camper and gathering fallen tree limbs for my firewood pile. When five thirty rolls around, I decide I should start getting ready for the barbecue.

I look at myself in the mirror, unsure of how much effort I want to put into getting ready. I'm still on the fence about whether or not I even want to participate in this event. I know Jalynn probably has a guy or two in mind that she wants me to meet. When Jalynn is put on a task, like helping me meet people, she attacks with full force and unwavering determination. It's both a blessing and a curse.

Thoughts of the man from the flower shop a couple of days ago trickle back into my mind. Just the memory of him makes heat course through my body and my mouth go dry. I push my thoughts of him away, though. I don't need to test the waters with a jerk to know that's not what I need.

I debate what to wear, finally settling on jeans and a gold graphic T-shirt. I tuck the front of it into my belted jeans and slide my favorite selection of leather bracelets on my wrists. Grabbing a light jacket to take along with me in case it gets chilly, I study myself in the mirror for a moment, then add a set of chunky gold huggie earrings and a delicate paper clip chain that barely hangs visible over the neck of my shirt.

It's already six thirty when I pull into Jalynn's driveway. The driveway and side yard are already full of pickups and a few SUVs. One thing I've noticed since being in Montana is that most everyone here drives a four-wheel drive vehicle of some sort. My two-wheel drive pickup might give me trouble this winter. I leave the truck in a spot where I feel certain I won't get blocked in and head inside.

Voices float around from the backyard as I walk up to the house, and I know I should probably walk around back to join the party. Suddenly feeling uncharacteristically shy, though, I opt for the front door instead. Making it inside, I find Jalynn and several other girls gossiping around the kitchen island.

"Lacey, you made it! I was beginning to worry." Jalynn gives me a hug and pulls me into the kitchen with her. "Ladies, this is Lacey. She's the friend I was telling you about."

Jalynn's introduction is followed by a chorus of hellos.

"What do you think of Montana? Is it much different than North Carolina?" the brunette with the round pregnant belly asks.

"It's completely different, but it's been great," I answer, slowly warming up to the group.

"What brought you to Montana, anyway?" asks a different woman, a blonde with bright red lipstick, taking another sip of her drink.

I try to think of a graceful way to answer, knowing it's liable to lead us into a discussion I don't want to have.

"Oh, you know, I needed a change. And Jalynn here, being pregnant with her first child and not knowing what to expect . . ."

Much to my relief, they take the bait, and the focus turns back on Jalynn, and I get to hear a rather disturbingly graphic conversation between the five women about pregnancy and birth.

Soon, George walks in from the back porch and ushers us outside with the rest of the group. I scan the crowd, taking in my surroundings. There are several good-looking guys here. Some of them clearly already have girls, but several appear to be single. Chances are, if they were invited to this barbecue, they already have Jalynn's stamp of approval.

I go through the line to get a plate of food and return to Jalynn's side, hoping I'll blend into the crowd and avoid intro-ductions for a while. Jalynn gives me a nudge, silently checking in while she continues listening to the story being recounted to her by another someone I haven't yet met. I respond with a wink and take a big bite of the burger on my plate.

"If you want an introduction to anybody, let me know," Jalynn offers once the storyteller walks away. "Anyone caught your eye yet?"

"Not so much," I say. "I'm so out of my depth."

"You are not. You're just nervous, and that's okay. Just start talking to people and try to have fun. Anything else will naturally fall into place."

I roll my eyes, feigning annoyance at her pep talk, and head to the porch to throw my plate away. A soothing melody floats through the yard, capturing my attention, and I slow my pursuit. My eyes wander, searching for the source, but I can't see through the group of people gathered around a picnic table. Whoever's playing the guitar is good. Without thinking, I move toward the music, feeling drawn in.

I find a lone chair out of the way of company but close enough to the melody being plucked from the guitar to soak in each note. I take a seat and close my eyes, allowing myself to melt into the music. I open my eyes as a couple among the group saunter away and I am given a clear view of the guitarist.

"Oh. It's you," I say. He looks up from his guitar, his eyes landing on mine, but he doesn't stop playing.

I stand from my seat and close in to fill the open gap. A strange beckoning fills me. The music giving me reprieve is being played by none other than the rude but devilishly handsome man from town.

"What are you doing here? And how do you know George and Jalynn?" I ask.

The music comes to an abrupt stop.

"Hi," he says. I take a step closer, feeling drawn by his warm, captivating gaze. "I was hoping we might cross paths again—"

"Hey, baby." A tall redhead appears out of nowhere and kisses him on the cheek. She takes a seat next to him.

His gaze slowly drifts away from me. Is that disappointment on his face? He begins picking the guitar again as he gives the redhead a nod and focuses back on his hands floating over the strings. The redhead is saying something, but I no longer hear the words. A throat clears behind me, snapping me out of the trance I'm in. I spin around and bump directly into a broad, hard chest.

"I'm sorry," I say to the massive figure towering over me. I stumble back a step, and the apprehension I've been trying to chase away takes a U-turn straight back into my soul.

They grow the men here in Montana like they grow the mountains. He has a bright smile on his clean-shaven face, and his big, happy eyes take me in. I self-consciously smooth my hair from the jolt of our collision and make a mental note of my escape route away from him if it becomes needed.

"My fault," he assures me with a genuine smile. His voice is smooth and friendly. "My name's Caleb. I work with George. Are you the friend from back east?"

"I am. My name's Lacey. Are you from here?"

"Basically. I grew up in the next town over but spent most of my time here. That's how I got acquainted with George. What do you think of our little town? Was it worth the drive?" He cocks an eyebrow at me. He reminds me of a Viking with his blond hair, broad forehead, prominent chin, and expansive chest.

"I love it here. Best choice I've made in a long time."

I slide my hands into the back pockets of my jeans, suddenly feeling vulnerable and unsure of what to do with them.

"Can I suggest another brilliant choice?"

"I suppose," I say, my curiosity piqued.

"Play a game of croquet with me."

"Say what now?" That isn't where I thought he was going.

"Croquet. You ever played? They have a course set up in the back of the yard. Come play a game with me," Caleb says, repeating the suggestion, unfazed.

I glance back over the yard to see where the croquet course is set up. It's far enough back in the yard that it's not getting unintentional foot traffic but close enough not to be secluded. I look back up into Caleb's eyes, debating which prompting to listen to.

I don't know him. I'm not even sure that I want to know him. But he seems nice. He's a friend of Jalynn and George. And I still want to know if Jalynn is right. Can I have better? Something about his demeanor washes away the anxiety I haven't been able to shake tonight and suddenly puts me at ease. I can do this, right?

"I can't agree to that until I know the answer to a very important question," I say as I walk slowly backward toward the porch steps that will lead us down into the yard. Caleb follows, still wearing the smile he greeted me with. "Are you a sore loser?"

"No!" He draws out the word like the question is offensive.

"Good. Because you should know something about me . . ." I give him a mischievous grin.

"What's that?" he asks, slowly closing the gap between us.

"I kick ass at croquet. Get ready to have your pride wounded."

I give him a wicked grin and turn away, leaving him with a view as I lead the way to the back of the yard for our match. Yes, I think I can.

Locating the croquet set, I make a display of inspecting the mallets while waiting for Caleb, who I'm pretty sure didn't mind being left to catch up with me. Surprisingly, I find myself feeling at ease with him. Caleb steps up next to me and watches me with a smirk as I finish my inspection. I look up at him through my lashes. He's so much taller than me. At least a foot. I wonder what I look like from his bird's eye view.

"Ladies first," Caleb says, gesturing toward the croquet set for me to make my selection from the mallets.

"I'll play with yellow," I say, "to match my sunny disposition."

I exaggerate batting my eyelashes at him, earning a chuckle.

"I'll take black."

"To match your dark and tortured soul?" I ask jokingly.

It couldn't be more evident that there is nothing dark and tortured about this affable man.

"No, because I'm so manly," he offers, flexing his arms to put his bulging biceps on display.

"We'll see how that manly mallet plays out for you."

I slide past him, place my ball, and strike it with my yellow mallet, sending it through the first hoop.

"That was pretty good," Caleb says, lining up his ball.

With a pop of the mallet, his ball glides over the lawn, passing just left of the first hoop. I arch a judgmental eyebrow at him.

"Give me time. I'm still warming up," he reasons.

After a miserable loss, Caleb restocks our mallets and balls with the rest of the set. He casually wraps an arm around my shoulders as we walk back toward the house, weighing me down with uneasiness again. But it doesn't stay long. Caleb continues making lighthearted excuses for his poor playing, not noticing that I tensed up from his touch, and soon I find myself relaxed again and laughing at his exaggerated explanations.

"Being tall definitely puts me at a disadvantage," he says.

"How do you figure?" I giggle.

"Obviously, having to hunch over like I did to reach the ground put me at a different perspective than you," he jokes.

"I thought you told me you aren't a sore loser?"

My laughter is quickly subdued by a strange sensation that resonates inside me. Glancing ahead of us to the porch, I see the guy with the guitar watching me closely. Nervousness sweeps over me again. The redhead is still sitting at his side, but she's too preoccupied by her cell phone to pay him any mind.

"I think I deserve a consolation prize," Caleb suggests as we come to a halt at the edge of the crowd.

I look back at him. There's no denying Caleb's attractiveness. The conversation with him tonight has flowed, and despite his mammoth proportions, I feel absolutely at ease with him.

"If you're about to ask me for a kiss, you should know I'm not that kind of girl," I tease him, putting my focus back on Caleb, though I can still feel another set of eyes on me.

"In that case, I'll settle for your phone number."

I hold out my hand for his phone. He pulls the phone out of his pocket and sets it lightly in my hand. I punch several buttons and hand it back to him.

Glancing at his phone screen he reads, "Lacey, The Exquisitely Beautiful Queen of Croquet." He chuckles. "A truer title may have never been ordained."

As the night grows late, people steadily begin saying their goodbyes and leaving. I yawn, wanting to retreat as well, but start gathering trash left behind by the other visitors and help Jalynn get her house back in order. I drop a final trash bag in the garbage can and collapse exhausted on the picnic table. Jalynn slides onto the bench next to me, nudges my side with her elbow, and gives me a grin.

"Looks like someone had a good time," Jalynn says.

"It was okay," I say, downplaying it. Truth is, it went better than I expected.

"No one would have guessed you've been out of the dating game as long as you have by that performance you gave tonight. Caleb is a sweetie. And not bad looking, either!" Jalynn wiggles her eyebrows at me.

"He seems sweet as pie. Who's the guy with the guitar?"

"Oh, that's Jacob. He's a veterinarian, so he's up at the ranch quite a bit. He's a sweetie, too. That girl who was sticking to him, though . . . she hasn't exactly won many friends around here."

"How come?"

"Girl, let me tell you. She put on this show, acting all sweet when she first came to town a few years ago. She was living in Bozeman but for whatever reason decided to apply for a job with Jacob. Of course, several of the girls in town were disappointed that she swiped Jacob up so quick, but then her true colors came through. She's got her damn nose stuck up so high it's a wonder she hasn't drowned in the rain. They broke up several months ago. I haven't heard anything about him taking her back, but I don't know why else she would've come tonight."

After getting the scoop on the redhead, I don't hang around much longer. I'm anxious to get home and sleep. Back at my camper, I check my phone before settling in for the night. A text from Caleb is already waiting for me.

Caleb: I'm glad we met tonight. I had a great time talking to you.

I smile to myself. He seems like a genuinely nice guy. I need nice in my life. And it certainly doesn't hurt that he's enjoyable to look at, either.

Me: I had fun. I hope your ego wasn't too bruised.

Caleb: If it was, would you help nurse it back to health?

Me: I suppose that would be the responsible thing for me to do. ;)

Caleb: In that case, I'll be sure to remind you to kiss it better when I see you next.

Me: I'm clearly gonna have to keep a close eye on you . . .

Caleb: I wouldn't have it any other way.

I chuckle at his reply and toss my phone aside. The night replays in my head while I undress and get ready for bed. I didn't have any expectations going into the night, but I was pleased with how things played out. It was a little surprising to see Jacob there, but I was even more surprised by the way I felt drawn to him, especially after the way he acted the other day at the shop. And the day he nearly ran me over in his truck. Evidently, he has a girlfriend, though. Even if he wasn't a jerk, I don't need to waste time dwelling on him. No, Caleb is the much better choice.

I climb into my bed, my routine complete, and plug my phone in for the night. Eventually, I drift off to sleep, only to find my memories awaiting me.

My lungs burned as I pedaled up to the riverbank. I slid off my bike onto tired and wobbly legs after rushing all the way from home. Ben didn't tell me what was wrong, just that it was bad, and he needed me.

I pushed my bike along with me, holding tightly to the handlebars while I scanned the riverbank for Ben. When I spotted his dark-haired head sticking up over the weeds, I dropped the bike and ran over to him.

"Ben!" I gasped, looking down on his bruised and bloodied face. "What happened? Are you okay?"

I dropped down onto my knees in front of him. Unsure of what to do, I wrapped my arms around him and hugged him tightly against me. When he winced, I loosened my grip on him, but I didn't let him go. We stayed wrapped up in each other on the riverbank until the tension began to leak out of Ben's body, and he was ready to talk.

"What happened?" I asked him again.

"Pissed off my old man," he said, his voice cracked. He still wouldn't make eye contact with me. "Made the mistake of breathing, I guess."

The crickets and bullfrogs sang, filling the air between us while I tried to find my words.

"Ben . . . I'm so sorry," I finally whisper. "You've got to tell your momma what he did."

"She don't give a damn. She watched the whole thing without so much as saying something. She never does. Just lets him go at me and Brian till he's worn himself out."

"Oh, Ben . . ."

I wrapped him up again in my arms and sat silently, his head resting against my chest and warm tears sliding down my cheeks for him.

CHAPTER NINE

I unload my guitar from the back seat of my truck and head inside. When I heard that George and Jalynn were having a barbecue for their friend to get to know other people in town, nothing could have kept me away. I was anxious for the chance to cross paths again with the little spitfire of a woman my mother had hired to help out at the flower shop. A smile tugs at my lips as I reminisce about my previous interactions with her.

I walked in to take that delivery to Bozeman in a foul mood. Again. Ashley has been up to her usual antics. It wasn't enough that she'd lied and cheated or that she'd turned my world upside down. After several days of her hanging around and begging for a second chance, I was angry and mopey and definitely not interested in entertaining niceties with someone new.

A few years ago, I would've been all about putting forth the effort to meet that beautiful dime piece. I would have hugged my mother for hiring her and putting her in my path. It's funny, though, how one snake in the grass can ruin the entire field for you.

Still, I know I should have handled that encounter differently. I've been a jerk to the poor girl, and she didn't deserve that. And the way she made such a common little phrase—"You have a nice day"—sound like a sweet goodbye with undertones of "go fuck yourself" jolted me out of my internal grumblings about Ashley.

I'm not sure if she meant for me to hear her call me an asshole, but when I heard the word spewed at me from those intoxicating lips of hers, I almost spun around to try to figure that woman out. It's just as well that I didn't since I'm supposed to be deciding if I'm giving Ashley a second chance or not. If I can forgive her, we still have a chance at the life I thought we were going to have together. If I don't forgive her, well, I don't know if I'd even try to get in that deep with anyone new. And it's awful hard to think about Ashley while my head is full of another woman.

Just the sight of Lacey tonight ignited a fire in my belly that I'm still trying to extinguish. Ashley showed up before I could make conversation with her. So I still owe her an apology for the way I acted. Caleb is a good guy for her. He's much better for her than I would be. I still didn't enjoy watching him with her, though. It could have been me talking with her and occupying her time, earning her smiles. For a minute, I thought he was going to steal a kiss. I was ready to jump off that table and punch him in the throat. Why? I don't know. I have no claim on the girl, just a feeling that I haven't figured out how to describe.

Kicking off my boots, I strip down to my boxers and slide into bed, ready to have the day over with. Ugh, I have a family dinner to attend at my parents' house tomorrow. Fuck it. They'll have to do the dinner without me. I need a day to unwind and clear my head. I'll make it for dinner next week.

I GRAB my hiking pack and fishing gear out of the back of my truck and ready myself for my day in Bear Trap Canyon. After the week I've had, my favorite fly-fishing spot is calling my name. I strap my pack on and head down the trail, making myself focus on watching for bears and rattlesnakes instead of the two women who have been in my headspace all week.

As usual, I send a text to my sister, Mia, before hitting the trail, per my standing agreement to let someone in the family know where I'm going when I head out on my trips. I told her I wouldn't be back in time for the family dinner tonight, and she kindly reminded me that our mother wasn't going to be very happy about that. Mia gets it, though. She understands that sometimes I need time and space for myself.

I hadn't taken the breakup with Ashley very well initially, and then when I bumped into her at a vet conference a month later, she was already living with the man she had cheated on me with. That's when it hit me the hardest.

I came home from that conference and told Mia I was going fishing, but I didn't come home for a week. No mother has aimed her wrath on an adult child as severely as my mother laid down her wrath upon me after I finally re-emerged into civilization. Looking back now, I understand why she was furious. For all she knew, I'd been eaten by a grizzly. I hadn't told them where I was going, so even if they wanted to search for me, they didn't know where to start.

Mia helped me dig myself out of my agony with a bottle of whiskey and a new dairy client needing a herd health check. As soon as I was sober enough to walk straight, Mia had me at the new dairy client's ranch doing pregnancy checks until my arm felt like it was going to fall off. Since Ashley and I broke up nine months ago, I've avoided the dating scene at all costs, determined to stay single and unattached.

Maybe that's why it's such a surprise that Lacey affects me the way that she does. From the moment I saw her in the middle of the street, I've had a fire coursing through my veins that I haven't felt since things were good with Ashley. Frankly, I'm not even sure I felt it with Ashley. Lacey has my head racing like a pubescent boy, making me want to claim her as my own.

I drop my pack and climb down the rocky bank to the river so I can look over my options and choose a fishing spot. Deciding to move further downstream, I grab my stuff again and walk it down to the spot I'd scoped out and settle in. I prep my line, then cast into the clear river. Already, I can feel the bottled-up tension I've been carrying zipline down my fishing line and drift away with the current.

In the canyon, a hiking path runs along the side of the river. The mountains loom over, creating a canyon, with pine trees growing up the sides. Spending time outdoors is a humbling experience. The clusters of yellow flowers growing in spots along the river and path remind me of Lacey at the barbecue. She used the yellow mallet in her croquet game with Caleb. I can't help but wonder if yellow is her favorite color.

Shit. I'm not supposed to be thinking about her. I'm supposed to be thinking about Ashley . . . forgiving her and choosing the family path I've always wanted or accepting the fact that life may be out of my reach.

The tip of my floating line dips down, telling me I've caught the interest of a fish, and I start my slow retrieve to bring the fish in. Gradually, I work the fish closer. When I'm getting close enough, I reach back on the bank behind me for the net to have it at the ready. Once I net the fish, I set my rod aside. I pull the rainbow trout out of the net and hold it in one hand while I snap a picture of it on my cell phone and then free it back into the river. Casting again, I patiently wait for my next catch.

With a successful day of fishing under my belt, I pack my gear up and get ready to hike back out of the canyon. I have about four miles to hike before it gets dark, and I didn't come prepared to stay the night here. I hike out and bask in the peacefulness of this beautiful canyon. It isn't busy with other hikers today, making it the perfect day for me to be out here.

Once I get far enough out of the canyon to receive a cell signal again, my phone goes crazy, buzzing in my pocket. Great. I don't even want to see how many messages I have. I take my time loading my stuff in the truck, and I climb inside and then make myself pull my phone out and face life.

> Mia: FYI Mom's pissed.
>
> Mia: I can't believe you made me go through family dinner alone.
>
> Mia: You owe me
>
> Mia: Do we need to have another whiskey night?
>
> Mia: Are you still lost in your feelings?
>
> Mia: You better let me know when you make it out so I know whether to send search and rescue after you or not.

Mia is obnoxious. She's one hell of a sister, though. I reply to let her know I'm headed home, and I put the truck into gear. I still don't know what to do about Ashley, but I've got to come to a conclusion soon.

On Monday afternoon, I walk into the flower shop, and I'm immediately greeted by Mom. Thankfully, she seems to have had time to cool off about me missing dinner. We chat for a bit, and she's telling me something about Dad's latest project that he's in way over his head with, but I can't focus on our conversation. I didn't actually stop by to see my mom. I need to see Lacey. After thinking about it, I've decided I need to explain myself to her.

Mom mentions Lacey is out in the greenhouse watering, and I head that way through the back of the shop. I don't owe Lacey anything. I know this. We've barely exchanged words with each other at this point. I know I'm walking on dangerous ground by seeking her out, but she is all I have been able to think about since I nearly hit her with my truck. Maybe if I make amends with her for my behavior, I'll be able to stop thinking about her and start focusing on the Ashley issue. At least, that's the excuse I keep telling myself.

It's hot and humid inside the greenhouse. My shirt instantly sticks to my skin. The fans on the back wall which circulate the air are so loud that Lacey doesn't even hear me come in. I slowly approach, not wanting to startle her.

Her thick, wavy hair is pulled up in a ponytail. She's wearing jean shorts and a T-shirt under her green flower shop apron, and she's barefoot. Smart, really. There's no way to avoid wet feet when watering the greenhouse. It's one of the disadvantages of the otherwise relaxing job. Lacey must have kicked her shoes off to keep them dry while she waters. It might not be OSHA approved, but OSHA's not here.

Lacey must have caught a glimpse of me from the corner of her eye, because those captivating eyes shoot up directly at me, surprise written across her face.

"Hey," I yell over the sound of the fans and approach her at a normal pace now.

"Hi," she replies, still watering the plants but giving me her attention.

I stop once I'm beside her. What did I come here for again? Damn, she's gorgeous. A few droplets of water fall from the bench of the watered plants and onto my boot.

"I want to apologize," I finally say, snapping back out of my head.

"For?" she yells back over the noise of the fans and continues watering.

"The other day. When I came to pick up the shipment. I

was a jerk. And for the time I almost ran you over. And then honked at you . . ."

Why did I think this was a good idea?

"You're right," Lacey replies, moving further down the bench to water more plants. "You were a jerk."

"It's just, I had a bad day . . . or . . . a bad week."

"Okay."

I'm not sure what I was expecting, but I do know I wasn't expecting her to be so nonchalant about it all. She isn't exactly making this easy on me.

"My ex showed up. She wants me to take her back. It was a whole thing. She hasn't been my favorite person for a while now." Lacey's looking at me like I should have more to say, but I don't, so I panic. "I told her I would think about it. About taking her back."

"Why did you break up?" Lacey asks without looking away from the plants.

"She cheated."

"That's terrible. Why would you take her back?"

Lacey looks up at me this time, watching me. She makes it sound so obvious. Lacey breaks eye contact and moves to the next bench. I follow close behind.

"We were engaged. She swears it was all a huge misunderstanding. She wants a second chance, and maybe she deserves one. I don't fucking know." I run a hand through my hair, the stress of the decision weighing on me again. "That's what I'm supposed to be figuring out."

The fans cut off, and it goes quiet in the greenhouse, aside from the sound of the water spraying from the hose Lacey is holding. I notice, suddenly, how close I'm standing to her, no longer giving her any space.

"She's manipulating you to get what she wants." Lacey speaks at a normal volume now, looking up at me. She takes a step to put some space between us and turns back to the plants.

"What do you mean?" I put my hands in my pockets, trying to deny the impulse I feel to pull her closer to me.

"She's making you question your perception of what happened that caused you to break up. And she has you questioning whether you owe it to her to give her another chance. It's not about what you experienced or what you feel. It's about you giving her what she wants. People like that are toxic."

"You know from experience?" I'm mere inches from her again.

"Yes. Years of experience. The longer you stay, the worse it will get, until it feels impossible to get out."

"How did you get out?" I ask in barely more than a whisper. She looks up at me through those long lashes, and we lock eyes.

"I ran away."

I hold her gaze, unable to pull myself from her. I want to reach out for her. I want to wrap her in a hug and just . . . be. What did she run away from? The thought of someone manipulating and taking advantage of this woman makes my blood boil over. I study her face and notice a thin scar shooting up from her eyebrow. The possibility of this woman experiencing pain is hard to reckon with, and I find myself hoping the scar stems from a good memory being made, rather than something upsetting. Every freckle looks intentionally placed over her slightly flushed cheeks, making her a masterpiece. Her lashes curl up from her bright eyes, and I'm jealous of her teeth that are nibbling on her lower lip.

"I should turn this water off," Lacey finally says, breaking the moment and backing away again.

I step back and take a deep breath, willing the blood to come back up to the head I'm supposed to be using right now. Lacey walks over to the spigot at the back of the greenhouse. My body can't resist the magnetic pull of the force that surrounds her, and I find myself following her, my hands still pushed deep in my pockets. Managing to stop a few steps away, I give her more space this time. I shouldn't have been all up in her business like I was, close enough to touch. Her song is too strong, and I need more distance if I have any hope of resisting her siren's call.

I watch Lacey hang the hose in its spot and reach for the knob of the spigot, closing the valve and shutting off the water. When she never seems to reach the end of twisting off the spigot, I take a curious step closer, ready to inspect it. Without warning, the spigot breaks off of the top of the pipe running up from the ground, leaving a geyser of water spewing into the air and soaking everything around it, including a squawking Lacey.

I rush to the rescue like a knight in fucking armor to reattach the spigot with no success. Lacey squeals next to me, her hands gripping the top of the pipe as she tries to stop the water from coming out. It causes the water to spray at us with a vengeance instead. The generous dousing of cold water helps calm the hard-on I've been fighting, and I'm finally able to get my wits about me enough to remember the main water cutoff to the greenhouse is only a couple of feet away. I reach for the cutoff from where I'm kneeling next to Lacey and the pipe. The water stops, and we collapse side by side on the wet cement floor, our clothing soaked through and clinging to our bodies.

After a moment of quiet, a bubble of laughter erupts from Lacey, coaxing a chuckle out of me, too. I study her, feeling the pull I've become accustomed to when I'm near her. Drops of water from her hair run down her face. A loose strand of wet hair is hanging down from her bun, partially plastered to her cheek. Without thinking, I reach across and tuck the feral strand of hair behind her ear. She stills, her giggles coming to a stop, and I think she might be feeling the same sensation that's clouding my judgment.

I want to pull her hair down from the ponytail and run my fingers through her beautiful, wavy mane. A droplet of water runs down her nose and rests in the dip of her cupid's bow, drawing my eyes back to the lips that I ache to taste.

Lacey bashfully lowers her eyes but only briefly. She must

feel it, too. She must feel us being pulled together. Is she leaning into me, or am I the one leaning, giving into temptation? Unable to keep my hands to myself anymore, I reach over again, this time stroking the back of my finger down her jaw, toward her lips. She leans into my touch, tilting her head slightly to the side. Our faces are only inches apart, her touch igniting the fire I've tried so hard to ignore. I don't want to ignore it anymore.

The thunderous rumble of the fans coming back to life jolts us both out of our spell, and we jump away from each other. The longing now replaced with an awkward tension, I clear my throat and rise to my feet, then offer a hand to Lacey. She hesitates briefly, then reaches out and takes it. The warmth of her touch spreads through my palm, climbing my arm as I pull her to her feet.

"I'm sorry," I mutter barely loud enough to be heard over the fans. "I may not technically be taken, but I'm not free to—"

"No, it's okay," she says. "We shouldn't."

I scoop up the broken spigot, give Lacey a nod, and walk out of the greenhouse.

After I locate my mother in the front of the shop, I try to explain the mishap in the greenhouse with the water spigot. She listens with a look of disbelief on her face. While she finishes processing my tale, I head for the hardware store to get a replacement.

Overall, that was probably the most disastrous apology I've given to date. I'm still not sure how I ended up soaking wet on the damn ground next to Lacey, touching her, and nearly giving in to my carnal need to taste her. Maybe if Ashley's apology to me went the same as this apology just now, I wouldn't have found myself with the self-control of a horny teenage boy in my mother's greenhouse.

Ashley. What am I going to fucking do about Ashley? I obviously loved her. I was going to marry her, after all. An apology from her doesn't fix anything, though, does it? Can I trust her again simply because she says that I should? Are her promises worth anything? I don't know. I want to make the right choice here, outside of the hurt I feel, but I don't know what the right thing is anymore. I'm confident about one thing, though. I need to stay away from Lacey while I figure it out. The rush of hormones she inspires in me isn't going to help me make a levelheaded decision about anything.

CHAPTER TEN

When I walk back into the shop looking like I've just competed in a wet T-shirt contest, Maddie gives me the rest of the afternoon off. I head straight to Jalynn's house, hoping she's home. Thankfully, her car is sitting in the driveway when I pull in.

I knock on her door and wait. Letting only a short moment pass, I knock again, harder this time. Jalynn hollers through the house that she's on her way, and I stand on the porch, soaked and flustered, when her door finally swings open.

"What is going on?" Jalynn asks. Concern is etched on her face. "Are you okay? What happened?"

"Can we talk?" I bite my lip.

"Yeah, of course. Come on in here. Let's get you changed out of those wet clothes and into something comfortable."

Jalynn motions me into the house and leads me straight to her closet for a change of clothes. She offers me a few different options, and I choose a pair of sweats and a T-shirt.

After the wardrobe change, Jalynn pours us both a glass of sweet tea, and I take a seat on the living room couch next to her. She looks at me expectantly, and I let the floodgates open. I tell her about Jacob coming by the shop to take the shipment of flowers to Bozeman. I try to explain the indescribable urge to be near him and the incident in the greenhouse. Jalynn sits quietly, for once, and listens.

"I don't understand what happened," I say, hugging a pillow to my chest. "He comes around, and I lose it. You'd think I'd never met an attractive guy. But it's more than me wanting to jump his bones. It's like I can sense him before I see him. I can feel him looking at me. I don't know him, but it's as though I've always known him."

"Bless your heart, Lacey. You sound like you're in love with him."

"Don't be ridiculous," I scoff. "I don't know him. Also, he's trying to work things out with his ex, from the sounds of it. I don't want to get in the middle of anyone else's drama. I've had plenty of my own."

"Oh no. I sure hope he doesn't get back with her." Jalynn rolls her eyes. "I can't stand the girl."

"I don't know the details," I say. "He just said they've been talking about it. And then there's Caleb . . ."

"Oh, yes!" Jalynn claps excitedly. "Tell me what's going on with Caleb."

"Nothing much. We've been texting back and forth. He's been flirty and has asked me out a couple times." I take a sip of my tea and set the glass back down on the coffee table.

"Wait, you went out with him and didn't tell me about it?"

"I turned him down."

"No, you didn't . . ." Jalynn says, leaning slightly forward in her seat.

"But I did," I say with a sigh.

"Why? I thought you liked him."

"I don't know. I do like him. He's incredibly handsome and sweet. This is just so hard. I don't know what to do." I rest my chin on the pillow still snuggled to my chest.

"Do you want to go out with him?" Jalynn asks.

"Yes. But no. I don't know. I'm just barely getting comfortable with texting him." I pull my feet up, crossing my legs in front of me.

"So what exactly did you tell him when he asked you out?"

A blush spreads to my cheeks, and I bite at my lip, remembering the conversation from the last time he asked to take me on a date.

"I told him I needed two to three weeks' notice," I blurt out and pull a throw pillow up over my face. Jalynn erupts with laughter, nearly rolling out of her seat. I can't help laughing along with her.

"Good heavens, Lacey, I'm gonna pee myself!" Jalynn squeals as her laughter begins to calm. "Are you a potential date or an employer?"

"I know! I don't know why I said that. I just got all nervous, and that's what came out," I say, still lightly bubbling with giggles. "See? I'm not cut out for this. I should just give up on a happily ever after and accept my fate of becoming an old cat lady." I grab my sweet tea for another sip.

"Lacey, honey, obviously you need to do what feels right to you, *but* for what it's worth, I think Caleb would be good for you. If you want to go after that, don't overthink it. Let yourself be happy. I have no doubt he's one that would treat you right."

"And he's such a good guy. I'm having fun talking to him. He's good for me. I just need to steer clear of Jacob and let the air clear for a bit, right?"

"I agree," Jalynn says. "Jacob's great, don't get me wrong, but if you ask me, the last thing you need right now is to get involved in a messy love triangle. Caleb is an excellent choice, and if he makes you happy, you should hold on to that." Jalynn reaches over and squeezes my hand. "Whatever you decide, though, I've got your back."

I don't know what I'd do without this girl. I finish off my glass of tea, slouch down on the couch, and rest my head on her shoulder.

"You're gonna be one hell of a mom," I say.

"Hello?" I answer my ringing phone while I'm getting ready for bed on Friday night after an evening of games at Jalynn's.

"Hey, pretty girl, what are you up to?" Caleb asks.

"Well, I was just sittin' here thinkin' 'bout you . . ." I say, throwing the twang in my voice on extra thick.

"I like the sound of that. I have a question for you."

"What's up?" I ask, though I'm pretty sure I know where he is headed.

"I know I'm short on giving you notice, but I want to see you this weekend. Are you free?" Caleb asks.

"Hmmm." I draw out giving him an answer, teasing him a bit. I've already decided, after my conversation with Jalynn and much internal debate, that if he asked me out again, I'd accept. "I think I can squeeze you in."

"I'll pick you up tomorrow around eleven. Does that work for you?"

"That's perfect."

The following morning, I step out of the shower, wrap a towel tightly around my body, pile my wet hair up on my head, and lather my moisturizer on my face and neck. I grab my phone and turn on my playlist while I do my makeup and hair.

I'm trying to let myself be excited for my date with Caleb. Talking to him has been a highlight for me, and I had a blast playing croquet at the barbecue with him. Something about Caleb puts me at ease. I'm not sure if I'm more nervous about the possibility of him turning out to be something different than he seems or the potential he has to be something great. Regardless, I hope I can put Ben behind me and give Caleb a chance.

After deciding on a jean skirt hitting about midthigh and a

feminine V-neck blouse, I slide into my boots. Footsteps on the porch catch my attention. I scramble to finish gathering myself as a couple of knocks sound on the door.

"Just a second!" I call out, taking one last look at myself in the mirror.

I run my fingers through my curls, loosening them into semicontrolled waves, and spritz myself with perfume. I slide my cell phone into my purse and lift the strap over my head, across my body. Doubt begins to overtake me as I approach the door. Am I rushing this? Will Caleb actually be any different than Ben? Despite my concerns, I push forward, determined to overcome the fear. When I open the camper door, Caleb is smiling on the other side. Just like that, the doubts and fear begin to melt away. How does he do that?

"I thought about bringing you flowers, but knowing that you work at a floral shop, I didn't know if that would be a good thing or not," Caleb confesses. "So I brought you chocolates instead."

He pulls a box of chocolates out from behind his back and holds them out to me.

"Thank you. Aren't you just sweet as pie? I've actually never been given flowers, either," I admit. I set the box of chocolates on the counter and shut the door behind me.

"I'll keep that in mind. So this is where you live, huh?" Caleb looks around while I lock the door.

"Yep. It's pretty peaceful."

"Looks like a nice little setup. You don't get nervous being out here all alone, though?" he asks, returning his gaze to me.

"I mean, it would certainly be nice to have a brave, strapping man I could call on if I got scared," I tease, trying to maintain a timid expression.

"Yeah?" Caleb asks, instantly seeing my performance for what it is. "I might know someone like that you could call."

"You do?" I look up at him eagerly, fighting the grin that's trying to break free.

"Yeah. I'm pretty brave. And I have the strapping part mostly down, too," Caleb says with a showy flex of his arms.

"My hero!" I say, clasping my hands over my chest.

"Get out of here!" Caleb chuckles and ushers me toward his truck.

He throws an arm around my shoulders, leads me over to the passenger side of his pickup, and opens the door for me to climb in. I look at the floorboard of the truck, down at my skirt, then up at Caleb. The floorboard is nearly hip-high on me with no running board to step up on.

"This could be a problem," I say, laughing. "Maybe I should go inside and change into pants."

"Hmmm . . . a bit of a leap for you, huh? That's okay. I think we can manage." Caleb wraps his massive hands around my waist and lifts me into the truck.

"Thanks," I say, adjusting myself in the seat. As Caleb hops in, now on the driver's side of the truck, I ask, "Where are we going?"

"You'll see," Caleb says with his typical grin. He backs out of the driveway.

"No, Caleb," I say, resting my hand over his on the gear shifter before he can move the transmission into gear, "I want to know where we're going."

Caleb pauses, looking over at me with an expression I can't read. My heart starts to pound in my chest, and suddenly, I wonder if it was a good idea to agree to this.

"I want to show you the scenery on our way up to this little lake I know about. Honestly, it's so small it's almost more of a giant pond, but people go up there to picnic and swim and stuff like that. Our lunch is in the basket in the back. But if you aren't comfortable with that, we can do something else," Caleb says in a gentle voice.

"No, sorry," I say, withdrawing my hand from his again. I shake my head, focusing my eyes on my lap. "A lakeside picnic sounds fun. I'd love that." I look back up at him and force a smile.

"Are you sure? Seriously, Lacey, if it makes you uncomfortable—"

"No, please. I want to go."

Caleb nods silently and shifts the truck into gear, and we head down the road further away from town. I control the radio on our drive to the lake, flipping through the stations between songs and rocking out to my favorites, the music soothing the nervous butterflies in my stomach. Caleb was right about it being a beautiful drive. Montana is a lot different from what I'm accustomed to but just as gorgeous as home. Instead of roads winding along the tree-covered Appalachians, the terrain is an open expanse of landscape, surrounded by formidable, bare Rockies.

We arrive at the lake, and I make a mental note of the other vehicles already here and remind myself that, though I haven't spent much time with Caleb, Jalynn and George know him well. When Caleb hops down out of the truck, I scoot over into the driver's seat. Caleb reaches up for me, grinning, and lifts me down, the muscles in his shoulders working under my hands as he lowers me to the ground.

I love his smile. I don't think anyone could be sad with Caleb around. He exudes happiness. Caleb grabs the basket out of the back of the truck, then takes my hand in his large, callused one, interlacing our fingers. My heart starts beating harder in my chest, and I examine my racing thoughts, trying to determine how I feel about holding his hand.

Can I do this?

"You're not shy, are you?" I ask, nodding toward our clasped hands.

"I just know a good thing when I see it," Caleb replies nonchalantly.

This isn't so scary. This is okay.

We stroll at a leisurely pace on the gravel trail around the lake. Conversation comes naturally.

"Do you have any siblings?" I ask.

"No. I'm an only child. My parents wanted more kids, but it wasn't in the cards for them, I guess. So, growing up, I spent every possible minute up at my friend Austin's house. He's like a brother to me, and we're always looking out for his little sister."

"And you work with George now?"

"Yeah, I came back after college and started working on the ranch with George. It's a pretty nice gig, and it allows me to be close in case my parents need anything."

I listen and nod along, encouraging him to keep talking.

"What about you?" Caleb finally asks.

"I was raised by my grandparents from the time I was seven. My granddaddy passed away while I was in high school, and then my grammy passed the summer after my freshman year of college."

"Do you have any other family? Are you related to Jalynn?" Caleb asks, concern showing on his face.

"No. Jalynn is like a sister to me, but we're just good friends. It's okay, though. It's easy to go where you want and do what you want when you're not tied to any family."

"That is possibly the saddest thing I've ever heard," Caleb says, looking down at me.

I ignore the pity that sweeps across his face.

"When are we eating this fancy lunch you packed?" I ask, holding a hand to my stomach as though I'm having hunger pains. The pity in his expression washes away as quickly as it appeared, replaced with a look of understanding.

"This looks like a good enough spot," Caleb says, following my cue.

Caleb spreads the blanket out and offers me first pick at a spot to sit. I sit and Caleb settles next to me, pulling out the contents from the basket. He has cold-cut sandwiches, chips, pickles, and a giant slice of chocolate cake to share. He hands me two clear plastic cups to hold while he opens and pours the sparkling grape juice he brought.

"Looks like you've done this a time or two," I say, giving him a look as though I've caught him in something. "I bet you do this with all of the girls."

"Just the special ones," Caleb replies with a wink, not skipping a beat.

"This is nice," I say. "It reminds me of my favorite spot back home."

"Oh yeah?" Caleb responds, encouraging me to continue.

"We have a river that runs near the town. Most of our free time growing up was spent on that riverbank, a local hangout of sorts. A lot of firsts happened there, too. Oh, the stories Jalynn and I could tell from those days." A grin spreads across my face at just the thought of our shenanigans.

"Maybe we can have some good firsts here," Caleb suggests.

With full bellies and good conversation, neither of us are too anxious to leave. We stroll down to the rocky beach of the lake, and Caleb teaches me how to skip rocks across the water.

"Person with the most skips wins," I say after only a few minutes of practice.

"I'm beginning to realize that you, Miss Lacey, are a very competitive person. You think you're ready to take me on?" he asks.

I approach Caleb where he's currently down on one knee gathering flat rocks for skipping and lean down toward him, gently pressing a hand to his cheek. Our lips are only inches apart. I stare into his eyes. His breath catches, and my gentle giant rigidly stays rooted to the spot, waiting for me to close the gap between us.

"Only the weak cower in the face of competition." I giggle as I spin away from him and start scooping up my own rocks. Caleb clears his throat behind me.

"Alright then, Exquisitely Beautiful Queen of Croquet, prepare to be humbled," he says, rising to his feet.

Several rounds of rock skipping later, most of which were won by Caleb, Caleb glances at his watch.

"I'd better get you back home," he says.

I help gather up our picnic, and we stroll back to Caleb's truck with his arm around my shoulders and my arm around his waist. I feel safe with him.

Maybe I can do this.

"That was a fun afternoon," Caleb says later, standing at my camper door.

"I had fun, too. Thanks for the picnic. And the rock skipping instruction."

"With more practice, I think you'll be pretty good competition. When can I see you again?"

Caleb steps in closer to me, and I'm acutely aware of his every move.

"Next weekend?" I suggest.

"You're not going to make me wait that long, are you?" Caleb's fingers gently trail up and down the backs of my arms.

"Patience is a virtue."

"A virtue I have very little interest in," Caleb says with a playful smirk.

He slowly inches in closer to me, undoubtedly hoping to end the date with a kiss. I debate my next move. This was good. He's good for me. He's a respectable guy, and I love spending time with him.

I slowly slide my hands up his shoulders and around his neck. Caleb takes the invitation and leans down toward me. Rising up on my toes, I close the space between us and lightly brush my lips against his. He leans further into me, deepening the kiss, but I'm quick to cut it off, not ready to push myself any further.

"Call me," I say and slide through the door.

That night, while preparing for bed, my phone dings, alerting me to another text message from Caleb.

Caleb: Goodnight, beautiful. Sleep well.

I collapse on my bed and touch my fingers to my lips. It was a simple kiss but significant just the same. Caleb is the first man I've kissed aside from my ex. Emotions swirl in my head as I try to process my new reality. Caleb's so sweet and gentle. I undoubtedly could've turned him away tonight, and he would've accepted it without retaliation. I'm sure of it. He wouldn't exploit his status with me to finagle physical intimacy.

I think about the way Ben felt entitled to every piece of me. I remember how he'd push and demand and manipulate until I finally gave him what he wanted. My stomach churns, and I break out in a sweat. With each second ticking by that I allow myself to dwell on the memories of him, anxiety grows within my belly. I push the thoughts of him away, grateful for the new reality I've been able to establish for myself here in Montana. Finally letting my body relax, I drift off into a restless sleep, the old memories playing over in my mind.

"Okay, class, this is your senior project. It's worth thirty percent of your final grade, so get used to looking at your partner's face, because you will be seeing a lot of each other if you do this project correctly," Mr. Huffcutt said. "Seventy percent of your project grade will be based on your work. The other thirty percent will be based on your presentation."

The bell rang, and Mr. Huffcutt's voice was drowned out by the bustling of students leaving the classroom. Ben pulled me out the side door to the parking lot. I hung back, letting my hand slide out of Ben's.

"Wait, Ben, I have to go this way," I said, motioning to the other parking lot.

"Why?" Ben asked.

"I'm going to the library with Gary. We're gonna get started on our project."

"I thought we were gonna hang out. Are you seriously choosing Gary over me?"

"No, Ben. Don't be silly. He's just going out of town this weekend, so we wanted to go ahead and get started."

"I can't believe you let Mr. Huffcutt pair you with that loser. Did you even try to switch partners?"

"You know I did. You saw me talk to him about it," I said and tried to pull Ben toward me. "I'll call you when we're done. You can come pick me up, and we'll go do something."

"Whatever," Ben said, clearly unsatisfied, and he turned away.

"Ben, don't be like this," I called after him.

As promised, I dialed Ben's number as I stepped out of the library. It rang a few times, then went to voicemail. I sat down on the front steps of the library and dialed again. This time it only rang twice before going to voicemail. He was ignoring my calls. I opened a new message and typed out a text to him.

> Me: I'm done at the library. Wanna come get me?

After pressing send, I noticed a new text on my phone from Chance, one of Ben's friends. I opened the message to see why Chance was texting me. Ben always got pissed when other guys would text me, and his friends knew better.

> Chance: Thought you'd want to see this.

The message was followed by a picture. In it, Ben was sitting on his tailgate down at the river with a bunch of other kids from *school. One of whom, Jessica Moore, he had his arm around. I zoomed in on the picture, trying to figure out whether he was whispering something in her ear or kissing her neck like he'd done so many times to me.*

Me: What the hell Chance???

I slid my phone back in my pocket and started walking home. Grammy was on night shift, so she couldn't come pick me up, but the library was just a couple of miles from home, anyway. As I walked, I debated calling Jalynn and telling her what happened. Jalynn was already not Ben's biggest fan, though, and I didn't want to risk driving that wedge any further between my best friend and my boyfriend. Or was it my ex-boyfriend now? I should break up with him, if it wasn't already his intention to end things with me. I didn't know what exactly was happening in that photo, but whatever it was, I knew it wasn't okay.

As usual, Grammy left the back door unlocked for me. She'd left a note on the counter, telling me my dinner was in the microwave. I pulled it out and stood at the counter, picking at it. Grammy had made one of my favorites, but I couldn't enjoy it. My mind was still on that picture.

My phone buzzed from my pocket, but when I saw Ben's name on the screen, I pushed the red button and slid it back in my pocket. It buzzed again. This time I turned the phone off, not wanting to talk to him. I just wanted to go to bed. Maybe with some rest, everything would seem simpler.

Too exhausted from the drama of the day for an entire bedtime routine, I pulled off my shoes and jeans and slid into the comfort of my bed. Instantly, my body began to relax. Just as I was starting to drift off to sleep, however, my bedroom door flew open, banging against the wall and startling me to attention. I sat up in bed in a panic to find a dark figure filling my doorway. Ben.

"What are you doing here?" I asked, half enraged and half-heartbroken.

"*Why weren't you answering my phone calls, baby? I tried calling you,*" *Ben said in an accusatory tone.*

He ignored my calls and was hanging on another girl, but I was the problem, per usual with him.

"*I don't have to answer to you anymore.*"

"*Why's that?*"

Ben slowly stalked into my room, approaching my bed.

"*Because we're done. Now kindly see your way out.*" *I pulled my knees up to my chest, the blankets covering me, giving me a sense of protection.*

"*That's funny. I don't remember having that conversation.*" *Ben stopped at the edge of the bed.*

"*Probably because your head was too far up Jessica Moore's ass to hear me!*" *I raised myself up on my knees so that he wasn't towering as high over me.*

"*What was I supposed to do? I have needs. She was willing to give me what I needed.*" *Ben leaned in closer, so close our noses were practically touching, and I could smell the booze and cigarettes on his breath.*

"*For the last time, Gary and I were just doing research for our senior project.*" *I shoved his chest away from me, but he caught my wrists and held his ground.*

"*I told you that I needed you to come with me, but you chose him anyway. What was I supposed to do? If you'd been there, I wouldn't have needed anyone else. This is your fault, Lacey. You caused this. And now you're trying to break up with me?*"

"*Ben, leave . . . I don't want you here.*"

"*Not until you tell me you're still my girl.*"

"*Ben—*"

"*Say it, Lacey. Tell me you're mine.*"

I quickly realized there was no point in arguing with him while he was drunk. That's when his temper was always the shortest. I fell back onto my butt and folded my arms over my chest.

"*Fine. I'm yours, Ben. Now leave. I'll talk to you tomorrow.*"

I sit upright in my bed, soaked with sweat and tangled in my blankets. Pulling my legs free, I drop them over the side of the bed, stand, and head into the bathroom to splash cold water on my face. It's easy to see the signs now, looking back. I feel sick as I think of the control I allowed him to have over me. I try to calm my ragged breath. Slowly, my heartbeat steadies, and my body begins to relax again.

CHAPTER ELEVEN

Switching off the TV, I rise from the couch to answer the tapping at the door. Against what may actually be my better judgment, I've invited Ashley over to talk things out once and for all. I've been stewing over her proposal to get back together for over a week now, and it's time to make a move, regardless of the direction.

"Hey, baby. I'm glad you called," Ashley says when I answer the door.

She brushes a kiss on my cheek, and if she notices my minor recoil at her touch, she doesn't let on.

I follow her into the living room, and she settles herself on the couch. She's wearing that blue dress I always loved to see her in. Intentional, I'm sure, and it's not a wasted effort. It still gets to me, reminding me of the weekend trip we took last year to Jackson Hole.

"You look good," she says, probably fishing for a compliment of her own.

I oblige.

"Thanks, so do you," I say.

The tension in the room is so fucking thick you could slice it with a knife.

"Have you made a decision?" Ashley presses after a few beats of silence.

"I'm not confident there's a future for us," I say. "I don't know if I'll ever be able to look at you the same. But I think we both would take back some choices if we could."

"I would," Ashley says softly, as hope inflates her body. "If I could go back and change it, I would."

"I still want the same things, Ash. And I want them with you. I don't want to give up on us if there's any chance that we can fix this. So, if that's what you want, I want to give it a try."

Ashley grins and rises back to her feet. She comes across the room and hugs me tightly against her, knocking me off balance. I stumble but catch us, my arms awkwardly wrapping around her. This might not be the right decision, but the worst thing that can happen by choosing to try is wasting a small amount of time. On the other hand, if it is the right decision, and I don't try, I could be losing my future.

lacey

The front door bells chime while I'm sweeping the shop. We've had a busy start to June. I glance up from my task to welcome the customer and find Caleb standing at the door, his familiar grin on his face. I wasn't expecting him, but I don't mind that he stopped by. I can't help but smile when I look at him. He is full of happiness. It's almost as though the joy just spills out of him. I lean the broom against a chair and wrap my arms around his neck, hugging him. He wraps me up in his arms and lifts me off the ground, spinning me around.

"What are you doing here?" I ask.

"I wanted to see my girl," Caleb says. "What time do you get off work?"

"In about fifteen minutes. Why?"

"I want to take you somewhere." Caleb sets me back on my feet.

"Sounds great."

"I'll pick you up from your place in about an hour, if that's enough time for you. You need to wear warm clothes. Nothing fancy that you don't want to get dirty."

"Oh"—I wiggle my eyebrows at him—"I'm liking the sounds of this."

Caleb kisses me on the cheek and leaves so I can finish closing up. I'm enjoying dating Caleb. He's lighthearted and fun, always making me smile. Still, something is missing. But is that to be expected so early on? Is the missing piece something that will grow into place eventually?

Back at home, I change into a pair of old jeans and a T-shirt, then tie a sweatshirt around my waist. I pull my hair up in a ponytail and go outside on the deck to wait for Caleb. My eyes roam over the little home I've created for myself here, and my chest fills with pride. The closest thing I've done to this was moving to college, but even then, I had Jalynn living with me. Looking back, it feels like our move to college was a lifetime ago.

"This place is starting to come together," Jalynn announced, wiping her hands off on her pants. We've been unpacking our final few boxes in our new college apartment, two hours from home.

"I know! I can't wait for Ben to come see it," I added.

"That was awful convenient for him to be too busy to help while we were unloading all of our stuff."

Jalynn gives an exaggerated eye roll in my direction, and I feel the need to defend my boyfriend's honor yet again.

"You know Ben wasn't happy about me moving in with you instead of him. Give him some time to get over it."

"Yeah, yeah, yeah. The green-eyed monster, always jealous of anyone who dares spend time with you. When I see him next, I'm telling him the apartment manager mixed up and gave us a one bedroom so now I'm sharing a bed with you, too."

Now it's my turn to roll my eyes.

"If you held onto any guys long enough, I'm sure they'd get jealous, too," I said jokingly, winning a nudge from Jalynn.

When Caleb's truck pulls into the driveway, the crunching of the gravel pulls me back from my college days. I hop up out of my seat and skip down the steps.

"Hey, beautiful," Caleb says when I open the passenger door and make the climb into his truck. He pats the middle of the bench, inviting me to slide over next to him. I hesitate momentarily. His smile warms me like it always does, though, and I scoot over next to my affable beau.

I'm not sure how long we've been driving when Caleb pulls off the road onto a dirt path leading to the middle of nowhere. Eventually, he slows to a stop. Caleb carefully leads the way, and we hike down into a canyon, to a dark opening at the base. He pulls a small head lamp out of his pocket.

"Now would be a good time to put that sweatshirt on," Caleb says. "It's only going to get colder from here."

I untie the arms of the sweatshirt from around my waist and pull it on over my head. Caleb takes the head lamp and straps it to my forehead, then pulls out another one and puts it on himself. He takes my hand and leads me into the opening, crouching as we go.

"What are you getting me into?" I ask, peering down into a dark hole about four feet across.

A rope is securely tied to a stake at the top of the opening. The incline down is sloped and frozen over with ice.

"You're taking me into a cave?" I ask, realization finally sinking in. My palms dampen from the nervous excitement that washes over me.

"Is that okay? I think you'll like it."

"We don't need special training for this?"

"This is a simple cave to navigate." Caleb reaches over and adjusts my head lamp. "It's perfect for beginners. You want to give it a try?"

"As long as we don't find any skeletons of lost spelunkers down there, I'm in."

"I'll go down first. You can follow me," Caleb says. "That way I can kick the skeletons aside so you don't see them."

"Hold up," I say. "You know that old expression 'Hold my beer?'"

"I'm familiar," Caleb says, peering down at me.

I pat his hard chest and smirk up at him.

"Hold my figurative beer," I say.

Without waiting for a response so that he has no chance to disagree with me, I take hold of the rope and slide down feet first into the icy hole. Caleb's chuckle follows me down into the cave, and he waits at the top of the opening till I make it to the bottom and move out of his way. Once he makes it in, I'm patiently waiting for him at the bottom of the slope.

Inside the cave, the ground is solid ice, providing very little traction. The walls and ceiling are a combination of rock and ice. I continue to lead the way, since there is only one direction we can go into the cave. With a hand on each side of the passageway, I take deliberate steps on the ice, careful not to slip, as the width of the opening narrows down to only about two feet. Soon, the width narrows more, and I have to turn my body sideways to continue through. I look back at Caleb. He's somehow still able to follow even with his massive build.

The passage opens back up again into a larger cavern, but the ceiling drops abruptly in front of us, only a couple of feet from the icy floor. I carefully lower myself to my knees so I can peer through the opening. The height is just short enough for me to crawl through on my hands and knees, and I army crawl through the opening.

I easily slide down the dips in the ice, and after about ten feet of army crawling, I'm back in another cavern, able to stand again. I wait for Caleb to catch up.

We're able to navigate the rest of the way on our feet. At the back of the cave, the wall of ice slopes down. Another rope is secured several feet up the wall. I grab the rope and am able to pull myself up to a small shelf of ice, several feet up. Caleb slides onto the landing beside me.

"Now what?" I ask him.

"Now," he says, wrapping an arm behind me, "you slide."

He gently pushes me over the ledge, and I squeal with delight as I go gliding down the icy slope.

After several trips down the wall, we begin our trek back out of the cave. Making it out is more treacherous in spots. Working against the slopes of ice, I search for something secure to grab onto as I crawl through the section of low ceiling. With no exposed rock within reach, I grab hold of a jagged lump of ice, hoping to have enough traction on it to keep my grip. Slowly, I pull myself forward, up the small incline of ice. Suddenly, my hand slips, and I fall back down the incline with a thud.

"Are you okay?" Caleb asks from behind me.

"I hit my head." I pause and touch my fingers to my forehead. I can feel it already beginning to swell. "I'm okay, though."

I try again, this time making my way though.

Finally out of the cave, we make our way back out into the dimming sunlight. We take off the head lamps and remove our wet sweatshirts.

"Wait," Caleb says, catching a glimpse of my forehead. He brushes the loose strands of hair from the front of my face. "Babe," he says, his voice full of remorse, "your head. You have a big goose egg on your forehead."

My fingers go to my forehead, feeling the large bump that has appeared, and I wince.

"It's not too bad," I assure him. "A small price to pay for that experience."

"No, it's not a small price. Do you have a headache or feel dizzy or anything?"

"No, Caleb, really, I'm fine."

Caleb turns his back to me, crouches down, and instructs me to hop onto his back. I do, after a slight pause, and he stands back up, holding onto my thighs to secure me. I wrap my arms tightly around him but protest him carrying me all the way back to the truck.

"This isn't necessary, Caleb. Really."

"It is necessary. I let you get hurt. The least I can do is make sure you're taken care of."

"It's too steep of a climb back to the truck, and I'm too heavy. You'll just end up hurting yourself in the process."

"Now I *have* to carry you back. You just called me weak," he scoffs, but the humor still in his voice tells me he's teasing. "I've got to prove my brute strength now."

BACK AT MY CAMPER, Caleb unnecessarily helps me inside and onto my bed, despite my insistence that I'm fine. He pulls a bag of frozen peas from the freezer and applies it to my head. Caleb climbs onto the bed beside me, setting off warning bells in my head. I suddenly feel clammy and closed in.

"Actually," I say, "I think I need some fresh air. Let's go sit on the deck."

Before he can reply, I'm off the bed and out the door of the camper. Caleb follows, and when I take a seat, he motions to the spot next to me. I nod, feeling more secure in the open space. Caleb monitors my symptoms while telling me stories about other caves he's visited. Eventually, I'm cuddled into his chest, enjoying the warmth of his body and the velvet of his voice until he's convinced that I'm not about to pass out or suffer from amnesia.

"I'll call and check on you when I make it home," he says.

"Caleb, I'm fine."

"I think so, too. But I'm still going to check up on you to be sure."

He kisses my forehead sweetly and turns to leave.

lacey

"How's it going with Caleb?" Jalynn asks me. "We never get much of a chance to talk about it. It seems like he's always with you, which I assume means things have been good?"

I'm sitting on a stool at her kitchen island, chopping vegetables to go into the salad Jalynn is making. Chopping vegetables is about all she allows me to help with in the kitchen, for good reason. The one time in college she allowed me to make dinner, the meal had been absent of any positive flavors, but we all choked it down anyway. Shortly after the meal, we came down with food poisoning. Jalynn hasn't left me unsupervised in the kitchen since.

"Caleb is amazing . . . and I can't deny I've been having a blast with him."

"Sounds like a 'but' is coming." Jalynn stops what she's doing and looks at me with narrowed eyes.

"But . . ." I say with slight exaggeration, "something's missing."

"What do you mean?"

"He's handsome, obviously. He says all the right things. And he's so gentle, like a gentle giant. You know I get a little uneasy sometimes, but I don't get that feeling very often with him anymore. I have an absolute blast when I'm with him. He's a good kisser, too," I add with a grin. "But there's no butterflies. His touch doesn't short-circuit my brain."

"Okay . . ."

"It's almost like a male version of you that I make out with on occasion. Does that make sense?"

"Maybe the fireworks will come later," Jalynn suggests, swatting George away as he picks at the cucumbers.

"Maybe. How long can I wait, though, without risking leading him on?"

I shrug and finish chopping the last of the peppers. I dump the peppers into the bowl of salad and slide off my stool to go answer the knocks at the front door. Caleb should be showing up soon for the dinner party Jalynn is hosting. Instead of Caleb, though, it's Jacob and Ashley. I greet them as they step inside. Jacob's arm brushes against mine as they walk by, and as usual, butterflies fill my stomach and overtake my body at his touch.

Memories from the greenhouse fill my head. I know I shouldn't let the memories stay. He's back with Ashley, and I'm with Caleb. I respect that. We got caught up in the moment in the greenhouse. That was all. I pull my eyes away from Jacob and start setting the table for our meal, ignoring the urge to be near him.

Relief floods my body when I hear knocking at the door again. This time it will be Caleb. I sidestep Jacob to get to the door, accidentally brushing against him again. Goose bumps run down my arm where we touched. I take slow, deliberate breaths, trying to steady my heartbeat as I wrap my fingers around the doorknob and pull the door open. As expected, a grinning Caleb stands on the other side. Caleb steps through the door. He grabs me up and spins me, pulling a giggle from me. He places me back on my feet and presses a kiss to my lips.

"Gosh, it's good to lay eyes on you," Caleb says.

"It's about time you got here," I tease and turn to lead him by the hand over to our group of friends.

I ignore Jacob's eyes burning into me and focus instead on Jalynn ushering everyone to the table to have a seat.

Dinner starts off smoothly. I'm the newcomer to the group but feel like I have melted in seamlessly. Well, except with Ashley. She glowers at me most of the time we're together and typically doesn't speak to me at all unless she has something snide to say. I thought maybe Jacob had told her about the close call in the greenhouse before they were back together, but after the last time we all hung out, Jalynn insisted it's just the way Ashley is.

"Is everyone going to the summer festival next weekend?" Jalynn asks during the meal.

"I still can't believe enough people go to that stupid festival to make it worth the trouble of doing it every year," Ashley scoffs.

"Ash," Jacob admonishes quietly, sitting back in his seat.

"I'm being serious. It's a ridiculous event," she continues. "I wouldn't recommend wasting your time with it," she says, directing her attention toward me. "You won't miss anything by not attending that redneck event."

"Actually, I'm gonna go. I'm pretty excited about it. I wish my hometown did something similar," I say.

I might be new, but even I have heard how important the festival is to everyone around here. Nearly the whole town shuts down for the night.

"The festival is nice," Jacob chimes in. "Don't let Ashley convince you otherwise. I've been going for as long as I can remember."

I feel his eyes linger on me.

"Me, too," George adds in, raising a fork in the air. He goes back in for another bite.

"We should all go together!" Jalynn suggests. "Make a big group date of it. It'd be fun."

"Sounds good to me," Caleb says. "What do you think, Lace?"

"Yeah. Let's do it."

"I suppose you do look the type to find a silly festival exciting," Ashley says to me, rolling her eyes.

I glance over at Jalynn. When her eyes leave mine, they go directly to her plate.

"Lacey, what happened to your forehead?" George asks, trying to move the conversation along. He has spent enough time with us to know the meaning behind our silent exchange. And he's heard me tell Jalynn how badly Ashley gets under my skin.

"I headbutted a block of ice," I say.

"I took her out to the ice cave," Caleb joins in. "She had a small mishap on the way out, but I nursed her back to health."

Caleb winks at me and goes back to eating the food on his plate. The muscle in Jacob's jaw flexes so briefly I'm not sure if I imagined it.

"It was so much fun, though. It was well worth it," I say.

I know without looking that Jacob is still staring at me. I can feel his eyes on me, making me sizzle.

"There's lots of good places to go around here if you like being out in nature," Jacob says. "Do you like fishing?"

"I haven't fished much," I admit. "But I'd love to learn how to fly fish."

"That's my favorite," Jacob says, his attention locked on me. "I could give you some incredible spots to go." Ashley is glaring at Jacob now, a sour expression on her face, but he doesn't seem to notice her. "Where else have you been?"

"Caleb took me to this super cute little lake. What's that lake called?" I ask Caleb, forcing myself to break eye contact with Jacob.

Caleb clears his throat and uncomfortably shifts in his seat. We all wait expectantly.

"Lover's Lake," he mumbles.

Jalynn giggles, and Jacob's jaw clenches again. Maybe I didn't imagine it.

"What?" I ask, reading the room.

"Lover's Lake is a notorious place for couples to go to . . . if you know what I mean." Jalynn giggles and winks at Lacey.

"Oh. In that case, I guess I don't have to say anything more about what we were doing up there," I say jokingly and nudge Caleb.

"That's fitting," Ashley snips at me. "You would be the type to brag about going to Lover's Lake with a boy."

I pause for a moment, letting my eyes linger on Ashley. She straightens in her chair, looking uneasy under my gaze.

"Aren't you precious?" I say with a sweet smile. Jalynn struggles to smother a giggle.

"Lacey's some serious competition when it comes to skipping rocks," Caleb says.

He drapes an arm around my shoulders and kisses the side of my face. Ashley rolls her eyes again.

"Gag me!" she mutters under her breath.

"How about you, Ashley?" I ask. "Are you any good at skipping rocks?"

"I can't say I've ever tried." Ashley sits up straighter in her chair and dabs the corners of her mouth with her napkin. "I'm usually much too busy with more important things."

"All work and no play? Bless your heart," I say, feigning pity.

"I'm sure I could give you a run for your money," Jacob chimes in. Ashley turns red beside him. "Maybe we should all go out on the lake one day. We could take my boat."

"We're free next weekend, aren't we, Jay?" George asks, earning a nod from Jalynn.

"Well, we *aren't*," Ashley says, giving Jacob a pointed look. "Remember, we're supposed to spend the day in Bozeman."

"Bozeman isn't going anywhere, and Lacey hasn't been out on the lake yet. We'll do Bozeman another day," Jacob says, his eyes not leaving mine, and I hope there's no evidence on my face of the heat building inside me.

"You've *got* to be kidding me!" Ashley's rage breaks the spell, and I quickly look away.

"What's wrong, Ashley?" Jacob asks.

"You're choosing her over me!"

George chokes on his water, coughing and sputtering to clear his lungs. Jalynn slaps him loudly on the back, trying to help him regain his composure.

"What are you talking about?" Jacob askes in an exasperated tone, leaning back in his seat.

"I thought I was imagining it, but I'm not, am I?" Ashley's voice screeches through the room.

"You need to chill out, Ash. You're blowing things out of proportion," Jacob says barely above a whisper, clearly uncomfortable with the direction the conversation seems to be headed. "Not everything is about you."

Ashley's face turns red, and her eyes bulge. Without a retort, she scoots her chair back and strides out the door. Caleb rests an arm across my shoulders, looking confused about what just transpired.

"I guess I'd better go," Jacob says, scooting his chair back too and slapping his hands on his knees. "Jalynn, George, thanks for dinner. Sorry to cut out early."

He nods to me and Caleb and follows Ashley's trail of fury out the front door.

"What just happened?" Caleb asks.

"I have no idea," I say with a shrug. I concentrate harder on my plate of food and shovel a bite into my mouth. Jalynn muffles a giggle.

I train my eyes on the table, hoping the guilt I feel will subside quickly. The stockpot of feelings I have swirling around inside me must have been more evident than I realized if Ashley picked up on it. I hope she was the only one. I shouldn't have allowed myself to get so wrapped up in Jacob.

Why couldn't I feel that same spark with Caleb that I feel just being near Jacob? Would that feeling ever come? If I'm honest with myself, I think I already know the answer. As much as I want things to work out between me and Caleb, it's not fair for me to keep stringing him along, waiting for feelings that are never going to come. I can't continue to hang on his arm while my heart is doing somersaults for another man, taken or not.

Caleb and I help clean up dinner. I wash the dishes while Caleb dries. Jalynn sits at the island, by order of me and George, and supervises our progress while giving George directions to put away the leftovers and wipe down the table and chairs.

Caleb puts the last dish away and hangs the dish towel on the hook inside the cupboard door. We say our goodbyes to Jalynn and George and head out to our trucks.

"Are you ready to call it a night, or are you interested in phase two of our evening?" Caleb asks me.

"Oh, phase two, please!" I say, giving Caleb's hand a small squeeze. I should go home, but I'm not ready to say goodbye yet. Even with my misgivings of our longevity, Caleb emanates peace and happiness. Both are things I've been in short supply of for the last several years.

"Let's drop your truck off at your place, then I'll drive us out."

We condense down to one vehicle and travel a few more miles down the dark, quiet back road leading into wild Montana. Caleb pulls the truck off the dark road, into an open field. The terrain makes for a bumpy ride. I brace myself with a palm flat on the roof of the truck as we bounce and rock, slowly creeping further into the field.

Finally satisfied with the spot, Caleb slows the crawling truck to a stop. I slide out of the cab, following close behind Caleb. It's incredibly dark. Caleb leads us around to the bed of the truck with his flashlight and lowers the tailgate. I take the flashlight from him and shine it into the bed of the truck.

Glancing over the contents, I give Caleb a quizzical look, waiting for his explanation.

"What's all this?" I ask when he doesn't immediately explain. I scrutinize him suspiciously. "What in heaven's name could we be doing out here in the dark, in the middle of nowhere, that would require a mattress in the bed of your pickup? Did you forget my name? 'Cause it ain't Jezebel."

Caleb throws his head back and laughs.

"No, nothing like that," Caleb says. "Think more along the lines of a drive-in movie theater." Caleb grins down at me. "Here. Climb on up. I've got to grab some stuff from the cab."

With his help, I climb into the bed of the truck and sit on the mattress while he grabs pillows and a blanket from the cab. He hands them over to me, then goes back for a laptop and a bag of snacks. Caleb climbs up and sits next to me, spreading the blanket over our laps and opening the laptop. With a few clicks, the opening scene of a movie is paused on the screen. Caleb reaches an arm around my shoulders and presses play.

"You brought me out in the middle of nowhere at night to watch a scary movie?" I ask him, wide-eyed.

"Maybe . . ." He looks down at me with a hesitant grin. "Is that okay?"

"That's awesome!" I smile back up at him. "Let's do this."

I cuddle into Caleb's side and soon, I'm screaming in unholy octaves as a terrifying creature overtakes its petrified victim.

Rolling out of bed, I try to wipe the sleep from my eyes. I'm exhausted. Sleep was difficult to find during the night as my mind was all too aware of the significance of the approaching day.

Six years ago, to the day, I received the phone call that Grammy had passed away. My rock, my compass, my comforter, and my only living relative was gone. Grammy had suffered a stroke while driving to work. Her car crashed into a tree, and she was pronounced dead at the scene.

I start the shower running, letting the water warm up, and climb in. I know I shouldn't dwell on the memory of that day. Rehashing it won't change anything. It only makes me ache for a family.

I massage shampoo into the roots of my hair as the warm water washes over my body, offering the only comfort available to me right now. I turn and hang my head back, rinsing the soap from my hair. Grammy loved my long hair. When I was a kid, she would fix my hair in braids every day. Even when I talked her into giving me a ponytail, she always French braided the top to wherever she intended to place the ponytail before pulling the rest of my hair up and securing it with a hair tie.

I dry my body and pull on the clothes I already set out to wear, readying myself for work. I try to keep my mind off the past as I do my makeup and put my hair up in a clip. I check my phone for the time and begin gathering my keys and purse but decide to take one last glimpse in the mirror as I walk out the door for the day. I stand in front of the little mirror hung on my wall, and I study my reflection. Pulling the hair clip back out of my hair, I brush my hair out again and part it to one side. Starting on the larger side of the part, I begin braiding my hair, wrapping the braid around the back of my head and down behind my opposite ear. Today, I'll wear a braid for Grammy.

Work drags on, not offering much mental stimulation to keep my focus elsewhere. Maddie is busy reorganizing the storage closet, and I settle for finding little tasks to do around the shop to keep myself busy.

I wonder what Grammy would think of my new life in Montana. Grammy wasn't known to be adventurous. She'd always told me that I got my free spirit from my mother, who'd gotten it from my grandfather. I like to think, however, that

Grammy is looking down on me and is proud of me for being brave enough to leave home.

I slide onto the stool behind the counter and pull out my phone. Opening the internet browser, I google the address of Grammy's house, the home I grew up in and owned for a short couple of years before Ben made me sell it. That was one of my biggest regrets. I miss that old house. The house carried that notorious old house smell but always with undertones of bacon. Maybe one day I'll buy it back.

My phone buzzes in my hand, distracting me from the pictures on my screen. A text message pops up on the top of the screen, and I tap on it to read the message.

Caleb: Hey beautiful. How's your day going?

Me: I've had better. You?

Caleb: Just thinking about you. What's wrong?

Me: Having a rough day is all. Feeling homesick. No big deal.

I slide my phone back in my pocket as the shop phone rings. It's an order. Finally, something for me to do.

With my workday over, I lock up the shop and head for my truck. My handsome Caleb is leaning against the side of my truck, waiting for me. My eyes meet his, and I can't help but smile. Just like that, a chunk of the weight I've been carrying around today is lifted off my shoulders. This man is going to make someone a very lucky girl one day. I wish it could be me, but I'm beginning to think I'm being selfish pretending like he could be the one for me. I want him to be. I just don't think that he is.

"Hey, you," I say, approaching him.

"Hey." He pushes off my truck and stands up straight.

"What are you doing here?" I ask.

I rise up on my toes and wrap my arms around his neck, hugging him tightly.

"I thought I'd try to brighten up your day," Caleb says.

"Oh yeah?"

Caleb hands me a small paper bag. It's heavier than I expected, and it almost slips from my fingers. I open the bag and peer inside. My smile grows brighter as I look back up at him and then give him another hug.

I hold up a chocolate Moon Pie and a cola. "I didn't even know you could buy these around here."

"I know a guy," Caleb says with a grin.

"Thank you!"

I let down the tailgate of my pickup and slide up on it, taking a seat. Caleb walks over and sits next to me, watching as I pull out the Moon Pie and open the wrapper.

"Mmmm. This brings back so many good memories," I say through a mouthful.

I hold the Moon Pie up toward Caleb, offering him a bite. He leans forward, letting me feed him as he bites off a piece. He nods as he chews.

"It's alright," Caleb says. "But it's not great."

"They're better when you microwave them but a delicacy nonetheless, so you better not speak evil of them." I chuckle.

Music floats softly to us from the radio of Caleb's truck while we finish sharing the Moon Pie and soda. I lean into Caleb, finally finding peace from the memories.

"I'd better get going," Caleb says eventually, nudging my side. "I hope the rest of your day goes better, though."

"Seriously, Caleb, you have no idea how much I appreciate this. You definitely made my day better."

I follow Caleb's lead, sliding off the tailgate of my pickup. He closes the tailgate for me and wraps me up in his arms, lifting me up off the ground like he usually does in a big bear hug. I kiss his cheek, and he sets me back on the ground.

"I'll call you later," he says.

At home, I change into sweats and wash the day off my face. I'm ready for a relaxed, quiet evening. In the bathroom, I grab my towel and pat my face dry. My scar catches my eye as I peer up into the mirror to make sure I got all of my mascara off. It's slight now in comparison to what it used to be. Instinctively, my fingertips trace over the thin white line.

I stretched lazily in my bed, slowly waking up after a night out with Jalynn. College life so far had been a dream. There was never a dull moment living with Jalynn, my classes were going well, and Ben had finally started to ease up on me choosing not to live with him. Next week was the last week of finals for the first semester of my freshman year, and the next couple of days would be spent with my head in my textbooks in preparation.

I stumbled out of bed, tripping over my shoes discarded from the previous night. I was thirsty, and my stomach rumbled, ready for food. I headed straight for my bedroom door, still in just the panties and tank top I'd slept in.

In the kitchen, I poured myself a glass of orange juice and took a big swig, then pulled out a bowl to mix up some oats. A door down the hall creaked open and feet pattered toward the kitchen. Jalynn must have finally woken up, too.

"Hey, sleepyhead," I say, turning to face her. Only, it wasn't Jalynn. It was the guy from last night, only now he was in his boxers—Brody, the one who had sent drinks over to us and spent the rest of the night flirting with Jalynn. Jalynn and I came home alone. She must have gotten his number and invited him over after we got home.

"Uh, good morning to you, too," he said gruffly. "Water?"

I pointed to the cupboard where our glasses are kept, my feet rooted to the floor, hoping he's too hungover to notice my lack of attire. Brody grabbed a glass from the cupboard, filled it with water, and slung an arm around my shoulders.

"So is this what you girls do? You share playdates?" He raised an eyebrow and began leaning into me.

At that moment, the front door of the apartment slammed

open and closed. My eyes darted in that direction, landing on Ben who had let himself in with the key I'd given him.

"Who the fuck are you?" he said, glaring at Brody who still had an arm draped over my shoulders.

"Well, that's not very polite," Brody replied. "Who the fuck are you?"

"I'm the last fucking face you'll ever see." Ben stormed toward Brody. "Get your fucking hands off my girl."

Ben grabbed my arm and slung me back in the opposite direction before throwing fists at Brody. Still not totally solid on my feet, I stumbled back and lost my balance. I fell, hitting the counter on my way down. Ben was on top of Brody, who was now laid out on the floor, repeatedly punching him. A scream echoed through the apartment as Jalynn rushed down the hall and rounded the corner to see what the commotion was.

"Ben, stop! Get off of him!" Jalynn shouted. "That's enough!" She stood over the both of them, pushing Ben away.

Ben stood, taking a few steps back but keeping his fury-filled eyes on Brody the whole time. Jalynn was helping pull Brody up off the floor, shoving paper towels in his face, when she spotted me still laying on the floor.

"Did you hurt her?" Jalynn yelled, motioning toward me.

Ben, looking confused, turned to where Jalynn was pointing and saw me just beginning to sit up. He rushed to me, dropping to his knees next to me.

"Lacey, baby, I'm so sorry," he said, tenderly helping me lean back against the cabinetry. "I'm so sorry, baby. I never meant to hurt you. I swear."

I reached up to my forehead just above my eyebrow where the pain was centralized and touched it with my fingertips. When I pulled my hand away, my fingers were covered in blood. Ben grabbed a towel and held it to the cut on my forehead.

"I'm so sorry, baby. Please forgive me," he said with a sob. "You have to forgive me."

"She needs stitches for that," Jalynn said, now standing over

us. "Come on, Lace, let's get you to the emergency room. Brody"—Jalynn looked back to where Brody was, now dressed and putting on his shoes—"do you need the emergency room, or are you good?"

"I'm getting the fuck out of here," Brody said. "The hell with you all."

Three hours and four stitches later, I was back at my apartment, Ben in tow. I sat down on my bed, waiting for the lecture that I knew was brewing. I watched Ben pace across my bedroom floor.

"I can't believe you," Ben finally said.

"Me? What do you mean?" I asked, confused.

"Did you sleep with him?" Ben demanded.

"Of course not! I'm with you."

"Then why were you half-naked, letting him hang all over you like that?" Ben asked, motioning toward my bedroom door.

"He wasn't here for me, Ben. He was here for Jalynn," I said, feeling like a scolded child.

"You told me you were studying all weekend for finals!"

"I was. I am. I was just getting myself some breakfast in my apartment."

"I can't believe you'd betray me like that," Ben continued.

"I didn't betray you," I insisted as he skulked toward me.

"I don't like you living here."

"Sorry." I folded my arms over my chest.

"I don't want you to stay here anymore."

"Where am I supposed to stay, then, Ben?" I asked, my frustration beginning to boil over.

"Move in with me."

"I'm not ready to live with you, Ben. We've talked about this. Not to mention I can't exactly just leave Jalynn high and dry with the rent."

"I don't give a damn what Jalynn has to do. You're not staying here anymore, and if you loved me, you wouldn't fight me on this."

"I don't have time to move right now. I have finals to prepare for." I pressed my hand to my throbbing head.

"If you have time to play with Jalynn's leftovers in your kitchen, then you have time to move in with me," Ben said flatly. "I'm going to go gather up some boxes. We'll get your stuff packed up when I get back."

"I'm not moving, Ben. You aren't listening to me."

"This isn't up for debate, Lacey. You'll either move in with me, or we're done."

"Ben, don't be ridiculous."

"I'm serious right now, Lacey. This is it." There was a warning tone in Ben's voice.

"Then I guess we're done," I said, not breaking eye contact despite the fear building up as the black fury in his eyes washed over me.

An angry bellow exploded from Ben, and he grabbed the lamp from my nightstand and smashed it against the wall, making me jump. Then, he stormed out of my room and slammed the door behind him hard enough to rattle the wall.

I exhale deeply and lean back against the bathroom wall. My hands are shaking from the adrenaline the memory sends coursing through my body. I breath in deeply again, filling my lungs to capacity, and slowly release it.

I'm okay. That's not my life anymore.

Feeling steadier, I flip off the bathroom light and lie on my bed with a book. Sometimes disappearing into someone else's world is the best medicine.

jacob

"Ashley?" I call out her name down the hallway. "You okay?"

She brought dinner over tonight after I got home from work. I haven't been making as much time for her as she wants. I'm not really avoiding her, but I'm busy. Most nights, I'm exhausted as shit by the time my workday ends.

Not getting a response, I walk down the hallway to check on her. While I was cleaning up after dinner, she went to the bathroom. She's been gone a while. Long enough for me to notice. I reach the bathroom, but the door stands open, and she's not there.

"Ashley?"

I walk into my bedroom, the light from the master bath catching my attention. Splayed out across my bed, I find Ashley in barely there blue lingerie. Nothing much has been left to the imagination with this outfit.

With my hand still on the doorknob, my body stiffens but not in the way she intended. I divert my eyes to the floor. It almost feels as though someone ripped back open the wound she left in my chest.

"Fucking hell," I say under my breath.

"Come here," Ashley's sultry voice calls softly to me from across the room.

"Ashley, this isn't a good idea."

Rather than going to her, I turn and lean my back against the doorframe, looking away from her. I hear slight shuffling on the bed as she rises and comes to me instead. Stepping in front of me, she straddles my legs and presses herself up against me. I refuse to look, despite her hand trying to pull my face toward hers.

"Come on, baby. We need this," Ashley says.

"I'm not ready to have sex with you, Ashley. I'm not there yet."

"I get it," she says, clearly *not* getting it, "but we need to rip off the Band-Aid. We need to connect again like we used to."

"Put your clothes back on, Ashley. I told you. I'm not ready." I say it more firmly this time, hoping she's listening.

She turns back into the bedroom, so I assume she's done, and I head back out to the living room while she dresses. When she finds her way to me, I think she can tell that I'm done for the night. She heads to the front door, and I follow behind. At the door she turns back to me, pressing a kiss to my lips. I kiss her back, but I don't let myself feel it. I can't. Not until I know that I'm enough to make her stay.

"We're still on for dinner tomorrow, right?" Ashley asks.

"I'll pick you up after work," I say.

Closing the door behind her, I let out the breath I didn't realize I've been holding. I'm not ready to jump back into a physical relationship with her. I turn out the lights and head back to my room to get ready for bed. There's a long day of herd health ahead of me tomorrow, and I need some rest. It's already later than I intended to get to bed tonight. Ashley reminded me, though, that I promised to try with her, and part of trying was seeing each other. She's right. So when she suggested bringing over some dinner, I agreed.

I'm trying to forgive her for her infidelity, but if we're being honest, I'm still brimming with resentment. I thought maybe if I started dating her again, the dam would finally burst, and I'd be able to move forward. Instead, it seems like the more time I spend with her, the more irritated I become. Simply put, it isn't going well. I want it to work with her, though, and I'm not ready to totally give up on the life we planned out for us. It's just not going to work if I can't get my head back in it.

My phone rings, pulling me out of my thoughts. I slide the phone out of my pocket, checking the caller ID. It's a client.

"Hello?"

"Hey, Doc, this is Diane Sturgill. Epona's been in labor for a while now. It isn't going well. I think we need your help."

"What stage is she?" I ask, pulling my boots back on.

"Still stage one. She's been acting colicky for several hours now, though, and I'm worried something isn't right."

"Can you get her on a trailer to bring her to the office?"

"We're getting her loaded now. Meet you there?"

"Yeah, I'll see you shortly." I grab my keys and wallet and head for the door.

"Thanks, Doc."

I rush to the office and start prepping for Epona's arrival. Once the lights are on and I have my tools and equipment on standby, I walk out to the unloading area to watch for Diane and her mare.

Diane pulls in, swinging the trailer around close to where I'm standing. Once the truck engine is shut off, I open up the trailer and prepare to unload Epona. Slowly, I walk her off the trailer and lead her to the prepared birthing stall.

"How long ago did her water break?" I ask.

"It must have happened on the way here," Diane replies.

I slide my hand into the mare, feeling for the foal. Epona dances around, trying to free herself of me. I reposition and continue the exam.

"The foal's head is tucked down under the legs. I think if we sedate Epona, I'll be able to get the foal repositioned."

"Will the sedation harm the foal?" Diane asks anxiously.

"No, but the longer it takes us to get the foal out, the lower our chances of delivering it live."

"Okay, let's do it."

I rinse off my hands in a bucket of clean water and begin preparing the medications for sedation. Diane stands at the head of the horse, rubbing Epona's neck and soothing her in a low voice. I approach with a shot prepared in one hand, rubbing down the mare's neck in search of a vein. Finding one, I inject the medication and snap the cap back over the needle, then glance at my watch for the time. I need to have this foal delivered in the next fifteen to twenty minutes or I'm going to have to resort to more intrusive means, like surgery.

A couple of minutes pass, and Epona is showing signs of sedation. I get to work repositioning the foal. Reaching into the mare, I feel around for the foal's head. Finding it tucked downward, I wrap my fingers around the jaw of the foal, pulling and lifting, trying to bring the nose up. With a few more minutes of manipulating the foal's position, I get it in the position it's supposed to be.

"How's it going down there?" Diane asks.

"We're good. I've got the foal in position, and I'm going to start pulling the foal in time with her contractions to help her get started."

With each contraction, I pull the foal's front legs, helping the mare along. Once the foal's front legs and head are protruding, and the foal's ribcage is in the pelvic canal, I wipe the foal's nose and allow Epona to try to finish the job on her own. With a few more pushes, the foal is free.

I immediately step back in, attending to the foal. I check for a heartbeat and listen to the lungs. Passing both of those checks, I take a blood sample from the umbilical cord to have it processed, and I check the foal's ribcage to ensure there aren't any fractures.

"You've got a boy," I announce. "Heart seems to be doing

okay. Lungs sound good. Epona's sedation should start wearing off soon."

"Thank you! I was really getting worried for a bit."

"I don't expect us to have any more issues, but I'll keep them here tonight, so I can make sure Epona gets the placenta out and these two start bonding." I stand and wipe at the itch on my cheek with my shoulder.

"Has anyone told you lately how magnificent you are?" Diane asks. "I'd hug you, but . . . you know," she adds, motioning to all of the birthing fluids covering me.

"Occupational hazard," I say. "Give me a call around eight in the morning, and we can make arrangements for them based on how the rest of the night goes."

I see Diane out, then return to the birthing stall to start cleaning up and to keep an eye on the new mother and baby. I check my watch, noting the time again. I can't wait to get a shower. I love this job, but I don't love smelling like the insides of a horse.

In no time, the placenta passes. I look it over, making sure the entire placenta has been expelled before I dispose of it. So far, so good. Things are progressing nicely now.

I stop and watch the foal for a minute as he tries to stand. His little legs wobble as he works himself up. Once standing, he takes a few shaky steps, then goes back down momentarily. Epona nuzzles him, encouraging him back up on his feet. This time, he makes his way over to her, latching on to nurse. I check the time again. As long as the foal passes the meconium in the next hour or so, we shouldn't have anything to worry about.

Making sure the two are settled, I head into the office to get cleaned up. I start the shower running to warm up while I pull a clean bath towel out of the cupboard. Times like this certainly make it handy having all of the accommodations I do at the office.

Sticking my hand into the spray, I check the temperature of the water again. Satisfied that it won't make me shrivel up, I strip off my clothes and climb in under the warm water. Rubbing the soap over my skin, my mind's no longer on the mare and foal. Instead, thoughts of dinner the other night at George's fill my head. Ashley did what she usually does so well and caused another scene. It's embarrassing the way she treats my friends. Lacey, though. She handled Ashley's jabs with grace.

The weak stream of water from the showerhead finally rinses the soap off my body, and I shut the water off. My towel hangs on the hook next to the shower, ready for me, and I wipe away the droplets of water clinging to my skin. Satisfied, I wrap the towel around my waist and head to the back room where I keep extra changes of clothes. I throw on a new pair of jeans and a T-shirt and pull my boots back on so I can check on Epona and her baby again.

The pair look good together. Epona keeps a close eye on her foal as he trots around the stall, testing out his legs some more. Everything still looks good, so I head back into the office and lie down on the couch to get some rest. I'll check on the horses again in a while, but right now, I need some fucking sleep. A yawn escapes me as I stretch out, settling into the couch.

Ashley in her barely there lingerie comes back into my mind. Maybe she's right. Maybe we do just need to rip off the Band-Aid and try. We aren't connecting. Not like we used to. Truthfully, Ashley was always high maintenance, and she never had any trouble being a bitch to people. The difference is she wasn't a bitch to people who mattered. She tried like hell to win over my mother and Mia. She was constantly on eggshells around them, which probably didn't help her cause any. Mia always thought Ashley was hiding something.

Ashley never was one to wear her heart on her sleeve. She was raised by a father who valued people for their tax statements rather than their character, and it was no different for his daughter. He expected her to succeed. There was no other option.

She always showed up for me when it counted, though.

Like the time on George's ranch when I decided to relive my glory days as a bull rider on a rank bastard George had just got in. That bull got a pretty good piece of me before the boys managed to pull me out, and Ashley was left to put the pieces back together. Okay, the doctor put the pieces back together, but Ashley stuck by my side and took care of me till I recovered, and it wasn't a glamorous job.

The way Ashley took control of situations was a turn on at the beginning. I loved the way she took charge and made things happen. Lately, though, it feels more like she steamrolls everything to get her way. I may never understand why she decided to run around on me, but I don't guess that part's too important for me to figure out. The part I need to figure out is if I can give her a fair chance to redeem herself.

CHAPTER FIFTEEN

I am exhausted and irritable as shit by the end of the day. Having worked a heavy schedule after only a few hours of sleep on the office couch, all I want to do is go home and shower and climb into bed. Ashley had a conniption when I called her to suggest rescheduling our dinner date. She went off on a rant about how I put everything else in front of her, and things would never work out between us if she wasn't a priority. She's probably right on both accounts. In the end, I agreed to stick to our original plans for the sake of trying to make things work and all that shit.

Ashley is staying in a condo in town while we figure things out. I leave my car in front of her condo and meander up to the door, not especially looking forward to expelling the amount of energy I know this evening is going to require of me. I knock on the door and wait, my hands thrust in my pockets. After a couple of minutes, Ashley finally answers the door. She looks me up and down, her smile deflating into a scowl.

"Are you kidding me?" she says angrily.

"What is it now, Ashley?" I ask with a sigh.

"You're late and you show up to take me out wearing that? Have you even showered?"

"I tried telling you on the phone it's been a long fucking day," I grumble despite myself. "I came here straight from the McGreer ranch where I spent the day sticking my arm up a bunch of cows' asses. I was up half the damn night delivering a foal, I'm running on only a few hours of sleep, and frankly, all I want to be doing right now is sawing logs in my fucking bed. But here I am, taking you out to dinner because it can't be pushed off till tomorrow, heaven forbid. So do you want to have dinner tonight, or do you not? Because once I get to the house, I'm not leaving again."

Ashley pouts all the way to my truck, not saying a word. She waits for me to catch up and open the door for her. I let out a sigh, look pleadingly up into the evening sky, and follow after her.

We trail behind the hostess through the dining room, weaving by tables. Approaching an empty table, the hostess lays down the menus and rolled silverware and steps aside for us to take our seats. I can tell by the look on Ashley's face that we're about to have trouble.

"You want us to sit here?" Ashley asks the hostess, pointing at the table.

"Ashley, don't. This table is fine. Let's just sit down and have dinner," I say, trying to bring her back down.

"Absolutely not! I will not eat my dinner next to the bathrooms!" Ashley says, her fists pressed firmly into her hips.

"You're being ridiculous. The bathrooms are way over on the other side of the bar. Come on and have a seat."

I pull out a chair for Ashley to sit.

"I will not! I demand a better table." Ashley turns back to the now wide-eyed and nervous hostess.

"Um . . . Okay . . . That's fine, just let me see . . ." The hostess spins around, glancing over the dining room. "How about over here?" she asks, motioning to a table in the middle of the room.

"That's more like it," Ashley agrees.

I mouth an apology to the hostess as Ashley sinks into the chair I pull out for her. Rounding the table, I take my own seat on the opposite side. I scoop up the menu and begin scanning the laminated booklet for the entrées.

"You realize you're the reason they tried to give us a crappy table, right? Because you smell like a barn," Ashley says, scrunching up her nose.

"Ash, please don't start."

A waiter steps up to our table for our drink orders. Ashley quizzes him on their wine selection, trying to make up her mind. By the end of the inquisition, the young waiter is flustered. Relief floods his face when I simply order water, and he rushes away.

Everything is a fucking production with her. Nothing can ever just be, and nothing is ever good enough. Ashley doesn't belong in Montana. She belongs in a big city with all of the other wealth-chasing, designer-wearing, uppity nitwits. I chastise myself, knowing I shouldn't be feeling that way about my . . . significant other? I don't really know what to call her anymore, but I know beyond a shadow of a doubt that she's significant—a significant pain in my ass.

The waiter returns with our drinks. After placing the appropriate glasses in front of us, he pulls out a notepad and visibly gulps, as ready as he'll ever be to try to take Ashley's order.

"I'll have the salmon Caesar salad, but I want it with the vinaigrette, not the Caesar. And I don't want the parmesan on it, either. Or the croutons. But I want cherry tomatoes added," Ashley says. "And I want the cherry tomatoes sliced in half."

"Yes, ma'am," the boy tells her, nervously scribbling her instructions on his notepad.

"Actually, does the chef caesar the salmon before or after it's grilled?"

I roll my eyes.

"After, I believe, ma'am. I'll have to check with the chef to be sure."

"If it's before it's grilled, be sure to tell the chef not to put the caesar on mine. Just cook it plain."

"Yes, ma'am. And you, sir?" The waiter turns to me.

"Oh, this wine is horrible," Ashley interrupts. "I want it replaced with a bottle of Roero."

"Yes, ma'am."

"I'll have the ribeye," I say, glaring across the table at Ashley. "Medium rare—"

"And just bring him a house salad with vinaigrette for his sides," Ashley interrupts again. She takes another sip of wine.

"No. No salad for me. I'm not a damn rabbit. I want a loaded baked potato and mac and cheese."

"Oh, no, Jacob. That's too many carbohydrates for one meal," Ashley says in a tone that suggests she's scolding a young child as the waiter retreats from the table.

"When I start giving a damn about my figure, I start being choosy about what I eat. Until then, I'll eat what tastes good. And that's not a salad."

Ashley leans back in her chair, swishing the glass of wine in her hand—the same wine she told the waiter needed to be replaced. Her eyes roam over me. What is she plotting? She sits up straight again and places her wineglass back on the table.

"I think I should move back in with you," she says matter-of-factly.

I arch an eyebrow.

"How do you figure?"

"We aren't getting anywhere like this. Work keeps you busy. Half of the time I get to see you, we're either out with your friends or you're a tired grump. There's no way we are going to make progress like this."

Ashley's point is valid, even if I don't want to admit it.

"How do you think us sharing a bed will change anything?" I ask her sincerely.

"Think about how much burden it would take off your shoulders. I'll handle the meals and the housework."

"Meaning you'll hire a maid and order out our meals." I take a sip of my water.

"Even so, it will be one less thing for you to worry about. And we can spend casual evenings together at home. We'll see so much more of each other."

Ashley leans forward and reaches across the table to take hold of my hands. I don't pull back but let her continue holding onto me. I let her words sink in for a minute. She's not wrong. Maybe I would be more patient with her if seeing her wasn't such an inconvenience.

It wasn't that long ago that I loved this woman sitting across from me. Surely I wasn't completely fooled about who she is. The woman I fell in love with has to still be a part of her. Maybe I'm too focused on the hurt still to find the bits of her I loved. But how can I trust her again?

"Can I think about it?" I ask, earning a soft smile from Ashley.

"Of course."

lacey

Caleb and I weave through the crowd of people at the rodeo, our fingers intertwined. I scan the stands of the fairgrounds for our friends. A mixed scent of livestock, earth, and popcorn fill my nose. Caleb leads the way, clearing a path for me through the throng of people.

"There they are," I say, pointing to a spot midway up the stands.

Caleb stops at the bottom of the stairs, letting me pass in front of him to climb the stairs to where our friends are saving seats for us. Caleb wolf whistles at my ass, and I turn around and smack his large shoulder playfully.

Jacob and Ashley are sitting in the row behind Jalynn and George with two empty seats next to Jalynn for me and Caleb to join them. I send Caleb into the row first so I can claim the seat next to Jalynn and give George and Jalynn a hug as I squeeze by them to my spot. My foot catches on something as I make my way by Jalynn, and to my horror, I lose my balance. My hands shoot out to my sides instinctively, trying to rebalance, but it's futile. I already know I'm going down.

But then, I don't. Strong hands grab me from above, and suddenly, I find myself wrapped up in unyielding arms. Heat washes over me and rushes through my veins. I know who my rescuer is simply by my body's response to him. I'm proven right when I look up to see it's Jacob who has wrapped me in his arms. And just like that, he lets me loose again and steps back into his seat, leaving me lightheaded.

Caleb grabs my hand, late to the party because his back was to me when I tripped, and helps me make it safely into my seat. I glance back at Jacob, but his focus is on the arena. Ashley sits next to him with a scowl on her face, undoubtedly upset by what just transpired.

"Are you okay?" Jalynn asks, looking me over.

"Yeah. I'm good. What'd we miss?" I ask.

I want everyone's focus back on the rodeo as quickly as possible. I don't need any more witnesses to the blush that has spread across my face.

"Nothing much," Jalynn replies. "They are getting ready to start the bull riding event."

The gate in the arena flies open and a large bull comes bucking out, the cowboy bending and weaving with the bull. The bull spins back in the other direction, almost throwing the cowboy from his back. The audience cheers when the eight seconds expire, and the cowboy hops off the bull, running to the side of the arena so the bull can't retaliate against him. The rodeo clowns work to get the bull out of the arena while the cowboy waits for his score to be announced and the next cowboy gears up for his turn.

"Do you miss it?" George asks Jacob, turning to look at him over his shoulder.

"Sometimes," Jacob confesses. "Until I see someone get completely obliterated by a bull."

"You're not riding again," Ashley says. "I won't have you put yourself at risk like that again." Jacob rests a hand on her knee, something private clearly passing between them.

"You used to ride bulls?" My brows furrow.

"Yeah. A lifetime ago," Jacob says.

His voice melts my insides.

"I had no idea," I say, holding our eye contact.

He sends chills down my spine.

"Why would you?" Ashley interjects, still wearing her typical sour expression. "Have you been having heart-to-hearts with my fiancé that I don't know about?"

"I'm not your fiancé anymore," Jacob corrects her, pulling his hand away and turning briefly to Ashley. "And don't start your crap tonight, Ash."

"Spoken like someone who has something to hide," Ashley spits back.

"You would know, wouldn't you?" Jacob asks.

"How's your dad doing, Ashley?" George asks, always the peacemaker. "I haven't seen him since we closed on our house."

"Oh, you know Daddy, he's busy making money as always. Just closed on another huge deal. He has a sense for those things. He can always sniff out an opportunity to make money," Ashley says smugly.

Caleb reaches over and pulls my arm under and around his own, lacing his fingers through mine. I'm suddenly concerned whether the static cling between me and Jacob is as obvious to everyone else as it feels coursing through me. I didn't mean to feed the current. It's simply always there when Jacob's around.

I watch the bull riding, quietly soaking in the charge radiating off of Jacob and seeping into my body, intoxicating my senses. I barely notice as the rodeo transitions from bull riding to bronc riding.

"I'm going to grab a drink," Caleb says, standing. "Do you want anything?"

"No, I'm good," I say.

"How are things going at the shop?" Jacob asks me as Caleb heads to the concession stand.

"Good," I say, turning again to look at him. "Diane was in today. She told me about the trouble with her mare. I was happy to hear that you were able to safely deliver the foal."

"It wasn't that big of a deal."

"It was to Diane," I say. After a beat of silence I continue, "And I love working with your mom—"

"Wait a minute," Ashley interjects. "You're working at the flower shop with Mrs. Jones?"

"Yeah, it's definitely my favorite out of the handful of jobs I've had. And Maddie is great." I direct my comment back toward Jacob. "If the stories she's told me about your childhood are true, the woman is a saint!"

Jacob laughs.

"She lets you call her Maddie?" Ashley asks.

"Yeah. She's a sweetheart," I say.

"You've barely known the woman for five minutes!" Ashley exclaims. "I've known her for years! I'm engaged to her son!" Ashley's frustration spews out.

"We do spend a lot of time together, though, since we work together," I say, trying to diffuse the situation.

"I should have figured she'd have a soft spot for the hillbilly minx."

"Ashley—" Jacob starts, but I interrupt him.

"Excuse me?" I ask, turning in my seat and zeroing in on Ashley.

"You show up one day out of the blue, and everyone is falling over themselves to get to you. I don't get it. I don't see what is so marvelous about you that has everyone fawning over you!"

"Nobody is fawning over me, Ashley," I say.

"Yes, they all are. And my fiancé is at the top of the list!"

"Ashley—" Jacob tries to interrupt again.

"I couldn't get your attention when she's around if I stripped off all my clothes and went walking naked across the arena," Ashley says to Jacob, now on her feet and drawing the attention of the people sitting around us. "So what's the deal, Lacey? Are you having sex with my fiancé?"

"Ashley!" Jacob barks at her.

"Bless your little heart. It's truly bewildering how your lovely disposition doesn't leave the whole world smitten with you," I say.

I stand and slide past Jalynn and George to the stairs, trying to ignore the embarrassment flooding over me as the spectators stare. Once on the stairs, I briefly glance behind me to see Jacob rising to his feet. Ashley grabs at his arm, trying to stop him as he slides past her to the stairs. He glares back at her and pulls his arm free as I turn away again to focus on the path ahead of me. I don't even know where to go.

I head under the stands where I'm free of people watching. Taking a breath, I lean back against one of the beams, trying to calm myself. I'm kicking rocks one by one across the concrete pad when Jacob finds me.

"Hey," he says, stopping next to me.

"Hey." I can't look at him. I chew on my bottom lip and focus extra hard on the concrete.

"Sorry about Ashley. I don't know what her deal is." Jacob leans against the beam next to me.

"It's okay. She's jealous. I get it." I fold my arms over my chest and study the man in front me as I breathe in his heady scent.

"What do you mean?"

"Tell me you feel it, too," I say, not giving myself a chance to filter the words.

"Feel what?" Jacob asks, but I can tell by his expression that he knows exactly what I'm talking about. He does feel it. I need to hear him say it, though.

"The sparks. The pull." I drop my eyes back to the ground, embarrassment creeping back again.

"Lacey . . ." Jacob steps closer and reaches up to sweep a strand of hair behind my ear, allowing his fingers to linger a little too long. I'm paralyzed by his touch, desperate to hear him confess.

"Lace?" This time it's Caleb's voice calling for me.

Jacob quickly drops his hand and takes a step back. His hands find his pockets as Caleb approaches us. I straighten where I am and slide my own hands into the back pockets of my jeans.

"Is everything okay?" Caleb asks, only a few feet away from us now. He glances back and forth between us, seeming unsure of what he has walked up on.

"Yeah," I say. "But I think I'm ready to go home. Jacob, will you tell everyone goodbye for me?"

"You don't have to leave," Jacob says, and for a moment, I think he's going to reach for me again.

"I think it's probably best," I insist. "Take me home, Caleb?"

"Sure thing, beautiful," Caleb says.

Caleb and I walk out of the rodeo to his truck, hand in hand. Caleb opens his truck door, then lifts me into the driver's seat, my body facing him. I pull him to me, straddling his body. My hand gently rests on the side of his face, and I run my thumb across his cheek. He really is a sweet, wonderful man.

"What's going on in that head of yours, beautiful girl?" Caleb asks, resting his hands on my thighs.

"Nothing much."

"No, it's something. I can tell. You look like someone kicked your favorite puppy."

"You're my favorite puppy." I run my fingers through his hair.

"Who kicked me, then?" He leans into me more, his smile beginning to fade.

"I'm afraid I might."

"Why?"

"I really like you," I say.

"That's not a kick. I really like you, too."

I sit in silence for a moment. Caleb furrows his brow. I try to remember if this is the first time I've ever seen him without a smile on his face.

"Did I miss something?" he asks. "Does this have anything to do with what happened in there?"

"No. I'm just afraid I've let things go further than I should've. I wasn't sure. But I didn't know I wasn't sure."

"Lace, you're worrying me. Just spit it out."

"I'm afraid we're better suited as friends."

Caleb steps back and leans against the side of his truck. His head hangs limply back over his broad shoulders.

"Caleb—"

"No, it's okay. You're allowed to feel whatever sort of way. Why do you think we should be friends?" he asks, his head turned toward me now.

"Do you feel a fire in your belly when I kiss you?" I ask, leaning my side against the back of the seat, closer to Caleb.

"Not in my belly, but—"

"Caleb!" I smack his shoulder.

"Do you really think it matters if we don't?" he asks, looking over at me.

"Is complacency all we should strive for?"

"I like you, Lacey."

I reach over and grab Caleb's arm, hugging it to me.

"But you may never have that burning desire for me. And you deserve to have that with someone."

Silence falls over us as Caleb contemplates what I just said. He pushes off the truck and turns back to face me, his hands on my knees.

"So where does this leave us?"

"Friends?" I suggest.

"Friends," Caleb repeats, only looking like a gently kicked puppy.

The ride back to my place is a quiet one. I silently hope I did the right thing, and I hope Caleb isn't taking it too hard. He seems to be handling it okay, though he's clearly disappointed. So am I. When we reach my camper, Caleb helps me down and walks me to my door as usual.

"So this is it?" he asks, his hands deep in his pockets. "Just friends now?"

"I think it's best." I shrug.

Caleb leans down and wraps me in his arms, picking me up off the ground as he always does. I hug him tight, my arms around his neck. He kisses my forehead before turning and walking back to his truck.

I'm quick to find my way to bed, and surprisingly, sleep isn't hard to find. What starts off as a peaceful slumber turns dark quickly, no doubt my challenging day stirring up a pain that overtakes me.

Sitting on the couch in Grammy's living room—now my living room—I tried to wrap my head around the fact that she was gone. I still wore the black dress from the funeral, my mind too numb to make my body go through the motions of changing my clothes. It was just me now, the last of my family. This was not what I'd expected from my summer break. I hadn't anticipated spending my last month of summer alone.

Knocking on the front door stirred me at last. I stared at the door, my mind and body still not quite connected. With another firm knock, my feet dropped to the floor, and I rose from the couch, starting toward the door. The world felt as though it was moving in slow motion, but I think it was just me barely inching toward the door.

By the time I finally pulled it open, my visitor had already begun his retreat back to his truck. He froze, apparently hearing the door behind him, and turned back to me.

"Ben, what are you doing here?" I asked. I'd barely seen him since we broke up last fall after the incident before finals.

"How are you holding up?" he asked.

A shake of the head was about all I could muster. Ben stepped into me, wrapping me in his arms. I buried my face into his chest, and the dam of emotions I'd been holding finally burst free.

My sobs wake me. I sit up and drop my legs over the edge of the bed and wipe my cheeks dry on my T-shirt. That summer, the summer after my freshman year of college, was the start of one of my most difficult years yet. When Grammy passed away, I let Ben back into my life. I guess those six or so months broken up was long enough for me to forget how hard it was to be with him.

It seemed like perfect timing. Jalynn and George started dating the second semester of our freshman year and had plans to move in together in the fall. I hadn't figured out what to do about my living arrangements at school. After Ben and I got back together that summer, though, he suggested I move in with him. It seemed like the perfect solution. If I could go back in time, there are a lot of things I wouldn't change. As for my sophomore year of college? Yeah, I'd burn that year down to ashes and wouldn't ever look back.

CHAPTER SEVENTEEN

I knock loudly on Jalynn's front door and walk inside. We're all supposed to be going to the summer festival in town together. That is, all of us but Caleb now. Jacob and Ashley plan to meet us at the festival.

I open the door and step inside. George is sitting on the couch watching TV while he undoubtedly waits for Jalynn to finish getting ready. Jalynn pops her head out from the hallway, putting her earrings in.

"You ready?" she asks, earning a nod from me. "Let's go, then."

Jalynn motions for George to get up. He turns off the TV, and we all head out the door.

Every summer the town holds a community dance in the large courtyard downtown. It's one of the most attended events of the year. The town hires a live band and sets up tables with refreshments from the local bakery.

We find a place to park a couple of blocks away and walk over to the courtyard. I don't mind the walk. It's a cool evening with millions of stars twinkling overhead. The town is filled with music and laughter. I follow behind Jalynn and George, taking in the joyful sounds coming from the square.

Jacob and Ashley beat us to the festival. Ashley glares at me as we approach, clearly still holding a grudge from the other night at the rodeo. Oh well. Jacob pats George on the back, then gives me and Jalynn each a side hug. My breath catches at his touch.

Did he feel the jolt of electricity, too? We were interrupted the other night before he had a chance to answer me. It was probably just as well. If he answered and agreed he felt it, too, what difference would it have made? He's still with Ashley, and despite what a struggle it is for me to be civil with her at times, I don't want to be the wedge that drives them apart. They need to figure out their relationship without any extra complications.

"It didn't take you long to chase poor Caleb off, did it?" Ashley asks me in place of a hello.

"I'm flattered that you care enough about me to keep up with my latest comings and goings, Ashley. Truly, I'm touched." I rest my hand over my heart for emphasis. "How are you doing?"

Ashley flounders over a response.

"Lace, I need to go to the bathroom. You want to come with me?" Jalynn asks. Once we make it out of earshot, she says, "I told you she was a piece of work."

"I don't like her," I reply.

"I do believe the feeling is mutual." Jalynn laughs. "I've got some tea to spill, though. Care to hear it?"

"About who?" I perk up.

We aren't ones to gossip. We just like to keep up to date on current events.

"Ashley, of course. I bumped into Jacob's sister earlier today, and she's always said Ashley is a gold digger and was with Jacob for his money. You see, his grandfather helped him pay for vet school, so he didn't have to take out any student debt, and then he handed his already successful veterinary business over to Jacob when he was ready to retire. Well, evidently this man she cheated on him with, who happens to be another vet, is known for boasting about having old money, too, and a lot of it."

"I guess that makes sense," I say, pulling open the bathroom door.

"That's just the background. This is where it gets good." Jalynn pauses briefly for effect, then continues. "The guy evidently isn't a very good vet and has been supporting his business with his family's money. But then he had a falling out with his family, and they cut him off. The guy is filing for bankruptcy. That's what Ashley is doing back here. She thought the grass was greener on the other side, and now that it's not, she's back trying to make up with Jacob."

"Does Jacob know all of this?" I ask incredulously.

"Mia told him, but she says he won't listen. He says it's just gossip, and if it were true, he'd have heard it through the grapevine of vets. Who knows. But Mia is convinced."

"I'm speechless. Honestly, I can't even," I say, pausing the touch-up on my lipstick to stare back at Jalynn in the mirror.

We finish in the bathroom and head back out into the crowd. On the way back from the bathroom, we bump into Caleb. He looks good. Not quite his same glowing self but still cheerful. When he spots us, he comes over to say hello instead of running the other way, which I take as a good sign. I really didn't want to hurt him. Giving me one of his typical bear hugs, he asks me to dance, and I happily agree. He takes my hand and leads me out to the dance floor.

The song changes just as we start dancing. The new song is slow, and Caleb pulls me close. I'm grateful he's taking the breakup so well. Maybe we'll be able to continue being friends. I hope so. I rest my head on his chest and let him lead me around the dance floor.

"Are you sure we made the right decision by breaking up?" Caleb asks quietly above me. I look up into his soft eyes.

"Yeah, I'm sure. I hate it, but it's what needed to happen. It's not right for us to use each other."

A strange feeling sweeps over me, and as I start to return my head to Caleb's chest, my gaze lands on Jacob, standing off to the side of the dance floor. His eyes glide around the dance floor with us, following each step we take. Next to him, a sour Ashley stands, swirling her drink in her hand and unsuccessfully trying to win Jacob's attention. Her gaze drifts onto the dance floor, and she undoubtedly realizes why she can't get a response from her boyfriend. His focus is fixed on me.

"You're right. Even if we can't have the ones we want," Caleb says, following my line of sight.

My cheeks flush at being found out by him, and I drop my eyes to the ground. Caleb spins me around and pulls me close again. Unable to stop myself, I search the perimeter for Jacob once more, only to find him walking through the dancers with a stern expression on his face, his eyes locked back on mine. Do I let him cut in if he tries? As bad as I want an excuse to be pressed close to him, I don't think I can. It wouldn't be right. Still, my heart flutters in my chest as he takes each step closer, and tingles run down my spine in anticipation of his touch.

He's almost to us, close enough to reach for me, but a couple slides between us, making him drop his hand back to his side. As they make their way past us, George appears out of nowhere, drapes an arm around Jacob's shoulders, and leads him off the dance floor while starting a conversation too low for me to hear.

I lean back into Caleb and focus on moving my feet, hoping it will help me clear my head of all thoughts of the man I can't dance with tonight. Caleb pulls me close, aware of what just transpired but gracious enough not to comment.

I WALK into the floral shop the next day to find Maddie humming and straightening the shelves below the front counter. I'm ready to start a new week and get back to work.

The weekend went pretty well, considering, but it's time to put it all behind me.

"Good morning, dear," Maddie says.

"Good morning," I say. "We have someone picking up an arrangement early?" I ask, eying the beautiful arrangement sitting at the register. Maddie looks up at the arrangement and back at me.

"Nope. That one is for you."

I blush, confused, and grab the card off the arrangement. Sure enough, my name is written in Maddie's flowy handwriting across the front of the envelope. I look back at Maddie.

"Sweet boyfriend you've got there," Maddie says.

"I don't have a boyfriend," I say, opening the card to read the message. It's from Caleb. "We're just friends."

"Good friend, then." Maddie says, staying busy with her task. "That arrangement wasn't cheap. But truthfully, I was hoping you weren't too smitten with him just yet. I've been hoping you would hit it off with my son. I think you two would make a great couple."

"I'm not sure I'm ready to get seriously involved with anyone," I say quietly. "I'll move this out of the way and get to work."

Maddie gives me a nod and continues working on the shelves.

Already off balance from the weekend's events, I try not to think about the flowers or Caleb all morning. Thinking about it only layers on my anxiety extra thick. I broke things off with him. Why would he send me flowers? Maybe he wasn't taking it as well as I thought.

My lunch break comes too quickly. I take the leftovers I brought for lunch out on the back patio to eat, but I'm still too unsettled to get any food down. My phone buzzes on the table next to me. I try to ignore it at first, but I give in and look. It's a text from Caleb.

Caleb: Hey beautiful, call me.

What is going on? I put the phone back down and lay my palms flat on the cool iron table, focusing on box breathing, hoping to shove down the anxiety overtaking my body. I haven't had a panic attack since I made it to Montana, but I feel myself spiraling toward one now. I slide my phone back into my pocket and head inside to work. I need to keep myself busy.

After work, I head to Jalynn's. I grab the flower arrangement strapped in next to me and carry it with me to the door. Jalynn opens the door, and I shove it more abruptly than I intended into her arms.

"We had an extra, so I brought it for you. Thought you could use some flowers to liven the place up."

I slide by her and step into the house.

"Lacey, these are beautiful," Jalynn gushes and carries them inside. She places them on her kitchen island.

"Hey, Lace," George says, walking through the kitchen. "Jay, I need you to come show me where you want this picture hung."

"Okay, I'm coming," Jalynn says, following close behind him.

It's not until I walk into the kitchen that I notice I'm not alone. Jacob stands by the island. He's wearing a smirk on his face and eating grapes from a bowl on the counter. I glare back at him.

"What?" I ask.

"I think you forgot your card," Jacob says, pulling the card out of the arrangement. I snatch it from him, a blush spreading across my cheeks.

"Thanks." I tuck the note in my back pocket.

I watch Jacob's expression soften as he studies me, and I squirm under his unyielding gaze. He holds the bowl of grapes out to me, offering me some. I shake my head.

"Don't like flowers?" he asks, nodding toward the arrangement on the counter.

"Don't like strings," I reply with a shrug. I'm still embarrassed that I got caught, but Jacob nods as though he understands. "Please don't say anything to Jalynn or George."

"Why would I?" he asks and pops another grape in his mouth.

"I don't know. I just don't want them getting any ideas about anything."

"Your secret is safe with me." He tosses another grape into his mouth.

"What are you doing here, anyway?"

"Dinner invitation. And I was helping George with baby furniture," Jacob says, still studying me. Silence falls over the room.

"Aren't you two just a talkative bunch?" Jalynn comments, coming back into the room and breaking our bout of silence.

"Did Caleb get a hold of you today?" she asks me. "He texted George a while ago asking if you were okay."

"I'll call him later," I say.

"Caleb is a cool guy, but he's kind of a chump," Jacob interjects and tosses a grape up into his mouth. Jalynn and I both shoot surprised looks at him. "What?" Jacob says.

"Why don't you tell us how you really feel?" Jalynn asks him.

Jacob shifts nervously on his feet.

"I don't know. I mean, he's fine. He's a good guy. And I know we all hang out, but I just have a hard time imagining Lacey and Caleb together as a couple. Not that I was imagining them *together*. I mean . . ."

"Uh-huh," Jalynn says.

"I best be getting back to work," Jacob says after clearing his throat, and he hightails it out of the room.

Once Jacob's out of sight, Jalynn and I burst into fits of giggles like little schoolgirls. The laughter finally releases the tension that has been building up inside me all day. I keep Jalynn company while she finishes fixing dinner. With the table set and dinner served, we call the boys to come eat.

After dinner, I make sure the mess is cleaned up for Jalynn, and I say goodbye to everyone. I head out to my truck, breathing in the crisp night air. The harsh anxiety from today has dissipated but has been replaced by the butterflies that fill me every time Jacob is near. Once I'm in my truck, I put the key into the ignition and turn it. The radio and lights flip on, but the truck doesn't fire up. I try to start the truck again with the same result.

I let out a frustrated groan and hit the steering wheel with the heels of my hands. This time, I hold my breath and twist the key, trying to start the truck one more time. Nothing. I collapse over the steering wheel, arms wrapped over the top and my forehead down on my forearms. Why? Why is this happening now? I just want to go home.

My cell phone buzzes in my pocket. I pull it out and Caleb's name flashes up on the screen. My thumb hesitates over the screen, but the red button wins in the end. I don't have time to make nice with him right now, and frankly, I'm not ready to face the drama I'm afraid might come with talking to him. Once I'm home, I'll send him a text to gauge his mood.

A tapping on my window scares the shit out of me, causing me to jump in my seat and squeal. By the light of the porch, I see Jacob on the other side of the glass. I reach for the knob and roll the window down.

"Car troubles?" Jacob asks.

"Yeah, it won't start," I say, feeling defeated.

"Try it again." I twist the key in the ignition. "It sounds like your starter is bad. How about I give you a ride home." He says it more as a statement than a question.

"How will I get to work in the morning?"

"I have to go down that way in the morning, anyway. I can give you a lift."

"Are you sure?" I ask. "I feel like it's too much to ask. I really don't want to put you out."

"Seriously, not a problem. Like I said, I'm headed that way in the morning, anyway."

Jacob opens my door for me and rolls the window up while I grab my stuff. I follow him over to his pickup where he opens the door for me to get in. At least I can get in his truck without assistance. When Jacob climbs in on the driver's side, I tell him where to go. He looks at me, confused, but he follows my instructions.

"Right here," I say, pointing out the driveway that has freshly laid gravel. Jacob slows down but hesitates to turn.

"You said here?" he asks.

"Yeah, that's what I said."

Jacob pulls into my driveway, his headlights illuminating the camper.

"You live here?"

"Yup."

Jacob regards me suspiciously. Getting out of the truck, he goes around to the other side and opens the door for me. He offers me a hand as I step out of the truck, then grabs the flashlight from his glove box and walks up to the camper with me, shining the light on the door as I unlock it. Once open, I reach inside and turn the lights on. As I do, Jacob peeks inside the door and looks around at my setup.

"Why?" he asks.

"Why what?" I begin to feel defensive. My phone buzzes. I look down at it in my hand. Another text from Caleb. I ignore it and look back at Jacob.

"Why do you live here . . . in a camper . . . by yourself? It's hardly safe."

I sigh loudly and roll my eyes.

"I mean, don't get me wrong, you've got a pretty nice setup here. I just don't understand why you would make this your permanent residence. Looks more like a weekend getaway or something," Jacob says, trying to lighten the offense I'm certain he can see growing in my eyes.

"I'm a grown-ass woman. I have no one to answer to and can do as I please. I happen to like my little gypsy wagon, so you can knock it all you want, but frankly, I don't care what anyone else thinks. It works for me. And I like it," I rant.

"Gypsy wagon?" Jacob repeats, a smile dancing on the corners of this mouth.

"Okay, so I did say that, but—"

"No, I like it." Jacob nods, still fighting off the smile. "I see what you mean. You're just a little gypsy floating around wherever you please." He wiggles his fingers through the air.

"Sure . . ." I say, waiting for the punch line. Jacob just stands there, continuing to nod and looking like he has a secret. "Okay, well then! I appreciate the ride. I will see you in the morning?"

"Sure thing . . . Gypsy."

"Excuse me?"

"I'll see you bright and early." Jacob rotates around me, heading for his truck without turning his back to me. I narrow my eyes at him. "Have a good night, Gypsy."

"This is not going to be a thing!" I call after him. "You're not calling me Gypsy! Be here at eight sharp!"

Jacob gives me a wave and backs out of the driveway.

"Why? Why did I have to run off at the mouth like that in front of him?" I ask out loud as I climb into the camper and trudge my way to bed.

As I undress, the card from the flowers flutters out of my pocket and onto the floor. I scoop it up, remembering that I need to call Caleb. Maybe I'll just send him a quick text instead.

Me: You sent me flowers?

Caleb: About that . . . I ordered them directly through Mrs. Jones on Friday before everything happened. I hope you can enjoy them anyway.

Me: Thank you. That's very sweet of you.

Relief sweeps over me, as I'm reminded yet again that Caleb isn't Ben. I settle onto my pillow, thinking about how different he is from Ben. Caleb hasn't once lost his temper with me a single time. In fact, in all the time we've spent together, I've never seen him mad. With Ben, on the other hand, I could never do anything right.

"Lace, what's wrong?" Jalynn's voice rang through my cell phone.

"Can . . . you come . . . get me?" I somehow got the words out between ragged breaths.

"Where are you? What's happened?"

"I'm . . . not . . . sure."

"Are you hurt, Lace?"

"No." This time a sob slipped out with my reply.

"Send me your location," Jalynn ordered.

I ended the call with shaky hands and sent my location to Jalynn's phone. Thank goodness for technology. I didn't have the mental capacity at that moment to try to figure out where I was exactly. Using the flashlight on my phone to see through the heavy darkness, I found a stump off to the side of the road to sit on while I waited to be rescued. It was wet, like everything else around me, but I didn't care. I'd be soaked through by the time I was found anyway.

The cold rain washed over my body, making me shiver uncontrollably. A low of fifty degrees wasn't cold enough for snow, but the large raindrops slid down my bare skin like ice daggers, and the wet cold clung to my clothes. I had thrown my coat into the back seat of Ben's car during our argument. With the heat blaring from the vents of his dash, and our anger and frustration flaring over our disagreement, it had been too warm in the car to wear it. I never expected him to kick me out of the car.

He'd pulled the car over on the secluded road, screaming at me to get out. When I'd refused, he'd reached across me and threw my door open, then proceeded to unbuckle my seat belt for me and had tried to push me out of the car. Proving to be more difficult than he had interest in dealing with, he'd wrestled me for my phone, popping me in the mouth in the process. The taste of blood had spread over my tongue, and I'd sucked my split lip into my mouth, trying to calm the pulsing pain.

Ben had tossed my phone out the door, to the side of the road. I'd made a dash for it, grabbing for it before the screen went dark again. My feet hadn't even hit the ground, though, when Ben had shoved me from behind, sending me to the ground, and the door had slammed shut again with the jolt of him accelerating away from me.

So there I sat soaked through with ripped up knees, skinned hands, and a busted lip, shivering and sobbing in the rain, when the headlights of George's truck illuminated my surroundings, and Jalynn rushed to my side. Jalynn threw her arms around me and pulled me to my feet. George was close on her heels, draping his own coat over my soggy shoulders and helping Jalynn get me into the front seat of the truck. Jalynn climbed in next to me and turned up the heat, pointing the vents toward me in attempt to warm my shaking body.

"THAT NO-GOOD, WORTHLESS BASTARD!" *Jalynn exclaimed, pacing the floor later that evening.*

George had driven us back to his and Jalynn's apartment. Jalynn had helped me get cleaned up and in warm, dry clothes. She settled on the couch next to me, waiting for an explanation. I stared at my bandaged hands in my lap, unable to look at either of them while I recounted the events of the evening.

George was being pretty quiet, occupied by his buzzing phone. Jalynn caught sight of the caller as she paced by, and she lunged for the phone.

"I don't think so," George said, holding the phone over his head.

"Let me talk to the slimy dick waffle. I have a few things to say to him," Jalynn fumed, still reaching for the phone.

"Is it Ben? Is Ben calling?" I asked, perking up from my seat. "He's probably looking for me."

I grabbed my phone from the end table next to me, but it didn't respond. The battery was dead. This wasn't good. Ben would be furious if he'd been trying to get a hold of me.

"Lacey, please tell me you're done with him," Jalynn said, abandoning her mission to get the phone from George to come sit next to me again.

"It was a bad fight," I said. "He lost his temper, but he still loves me."

"Lace . . ." Jalynn said, disappointment washing over her face.

We were interrupted when someone pounded on their front door. George hopped up out of his chair to answer it. Ben's voice came from the other side, and he tried to push past George to get in. George reared back and slammed his fist into Ben's face, knocking Ben off his feet. I jumped off the couch, screaming, and grabbed onto George's recoiled arm before he could punch Ben again.

Wedging myself between them, I helped Ben back to his feet. Ben glowered at George, and Jalynn reached around George to grab hold of my hand.

"Please, Lace. Don't go with him. Stay here with us," she pleaded, desperation in her eyes.

"I can't, Jay. I gotta go. It's okay, though. Thank you for picking me up. I'll call you tomorrow," I said.

I pulled my hand free from her grasp and took a few steps backward, then I turned and followed Ben to his car. I adored my friends. They didn't come much better than Jay and George. Not all of us got to have the storybook romance like they did, though. They didn't want to believe that, but I'd already accepted it. Ben was my future, despite his imperfections.

Maybe I'm wrong to believe Jalynn. Maybe that's why the sparks weren't there with Caleb. He was too good for me. I was trying for something that's just not meant to be.

I turn on the shower and begin to undress while the water heats. When all else fails, I always feel better after a shower and clean clothes.

jacob

On the drive toward Lacey's to give her a ride to work, I think about last night. Last night was a mess. I still haven't figured out the deal with the flowers. Did Lacey and Caleb get back together? Maybe it was Caleb's attempt to win her back. She didn't seem to be having it.

My attraction to Lacey has been on the rise the last couple of weeks, even though I'm trying to keep my distance. Lacey is everywhere, though. Even when I talk to my parents, the subject of Lacey comes up. My mom raves about how much help Lacey has been at the shop. From the sounds of it, she and Lacey are getting pretty close.

There was a time I wanted the house and the wife and the kids, too. That pipe dream left with Ashley, though. Maybe I'll be able to fix things with her, but it's not looking promising. And if not, I'm not wading back into the dating pool. Even if Lacey and I were both single, even though being in the same room as her makes me feel alive, I still couldn't do anything about it. I'm calling it quits and committing to being a bachelor. The family life just isn't in the cards for me.

Back at Lacey's camper, I knock on her door. I don't hear

any movement inside, so I try again, pounding harder. This time I hear a loud thud.

"Just a second!" Lacey calls out to me.

A moment later, the door flies open, and Lacey appears with her bathrobe wrapped tightly around her. I look her up and down, eying the robe. I must have woken her.

"Morning, Gypsy. New work uniform?"

"I forgot to set my dang blasted alarm last night."

Lacey holds one arm wrapped around her stomach to secure the robe. My mind begins to wonder what's under the robe, but I push the thoughts away. Instead, I force my eyes to her bedhead. It doesn't do much to help my wandering thoughts, though, because her hair looks like she was thoroughly . . . entertained last night.

Shit.

I don't need to be thinking about that, either. I'm here as a friend, giving another friend a ride to work. That's all. I'm focusing on my relationship with Ashley. Let's face it, though. That hasn't been going anywhere fast. Ashley is driving me crazy.

"Come on in," Lacey says, combing her fingers through her wild hair, trying to calm the mess. She gestures toward the bench. "I'll just be a minute."

I climb into the camper and have a seat. Lacey grabs her clothes off the bed and crams herself into the tight space of the bathroom to change. I explore the camper with my eyes from where I'm sitting while I intentionally focus on not thinking about the woman who is probably naked right now, approximately six feet away from me.

The interior of the camper is very feminine. It is cozy, though. I can see why she likes the place. She has it painted in lots of girly colors. I glance over the throw pillows sitting next to me on the bench and can't help but run my hand across them. These ones are funky textures and colors and give the camper a homier feel than the cold, neutral ones Ashley always kept on our furniture.

I guess the same could be said of Lacey and Ashley, too. Lacey is warm and full of life and personality. She doesn't care about current trends. She does what makes her happy. Ashley, on the other hand, bases every decision on what will get her further ahead. She's cold and methodical in the way she does things. To Ashley, joy is nothing more than wall art she'd never dream of decorating her home with.

"So this is how the gypsies live, huh?" I ask loud enough for Lacey to hear me through the bathroom door.

"It's not so bad," she yells back to me. Her speech is muffled, and I assume by the sounds coming from the bathroom that it's from a toothbrush in her mouth. She spits into the sink and continues. "Couldn't ask for cheaper rent, either."

"I can imagine. You know, you've taken over one of my fishing spots."

"What do you mean?"

She opens the bathroom door, dressed now. She's focused on finding her phone and her purse. My eyes slide down her body, liking how good she looks in something as simple as shorts and a T-shirt.

"I used to come down here in the evenings when I didn't have time to hike out anywhere else. I'd fish in the creek back there."

"Oh. Well, I don't guess I'd care if you came fishing. I can hardly stake a claim on the property."

"Maybe I will. You ready?" I stand from the bench as she approaches.

Lacey nods.

"Let me grab my keys."

I stand aside as Lacey locks the camper door, then I follow her down to the truck.

Eyes up! I keep reminding myself.

I don't need to be checking her out. At the truck, I reach

past her to open the door for her. I catch a whiff of vanilla off of her that shoots fire straight to my groin. She slides into the seat, and I close the door behind her. I take deep breaths as I walk around the truck, trying to clear the dirty thoughts from my mind. Why am I having such a difficult time keeping my mind out of the gutter around her?

I get in the driver's seat and start the truck. The radio instantly begins playing. Great. A song about sex. I switch the station without even caring what it lands on.

"How're things going at the flower shop?" I ask.

"It's great. Your mom is amazing. I wish my mom was still around."

"When did she pass?"

"My parents passed away when I was seven. My grandparents raised me after."

Another sultry song starts to play on the radio. I reach over and flip the channel again.

"Are your grandparents still in North Carolina?"

"They've passed as well."

"Oh. I'm sorry."

I switch the music away from another suggestive song again.

"My truck was Granddaddy's before he passed. That's why I haven't just dumped the old thing and bought something more reliable. He loved that truck."

I reach for the radio again, this time switching it off completely. Is every song these days about sex?

At the floral shop, I get out of the truck and make my way around the front to open the door for Lacey. She steps out of the truck and gives me a quick hug. I have to consciously make the decision to let her go, my whole body engulfed by the fire of her touch.

"Thanks for the ride," she says.

"No problem," I reply. "So I'm probably not going to be around when you get off work. You might see if Jalynn or someone can pick you up."

I had way too much confidence in myself, agreeing to drive her to work. I'm ashamed of the lack of control I feel around her. I need to keep my fucking distance.

"Okay. Well, thanks."

I watch silently as she disappears through the shop door. I get back in my truck and drive over to my office, a few blocks down. Ashley is supposed to meet me at the office to help out with some paperwork and filing today. She says we need more time together and has been pressing for an answer on her proposal to move back in together. I'm not ready to take that leap of faith. I suggested she come back to work for me instead. That's where it all began, after all. I'd hired her for office help.

At the office, Ashley hasn't made it in yet, but she should be showing up at any moment. I ready the files I want her to handle for me and start going over my inventory of medicines and supplies.

Not much has changed for me over the last couple of months since Ashley's been back. I've tried to forget all of the hurt, but every time I look at her, I'm reminded of her betrayal. My family never liked her, even from the start of our relationship. They put up with her because I loved her. Now, without the rose-colored glasses, I think I see her in the same way that my family has this whole time. It's a struggle to be around her. Even though she's just as pretty as ever, and her little dresses fit her just the same, I don't know if I'll ever be able to trust her again.

I finish the inventory and move over to my computer to begin putting in an order for the supplies that are growing low. I glance at my watch to check the time. Ashley should've already arrived. I log on to my computer and pull up the website I need. Slowly, I add items I need to the cart, making sure I haven't overlooked anything.

I'm not sure why Ashley ever applied to be an administrative assistant for a veterinary office. I was quick to deduce she hates animals. There are plenty of other jobs that would have been more suited to her high-maintenance personality than a vet office.

Once we were living together, she wasn't very tolerant of me coming home in the evenings smelling like my patients, either. She convinced me to shower at the office every day before coming home. That quickly led to having a washer and dryer installed at the office so I could do my laundry at work, too. Mia, the loving sister she is, was quick to tease me about being homeless and only a visitor at "Ashley's place."

The creaking of the front door pulls my attention up from the computer. An hour later than expected, Ashley walks in, shattering the silence. She's laughing and talking to someone on her cell phone. She plops her designer purse on the counter and taps her long, manicured nails on the stack of files waiting for her while she finishes her call.

"I'm so glad you were able to work things out with your family," she croons to the person on the other end of the phone. "I'm sure it's a relief not to lose your business, either."

My ears perk at the comment. Is she talking to him again? Mia tried telling me Ashley was only back because her new man went broke. I dismissed her accusations, but was she right? Had Ashley come running back to me all of a sudden because of the money?

"What is that smell?" Ashley asks, hanging up the phone and setting it face down on the counter.

"What smell?" I ask, my focus back on the computer screen.

"It smells like a barn in here! I don't know how you can stand it."

I let out an audible sigh, already regretting having her in the office today. Everything is such a damn ordeal with her.

"Those are the files I need you to work on," I say, nodding toward the files next to her phone.

"I'll get to them, but right now I need to deal with this smell. I can't stay here with it smelling like this."

Ashley walks back into the storage room. The sound of her rummaging through my things attacks my nerves.

"What are you looking for?" I call out, annoyed.

"Where did you put all of those wall flowers I had in here?"

"I threw them away."

"What?" She pokes her head out of the storage room, horror written across her face. "Why would you do that?"

"I didn't like them. You weren't here anymore. They were just taking up unnecessary space."

"I can't believe you," Ashley says, moving into the kitchen in search of some air freshener to spray around the office instead.

Finally finding a forgotten bottle in the back of a cupboard, she walks through the office leaving a trail of mist behind her. I cough and sputter on the heavy scent as she walks by my desk with her finger still pressed down on the sprayer. She sets the spray down next to the files and finally starts on her work.

A few minutes later her phone buzzes on the counter next to her. She picks it up and glances at the screen. Smiling, she opens the message. She types out a reply, presses send, and lays the phone back down. Seconds later it buzzes again. At this rate, she will never finish the stack of files.

I submit my finalized order and close down the computer. My level of annoyance grows with each buzz of Ashley's phone. I pick up my coffee mug and walk into the kitchen to refill it. As I'm putting the lid back on my mug, I hear the front door creak open again. I poke my head around the corner to see who it is.

"Hey, Freddy," I call out, grabbing my mug and walking back out into the reception area again. "How's things going out your way?"

"Oh, we're doing good. I wanted to come show you our new addition," the gruff man says.

As I approach him, I catch sight of his youngest daughter attached to his leg. I crouch down in front of the girl, who couldn't be more than five years old.

"Hey, Emmaline," I say.

She tightens her grip on her daddy's leg, holding on for dear life as she hides behind him. I reach into my pocket and pull out a piece of candy, offering it to her, and she pokes her head around to see what I have. A grin spreads across her face. In a quick motion, she snatches the candy from my palm and retreats again behind Freddy's leg. I chuckle and stand to talk to Freddy.

"What'd you get?" I ask.

Freddy steps back, pushing the office door open again. His son walks in guiding a tiny pony. I throw my head back and laugh, instantly understanding what has transpired. I crouch back down to Emmaline.

"Did you get a pony?" I ask.

Emmaline grins and bobs her head up and down in an enthusiastic nod.

"She's been begging me for a pony, and I came across this little guy and thought, why not?" Freddy says above us.

"He's a Falabella, right?" I ask, petting on the pony.

"Yep. Sure is."

"I love that you found a pinto, too." I stand and turn, looking for Ashley who is now looking through a file. "Ashley, come see this."

"Sorry, I'd rather admire him from afar," Ashley says. Her nose crinkles. "Actually, I think I'll get out of the way and take these files into the kitchen."

Ashley swipes up her work and leaves the room. I shake my head, frustrated by her inability to even feign interest.

"She's not a big animal person," I say to Freddy, hoping she hasn't offended him.

A buzzing across the room grabs my attention. Looking over to where Ashley was working, I see her phone still sitting on the counter. Another text message, no doubt. I stoop back down to examine the pony. I pull back her lips to get a look at her teeth and rub down her neck and mane. I take a quick look at each of her hooves. Ashley's phone continues to buzz from the counter. I stand and look over at it again.

Turning my attention back to Freddy, I ask, "Do you need a workup done on him or anything?"

"No, he should be good. Just wanted to come show him off to you," Freddy replies.

"Well, he sure is a pretty thing. You gonna take good care of him, Emmaline?"

The little girl nods her head, loosening her grip slightly on her father's leg.

Ashley's phone emits a few more buzzes in the time it takes Freddy to make it out the door. Ashley's still in the kitchen and hasn't seemed to notice yet that she's missing it. I walk over and look down at the phone. Per her usual, the phone sits screen down on the counter. It buzzes again. Finally, I pick it up, deciding to take it to her so I don't have to listen to the constant buzzing anymore. I turn the phone over and glance at the screen. There are eight new messages from Clyde.

Clyde.

The "friend" she'd sent the skimpy photos to.

Without even thinking, I slide my finger across the screen to open up the phone. As Ashley promised, there's no passcode on it now. It opens directly into their messages. I slide my finger over the messages, scrolling up, not even having to stop to read the words on the screen. The few words I catch tell me everything I need to know.

I toss the phone back down and lean over, my hands resting on the edge of the counter for support. Bile rises in my throat, and I will it away.

Same story, different day.

I'm a damn fool for letting her talk me into taking her back. Deep down I knew nothing had changed.

I scoop the phone back up again and march into the kitchen. Ashley is sitting at the table with her legs crossed, the stack of files in front of her. I slap the phone down on the table, making her jump in her seat. Leaning down toward her, I rest my hands on either sides of the stack of folders on the table. Ashley stares wide eyed at me.

"Get your shit together and walk your slimy, lying ass out that fucking door right now!"

Ashley scoots her chair back away from me and stands. I scoop up the files off the table and continue to glare down at her.

"Excuse me?" she snaps back.

"Your act is up, Ashley. I know you're back to talking to him, assuming you ever even quit talking to him in the first place."

"I haven't done anything. He's just a friend. Jacob, we've been over this, and you said you would try."

"I was trying, but I'm not going to bury my head in the fucking sand and pretend like I'm okay with you talking to him again."

I'm shouting now, my anger steadily building.

"You weren't trying. You haven't tried at all. You've been too busy mooning over Lacey to actually try to make things work between us," Ashley yells, matching my volume.

"Get the fuck out of my sight," I say through clenched teeth.

"You don't want to do this," Ashley says, settling her hands on her hips.

"Oh, I'm pretty damn sure that I do."

Ashley stares back at me, pouting, and folds her arms across her body. She must finally see the loathing in my eyes and realizes that her façade is up because she grabs her phone and purse and storms out of the office. Once I hear her car fire up, I collapse in her vacant chair, surprised to find the rage has been replaced with relief. Finally.

CHAPTER NINETEEN

I climb into my truck and try the ignition again. Sure enough, it still won't start. Jalynn picks me up from work, and after a few YouTube videos and the purchase of a hammer from the hardware store, I am ready to tackle the problem with the starter on my pickup.

I wiggle my way under the truck and locate the starter. Just like the videos suggested, I lightly hammer on it, roll out from under the truck, and try to start it again. Like magic, the truck rumbles to life. I grin to myself and toss the hammer in the passenger seat. It's not pretty, and it's not permanent, but it will do for now until I can afford the labor and parts to get it replaced.

I drive home, park the truck in the driveway, and head down to the creek. I haven't been down to the creek since moving here, and I'm craving some time in nature. A narrow dirt path leads the way down to the creek bank. Little white and yellow flowers grow in spurts near the water's edge. A wooden swing hangs from a tall tree limb overhanging the bank. I slowly ease down onto the swing, making sure it will hold, then settle all of my weight on it. With a gentle push off the ground, I swing back and forth over the bank.

My phone buzzes in my pocket.

Billy: Ben is causing a stink around town.

Me: What now?

Billy: He's doing his damnedest to get your phone number. Says he's a changed man and needs to talk to you.

Me: What do you mean a changed man?

Billy: He claims he's found Jesus.

Me: I don't care who he's found as long as it ain't me. You didn't give him my number did you?

Billy: Of course not. Just wanted to keep you in the know.

Me: Thanks Billy. Miss you.

I slide the phone back in my pocket and push off again, swinging higher this time. It'll take more than a little bit of Jesus to convince me to give him another chance.

Eventually, unable to shake off the anxiety Billy's update brought me, I head inside. I lock the door behind me and tap my fingers on the kitchen counter, trying to decide what to do with myself. Remembering some books I brought with me, I head for the back of the camper to choose one off the shelf above my bed.

I run my finger across the spines until I come to one that sparks my interest and stretch out on the bed with it. A folded slip of paper falls from the pages of the book as I open it and lands on the blanket. Picking it up, I quickly recognize what it is. It's the funeral program for Ben's little brother. My eyes rest on his picture on the front of the paper, and I study his sweet face. Without warning, the emotions and memories take over my thoughts.

Ben rolled over toward me and wrapped an arm over and across my torso, pulling me back against his chest. I knew what he wanted, but I still hadn't gotten over our argument from last night. He kissed and lightly nipped at my ear. I was grateful when the ringing of his phone sitting on the nightstand inter-rupted him. He rolled over and picked up the phone, answering it with a gruff "Hello."

Ben sat up abruptly on the edge of the bed. Despite the anger I was still holding on to, I could feel the new tension wash over the room. I rolled over to look at him, trying to figure out what was going on.

His mom's panicked voice came through the speaker of the phone. There was an accident. It was Ben's little brother, Brian. Something about a tractor. Ben jumped out of bed and started throwing clothes on. He told his mom we would leave right away and tossed the phone on the bed.

"Get up and put some clothes on," Ben said. "Brian's hurt bad. We've got to hurry." Already dressed, he grabbed his wallet and keys from the top of the dresser and slid a pack of Pall Malls in his pocket.

"Is he going to be okay?" I asked, pulling on the first clothes I touched.

I'd always loved Brian. He was a cute kid and had the sweetest personality. He was like the little brother I never had.

"No," was all Ben said.

I wipe the tears off my cheeks and sniffle as I run a finger across the picture of Brian's face. Twelve years wasn't enough time for that sweet soul. He should have had many, many more. His death was hard on all of us.

I tuck his funeral program into the back pages of the book and flip open to the first chapter to read.

"Mia had an employee call out sick this morning. They have a big wedding to set up for, and Mia needs all the help she can get," Maddie says. "I've got to go to Bozeman to help her with the wedding setup."

"Okay. I'll handle things here," I reply.

"Put this number in your phone." Maddie pauses for me to get my phone out and recites a number to me. "That's Jacob's number. He should be here shortly. He's going to be working on some projects around the shop for me today so you don't have to be here alone. I don't like having only one person at the shop all day, though I don't expect anything to happen that you couldn't handle on your own."

I save the number in my phone.

"Is there anything special you want me to accomplish today?"

"Nope, just do your thing. You can help Jacob out if he needs extra hands on any of his tasks."

"Okay. Good luck with the wedding stuff. I'll see you tomorrow?"

"I'll be back," Maddie says and walks out the door.

I tie on my apron and start setting up for the day, writing the special on the sidewalk sign and unlocking the door. This is going to be an interesting day.

Jacob strolls in looking all manly and sexy with his stubble and mischievous grin. The sleeves of his green T-shirt bunch slightly over his biceps earned from regular manual labor. A brown leather belt holds his light wash jeans over his hips, the denim loose but fitted over the muscles of his thighs and resting on the vamp of his boots. I have to remind myself to pick my chin up off the floor and not to drool over a taken man, though I try to casually sneak another look as he approaches.

"Hey," Jacob says. He leans against the counter.

"Hey. How's my bestie?" I ask, wiping chalk from my hands.

Jacob chuckles.

"Honestly, I wouldn't know."

I forget to act like I'm busy, my curiosity getting the better of me. Butterflies assault me when my eyes lock back on Jacob's.

"What happened?" I ask.

"You were right. She's manipulative and toxic. I told her to hit the road."

"I'm sorry I was right."

Jacob shrugs.

"I'm going to get to work," he says and brushes by, his touch making my head spin.

I bite my lip, trying to kill the smile overtaking me as I go back to my work. That was an interesting tidbit of information. I wonder what happened to finally make Jacob call it quits with Ashley. It doesn't hurt my feelings that they ended things.

I look over the orders that need to be assembled today, take the list with me to the back room, and start gathering my supplies for the first one.

I'm acutely aware of Jacob's comings and goings as he moves through the shop doing general maintenance and working on specific projects. I'm busy cleaning up my mess from the orders I assembled when Jacob walks back in with a large box. He sets the box down on the work table and begins opening it.

"If you have time, I could use some help with this one," Jacob says looking back at me.

"Sure. What do you need?" I ask, coming around the table to take a closer look

"I've got to change out the light fixture over this worktable. I'll need you to hold the fixture while I do the wiring."

Chills run over my body when Jacob looks at me as he's explaining.

"Okay."

"Think this table can hold the both of us?" Jacob asks with a smirk. He holds out a hand to help me climb up.

"I'm light as a feather, obviously, so if it breaks it's all your fault," I tease. Jacob climbs up on the table behind me.

"Are you calling me fat?" he asks, straightening up.

"No. It's all your big muscles that make you weigh more," I say, reaching over to squeeze one of his firm biceps.

My mouth goes dry at our proximity, and I lick my lips. Jacob's eyes stay locked on mine. He doesn't bother with a reply.

"So," I say nervously, trying to cut through the tension I feel between us, "what do you need me to do?"

Jacob clears his throat and shifts his focus to the task at hand. He grabs the drill sitting at our feet and motions toward the fixture.

"Start by holding this," he says, showing me where he wants me to hold while he works.

Much too soon, the light fixture is changed out. Jacob jumps off the table, then turns back, grabs me by my waist, and lifts me down to the ground. My feet reach the floor, but his strong hands linger on my hips, his body only inches from my own. My breath catches, and I lift my eyes slowly to meet his. I succumb to the magnetic pull radiating off him and slowly allow my body to lean in toward him, ever so slightly closing the space between us. The heat in Jacob's eyes warms my body.

Jacob's hands drop from my hips. He turns from me, gathering the pieces of the old light fixture to discard. He whistles a tune as he drops the pieces into the box. Embarrassment and shame sweep over me. Of course, I was misjudging the moment. He just ended his relationship with Ashley. That was thoughtless of me to make assumptions.

I escape to the greenhouse, kicking off my shoes outside the door, and head inside to water. I pull the nozzle off the hook and twist the water on, my mind drifting away to the day not so long ago when the spigot broke off and things got steamy between Jacob and me in the back of the greenhouse.

The greenhouse door swings open and Jacob walks in with

a ladder. He sets the ladder up a couple of rows up from where I'm watering and retreats back out the door. Minutes later, he returns with a pane of glass. I watch as he climbs the ladder. I drift back into my head while I move down the row, watering plants, as Jacob replaces a broken glass in the greenhouse.

Shattering glass around my feet startles me out of my daydream. I stumble backward without thinking, and a sharp pain bites into my foot. My legs want to give out under me to remove the weight from my bare feet, but I catch myself on the workbench at my side. Blood seeps into the crevices of the cement under me.

"Don't move!" Jacob yells down to me over the noise of the fans.

He quickly descends the ladder and rushes to my side. Without a word, he scoops me into his arms and carries me out of the greenhouse. He sets me on the worktable in the back of the shop.

"Sit here while I get the first aid kit," Jacob orders me. I couldn't argue even if I wanted to. My voice is strangled by the tears I'm trying to keep down.

When he returns, several drops of blood are pooling on the floor beneath my feet. Jacob looks at my watery eyes, his own face pained, and he swipes away a lose tear from my face that manages to spill over. He pulls a stool over to sit on and reaches down for my feet, inspecting them both for cuts.

Addressing the large gash on one of my feet, he opens a sterile pair of tweezers and dabs the blood trailing down my foot from where a shard of glass still sticks in my flesh. He uses the tweezers to carefully remove the glass from my foot and gently dabs my foot again. Jacob inspects the gash, making sure he got all of the glass. Satisfied, he treats the cut with antibiotic cream and covers it with a bandage. Jacob stands from the stool and closes the space between us.

"I think I got it all," he says quietly, his hands resting on the table, on either sides of my legs.

"Guess I'm lucky I had a medical expert close by," I respond breathlessly.

"Not the hooves I'm used to working on, but I figured it out," Jacob says with a smirk, easing the tension.

Slowly, he moves closer. I bite at my bottom lip, the anticipation rising as I feel his hands on my thighs now. Will he kiss me this time? I hold his gaze, but I don't lean in, not trusting my judgment. His warm breath dances over my skin, leaving goose bumps in its wake.

Softly, his lips finally brush over mine, so lightly at first that I might have imagined it. Hungrily, I raise my chin, pressing further into him, urging him on. He takes the hint, and his hand slides up to my hair, grasping a handful, and he deepens the kiss. My fingers rub over the stubble on his jaw, and I graze his lip with my teeth, earning a low moan from Jacob. Heat floods my body, pooling low in my belly. I wrap my legs around his, pull his body flush against mine, and feel his excitement as our bodies press together.

The chime of the bell over the front door breaks us apart. My heart is beating wildly in my chest and a flush covers my cheeks. Jacob clears his throat and steps back from the table.

"You don't have shoes on," he says. "I'll go up front and take care of the customer."

Jacob turns, adjusting himself as he walks through the door leading to the front of the shop.

I carefully slide off the table, being cautious at first with my injured foot. Did that really just happen? And what did it mean? I head back out to the greenhouse and slide my feet into my shoes. Inside the greenhouse, I clean up the broken glass. Sweeping up each piece, I hope my heart isn't the next thing to shatter all over this floor.

Jacob seems to be keeping his distance as the afternoon drifts by, filling me with anxiety. Finally, at closing time, I lock the front door and approach him. He's busy gathering his tools, getting ready to load up and leave. I watch him for a moment.

"Thanks again for doctoring me up," I say, walking up to him, unsure of how to start the conversation I want to have.

"Since I'm the reason you got hurt in the first place, I don't think thanks is necessary, but you're welcome."

"Your bedside manner is beyond this world. Do all of your patients get that treatment?"

Jacob chuckles. He stops what he's doing, turns toward me now, and leans back against the workbench in a relaxed manner.

"No. You are the first. Think I should make a thing of it?"

"Only when I'm the patient," I say. My cheeks burn with the confession.

"About that—" Jacob starts.

"Uh-oh. It's never good when someone starts with those two words."

Jacob gives me a sympathetic look, and his hands slide into his pockets. I fold my arms across my chest and wait for him to speak.

"Gypsy, don't get me wrong, I think you're gorgeous and funny. You are a remarkable woman. I shouldn't have kissed you, though."

"Why not? Neither of us are taken." I chew at my bottom lip, a nervous habit I haven't been able to break.

"I just ended things with Ashley. I'm not in a state of mind yet that would be fair to you for us to get involved. I like you. I just need some time to get things straight in my head and figure out if I'm even interested in getting in a relationship with anyone."

"Alrighty then." I slowly back away, beginning my retreat. "I've already locked up. I'm just going to head out and go nurse my wounded pride in private."

"Gypsy—"

"Nope, we're good. It was just a kiss. You don't owe me anything."

I walk out the door before Jacob can stop me.

jacob

"Thank God you came to your senses and broke up with her again," Mia says, rounding the pool table and lining up her next shot. "Honestly, I can't believe you agreed to give her a second chance in the first place."

"So I keep hearing," I reply dryly.

"Actually, strike that. I can't believe you gave her a first chance. She was a bitch, and I hated her from the start."

"I know," I say and take my shot.

Mia has never been shy about giving me her opinion on the women I date.

"Mom keeps telling me not to ask you about it, but I'm not as patient as she is," Mia says. "Please tell me Mom's little stunt a couple of weeks ago was successful to some extent at least."

"What little stunt?" I ask, having no idea what Mia is referring to.

Mia spins around to look at me.

"Oh my gosh. She actually duped you?"

"What are you talking about?" I pause, giving her my full attention now.

"That day, about two weeks ago," Mia says, dropping a ball

in the corner pocket, "when she had you fill in for her at the shop?"

"I remember. What about it?"

"It was a setup." Mia laughs incredulously.

"What do you mean it was a setup?" I lean against the edge of the pool table, my interest in our game waning.

"You are so damn gullible! I didn't need her in Bozeman. She's been dying for you and Lacey to get together. You're both finally single, and she jumped on the opportunity before it passed again. She fabricated the whole thing to get you and Lacey to spend the day together."

"You're kidding."

Mia straightens, resting the end of her pool cue on the floor in front of her.

"No. I'm not. And we've been dying to know how it went. Please tell me you didn't let the opportunity go to waste."

I exhale and run my fingers through my hair.

"I'm pretty sure I only made things worse," I say.

I've been actively avoiding Lacey since that day. I feel awful for giving in to the fucking horndog she brings out in me by kissing her.

"What do you mean you made it worse? Made what worse?" Mia asks.

"I kissed her. Then I told her I wasn't ready to get involved with anyone . . . And I've avoided her since."

Mia smacks my arm.

"Dumbass. What is wrong with you?" Mia scolds me.

"I'm not interested in being in another relationship, and Lacey doesn't want a fling. We might both be single but we aren't in the same place. And I don't want to hurt her."

"Or you're a pansy and afraid she'll break your little heart," Mia says.

"Or that, too." I focus back on our game, clearing a couple more balls.

"I can't even with you right now," Mia says and rolls her eyes at me. "Come on. You owe me a drink."

I take our pool cues and place them back on the rack. Mia leads the way through the pool hall to the door. When we get there, Mia takes a step back toward me as a wave of people come in through the entrance, and I instinctively place a hand on Mia's back. That's when I see Lacey filter through the door with the group of newcomers. She falters when she spots me. I give her a nod, and her eyes drop down to the hand still resting on Mia's back. She recovers quickly, though, and follows her group to the counter.

Fresh guilt washes over me. I wish I could go back in time and take back that kiss. It was selfish of me. I knew before I kissed her that I wasn't interested in dating anyone. And I was already pretty confident about how she feels about me. I wasn't sure she felt the same until that night at the rodeo when she asked me under the stands if I felt it—that electrical spark between us—too.

Even if I wanted to jump into another relationship right now, it wouldn't be fair to Lacey. I'm a shell of what I was before Ashley. She destroyed me. I have nothing left to offer any woman, and Lacey deserves more than that.

It's the right thing to keep my distance from her, especially now. I don't fully trust myself around her, and until I do, I don't need to put us in a situation where I might give in to her again. The temptation to be with her is too great, and the only thing that will come of it is mutual obliteration. I don't know Lacey's story yet, but I can still see a void in her eyes. She's healing from something that cut her deep. There isn't enough of me left to help her heal. I'll only pull her down my own path of destruction.

Mia and I head back to my place for a couple drinks. Mia pipes on about how ignorant I am and tells me in great detail all of the ways I've screwed up. I can always count on Mia not to sugarcoat her opinions about my personal life.

lacey

I'm sitting at the front counter making bows when the bells over the shop door jingle. I hop off my stool and greet the customer. It's a young man with sun-kissed skin and clothing suggestive of manual labor employment.

"Hi, what can I do for you today?" I ask as he approaches the counter.

"I ordered some flowers for my mother," the man says.

"What's the name on the order?" I bring the computer screen back to life and click over to look up the customer's name.

"Jared Compton."

"Perfect. I'll grab those for you," I say with a smile. I head to the cooler where his arrangement sits ready to go and bring it back to the counter with me.

"Have you worked here long?" Jared asks me.

"I've been here for a few months."

"I thought I would have remembered a beautiful face like yours," he says, making me blush.

With some flirty banter back and forth, Jared eventually asks me for my phone number. I hesitate momentarily. The whole dating thing hasn't gone well for me. Then again, that's mostly been my own fault. Jalynn's words about not all men being like Ben ring in my head. Maybe it's worth giving it another chance. I end up jotting my number down for him on a notecard. He's barely gone for five minutes when my phone buzzes in my pocket.

Jared: Are you free tonight?

Me: Depends . . .

Jared: Go out with me.

Me: What do you have in mind?

Jared: Dinner and a movie?

Me: Sounds great.

I rush home after work to get cleaned up and changed for my date. Jared didn't want to drive out to my place to pick me up, so we made plans to meet at the gas station in town. With nearly an hour's worth of driving to get home and back to town, I don't have a lot of time to get ready.

I hurry inside my camper and head straight to the bathroom to refresh my hair and makeup. I sort through my limited wardrobe for something date-worthy. Finally settling on an outfit, I finish it off with a pair of stilettos and head back out the door. My stomach grumbles as I climb back into my truck. Hopefully dinner is first on the agenda.

Jared is already at the gas station when I pull in. I leave my truck in one of the spaces off to the side so it will be out of the way and climb into Jared's truck.

"What do you want to do tonight?" Jared asks, preparing to pull out of the gas station.

"I thought we'd already decided to go get dinner and see a movie," I reply, thinking back to our conversation via text.

"I was hungry so I already ate. You can't talk and get to

know each other in a movie, so I thought maybe we should do something else."

"Oh. That's fine." My stomach growls in protest. "What did you have in mind?"

"I don't know. I do need to go to Walmart, though. Do you care if we run out there really quick? Then we can do something in the city since we will already be out there anyway."

"Okay. That sounds good."

The entire drive to Bozeman, Jared talks incessantly about himself, telling the same stories repeatedly—each time painting himself as a hero. My stomach rumbles again, wanting food.

"A good woman is hard to find these days," Jared says, finally moving away from the stories of grandeur. "I need a good woman. She wouldn't have to work or anything. I would take care of her. She could lounge all day by the pool if she wanted to while I'm out working hard. All I would ask from her is that she cooks me dinner and warms my bed. I'd take care of everything else for my queen."

"Oh. Sounds like you have it all figured out," I reply, feeling awkward and unsure of what to say.

We finally make it to Walmart, and I'm already weary of this date. Inside the store, Jared walks at a fast pace, leading the way. I'm struggling to keep up on the slick floors in my stiletto heels. They look good, but they aren't made for running marathons. Jared finds the items he needs and we check out.

"Have you decided what you want to do?" Jared asks.

"We could go bowling," I suggest.

"Nah. I don't feel like bowling, either."

"We could go for ice cream or something."

"Is that really what you want to do, Lacey?" he asks.

His eyes bore into me, making me shift in my seat. At this point, I can't deny my discomfort. Even if I could look past his obsession with himself, this whole date is rubbing me wrong.

"Honestly, I don't care. I'm fine with almost anything," I say, giving up on finding a solution.

"I know a park just down the road from here. Let's go see what's going on down there tonight," he suggests.

The park is completely dark. The top parking lot has a single lamp that allows us to see the last family packing up the car to leave. Jared drives down to the lower lot, though, where it's completely dark and abandoned. He stops the truck and leans over toward me, looking deeply into my eyes. My palms are sweaty, and nervous energy is burrowing into my bones.

"Lacey?"

"Yes?"

"Do you want to know what I want to do?" Jared asks.

"Sure," I say, all patience out the window.

"Do you really want to know?"

"Yes, Jared. I really want to know."

I'm drowning in regret over agreeing to this date. I've really been batting a thousand lately. Jared motions for me to come closer. Rolling my eyes, I lean in so he can whisper his secret into my ear like a damn child. My heartbeat becomes more rapid as I get closer to him, my whole body screaming at me to get away.

As his vulgar wish is whispered into my ear, I freeze in terror, not knowing what to do. This man is not stable. I silently assess my odds of getting away from him. It's too dark for me to see where I'm going if I get out of the truck. Plus, I'd have to kick these damn high heels off if I have any hopes of making a run for it.

Jared tries to plant a kiss on my mouth, but I shrink away to dodge it. Annoyed, he leans in to try again. When I resist, he grabs hold of me and starts climbing over on top of me. The hairs on my arms stand at attention, and a paralyzing chill trickles down my spine.

"I need to pee," I blurt out. "Can you take me somewhere with a bathroom?"

"Later," he says, close enough now for me to smell his rancid breath.

"Dude, I'm telling you, I've been drinking heavy all day trying to fight a urinary tract infection which means I'm ready to piss like a racehorse. If you don't get me to a bathroom now, my ammonia-smelling pee is going to seep into the seat and carpet of this truck, and you'll never be able to wash away the smell."

"Um . . ." Jared sits back, momentarily processing my warning. "Yeah. Okay. I guess we can take a quick bathroom break."

Jared settles back in his seat. He puts the truck into gear and heads toward the lights again. A few minutes later, Jared pulls into a Starbucks and insists on walking me inside. Once inside, I convince him we can't use their facilities without making a purchase and persuade him to get into the long line. That will hopefully buy me extra time to figure out what to do next.

Once inside the bathroom, I lock the door and pull out my cell phone. With shaking hands, I select Jalynn's name in my phone. No answer. I move up to George's number. No answer. I haven't talked to Caleb in a while, but I'm sure he would help me. I dial his number, but again, no answer. Not knowing what else to do, I go to Jacob's number and press the call button.

"Hello?" Relief washes over me when I hear his voice.

"Hey, Jacob. It's Lacey. I need help, and no one else is answering the phone."

"What's wrong?" Jacob asks, and I can hear the concern in his tone.

"Can you come get me? I'm out with a guy, and I'm not safe. I'm hiding in the bathroom of a Starbucks. Can you please help me?

"Send me your location, and I'll be right there. Just stay in the bathroom until I call you, you hear me?"

"Yes. Please hurry."

I'm not sure how long it took Jared to get through the line, but after about thirty minutes of occupying the bathroom, his big paws bang on the door, startling my nerves all over again.

"Lacey? Are you in there?"

"Yeah, I'm here. I'll be out in a minute," I say.

"You've been in there a long time. What are you doing?"

"I'm not feeling well."

"Lacey, open the damn door!" Jared demands.

"I told you I'm almost done."

"I'm going to get someone to unlock this door," Jared says. I hear his footsteps trail away from the small alcove of the bathroom door.

Shit.

Panicking, I look around for an escape. There's no windows to climb out. Nowhere to hide. I could try to sneak out the door, but I don't know where Jared is exactly or if I could get by without him noticing. I have to figure something out.

CHAPTER TWENTY-TWO

At the Starbucks, I dial Lacey's phone. She picks up on the first ring. I can hear the panic in her voice.

"Please tell me you're here," she says.

"Just pulled in. Are you still in the bathroom?"

"Yeah, but he went to get someone to open the door. What should I do?"

"Hang tight. I'm coming inside for you. Don't unlock the door until I tell you to."

I walk in and scan the space for the direction of the bathrooms. Catching sight of the sign, I push my way through the crowd. A large man is arguing with an employee about unlocking the women's bathroom for him. That must be her date. I bypass them and head straight for the bathroom where I bang on the bathroom door.

"Lacey, it's me," I call through the door.

I hear the click of the lock, and the door barely creaks open. Lacey peers out at me through the crack, and then she pulls the door open the rest of the way. I slip my jacket off and wrap it over her shoulders. Then I help her tuck her hair up inside my baseball cap that I've placed on her head. Once she's ready, I drape my arm over her shoulders and lead her out the door, right past the man still arguing about unlocking the bathroom door.

"Are you okay?" I finally ask, a couple of minutes down the road.

"Yeah. Thanks for coming. I don't know what I would have done . . ."

I glance over at her. Her hands are shaking. She hugs her arms tightly around her body. I reach over and grasp her trembling fingers on the hand closest to me.

"What happened?" I ask.

I'm honestly not sure I want to know, but I listen intently as Lacey retells the story to me from the beginning. My jaw tenses when she tells me the slimy words he uttered in her ear. Fury sweeps over me at the thought of him even considering forcing himself on her. My fist lands forcefully on the dash of my truck.

"What a fucking creep!" I say. "I'm going to turn around. Let's go see if the douche is still there. I have a few things I'd like to whisper in his ear . . ."

"No, Jacob. Please don't. Just take me home."

She's sobbing now. Clearly the adrenaline has worn off. Even knowing the emotions washing over her right now aren't my fault, remorse fills my body.

"Hey, Gypsy, don't cry. Scoot over here."

I pat the bench seat next to me. She unbuckles her seat belt and slides down the bench, up against my side. I wrap my arm around her and hold her tight for the remainder of the drive.

When we arrive in her driveway, I'm surprised not to see her pickup sitting there.

"Where's your truck?"

"It's at the gas station," she says.

"So he doesn't know where you live?"

"No, he knows the general area, but he hasn't been here."

"Good. I'm going to stay here tonight with you, anyway. Just in case."

"You don't have to do that. I'll be fine."

"Not a chance I'm leaving you here alone," I say, holding the door open for her.

"Thank you," Lacey says.

We make it inside, and she wraps her arms around my neck. I hug her tightly, my hand rubbing up and down her back, trying to calm her tears. I'd really love to pummel the fucker for making her cry.

Once she is calmed, she climbs into her bed. I take my spot on the floor of the living area, using one of the throw pillows from the bench as a pillow. We lie in our separate beds, only feet away from each other, and try to fall asleep.

"Hey, Gypsy?" I call out into the darkness.

"Yeah?"

"When you called me, you said you were calling me because no one else would answer the phone."

"Yeah?"

"Why didn't you call me first?" I ask, staring up into the darkness.

"I didn't think you would answer my call. I didn't think you wanted to have anything to do with me."

"Why would you think that?" I ask, but I already know the answer.

My hand rubs against my sternum as though it may be able to massage away the hole her words just gouged into my chest.

"You've stayed clear of me since the day we kissed at the flower shop. I'm either the world's worst kisser, or I must've gravely misjudged the situation."

Guilt washes over me, and I hate myself for making her feel at fault for my shortcomings.

"It wasn't you. I swear, it's all me."

As soon as the words leave my mouth I roll my eyes at myself. Did I really just use the "it's not you, it's me" line on her? My hand rises from my chest to my face where the tips of my thumb and middle finger massage my temples. I take advantage of her silence and try again.

"What I mean is I'm no good for you," I say.

"It's okay, Jacob. You don't have to explain."

Her voice floats over to me, barely above a whisper. Silence fills the camper as I fight the urge to get up off this floor and go to her.

"Gypsy?"

"Yeah?"

"Next time, call me first. Always call me first."

"Okay. Good night, Jacob."

I hear Lacey yawn, and the camper goes quiet again. I lie awake until I hear slow and steady breaths coming from her direction. Knowing she is okay now, I begin to relax and let sleep fall over me.

LACEY HASN'T BEEN PARTICULARLY happy with me the last few days. She refused to take a couple of days off work, so I told Mom to keep her working in the back of the shop in case her new friend came by to visit. I also recruited the help of Jalynn and George. We outnumbered her and forced her to stay with George and Jalynn for the next few nights to ensure her safety.

"I wasn't going to say anything," Lacey says. "But now I'm wondering if I should."

"What?" I ask, shifting forward in my seat.

We're having dinner with Jalynn and George. George invited me to join them for Taco Tuesday at their house tonight. He's been telling us what he knows about Jared.

"He sent me a text yesterday," Lacey says.

"What the hell did he want?" I demand.

Lacey pulls her phone out of her pocket. She opens the message from Jared and passes her phone over to me. George leans in to read it over my shoulder. My eyes scan over the words on her screen. Fresh anger courses through my veins.

"If you get any more calls or texts from that pervert, let me know. I'll take care of him," I say through my clenched jaw.

"I think we are going to ignore him unless it gets to the point that we can't," Lacey says. "Oh, George, I've been meaning to ask you. Do you have a C-clamp I can borrow?"

"A C-clamp?" George repeats with a furrowed brow. "What do you want with a C-clamp?"

"I need new brakes on the truck," Lacey says and takes another bite of her taco.

"And?" George waits for her to expound.

"And I don't want to pay someone to do something I'm perfectly capable of doing myself."

I lean back in my seat across from Lacey and chuckle. George and I exchange amused looks. I fold my arms across my chest.

"You're not changing your own brakes," I counter.

"Why not?" Lacey asks, and I can tell she's ready for a stand-off. Stubborn woman.

"First of all, what do you know about changing brakes on a vehicle? Have you ever done it?"

"No. But I did watch a video on YouTube, and it doesn't look like anything too difficult for me to manage. I just need some tools."

"And when something isn't done right and you take off down the road without working brakes, what are you gonna do then?"

Lacey shrugs. She leans back in her seat and folds her arms across her chest, too, mimicking my body language.

"I guess I'd better just do it right from the start so I don't have to find out," she states matter-of-factly.

"When do you want them done?" I ask her. "I have the tools you need. I'll come by and help you with it."

Lacey straightens in her chair, trying not to let the smile tickling her lips spread across her face.

"Tomorrow?" she asks.

"Tomorrow it is."

T**RUE TO MY WORD**, I pull into Lacey's driveway after work to help her change the brakes on her truck. She stands to the side and supervises my work. I'm pretty sure by the coy look in her eye that she is enjoying the view. I'm wearing my favorite baseball cap today, a T-shirt, and a pair of relaxed jeans pulled over my cowboy boots.

"Are you sure that's the way to do it? The video I watched said to do it a different way," Lacey teases, earning an unimpressed look from me.

"Hand me that grease packet, would you?" I ask, motioning toward the small packet of grease with a nod.

"Sure."

She hands me the grease packet, her eyes glued to me as I tear open the packet and apply the grease. I offer to let her spread the grease on the last one, but she just scrunches up her nose at it and insists I am doing too good of a job for her to interfere.

"So," she starts, "that blonde you took to the pool hall was really pretty. Is she Ashley's replacement?"

She's kneeling on the ground next to my tools now, making herself look busy as she pretends to organize them. I give her a sideways glance but continue working on reattaching the caliper. She must be talking about the night she saw me at the pool hall with Mia.

"No," I say firmly.

"Why not?"

Lacey knows I have a twin sister, but she hasn't met Mia, yet. I should probably tell her it was Mia with me at the pool hall, but I'm curious to see where she's going with this, and I'd be lying if I said I wasn't enjoying the jealous twinge in her voice.

"She's not my type."

"Long legs and big boobs aren't your type?" Lacey questions.

She leans toward me now, propping her hands on the tire lying between us. I'm guessing she's intentionally pushing her breasts out, trying to make them look bigger than they are. I unabashedly lower my gaze down to her insignificant cleavage. My eyes pause on her chest for a moment. I lift my eyes back to hers. A blush spreads across her cheeks.

"Nah," I say. "More than a handful is a waste."

I turn back to my work with a smirk on my face.

"Aren't you full of yourself?" Lacey says, pretending to be offended, and leans back on her heels again. I know she's secretly satisfied with my answer.

Within a short time, the brakes are finished. I clean up the mess, packing the old brakes and rotors into the boxes and loading them into the back of my truck so I can dispose of them for her.

"That didn't take long," she says.

"We still need to break them in," I say, wiping off my hands.

"How do we do that?"

"I'll tell you what to do. Hop in. I'll ride shotgun."

I climb in the passenger side of her truck, and Lacey gets behind the wheel. Damn girl's got a hammer on the floorboard. I can only imagine what that's about.

"Okay, get going about thirty-five miles per hour, then use medium pressure on your brakes to slow down to about five miles per hour," I instruct her. "We need to do that a couple of times."

She follows my instructions, speeding up and slowing down. After a couple rounds, I have her repeat the process a few more times from a higher speed. Satisfied that the new brakes are well bedded, I tell her to keep driving toward town.

"Let's get dinner," I say. "You hungry?"

"I could eat."

In town, she parks the truck in front of the diner. I come around and open her door for her. With a hand on her lower back, I lead her inside. We follow the hostess to our booth. I take the seat facing the door. I always make a point of sitting where I can keep an eye on the door, just in case some crazy wanders in.

I shouldn't be sitting here with her right now. I know this. I should have packed my shit up and left when the brakes were done. I'm not trying to get into another relationship, and hanging around Lacey is bound to make things dicey. I'm asking for trouble, but I'll certainly enjoy the view in the meantime.

The hostess gives us each a menu and briskly walks back to the front counter to help the next set of guests. Our waitress stops by for our drink order, and Lacey peruses the menu. I don't need a menu. The establishment hasn't changed their menu for the entirety of my recollection. Plus, I almost always order the same burger and fries every time I eat here.

Lacey sets her menu aside and looks up at me almost expectantly. Damn, she's beautiful. My hand itches to reach across this table and grab hold of that soft vanilla-scented mane of hair. The waitress shows back up, setting our drinks down in front of us, and takes our orders.

"How long have you two been married?" she asks.

My eyes dart over to Lacey.

"Oh. We're not married," I tell her. "Just friends."

"I remember those days. It won't be much longer before you are," she says, giving me a knowing look.

When she leaves, I turn back to Lacey. Her eyes are fixed on the table, a light blush flooding her face. My stomach flips. A part of me wants it. Hell, if I'm honest with myself, I want her badly. But I'm barely recovered from Ashley breaking my heart the way she did. I can't survive a repeat. And Lacey is way out of my league.

After a good meal and even better conversation, I pay the

bill and we walk side by side back out to the truck. The conversation always comes easy with Lacey. I take the keys from her, open the passenger door for her to climb in, and round the hood of the truck, climbing into the driver's seat. Lacey sits in the middle, just close enough for us to barely brush skin along the bumpy road back to her place.

"Thanks for helping me with the brakes," Lacey says when we make it back.

We are standing at her camper door. If I dared to steal a kiss, I'm pretty sure she would let me. I hover close, too close, slow to say goodbye as I internally debate whether or not to give in to this tantalizing woman standing in front of me.

She gazes up at me with those big hazel eyes that I could so easily lose myself in. I take a step closer to her, raising up a hand to brush back her hair. She closes her eyes and slowly rises up on her toes, leaning into me.

Shit.

I don't want to hurt her feelings. I don't want her to feel rejected or used. She doesn't deserve that. She shouldn't be punished because I can't fucking make up my mind. I quickly kiss her forehead and retreat back to my truck.

"See you around, Gypsy," I say and climb into my truck.

I drive home with nothing but Lacey on my mind. It would be so easy to give in to her. But I'll be damned if I'm ever the reason that woman sheds a tear.

CHAPTER TWENTY-THREE

jacob

I stomp a foot down on the paver stepping stone, making sure it's securely placed, and stand back to inspect my handiwork. Lacey wanted stepping stones from the gravel lot to the deck. I have a feeling she mentioned it to me because she knew I would end up doing the labor for her. She knows I like to help out with her projects. And that's all it is. I'm not looking for excuses to spend time with her like Jalynn evidently suspects. I just want to help Lacey out. She doesn't have many people in her corner, but I can be one of the few who are.

"It looks good," Lacey says from up on the deck.

"I think it should do," I say, looking over the stones.

"How much do I owe you?" Lacey leans down, resting her elbows on the deck rail.

Lacey knows I won't take her money, but she offers anyway. Every single time. Honestly, I don't know why she insists on asking. George says it's a Southern thing.

"You said the stepping stones would make it easier for you to wear those fancy high heels, right?"

"Yeah, it's hard to walk in the yard with stilettos on."

"So you're going to be wearing them more often, right?"

"Right."

"That's payment enough," I say with a wicked smile.

Lacey rolls her eyes at me, but I can tell she's amused. She enjoys the flirty banter, almost as much as I do.

"What am I gonna do with you?" she asks playfully, shaking her head at me. "You should probably come inside and have a cold drink after all your hard work."

I step up on the deck and follow Lacey inside. She's already examining the options in the fridge when I make it inside. She spins around, a water in one hand and a Coke in the other, and waits for me to choose. I take the Coke, letting my fingers brush against hers, and crack it open. My phone buzzes in my pocket, and I pull it out to see who's interrupting my day. It's vet business.

"Looks like I've got to go," I tell her after my brief conversation on the phone. "Some folks have a bloated cow that needs my attention."

I could be wrong, but I'm pretty sure it's disappointment that flashes in her eyes. Or maybe it's just a reflection of the disappointment I'm feeling.

"Let me come with you. I've always wondered what to do about a bloated cow," Lacey says.

"You've always wondered?" I raise an eyebrow at her.

"Who knows, I might run into a wild cow one day who needs rescuing from bloat."

"Fair enough," I say after a slight hesitation. "You never know when you might come across a cow in the wild needing rescuing. You're going to have to put some shoes on, though. And unfortunately, those high heels we were just talking about won't do it for this one."

Lacey is grinning from ear to ear as she skips back to her closet to grab her boots. All can be made right in the world by that smile.

FORTY-FIVE MINUTES PASS BY, and we're pulling up to a barn. The old farmer walks out of the barn and greets me as I exit the truck, and I grab my vet bag from the back. The farmer leads us around the back of the barn where his sick cow is contained away from the rest of the herd, her stomach swollen and distended. I look the cow over, examining her.

"Looks like we have more than bloat going on here," I observe. "Looks like she's got pneumonia, too."

"How can you tell?" Lacey asks.

Lacey is standing on the other side of the cow's head. She's petting the bovine, while talking to her in soothing tones. It's such a different experience out here with her.

"You see all that mucus coming out of her nose? She's got a high temperature, too. We'll give her a shot of antibiotics, though, after we release some of this bloat, and she should be good to go."

I make an incision in the cow's tough hide while Lacey continues petting her as though our patient is a little puppy.

"Can you hand me that trocar?" I ask her.

"Tro-who?" she asks.

"The red corkscrew-looking thing in my bag."

Lacey reaches into my bag, pulling out the trocar, and hands it over to me. She peeks over the cow's back to see what I'm about to do. Quickly, I shove it into the incision and pull out the center allowing the trapped gas to escape from the cow's belly. After a couple of minutes and insistent pleading from Lacey to be allowed to help "with the doctoring" as she calls it, I instruct her on administering the shot of antibiotics.

"That should do it," I tell the farmer. "Give it about a week. If everything has gone back down then you can take the trocar out. It should finish healing up on its own."

"Look at you, out here saving lives," Lacey says back in my pickup, out of earshot of the farmer.

"Somebody's got to be the hero," I joke. "It's just what I do. Saving humanity one gassy cow at a time."

Lacey yawns as I pull back onto the road. Soon, her eyes drift closed, and her head slowly relaxes over on my shoulder. I take in the sight of her in a peaceful slumber. Goose bumps break out across her skin from the cool evening air. I reach between my seat and the door, into the back of the cab, and pull my jacket back through. I lay it over Lacey, tucking it around her shoulders. Without thinking, I kiss the top of her head. She stirs momentarily and links her arm through mine, snuggling into my side. I let my right hand slide off the gear shifter and onto her thigh as I drive us down the road, headed for Lacey's gypsy wagon.

I TAKE a swig from the carton of orange juice in my parents' fridge, and Mom glowers at me. I close the carton and set it back in the fridge.

"I thought once you were grown I wouldn't have to worry about you drinking straight out of the cartons in my fridge anymore. I thought maybe you'd be drinking out of the cartons in your own fridge," Mom says.

"You have better stuff in yours, though," I say.

I've spent the morning helping Dad with a remodel on their bathroom. Finished for the day, I pull my phone out of my pocket to send a text to Lacey. I haven't heard from her today.

> Me: What are you up to?

> Lacey: Not a dang thing. You?

> Me: Just finished helping my parents.

> Lacey: I'm bored.

> Me: Want me to come over?

> Lacey: Let's go see a movie!

> Me: Pick you up in 20.

I say my goodbyes to my parents and leave to pick up Lacey. I'd told myself I wasn't going to see her this weekend, but clearly, I have no fucking self-control. I've only been to her place twice this week, though. And I saw her at work one day. I could have just called my mother to let her know I'd be bringing the load of fertilizer for her garden next week, but I was near the flower shop anyway, so it made sense just to swing by. It had nothing to do with the high probably that I would run into Lacey in the process.

I tap on her door and wait. I hear a loud thud, followed by a muffled expletive, and I chuckle to myself. The door swings open, and Lacey stands there looking as beautiful as ever, bent over and sliding her foot into one of those spiky high heels that make her ass look delicious. It's a good thing we're on our way to a movie so I don't have to worry about trying to keep my eyes off her.

"Hey," Lacey says, pulling me from my thoughts.

"Hey. Do you need more time getting ready?"

"Should I take more time? Are you telling me I look bad?" Lacey asks, straightening. She looks down at her outfit and raises her eyes back to me inquisitively.

"Nope. You look great," I say, backpedaling. "You seem rushed is all. Let's go."

I hold the door for her as she steps out onto the deck and wait for her to lock up. With the door locked, I motion for Lacey to lead the way down the stairs. That was a mistake. My eyes keep drifting down to the view as she walks ahead of me, which in turn prompts a series of thoughts I'm not supposed to be having about her. I reach past her and open the door for her to climb into the truck, then round the hood to the driver's seat.

"What movie do you want to see?" I ask.

"Have you heard about the one called *Meet You in My Dreams*?" Lacey asks.

"I'm not going to a chick flick. Next?"

"Technically, it's a romance, but there's a lot of action and violence in it. It's one of those movies that everyone enjoys."

"I don't want to be the only guy in the theater."

"You won't be. I went to see it with Jalynn last weekend, and it was so good! And there were a ton of guys watching, too. Honestly, I'd say it was about fifty-fifty," she insists. "Please?"

I groan, looking down into her pouty face, and begin to feel my resolve waiver. When did I become such a pushover?

"You swear?" I ask, unamused.

"Scout's honor!"

I BUY two tickets to *Meet You in My Dreams*, a large popcorn to share, two drinks, and a box of Milk Duds for Lacey, but I'm pretty sure I really just paid for my castration. Lacey leads us to the theater our movie is showing in and hands our tickets to the attendant, conveniently leaving me with the chore of trying not to look at her ass again.

"I thought you said there would be other men here," I whisper into her ear as we scan over the theater for our seats. Her hair tickles my nose, and her vanilla scent almost sends me to my knees. I'm in big trouble.

"It hasn't even started yet. I'm sure more men will show up."

We find our seats midway up the stairs and settle in. Lacey lifts the armrest between our seats so the bucket of popcorn can rest in the middle. I lean back in my seat, debating my life choices as the commercials and previews play. The opening credits roll, followed by a very heated love scene that leaves little to the imagination.

Fuck.

In an effort to keep the combination of Lacey and sex out of my head, I look around the theater at the other attendees. Almost every seat is taken, but I'm the only penis-wielding spectator in the place. I pull my phone out, turn the brightness down all the way, and start scrolling social media.

"Put your phone away!" Lacey scolds me.

"How did I let you talk me into this?" I groan in response but do as I'm told.

After 107 more minutes of romance, tears, and sex, the movie finally comes to an end. I don't waste any time gathering our trash and joining the slow-moving throng of people exiting the theater. Lacey walks beside me, her arm linked in mine.

"What a sweet husband to come watch this movie with your girl," gushes the lady behind us in line. I don't have a chance to speak up.

"He loves to spoil me," Lacey says.

"You better hold on to that one. The good ones are hard to find," the lady adds.

I dump our trash in the trash can at the door of the theater and lead us through the crowd and out to my truck, fuming the whole while. I catch Lacey chewing her bottom lip like she does when she is nervous. She probably thinks I'm mad about being tricked into sitting through that movie, but that's not it entirely. I'm pissed that I want her badly enough to sit through a miserable fucking movie.

"Are you mad?" Lacey eventually asks, once we are in the truck.

"I'm annoyed," I say, hoping she doesn't press for me to expound.

"Let me make it up to you. Let me buy you some ice cream."

I sigh and shift in my seat to look at Lacey. She's watching me with those gorgeous eyes, still biting her bottom lip. I've got to learn how to say no to this woman. I don't want a relationship, and all I'm going to do by humoring her is get the both of us hurt.

"Okay," I say and fire up the engine of the truck.

I SIT across from Lacey and try not to watch her too closely as she works each spoonful of ice cream into her mouth. It's too easy to get lost in thoughts of things I want to do to that mouth.

"You should have let me pay. I said I would," Lacey says.

"I know, but if my dad taught me anything, he taught me to always hold the door and never let the girl pay on a date."

As soon as the words leave my mouth, I wish I could stuff them back in.

"A date, huh?" Lacey asks. "Are you saying this is a date?"

"No. The same principle applies, though."

"You know, it could be a date." Lacey digs intently at the ice cream in her cup.

"Could be. But it's not."

"Why not? Is there someone else you'd rather date?" She's looking directly at me now.

"Gypsy, I like you. We spend so much time together, I don't have time to meet any other women. And I'm okay with that because I don't want a relationship with anyone right now."

"Okay."

She looks slightly deflated and is suddenly focusing very hard on her ice cream cup. And I feel like a complete douche.

"Lace—"

"We should get back. You ready to go?"

Lacey gives me a weak smile. I hate myself right now. I hate that I'm the cause of the disappointment on her face.

"Yeah, let's get you home."

lacey

Sitting around the table at Jalynn and George's, I push the conversation over to Jalynn and her pregnancy. She's reached the latter part of her pregnancy and could be welcoming their new addition soon. Jalynn and George almost have the nursery set up and decorated. They only have a few more pieces of furniture to assemble. And today, Jacob is giving George a hand.

George makes another joke about Jalynn's mood swings and food cravings. She's been a good sport in all of it and laughs at herself along with the rest of us.

"Oh, do you remember that eating contest you insisted on competing in in our sophomore year of college?" George asks Jalynn. Jalynn buries her face in her hands, laughing at the memory. "Do you remember that?" George asks me this time. "She would not be talked out of it, either. She got four hamburgers down, and then her face just went green."

"Babe, that was after Lacey moved back home," Jalynn reminds him.

"Oh. Oh yeah."

Nothing to kill the moment quite like digging up old history. Jalynn clears her throat and takes a drink of water.

Shame immerses me as I recollect the day that I broke the news to Jalynn.

"So you're throwing it all away just like that?" Jalynn asked, her foot tapping on the floor as an alternate outlet for all of the things she wanted to say to me but was holding back.

"Just because he asked me to marry him doesn't mean my life's goin' to hell in a handbasket," I argued.

I zipped up my suitcase and set it aside.

"Excuse me? He's making you drop out of college. And move back home."

"I'm just pressing pause on classes right now. He's still having a hard time with Brian's death."

"I don't like it, Lace. Something's not right, and I'm convinced you're keeping something from me." Jalynn folded her arms, anger still radiating from her countenance.

"Can't you just be happy for me?" I pleaded.

"No. I'm sorry, I love you, but I can't be happy about something that's bad for you . . . even if I can't quite put my finger on what's wrong."

"Jay—"

"Ben is a rotten apple, Lacey. Throw him back, and let the worms have their way with him."

"He loves me. And I love him. I want you to be my maid of honor."

"No. I will not support this. Don't do this, Lacey. I'm begging you." Jalynn took my hands in hers, making sure I heard her pleas.

"I have to. Ben needs me."

"You know what we need to do before the baby comes?" Jalynn asks everyone, startling me. "We need to go out on a double date."

She claps her hands with excitement and bounces in her seat.

"Seriously, Jay?" I ask. "I don't want to try to find a date. You know the type of luck I've had lately."

"I thought I was clear when I said *we* need to go on a *double* date."

Jalynn glares back and forth between me and Jacob.

"I don't think that's a good idea," Jacob says.

I don't get it. Jacob and I are practically inseparable. I spend more time with Jacob than I do with Jalynn these days. He's even commented on how much time we spend together. I go weak at the knees every time I see him, and he instantly boosts my mood without even trying. Not to mention all the sweet things he does for me. Jacob is a better boyfriend than Ben ever dreamed of being, and Jacob isn't even my boyfriend.

Is it me? I thought he was drawn to me the same way I am to him, but I'm starting to wonder. I thought after that kiss, with as much time as we've been spending together, a relationship would naturally form. I don't want to just be his friend. I want to have it all with him. Something's got to give.

"Okay, then," Jalynn says, stirring me from my silent sulking, "we can make it a triple date. Lacey, I'll set you up so we can avoid any more stalkers or perves, but Jacob, you have to find your own date."

"Jay—" I start.

"Come on, Lace. One date. That's all I'm asking. I want to go out and have a fun night with my besties before the baby comes. We wait any longer and I might not be able to move."

"What is this date going to consist of?" Jacob asks. He seems to know well enough that there's no point in fighting it.

"I'll come up with a plan."

Jalynn gives me a wink, and I get the impression she just might be up to no good. I'm not sure what yet, but she's got something up her sleeve. I'm sure of it.

WE MEET up at George and Jalynn's house on the night of our group date so we can carpool to a nearby farm for some fall fun.

Jalynn answers the knock at the door and returns with Russell, a tall, decently handsome ranch hand who'll be playing the part of my date for the evening. Jalynn makes the introductions, and Russell and I get acquainted while we wait for Jacob and his date to arrive.

Jalynn goes to answer another knock at the door, and she comes back into the room a moment later with Jacob behind her, but he's alone.

"I wasn't able to find a date," he says unapologetically.

I steal a look at Jalynn, trying to silently communicate the apprehension this turn of events has inspired in me. I lock eyes with her, and Jalynn turns back to Jacob, barely hiding the amusement on her face.

"That's okay," Jalynn tells him. "You can come along as our fifth wheel."

"I'm sure he doesn't want to come stag," I speak up, hoping my dismay about the situation isn't too obvious. "Jacob, it's okay if you don't want to go."

"No worries. I'll be your spare tire," Jacob says, giving me a wink.

Dread spills down into my feet, filling my body and making movement seem like an impossible task as everyone grabs their jackets and heads out to the car. What is Jacob thinking? Why didn't he just bring a damn date like we all agreed?

We decide to ride in George's truck together since everyone can fit. George and Jalynn sit in the front, while I'm in the back, flanked by Russell and Jacob. Thankfully, it's a short ride over to the farm.

We all stand in line for tickets to the haunted corn maze and hayride. It's awkward now, being on a date with Jacob here, but he and Russell are getting along surprisingly well, occupying most of the conversation. When we step up to the ticket booth, Jacob speaks first.

"Two for the corn maze and hayride," he says.

Jalynn and I glance at each other, bewildered. Jacob takes

the tickets and his change from the attendant. As he turns from the window, he holds out a ticket to me.

"Um, that's okay. I'll get Lacey's ticket," Russell says.

"No, man, I've got it," Jacob replies and steps out of the way of the window.

Russell steps up and buys himself a ticket.

We make our way to the corn maze. I lead the way with Jacob and Russell on either sides of me. Russell reaches over and takes my hand as we enter the maze. My cheeks burn with guilt, and I have to remind myself that it's okay for me to hold his hand.

With each scare in the maze, I naturally cling to Jacob for protection. As the fright leaves my body, I remember it's Russell I'm supposed to be here with, and I go back to holding Russell's hand. Toward the end of the maze, while I'm clinging to Jacob's arm, Russell drops back behind us to George and Jalynn. He's trying to whisper, but I'm still able to make out his complaint.

"What's his deal?" Russell asks in a hushed voice. "Am I supposed to fight him for her or what?"

Russell grabs my hand outside of the corn maze and pulls me along toward the hayride. I'm pretty sure he is trying to put some distance between us and Jacob. We find a spot to sit on the hay-covered wagon and wait for the others to catch up. Jacob is walking with George and Jalynn now, but as soon as they make it to the wagon, Jacob takes the vacant seat on my other side.

By the time we make it to dinner, I can tell Russell's patience is growing thin. Despite his efforts, Jacob is constantly vying for my attention. Russell tries to maintain physical contact with me during dinner, and I do my best to ignore Jacob's hand resting on my thigh. When the waitress inquires how to split the check, again, the boys argue over who is paying for me.

"I'll be on my own check," I tell the waitress, ready to be out of this predicament.

Once we make it back to Jalynn and George's house, Jalynn

turns on a movie for us to watch together. Russell watches me and Jacob wearily. I can tell that I'm no longer worth the effort to him. He's about to forfeit.

"You know what?" Russell announces after the first few minutes of the movie. "I think I'm going to go home."

"Are you sure?" Jalynn asks.

"Yeah," he says, nodding his head, lips pursed. "When you asked me about coming on this date, this wasn't exactly what I had in mind." He walks out the door. Slowly, laughter bubbles up and erupts after his exit.

"You two are ridiculous," George says after the laughter dies down. "I'm surprised he lasted as long as he did. Come on, Jay. Let's go to bed and let these lovebirds figure things out."

He stands and holds a hand out to help Jalynn out of her chair. Jacob and I look at each other, each of us feigning confusion, but we know good and well what George is talking about. They disappear down the hall, and I turn back to Jacob. His eyes are now focused on the TV screen.

"What's the real reason you didn't bring a date tonight?" I ask.

"I didn't want one." When I continue to watch him, he adds, "Are we watching this movie or what?"

"Why?"

"Because I haven't seen it," he says. I glare at him. "Because the only date I wanted was already taken."

"And who was that?" I ask, afraid of his answer.

He turns to me now and locks eyes with me.

"You seriously have to ask?" He pauses, but I don't say anything. "You."

"But you had your chance to go with me, and you said no," I point out.

"I know. I realized too late that by not taking you myself, I was signing you up to go with someone else. I liked that idea even less."

"So, what now? Neither of us date? You don't want to date me, but you don't want me dating anyone else, either?"

"I don't know," he replies and turns back to the movie.

After several seconds of silence, I turn back to the movie as well. I can't concentrate on it, though. I'm too caught up in my head trying to figure out Jacob to focus on anything else. The longer I sit here, the more my frustration builds.

"Jacob?" I finally break the silence.

"Yeah?"

"What's your plan here?" I shift in my seat, turning toward him, and wrap my arms around myself, hoping it will ease my nerves.

"What do you mean?" he asks, finally turning from the TV screen to look at me.

"If you have a move to make now would be a good time to make it," I prompt him.

"Lacey, I like you a lot, but I don't want to move things too quickly. I don't want either of us getting hurt."

"I don't know if you've noticed, but the only direction we've been moving is backward." I arch an eyebrow at him.

Jacob turns back to the TV. I know he's trying to pretend to be calm and unaffected, but I can see his nervousness pouring out through the tapping of his fingers on the arm of the couch.

"It's late," I finally say. I can't sit here with him any longer. "I'm gonna head home for the night."

I rise to my feet, prompting Jacob to sit up straight.

"Wait, Lace. Don't go," he says and stands.

Jacob grabs hold of my hands, but I pull away and sidestep him to the door. I know he's following me outside, but it's too late. I'm tired of waiting on him to notice what I can already see.

"Good night, Jacob," I say over my shoulder.

"I don't want you to leave here mad at me."

"I don't want to sit here pretending like everything is fine," I shoot back, not stopping.

I climb into my truck and slam the door closed for added emphasis. Jacob reaches to open it again, but I press down the lock before he can. The sides of his balled fists tap the doorframe and his frustrated exhale is nearly a snarl.

"If you want to have this conversation get out of the truck, and let's have it," Jacob grumbles through the closed door.

I slide the key into the ignition and twist. Nothing.

Shit.

Of all the times not to start, of course this would be the one. I reach down into the passenger floorboard where the hammer waits. I climb back out of the truck armed with the hammer and fury coursing through my veins.

"What are you doing?" Jacob asks.

"It's none of your concern."

I push away from him, but before I can make my move to climb under the truck, Jacob has me cornered, his arms blocking me, making me lean back against my truck to maintain some space between us. In a quick, fluid motion he pulls the hammer out of my hand and tucks it head down into the back pocket of his jeans.

"Would you stop for a minute and talk to me?" When he gets nothing more than a glare from me he continues. "We aren't good for each other."

"How do you even know if you won't give us a chance?" I spit back. "Is it that miserable for you to spend time with me? Because if so, what are you doing here? Why is it that every time I turn around you're here? I don't need you. I can manage just fine on my own. I let you help me because I thought it was just an excuse for you to spend time with me. If that's not the case, if I'm only a burden to you, then I don't want you here!"

"You are not a fucking burden. I want you more than I care to admit, but if things go sour with us, neither one of us will survive it," Jacob says inching closer, pinning me between him and the truck. His body pressed up against mine begins to chip away at my resolve. My fury turns into a boiling river of want, a mirror of the longing I see in his eyes, too. "I barely made it through my breakup with Ashley, and frankly, what I felt for her is only a fraction of what I already feel for you. And if I did something to break *your* heart, I couldn't live with myself." Jacob shakes his head, determined that he's right. "And when you decide that I'm not enough for you, there will be no coming back from that."

The pain in his eyes is undeniable, and I know there's no changing his mind. Yet our bodies are too close, confusing my senses. The emotions floating between us are too raw. If I stay here any longer, I won't be able to hold myself together, and I can't let him see me weak.

I reach around Jacob, grabbing the hammer from his pocket and pushing him off of me. Before he can respond, I'm on the ground and sliding under the truck. After giving the starter a couple of good whacks, I slide back out, my shirt riding up my body as I do, which pisses me off even more. I sit back in the truck and try the ignition. Nothing. This time it's my turn to let out a frustrated yell. Jacob stops me on my way back to the ground.

"Hold on," he says. "You haven't fixed your starter, yet? Hand me that hammer."

I try to protest, not wanting to accept his help, but he slides it out of my hand and climbs under the truck. After a couple of thuds, Jacob tells me to try again. This time the truck fires to life. I buckle my seat belt, ready to go.

"Wait for me to get out from under you!" Jacob hollers up at me in a panic.

"You really think I was going to run you over?" I ask after he rolls out from under the truck.

"I wouldn't blame you if you did."

I shake my head and slam the door closed again. Without giving Jacob another look, I put my truck in reverse and drive away.

THE NEXT MORNING, I step out of the camper and find Jacob's truck sitting next to mine. He's leaning against the hood of the truck, his legs crossed and his arms folded, waiting for me no doubt. I pause for a beat, remind myself I'm mad at him, fix my eyes on my truck, and trust my determination to carry me right past him. As I'm passing, he reaches out and gently grabs my arm.

"Lace—"

"What are you doing here, Jacob?" I ask. I pull my arm away from him defiantly, but I don't move.

"I'm taking you to work."

"I don't need a ride."

Jacob pushes himself off the hood of his truck and stands so close I can feel the warmth radiating off his body. Shivers run down my spine, and as I breathe in the leather and cedarwood that always accompany him, my anger evaporates.

"Please don't make this harder than it has to be, Gypsy." Jacob reaches up and gently tugs a strand of my hair. "Come get in my truck."

I raise my eyes to his, debating my next move. I can't deny the pleading in his eyes, but I'm not ready to make nice with him. Stubbornly, I tramp past him to the passenger side of his truck and climb in before he can open the door for me like he always does.

jacob

Lacey is still pissed at me, and to be honest, I can't blame her. I deserve it. She doesn't speak a word to me the whole way into town. I drop her off at the flower shop and drive over to my office to call around for a starter for Lacey's truck and to rearrange my day. Luckily, I find a place in Bozeman that has one in stock. It's close to lunchtime when I make it to Bozeman, so I stop by Mia's shop after and take her to lunch.

"Obviously, I'm always happy to let my brother buy me lunch . . ." Mia pauses, knowing I technically didn't offer to pay yet.

"Yeah, I'm sure you are."

"But what is this secret errand that brings you to Bozeman in the middle of the day on a weekday? Shouldn't you be kicking shit in a barn somewhere right now?"

Releasing an audible exhale, I observe Mia, debating the safest way to answer her question.

"Don't blow this all out of proportion and try to turn it into something it's not," I say, "but I'm fixing Lacey's truck and had to come to Bozeman for a part."

"Jacob," Mia says as she leans back in her chair, "this is

significant. You're finally making a move on Mom's new employee?"

"We're just friends," I insist. Mia raises an eyebrow at me. "I'm helping a friend. Don't read into it."

"You forget we're twins." Mia picks up her fork and takes another bite.

"So?" I drop my napkin on my plate, finished with my lunch.

"So I can see right through your bullshit. You really like her."

"I hardly know her," I lie.

"Okay, then you really want to bone her."

"Mia . . ."

"See? You're making a move."

"It's just a good deed. That's all."

I don't want Lacey to be upset with me. I promised myself I wouldn't hurt her, and I've got to make this right while I still can. My plan is to show her I'm sorry by doing something for her. Then, just maybe she will forgive me, and things can go back to the way they were.

I drive back to Lacey's and get started on her truck repairs. I've got the battery disconnected, and I'm lying on my back removing the old starter when the gravel crunches in the driveway behind Lacey's truck. Someone gets out of the vehicle and their footsteps approach. A not so gentle kick to the bottom of my boot causes me to yank my leg up and ram my knee against the truck.

"Damn it to fucking hell!"

I roll out from under the truck, rubbing my throbbing knee. Jalynn stands back, hands on her hips and her little foot tapping away impatiently. I'm not going to lie, she's pretty damn intimidating. I've listened to George's stories about the pregnancy hormones running rampant in her body, and it looks like I've got some angry ones focused on me right now.

"Yes?" I ask, looking up at her.

"I thought I saw you drive by. What are your intentions with my bestie?" Jalynn asks.

"I don't have any intentions. I'm just trying to fix her truck."

"Wrong answer." Jalynn's hands move from her hips, and she folds her arms above her pregnant belly.

"What's the right answer, then, Jalynn?" I rub my knee some more, trying to work the soreness out.

"There are several acceptable answers, frankly." Now she's pacing back and forth in front of me and counting out the acceptable answers on her fingers. "Date her, marry her, ravish her beautiful body, just to name the most obvious ones."

Jalynn turns back to me and shrugs. She watches me expectantly.

"I can't date your friend." I pick at the dirt sticking to the sole of my boot with the rachet I was just using to remove the starter.

"Why not?"

"There are several acceptable answers," I say, mimicking Jalynn. I count the reasons out on my fingers as I continue. "I break her heart and you murder me, you forbid George to associate with me, she breaks me, or I become addicted to her and can't let her go."

"Let's shoot for the latter," Jalynn says, grinning. "Seriously, though, Jacob, I don't know what your deal is, but you are an absolute moron if you don't ask Lacey out."

"I don't want a relationship. It will change everything. And what's to say she won't just break up with me after a few weeks like she did with Caleb?" I reach over to the box with the new starter and pull it out. This conversation is getting too personal, and I need something to busy my hands.

"She doesn't want a relationship with Caleb." Jalynn's hands are back on her hips.

"What makes me any different?"

"If you were paying any attention you wouldn't have to ask

me that right now. Trust me, this isn't an opportunity you want to miss out on because you're too chickenshit to ask her out. Lacey is one of those once-in-a-lifetime girls. You won't get a chance with another one. I don't know what's been up your ass, but it's time to pull it out and be a man."

Jalynn turns and leaves without waiting for a response. I swipe my forehead with the back of my dirty hand and lie back down on the ground to continue the repair. I attach the wires to the new starter, then smash the hell out of my finger as I try to get it positioned right to bolt it in. I let out another expletive, pick the ratchet back up, and begin tightening the bolts down.

Confident that the new starter is secure, I climb out from under the truck. I hook up the battery again and close the hood of the truck. I don't have Lacey's key, so I'll have to wait to see if I fixed the problem or not.

Maybe Jalynn is right. Maybe Lacey *is* a once-in-a-lifetime girl. I know I already don't want to let go of her, and she's not even mine, yet. I wipe off my hands and check the time. Lacey will get off work soon, so I gather up my tools and drive into town.

I walk into the flower shop as Lacey's gathering her stuff to leave. She looks me up and down, her eyes pausing over the grease stains on my dirty T-shirt. I probably should have changed before I came to pick her up. Observing her expressionless face, I try to judge if it is safe for me to approach.

"May I come in?" I ask.

"Yeah," she says and rolls her eyes.

I slowly walk up to the counter, not taking my eyes off of her. I'm still not sure if I'm about to be attacked by this tiny little gremlin or not.

"I just need to run this deposit over to the bank really quick," she says.

"Let's go, then, Gypsy."

In the truck, Lacey scoots toward the center of the bench seat and takes control of the radio. That's a good sign. In no time, I have her chatting and joking like usual. She seems to be over our argument from last night. Stopping next to her pickup, I shift in my seat to look at Lacey.

"You ready to give her a try? See if my mechanic skills paid off?" I nod toward her truck.

"You fixed my truck?" she asks in surprise.

"I gave it my best shot."

I climb out of the truck and hold open the door for Lacey to follow. She slides out and rushes over to her truck. Looking up at me, she twists the key in the ignition. The truck roars to life.

"You did it! I can't believe you fixed my truck!" she says, practically jumping into my arms to hug me. I stumble back a half step, then catch my footing and hug her back. "What do I owe you?" she asks.

She leans back to look at me but stays within my grasp. All of the anger and hurt in her eyes from last night and this morning are gone. I tighten my hold on her, liking the way she fits against my body.

"Go on a date with me," I say quietly.

"Come again?"

"Let's start over, you and me. Go on a date with me."

She's studying my face, either trying to decide how to respond or waiting for me to take it back, but that's not going to happen.

"Okay," she finally says.

lacey

I give the front door a couple of taps, open it, and step inside. I bellow a hello through the house, even though only Jalynn's car is in the driveway, to ensure I don't walk in on anything I might regret seeing.

"I'm back here," Jalynn calls back to me from down the hallway.

I follow her voice to the room currently being decorated and set up as a nursery.

"I need your help. It's an emergency," I say in a rushed voice, stepping inside the room. My nerves make me jittery, and I can't stand still.

"What's wrong?" Jalynn stops folding the baby onesie she's holding, focusing on me now with big, serious eyes.

"I've got myself in a pickle. Jacob is picking me up for our first date in thirty minutes, and I don't have a damn thing to wear!"

Jalynn exhales and shakes her head at me.

"Gosh, Lace, you scared the shit out of me. I thought it was something serious."

"This *is* serious!" I insist. "I don't even know what I'm doing."

"Okay, don't worry. We'll get you all fixed up. I'm sure you're going to have an awesome time." She finishes folding the onesie and sets it on the pile of freshly washed baby clothes.

I start pacing the room to work some of my anxiety out.

"Lace, it's just a date. Right? Am I missing something here?"

"It's not just a date," I say. "It's a date with Jacob."

"Uh-huh." Jalynn eases herself up out of the rocker.

"I'm serious, Jay. I'm really freaking out right now. I want this date to go well."

"It's going to go just fine, Lace. Jacob is already smitten with you. You could show up in a gunnysack, and it wouldn't hurt Jacob's feelings in the slightest." Jalynn takes my hand and pulls me with her further down the hall and into her bedroom. "But come on, darlin'. We'll get you all fixed up. What are you all doing on your date?"

Jalynn motions for me to have a seat on her bed while she digs in her closet.

"He said something about riding horses."

"Does he know you don't know how to ride?"

"I know how to ride," I protest.

"Jumping bareback on random horses in random fields while we were in high school hardly counts." Jalynn comes back over with a couple of outfits in hand. "What's the goal for your outfit today? Do you want something practical for riding, some-thing cute, or are you just trying to look sexy?"

"I don't want him to confuse me with one of the farm hands," I reply, rolling my eyes at the suggestion of wearing something practical. "Make me cute. And hurry. I'm running out of time."

"Why don't you text him and tell him to pick you up over here instead of at your place?"

"That's a good idea." I pull out my phone to text him.

Minutes later, we hear a knock at the door. I lock eyes with Jalynn and freeze. Jalynn starts for the door.

"Sounds like he's ten minutes early," Jalynn says. "I'll occupy him while you finish up."

Twenty minutes later, I check myself one last time in the mirror. Jalynn's jeans hug my curves and the floral scoop neck blouse she chose, tied in the front, is casual but classy. I run my fingers through my wavy brown hair, lifting it on top of my head as I debate whether to pull it all up into a ponytail or not. Jacob seems to have a thing for my hair, though, so I opt to pin a small section back out of my face but leave the rest cascading down my back. I hear Jacob and Jalynn's voices as I walk down the hall to the living room.

When I walk in, Jacob forgets about his conversation with Jalynn. He stands from his seat, and I shiver under his gaze as his eyes wander over my body. I approach him, pushing aside the butterflies trying to dominate my senses, and give him a hug.

"Sorry for making you wait," I say.

"It was worth it," Jacob says. "Are you ready?"

"I believe so."

Jalynn follows us to the door. As we make our way to Jacob's truck, she hollers after us, "Y'all be careful and have a good time. And Jacob, you'd better treat her like a freakin' lady!"

Jacob looks over at me with an unreadable expression. He's probably getting cold feet now about taking me on this date.

"Don't mind her," I say. "She's off her rocker."

"It's okay. She and I already had our heart-to-heart," Jacob says. "We're on the same page."

He gives me a grin that lets me know I have nothing to worry about. I slide up into his truck and claim the middle seat. I'm still nervous about how the night is going to go, but having Jacob next to me already feels like home.

After a short drive, Jacob parks the truck in a gravel lot. I stand back and watch him do his thing as he unloads the horses from the trailer. My nerves begin acting up again as I take in the size of the horses. Do they grow them bigger in Montana, too? I don't recall horses being this large back home. Then again, I was rarely toe-to-toe with any of the horses I rode in high school. Typically, I'd hang out on the fence until one got close enough for me to leap onto.

"You're biting your lip," Jacob observes, closing up the trailer. "Are you nervous about the horses, or are you already regretting coming on a date with me?"

"No regrets," I say. "I just don't recall horses being this big. There isn't a fence here. I've only mounted from a fence."

"You'll do fine," Jacob assures me. "I'll show you what to do." He grabs the reins of one of the monstrous beasts and leads it over to me. "This is Curly. She's big, but she's gentle. As long as you treat her right, she'll treat you right."

"I don't think she likes me," I say. "I'm pretty sure she's mean-mugging me right now."

"Get over here," Jacob says with a chuckle. "You're going to be just fine. Mount and unmount from the left side. She'll park out for you to make getting on easier. Just tap her over here on her shoulder."

Jacob gives Curly a tap, and the horse takes a couple of steps forward with just her front legs, lowering the stirrup to a more reasonable height. Jacob stands close behind me as I slide my boot into the stirrup, grab hold of a handful of mane, and pull myself up onto the horse. Jacob hands me the reins and checks my stirrups to make sure the length is right.

"See? That wasn't so bad," Jacob says.

"I still don't think she likes me."

Jacob mounts his horse, and we head off side by side on horseback through the open field. Curly's bulbous muscles work beneath me, and I am instilled with a certain respect for the strength of this beautiful creature. Following Jacob up a broad hill, I imagine what it must have been like in earlier times when horses were the only means of transportation. It was no wonder cowboys were associated with being bowlegged. Only twenty minutes of riding in the saddle has a soreness growing in my legs and butt that I'm not at all accustomed to.

"Stop that!" I fuss at Curly as she turns and nips at me again. "What did I ever do to you?"

"We're almost to the spot I wanted to show you, and we'll take a break," Jacob says, and he leads the way until we make it to the clearing on the other side of the hilltop, prior to the descent back down.

I gasp at the view. We stand above a beautiful valley with majestic mountains standing firm and immovable in the background. Wild bison are grazing in the valley, the calves sticking close to their mothers. The sun is slowly working toward its nightly descent behind the mountaintops.

Jacob ties up his horse to one of the nearby trees and stands at the ready next to Curly as I tap at her shoulder with my foot, signaling the horse to park out for my dismount.

With both horses settled, Jacob pulls out our dinner from his saddlebag and sits next to me in a spot, overlooking the valley below. He offers me a sandwich. I unwrap it and take a bite.

Chewing, I say, "I could stay in this spot, admiring this view forever."

"It's almost as beautiful as you," Jacob replies. I glance over at him, a smile tugging at my lips. "Ugh, that was pretty cheesy, wasn't it?" he grumbles, rubbing his hand down his face in embarrassment.

"It was," I agree with a laugh. "But thanks. I'll take the compliment, anyway." I take another bite of my sandwich. "How'd you know about this spot?"

"My brothers and I used to go riding a lot. We've probably covered most of this area on horseback over the years."

"You have two brothers, right?" I ask, trying to remember what Maddie told me.

"Yeah. They're both married and have kids. They live a few hours away, which Mom hates, because she doesn't get to see her grandkids often enough."

"She talks about the grandkids all the time at work."

"She can't wait for me or Mia to get married so she can have some grandkids close by."

"You and Mia are twins, right?" I ask.

"Yep. I don't know if you can meet her though. I'm afraid you two will be thick as thieves if you get the chance to know each other," Jacob teases.

"That could be dangerous for you."

Jacob changes the subject.

"So why did you choose to leave your home and move across the country to a place you've never been?"

"I just needed a change of scenery, I guess," I say, giving him my standard response.

Jacob arches an eyebrow at me.

"That seems extreme for a mere change of scenery. What's the real reason?"

"I needed to get away," I say after a slight hesitation.

"From?"

"Someone I don't like talking about."

I try to ignore the anxiety building up in the pit of my stomach as Jacob unknowingly summons the memories that I work so desperately to bury.

"A little heavy for a first date," Jacob says. "I get it. Just answer me this, what's the likelihood of you waking up one day and deciding all is forgiven and moving back to North Carolina?"

"That won't happen," I say, studying my sandwich. My appetite lost, I wrap the remainder of my sandwich and set it aside. "Too many lines were crossed."

Jacob nods and scoots in closer to me till our bodies are barely connected. I try to refocus on the scene in front of me and push the memories back inside.

"Did you know that bison are the largest mammals in North America?" Jacob asks, changing the subject again as we turn our attention back to the view below in the valley. He continues. "They are very intelligent animals. They're fast, too. Bison can run up to forty miles per hour and can jump six feet high."

Jacob's smooth, deep voice soothes the anxiety that was threatening to overtake me. I lean into his chest and listen to him talk, following along as he spouts out facts about the animals in front of us.

With the sun nearly set, Jacob stands and helps me to my feet. He tucks our trash back into his saddlebag while I prepare to mount Curly. Tapping Curly low on the shoulder, Curly takes a couple of steps forward with her front feet, parking out for the mount. I stick my boot in the stirrup, but before I can pull myself up, Curly backs out of the park and I lose my balance, stumbling backward. Undeterred, I try again. Curly cooperates until I grab the stirrup, and she steps back again.

"Need some help?" Jacob asks.

"No, I've got this. Curly and I are just figuring each other out."

I tap on Curly again, and she steps forward. I get my foot in the stirrup and grab hold of her mane, but again, she steps up and walks away. I stomp my foot and let out a frustrated noise. Jacob stifles a chuckle.

Dismounting his horse, Jacob grabs Curly's reins and leads her back over to me. He tells Curly to park out and stands beside her, rubbing down her neck while I climb into the saddle. Jacob hands me the reins and gets back on his own horse. Slowly, we start the trek back to the truck. I follow behind Jacob as he leads us down the slope of the hill, down into the open field. I pull on the reins to pull Curly's head away when she turns and nips at me again. The more frustrated I become, the more Curly acts out. After a while, Curly stops and refuses to move.

"Come on, you big dumb mule," I say, slapping the reins. "Let's go!"

Curly doesn't budge.

I kick her with my heels and slap the reins like they do in the movies. Curly takes offense and jumps to a start, trotting at first, then spinning and rearing back. My ass slides right out of the saddle, and I fall to the ground with a solid thud. Curly, clearly pleased with herself, prances off across the field. Jacob jumps down from his horse and rushes to my side.

"Fuck. Lacey, are you okay?"

He brushes the hair out of my face and gently pulls me up to a sitting position. He looks me over for injuries, concern on his face.

"Damn blasted mule!" I seethe.

"Nothing broken?" Jacob asks, inspecting my limbs.

"Just my pride," I reply and slowly get to my feet. I dust myself off. "I'm not getting back on that fucking horse."

"Okay, I'm just glad you're alright."

Jacob convinces me to get onto his horse and climbs up behind me. Riding over to Curly, he reaches down and grabs Curly's reins, leading her through the field behind us. I let myself relax and lean back into Jacob's strong chest, his arms around me guiding the horse, and soak in his warmth.

"You know you didn't have to get yourself thrown from a horse for an excuse to cuddle up to me," Jacob teases.

"It's a good thing you're not too big for your britches, or there might not be room for me on this horse," I quip in return.

Darkness sweeps over the valley before we make it all the way back to the truck. Without street lamps or city lights, the stars fill the sky, and the moon illuminates our path. I lean my head back, resting it against Jacob, and take in the expansive open sky speckled with stars. Jacob's body keeps away the chill of the August night air.

"Hey," Jacob says in almost a whisper. I turn and look up at him over my shoulder. "You doing okay?"

"Yeah. This evening has been remarkable," I say, holding his gaze.

"Good," Jacob replies.

His eyes drop down to my lips. Slowly, he leans down and presses his lips to mine, and I know I'm right where I want to be.

CHAPTER TWENTY-SEVEN

jacob

I finish putting the horses up and unhook the horse trailer from my truck. Aside from Lacey getting thrown from her horse, I couldn't have asked for our date to have gone any better than it did. She is perfect, and Jalynn is right about her being a once-in-a-lifetime-type of girl. I should have asked her out a long time ago.

I'm still curious about the person she left in North Carolina. It was most likely a boyfriend, but she didn't say. Her growing trepidation was palpable as the conversation continued. I fucking hated seeing her like that, so I did the first thing that came to mind in the moment and started spouting off random facts like I was a damn *National Geographic* reporter or something. It seemed to work, though. Her body began to relax, and she even snuggled into me, surrounding me with her fresh vanilla scent.

I would move mountains to protect her. She's strong and brave and has a mind of her own but at a moment's notice can turn hesitant and uncertain. I'm certain the person from her past is the reason for it somehow. Maybe I'll ask Jalynn about it when I get a chance.

The next morning I wake up with a smile on my face and

Lacey on my mind. I roll over and reach for my cell phone charging on my nightstand. Pulling up Lacey's name, I shoot her a text. I should probably play it cool and not make myself appear so eager, but I think we are past that already.

I get dressed for work, still on my high from last night. On my way into town, I check my phone to see if Lacey has responded. Nothing. She should be on her way to work right now. Hopefully she didn't oversleep. Finally, I decide to give her a call, but my call is sent straight to voicemail. I frown at the phone and drop it in the seat beside me. Did I misread her last night? Is she having second thoughts?

I only allow myself to text Lacey once more and then busy myself with work. It's proving to be an ineffective way of getting my mind off her. I'm distracted and can't seem to stop checking my phone. Unable to hold off any longer, I jump in my truck and head across town to the flower shop.

Lacey spins around to face me as the bells over the flower shop door ring. A smile spreads across her face. That's a good sign.

"Hey, is everything okay?" I ask as I walk up to the counter where she's standing.

"Yeah, why?"

"Are we okay? No second thoughts from last night?"

"No, no second thoughts. Why?"

"I've been trying to get in touch with you this morning."

"Oh . . . Oh!" Lacey pulls her phone out of her back pocket. I watch her press the power button and her phone chimes. "I had my phone off. You remember Jared? Apparently, Jared has a girlfriend. She found my number in his phone and isn't very happy about it."

I walk around the counter to where she's standing, wrap my arms around her waist, and kiss the top of her head. Lacey snuggles into my chest.

"Here, let me see your phone. I want to see what this chick is saying."

Lacey hands me the phone. I take a couple of minutes to listen to the long, threatening voicemails and to read the crazy text messages. Finishing the last message, I shake my head, block the number on Lacey's phone, and return it to her pocket for her.

"You sure know how to pick them," I say.

"What does that say about you?" she asks and turns in my arms to face me.

"No, you see, I chose you."

I lean down and plant a soft kiss on her lips.

"Oh!" My mom's surprised voice rings out.

She's just walked through the swinging door into the storefront. Lacey pulls away, a blush spreading across her cheeks. She's fucking cute when she's embarrassed.

"I'm sorry, dears. I didn't mean to interrupt," Mom says, her eyes darting back and forth between the two of us curiously.

"It's okay, Mother," I say. "I was just about to head out."

I can tell she's internally celebrating this new development. I give them each a hug and go back to work.

HOLDING OUT A HAND TO LACEY, I help her down from the cab of my truck. Her touch sends sparks down my arm and into my core. Lacey slides out of the seat, her boots land on the dirt lot, but her eyes stay locked on mine. I give her a gentle tug, and she lets herself fall into me. I wrap my arms around her and press a kiss to her lips. She kisses me back, then pulls away toward the bed of the truck, her hand still firmly in mine.

Lacey rises up on her toes, trying to grab our packs from the bed of the truck. I step up behind her and rest a hand on her hip while I reach over her into the truck and grab both packs with one hand. I slide the straps of my backpack over my shoulders, then turn Lacey to face me and fasten the straps around her waist for her.

"How does that feel?" I ask, my fingers making adjustments to the fit of her backpack.

Lacey reaches up to grab the straps running down my shoulders and pulls me down to her. She kisses me, gently biting at my bottom lip, her hunger matching my own. A groan escapes me, and she takes it as encouragement to press her body firmly against mine.

"That feels perfect," Lacey whispers, her lips still hovering next to mine. I close the space between us again for another quick kiss.

"We'd better get going," I say. "I'm trying to behave myself."

"That's no fun," Lacey teases, nipping at my lip again.

"You're not making it very easy for me."

I kiss her hard, then pull her down the trailhead with me. Lacey falls in pace behind me, walking down the narrow, rocky dirt trail that winds parallel to the river. With senses already heightened from Lacey's presence, I breathe in the fresh air deeply. The river rushes by us, and occasional fish hop up for an insect hovering at the surface. The yellow flowers and tall grasses bow in the gentle breeze. A western meadowlark puffs his yellow breast from where he sits on a branch of a bush and chirps a cheerful tune. It's stunning. It never gets old coming down to this canyon.

I glance back at Lacey, checking to make sure she is managing okay, and am surprised by how naturally she fits in to the magnificent scene around her. It's almost as though we're on a movie set, every minute detail carefully thought out and placed. I can't help smiling to myself. Somehow I've captured this alluring woman's attention, and somehow she's stolen my heart. As if on cue, Lacey looks up with a wide grin on her face, clearly as content in nature as I am. This girl is trouble.

I take a step off the side of the path, pause to offer Lacey my hand, and help her down the rocky bank toward the river. We set our gear down, and I prepare the line for fishing. Lacey watches quietly as I get everything set up for her. Leading her down to the water, I hand her the rod and stand behind her, my hand over hers.

"Start with the rod up close to the water," I say quietly into Lacey's ear. She relaxes into me. "Give yourself about four feet of fly line but no slack. You're going to bring it up to about here"—I show her with my hand—"then flick it forward again. That will give you a good backcast." I guide her through the backcast, then pause to let the line unwind behind us. "Now we're going to cast forward. We're going to swing it back forward and point where we want it to land."

With another flick of our joined hands over the rod, the line goes hurling forward again and plops onto the water. Lacey tries casting several more times. Eventually, she hands the rod over to me, letting me take over.

"You done already?" I ask, concerned that she might want to leave.

"I'm ready to watch the master at his craft," Lacey responds.

Lacey heads over to our packs and has a seat on the ground. She leans back against a large rock and watches me. The worry that she is ready to head back home slowly drifts off as I study her. She flips her backpack over and unzips the front pocket. She pulls out a sketchbook and some pencils that I didn't see her pack. Propping the sketchbook on her thighs, she picks a pencil and focuses on the white page in front of her.

I go back to fishing, but I can feel her eyes watching me. I wonder what she's sketching. I haven't seen her sketch and didn't know it was something she knew how to do. Eventually, the sketchbook is set aside, and I watch her slink toward me. She stops on the edge of the riverbank, an impish grin slowly taking over her face. When I glance back at my line, she takes the opportunity for a surprise attack.

The next thing I know, she's landed on my back, twisting me down into the water with her. Sputtering but still grasping the rod in one hand, I resurface and pull Lacey back up with me. Lacey cackles and grabs for my baseball cap that is trying to float away down the river. She puts the soggy hat on her head and tries to make a quick escape to the bank.

"What was that for?" I call after her over the sound of the rushing water.

"You were looking too sexy down there in the water. I thought I'd help cool ya down."

She stands still in the water, several feet away from me, apparently afraid to get too close.

"Hmmm." I nod my head, plotting my own attack. "Come over here."

"I think I'm just fine down here," Lacey says, stifling a giggle.

"You're wearing my hat."

"It looks better on me" She shrugs, not missing a beat.

"I can't argue with that," I agree. "I think we are done with fishing."

I walk to the bank to put up our fishing gear, and Lacey follows along at a safe distance, undoubtedly feeling like the champion of our unspoken war.

Back up on the bank, I open my backpack and pull out the small insulated pack with our cold food. Lacey takes her seat again as I lay out the food, and she divvies it up between our two plates, giving me an unguarded moment to retaliate. Grabbing a handful of ice from the insulated pack, I make quick work of dropping it down the front of her shirt.

Lacey jumps to her feet, dancing and hollering, as she tries to untuck the wet shirt from her pants. Now it's my turn to laugh. I'm a good sport, though, and graciously offer my assistance.

"Come here. I'll dig the ice out of your shirt for you."

"You, sir," Lacey says, pointing an accusatory finger at me, "can keep your grubby paws to your damn self."

Lacey finishes shaking the ice out of her shirt and gives me a dirty look as she sits back down to finish dishing out our lunch. I laugh and lean in to kiss her cheek.

"It's a good thing you're cute," she says.

"Oh yeah?"

"Yeah. Otherwise, this day might have a completely different ending for you," Lacey teases and hands me a plate.

That's when I notice her sketchpad again. This time it's sitting off to the side of her, open. I scoop it up and study the page.

"Gypsy, this is really good," I say. "I didn't know you draw."

Her page shows the image of a man fishing in the river with the mountains behind him. She's captured every last curve, shadow, and wrinkle. It's clear from the details of the sketch that the man is me.

"I used to sketch all of the time. It's been a while."

"Why did you stop?"

"I only draw when inspiration hits," she says with a shrug and focuses on her plate. "It's been a while since I've felt inspired."

"You should feel inspired more often. You're too good to let this talent go to waste."

"Then I guess you'd better stick around."

I respond with a kiss. Hell yeah, I'm gonna stick around. I've never had this much to lose before she came along and conquered my heart. Now, I can't imagine myself anywhere but with her.

lacey

We pull into my driveway at the end of another date, my hand in Jacob's, my head resting on his shoulder. It's late and I'm tired, but I'm not ready to say goodbye. We've been dating for about a month now, and no matter how much time we spend together, it never feels like enough.

Jacob pulls his truck in next to mine and turns down the radio. We sit quietly for a moment, neither of us wanting to move. I look up at him and fight the desire to reach up and kiss him. Not that he would mind, but damn, how does he turn me to butter? Every. Single. Time.

"Do I have to go home? If I go home, I'll go to bed. And if I go to bed, the morning will come. In the morning, I have to be responsible and go to work," I ramble.

"You don't like working with my mom?" Jacob teases. He knows I adore her. He pokes at my side, and I giggle and grab his finger to keep it away.

"I love your mom. She's awesome, but it is somewhat awkward now working next to her while I daydream about her boy."

We've slowly made it up on the deck, and I'm stalling in front of the camper door.

"So you daydream about me, huh?" Jacob teases, leaning more in my direction.

"You wish," I say, realizing my slip of the tongue. "Do you daydream about me?" I ask breathlessly.

I raise my head to look at him now. Jacob locks eyes with me and continues to inch closer until our foreheads touch, and his arms wrap around me.

"All of the time," he says and brushes his lips across mine.

He pulls me closer still and deepens the kiss. My arms slide up his body and around his neck, my fingertips playing in his hair. Jacob leaves a trail of kisses down my neck where he nips and teases at a sensitive spot. I'm practically purring for him but somehow find the strength to pull away.

"Would you like to come in for a minute?" I ask, not wanting him to leave.

"You talked me into it," Jacob says.

He follows me inside, and I remember my camper doesn't have the space for entertaining. The only seating is the bench.

"Sorry. I need to replace this bench with something more comfortable," I say.

"It's fine." Jacob takes a seat.

I slowly approach him, feeling awkward and shy. Jacob reaches for me, taking my hands and pulling me closer. I take a seat on his lap, straddling him, and rest a hand on the side of his stubbled face. Jacob tugs me into him again and takes possession of my lips, this time nudging my mouth open with his tongue. His hands slide up the sides of my legs until his arms are around my hips, pulling me into him.

I turn my mouth away, and he makes a tantalizing trail of kisses back down my neck, the scratchiness of his stubble heightening my anticipation. Lost in the spine-tingling sensations he makes me feel, I arch into him and let out a soft moan.

My phone buzzes in my back pocket, interrupting us. Jacob pulls it out, turning it to see who is calling.

"It's an eight-two-eight number," he says.

I know the number on the phone. It's a number I've dialed countless times since high school. The heat that has been coursing through my body turns instantly to ice as I stare down at Ben's number on the phone screen. My stomach churns, and I think I might be sick. I push myself up off Jacob's lap and straighten my clothes. My breathing is heavy, and I wrap my arms tightly around myself and step back to give Jacob room to rise from his seat. His expression is wracked with confusion, but he follows my lead without question. He stands and adjusts the stiff appendage in his jeans.

"Thanks for tonight," I say without making eye contact. "But it's late, and I need to get to bed."

"Lacey, are you okay?" Jacob asks, reaching for me. I step back out of his reach, still unable to look at him. He opens the door and steps onto the deck to leave but turns back again. "Did I do something?"

"No. Good night. Please let me know that you made it home safe," I say and promptly close the door in his face.

I know he is standing on the other side of the door debating whether to knock because I don't hear any footsteps. I stare down at my phone, now sitting on the counter. It's no longer ringing, but the phone buzzes again, signaling the arrival of a voicemail. After a moment, footsteps fading outside tell me Jacob has finally left.

I move to the sink and splash cold water over my face. With my breathing normal again, I pick up the phone, and with shaky hands, I click on the voicemail and raise the phone to my ear.

"Lacey, I hope you're waiting for me. Tell me where you are. We need to talk."

I delete the message and set the phone back down, leaving it on the counter while I change for bed. There's no way in hell

I'm calling him back. The phone buzzes again, making me jump. I grab for it. This time a text message shows on the screen.

Jacob: Made it home. Sleep well. I'll check on you tomorrow.

Me: Good night.

I plug in my phone and straighten the books that have fallen over on my shelf. Anxiety still fills my belly from the voicemail. His voice, his words. What does he mean, he hopes that I'm waiting for him? Waiting for him to appear? Or he hopes I haven't moved on from him?

I pull my phone back out and send Billy a message. They're two hours ahead of us here in Montana, but it's not too late for Billy.

Me: How did Ben get my number?

Billy: Shit, Lace, I don't know. Did he call you?

Me: Left me a voicemail. Please tell me he's still in town.

Billy: I saw him at the diner tonight.

Me: He doesn't know where I am does he?

Billy: I don't know.

I toss my phone. I can't do this. Climbing back off the bed, I go straight to the camper door to make sure it is secure and locked. Pacing back and forth, I try to figure out what to do. Should I leave? I don't want to. Knowing Billy saw Ben in the diner tonight calms my nerves slightly. He hasn't figured out where I am. He wouldn't have given me a heads up by calling first. I go back to my bed, lay my head on my pillow, and do my best to fall asleep. It's pointless though. I can't escape him, not even in my dreams.

"Gosh, it feels good to be back out here again," Jalynn said.

We were sitting side by side on the tailgate of George's pickup, down by the river. George and Ben were fishing about fifteen yards down the riverbank.

"We haven't been down here since the summer before we went to college," Jalynn added to fill the silence.

"Yeah, Ben and I never really come down here anymore, even though we're living back in town. We mostly just stay at the house."

"Are y'all doing alright? You seem really down."

Jalynn could always tell when something was on my mind.

"Yeah, I'm fine. Just still bummed from a fight Ben and I had last night."

With my thumb and forefinger, I flicked a bug as it crawled across the tailgate between us.

"What did y'all fight about?"

"He wants me to sell Grammy's house."

"What? Why? Don't you own it outright?" Jalynn asked.

"Yep. But we've been staying with his mom, trying to help her out, and he says there's no point in keeping it and paying taxes on it every year. That's where I grew up, though, Jay. I know it's not much, but I love that little house."

The boys began walking back up toward us, finished trying to catch any fish. Ben never was much of a fisherman. George loaded the fishing gear behind us in the bed of the truck, and Ben came over and stood next to me. He rested a possessive hand on my thigh, and I prayed Jalynn wouldn't say anything about Grammy's house in front of him.

With his free hand, he pulled the cigarette out of his mouth and dropped it to the ground. He smothered it with the toe of his boot, like he always smothered my ideas.

I watched as George leaned in and kissed Jalynn on the cheek, envious of his tenderness toward her.

"Did Jalynn tell you the news?" George asked me.

"No, I don't guess she did."

I tried to put a smile back on my face. I saw Jalynn try to discretely signal George that right now was not the time, but he must have missed it.

"We're engaged!" he said proudly. "We're getting married next month."

"No way!" I leaned over and hugged Jalynn to buy myself a few more seconds to respond. "That quick? But that's amazing! I'm so happy for you two."

"Thanks, Lacey. I was hoping you'd be my maid of honor," Jalynn said. "Sorry about the timing," she added in a whisper.

"Don't you worry your pretty little head about that. You deserve to be happy. I would love to be your maid of honor!" I said, doing my best to emanate the happiness I was lacking.

I stumble into the bathroom the next morning after a restless night of sleep. I'm not ready to hold my eyes open, but I need to get ready for work, and sleep proves to be elusive anyway. With eyelids open just enough not to run into the wall, I yawn and pull my hair up in a knot on my head so I can wash my face.

It's while I'm brushing my teeth that my blurry eyes have finally cleared and focused enough to notice the speckles of purple on my neck.

Shit.

Instinctively my fingers fly to the rueful hickey, my eyes wide. How am I supposed to work beside Maddie all day wearing the love bite left behind by her son? Just the thought of it makes me cringe. First impressions came and went a long time ago, and Jacob and I are both adults, but we're still trying to find our footing in this new dynamic, and I'm not sure where her lines fall. I dig into my makeup bag for some concealer, hoping I have something to cover the hickey with.

Much to my relief, it turns into a busy day at the floral shop. We are helping our sister shop in the city prepare for a wedding tomorrow. Maddie and I are busy getting the arrangements together and ready to take to Bozeman this evening.

"I hear that you and Jacob are getting along lately," Maddie says, breaking the silence.

I glance up from the arrangement I'm working on, wondering where Maddie is trying to take the conversation. Has she noticed the poorly covered hickey?

"Yeah. I really like spending time with him."

"I'm glad he made amends. He doesn't always think things through before he acts. It's ended him up in a scuff or two over the years."

I smile, thinking of some of the stories Jacob has shared with me about his rambunctious childhood. He and his brothers did not take it easy on their parents.

"He's been great," I offer, not sure what to say.

"I was hoping you might come over for dinner with the family Sunday evening. Are you free?" Maddie glances up briefly but continues working on her arrangement, trying to keep the conversation easy.

"Sure. I think I can do that," I say, though I'm not sure at all.

It seems somewhat quick to have earned an invitation to their family dinner. I make a mental note to talk to Jacob about it later and get his take on it. I don't want to make him uncomfortable.

I LEAN into Jacob that evening, resting my head on his shoulder as we sit side by side on the tailgate of his truck. The creek burbles, and we wait for a fish to be enticed by Jacob's fishing lure. I tell Jacob about Maddie's invitation, but he seems surprisingly unfazed.

"We haven't been seeing each other very long. I don't want

to ruin what we have by jumping the gun," I say to explain my trepidation.

"It won't be the whole family. Just me and Mom, who you already know, and you'll meet Dad and Mia. You think meeting family would change the way we feel about each other?" he asks.

"Everything changes when people get serious."

"Are we moving too fast? Is that what last night was about?"

"I'm not sure what you mean," I reply, pretending to be oblivious. One minute I was urging him on and the next I slammed the door in his face.

"Either way, if you want to come you should. Mom really likes you. I'm pretty sure she would have invited you to our family dinner at some point regardless of what is or isn't going on between us."

We fall silent again, letting the chirping birds take over the conversation.

"Jalynn mentioned something happened with your ex before you moved out here," Jacob says after a couple minutes of silence, trying to take a different angle at the conversation.

"She shouldn't have. It's none of her business." I sound snippier than I mean to.

Jacob nods.

"I take it that's not a conversation you want to have with me, either?" he asks.

"Nope. Definitely not," I say flatly. "It's not something I carry on about with anyone."

"Okay." Jacob doesn't even try to hide his disappointment.

"Look"—I suck in a deep breath and release it in a rush— "I'm not proud of my part in that relationship."

"What do you mean?"

"I stayed too long. Things started out pretty normal, but the longer we were together, the worse it got. I allowed it to get as bad as it did."

"It's difficult to clearly see things when you're on the inside. Even I know that. It was the same for me and Ashley."

"Yeah, but it wasn't the same. And you ended it way before I did. You did the right thing. I didn't. And Ashley isn't Ben."

I slide off the tailgate of Jacob's truck and slowly wade barefoot into the creek. I turn toward him again, pushing the memories away, but continue slowly walking backward into the creek with a playful smile on my face.

"You were done fishing, right?"

Jacob chuckles and pulls in his line. Setting the fishing pole in the bed of the truck, he kicks off his boots and socks and follows me into the creek.

SUNDAY EVENING, I focus on each step I take in my stilettos on the stone sidewalk to Jacob's childhood home. We walk hand in hand, but the slightly unlevel stones and the nervous butterflies fluttering around in my stomach have me worried about face-planting in Jacob's parents' lawn. I should have worn flats.

Jacob reaches for the doorknob, but the door swings open, and the beautiful blonde I saw with Jacob at the pool hall stands in front of me, greeting us boisterously.

"Hey, brother! Where were you last week? Oh . . . that's right. You skipped out on dinner again because you found a new lady friend!" She pulls him into a warm hug and then turns to me next, wrapping me in a tight hug, not even waiting for Jacob to introduce us. "I'm this goon's sister, Mia. I'm the older, smarter, and prettier twin. The extra couple minutes of baking didn't do him any good. It's good to finally meet you, Lacey."

"Good to meet you, too," I say almost in more of a question than a statement.

Mia leads us into the house and straight back to the kitchen where Maddie is cooking, and Mr. Jones is taste-testing. Mia leans in to whisper in my ear.

"You didn't quite get that hickey covered up. A little yellow will do wonders. I can show you sometime," Mia says.

"I was all out of yellow," I reply, and without thinking, my fingers instinctively go to my neck. A quiet giggle slips out from Mia.

"You have that many to cover?" she whispers back, an eyebrow cocked. "Alright, little brother, way to go," she says quietly to Jacob.

Maddie looks up from the stove, realizing we've made it into the kitchen. She leaves the stove and rushes over to give both Jacob and I a hug. I'm suddenly acutely aware of how much more hugging happens in this family than in mine. My grandparents were great, but they weren't overly affectionate.

"I'm so glad you were able to join us, Lacey," Maddie says. "This is my husband, Larry."

Maddie motions for Larry to come over. Larry is a tall gentleman with a beard that reaches down almost to the hint of a belly on his slender frame. He gives me a warm smile as he comes over to join the group.

"Hello, Lacey. It's good to meet you. You've been a frequent topic of conversation in this house. It's nice to finally put a face to the name," Larry says.

"No wonder my ears have been burning," I say, hoping I'm hiding the discomfort I feel about being the center of attention. "Do I dare ask?"

"Only good things, sweetheart, I promise," Larry says reassuringly.

I look up at Jacob who, if I'm not mistaken, is trying to hide the flush of embarrassment spreading across his cheeks.

Mia basically attaches herself to my side throughout the whole evening. By the end of dinner, we're essentially best friends. We team up on Jacob and tease him whenever the opportunity presents itself, which, with Mia around, is pretty much constantly. He takes it on the chin like a champ, clearly used to Mia's loving abuse. Maddie and Larry laugh along with us, and Larry joins in the banter with us girls from time to time.

After so many years together, Larry and Maddie still carry a magnetic pull between them. Larry's expression softens each time he looks at his wife. Maddie can't hide the sparkle that lights her face every time Larry takes her hand, even if she tried. I'm in awe of it. As a child I would often daydream about my parents, imagining them having a similar connection. I don't remember enough to know if they did or not. A tiny part of me is jealous of Jacob and Mia getting to grow up in this loving environment that can only be produced by a close-knit family like the one Maddie and Larry have grown.

After dinner, we move to the living room to continue visiting. I sit on the love seat next to Jacob and snuggle into his side. His arm wraps around my shoulders. No sooner than we get settled, I feel the familiar vibration of my cell phone in my pocket. I pull it out to discover a text message. It's from Ben.

> Ben: Don't forget about me. I need a phone call from you, Lacey.

I close the message without responding and shove the phone back in my pocket, a slight unsteadiness to my hands now. Jacob peers down at me, concern and confusion on his face, but whatever thoughts are going through his head, he pushes them aside and pulls me in tighter.

On the ride home, I silently debate what to do about Ben. I still wonder how he got my number. And what else does he know? I pull my phone out of my pocket and pull his number up to block it. My finger hovers over the button, though, and I debate whether blocking him is the best move or not. If I block him, I won't have to worry about him texting or calling me anymore, unless he figures out that he's blocked and starts harassing me from a different number. Then I'm back at square one. If I don't block his number, I have to deal with the texts and phone calls, assuming he continues trying to get ahold of me, but I can keep ignoring them. Plus, any information he leaks to me in the messages could be helpful. If he figures out where I am, will he say something and unintentionally give me a heads up that he's on his way here?

"What are you stressing about over there?" Jacob asks.

"It's nothing important," I say.

I think I'd rather know what Ben is potentially up to than to block him completely. I close out everything on my phone and slide it into my pocket. Sudden nausea overtakes my stomach as the memory of the first time he struck me floods into my mind.

I was working my shift at the diner. Employment opportunities in town were limited, but I'd worked at the diner through high school and went back to working there when I moved back to town with Ben.

Sheriff Tate walked in accompanying a very intoxicated Ben. He sat Ben down at a table in the back of the diner, away from all of the other customers, and made his way through the tables to the counter where I was putting in an order.

"Hey, Lacey. He needs a coffee to help sober him up and someone to keep an eye on him. If this happens again, I'm going to have to take him in."

"I understand. I'm so sorry. I'll take care of him. He won't be a bother to anyone else tonight, I promise," I reassured him.

Ben had been drinking a lot lately. It was a definite problem, affecting both of us. The Sheriff stood in place a moment longer looking like he had something more to add but seemed to decide against it. I knew he was worried about me. He'd been close to my parents, and after the accident, he'd given me extra attention to try to help fill the void for me and help out my grandparents.

Sheriff Tate patted me on the shoulder. After he left, I took a mug of coffee over to Ben's table.

"Hey, baby . . ." Ben's speech was slurred. "I came to see my pretty little lady at work. How you doin'?" He reached for me,

trying to pull me into him. I set the coffee on the table and pushed myself away from him. "You gotta light on you?" Ben asked, pulling a pack of cigarettes from his pocket.

"You know you can't smoke in here." I grabbed the pack of cigarettes from him and pushed the mug of coffee toward him. "Drink that. Sit here, and be quiet before you cause any more of a scene than you already have."

Tim, a flirty guy we went to high school with and now a frequent flier at the diner, waved me down. I put a smile back on my face and walked over to his table to see what he needed. He already had his order, and as usual, he wanted some conversation to go with it. I laughed at his jokes as I always did. It was part of the job to get higher tips.

Ben got up from his seat and stumbled his way across the diner to where Tim sat doing his best to flirt with me. With no warning at all, Ben punched Tim right out of his chair. I screamed at Ben and tried to help Tim back up, but Ben grabbed hold of me and pulled me out of the diner with him.

I fought against him, trying to get loose from his grip, but he wouldn't let go. Once at my truck, he pressed me against the passenger door and ordered me to get in. When I protested, he opened the door and shoved me into the cab.

Jacob turns to me, concern on his face. We're back in my driveway now, and I'm trembling. There's no way he doesn't notice the trembling.

"You okay?" he asks.

"Yeah," I lie. "All good."

I climb out of the truck, and Jacob follows my lead, walking me up to my door. He shines his phone's flashlight for me to see while I unlock the door. I turn back to him, dangling the keys in my hand, not ready to tell him good night. I don't want to be alone tonight. He wraps me in a hug and kisses the top of my head.

"Don't leave yet," I say, squeezing him tighter.

"You don't have to convince me to hang around, Gypsy."

I smile up at him and pull him into the camper.

"Your family is great."

"We get along most of the time," he replies, more focused on me than he is on our conversation.

"Want something to drink?"

"What do you have?"

"Eh . . ." I open the door of the mini-fridge and examine the sparse contents. "I have part of a bottle of water we could share. Supplies are getting low here. Someone has been keeping me busy lately."

Jacob examines my barren fridge. It holds a partially drunk bottle of water, a box of baking soda, and an apple. Jacob doesn't say anything, but his expression hardens. He begins opening the few cupboards I have, only to find a nearly empty bag of chips and a can of baked beans.

"Is my mom not paying you enough?" Jacob asks with genuine concern.

"What? No, my pay is fine. I just haven't been to the store." Jacob gives me a questioning look, almost like he doesn't believe me, and begins inspecting the rest of the camper more closely. "Jacob . . ."

I feel strangely exposed and inadequate. He checks the stove to make sure it's in working order, then the tap to make sure I have running water. He checks out each of the windows and pokes his head inside the bathroom, giving the toilet an unnecessary flush.

"Does your heat work? It's going to start getting cold enough to need it soon."

"I don't know," I say, answering him honestly. "I haven't tried it."

Jacob turns back to me, wrapping me in his arms again. I smile up at him, hopeful that his poking around is done, and rise up on my toes to kiss him. He kisses me back, slowly stepping us backward until his legs are against the platform of the bed. Bending at the knees, he pulls me down with him, letting his body free fall back onto the bed with me on top of him. We land with a camper-shaking thud.

"Ugh . . ." Jacob grumbles once he gets his breath back. "This is where you sleep?" I giggle. "Your bed just knocked the wind out of me, Gypsy."

I roll off of him, laughing, and allow him to sit up. He immediately pulls back the covers to expose the wooden platform beneath, no mattress in sight.

"You don't have a mattress?" He looks at me incredulously.

"I'm getting one. I just haven't yet. I was waiting until I got a job and, well, to be honest, I just got used to sleeping on it the way it is. I guess I forgot."

"You forgot that you don't have a mattress to sleep on?" Jacob asks in disbelief.

"Yeah?"

"You can't stay here like this."

"Actually, I can, I have been, and I'll continue living here," I insist, stubbornly folding my arms across my chest.

"Why?" Jacob rolls onto his side to face me, clearly unhappy with my living situation.

"Because I'm a grown-ass woman. It's home, and it's mine, and I can do whatever the hell I want to do." Patience is leaking out of me like a sieve.

"Either you call Jalynn and ask to stay with her, or we pack you a bag and you can move into my place." Jacob sits up on the bed, completely serious about making me leave the camper.

"Jacob, this isn't up for debate. I'm not leaving. You, on the other hand, probably should as you seem to have overstayed your welcome."

Jacob glares at me, never dropping eye contact, and if I know him at all, he's debating his next move. Lucky for me, he doesn't have one. Check. Mate. I grin, and he knows that this conversation isn't going anywhere right now.

"Fine. I'll drop it for tonight. But this isn't over. I won't have my girl living like she's destitute."

"I'm not destitute." I roll my eyes at him. "Not every girl needs a big ole castle with a moat and handmaids."

"Just because you don't need them doesn't mean you don't deserve them," Jacob counters. "Come on. Let's go sit on the hammock outside and enjoy some fresh air. I've got to forget about where my girl is sleeping tonight."

CHAPTER THIRTY

Sharp stabs gyrating in my arm pull my groggy brain to consciousness. I'm lying in the hammock with my tingling arm wrapped under Lacey. Despite the need I feel to pull it out and get the blood flow back, I don't dare move. I don't want to wake her.

The morning air is chilly, but we successfully cocooned ourselves in the blanket we brought out with us last night. I pull the blanket up over Lacey's shoulder. Her hand slides innocently down my torso, just low enough, and suddenly, other parts of my body are waking as well. It's while I'm trying to shift my body so I'm not jutting into her that Lacey begins to wake.

"What time is it?" she asks.

"I'm not sure. Close to seven, I'm guessing."

"Mmmm." Lacey snuggles back into me.

"I hate to, Gypsy, but I should probably go."

"No, don't."

"I've got appointments to keep." I kiss the top of her head and pull my arm free.

She clings to me as I climb out of the hammock. After getting on my feet, I help her up, too, making sure she makes it safely inside. Ready for a change of clothes, I hop in my truck and head home.

I unlock my front door and step inside. Something is off. The light is on in my living room. I know I didn't leave it on. I step into the room and encounter a smug-looking Ashley sitting in the armchair with her legs crossed. She sips on a mug of coffee and stares at me closely. I forgot she still has a fucking key.

"You were out late," Ashley says, checking the time on her watch. "Who did you stay the night with?"

"That's none of your business, Ashley. What are you doing in my house?"

I stay standing, ready to escort her out and strip her of her key.

"About that . . . as it turns out, this house actually belongs to my daddy," Ashley says, a smirk spreading across her face.

"I'm paying for the house. I haven't defaulted on any of the payments."

What game is she trying to play?

"Yes, but Daddy's decided since I'm not living here anymore that he's breaking the contract with you. You're officially being evicted."

Ashley pulls out a paper I didn't notice and slaps it down on the coffee table. I swipe it up and scan over the document. So this is what she's been up to. I should have foreseen it, but my brain doesn't process things like a slimy, vindictive bitch.

"You've got to be fucking kidding me," I grumble.

Ashley stands. She sets her mug on the coffee table and saunters over to me. She stands so close that our bodies touch, and she slithers a hand up my chest.

"If I moved back in, though, I could talk to him. I'm sure I could work something out with him. You know how Daddy listens to me."

Her hand leaves my chest, headed for my face. I catch her wrist and stop her. She looks up at me, startled.

"Not a chance in fucking hell," I say. "We're done, Ashley."

I drop her wrist and take a step back from her, motioning her to the door. She scowls at me, knowing she's lost. Ashley grabs her purse off the couch on her way to the front door.

"Then you'd better get packing. You're to be out by the end of the month," Ashley says and walks out the front door, slamming it behind her.

I go to the kitchen to get a drink while I process what just happened. I open the fridge door, examining my options. I can't believe Ashley. What did I ever see in her? I slam the fridge door shut again, too pissed off to drink anything, and head to my bedroom to start packing. The fuck if I'm going to stay in this place until the end of the month. If she thinks she can get me back by threatening to kick me out, she needs to realize just how done with her I am. None of the furniture in the house is mine, so it won't be a difficult packing job. I'll be out before I start my day. The house was a rent to own from Ashley's dad. The place was already furnished when I moved in. I only had to worry about my clothes and personal possessions.

The big question is where am I going to go? Real estate is limited in a small town like ours, and I'm not going to be a twenty-eight-year-old living in my parents' basement. I could live in my office, but all I have to sleep on is a couch. I should've been putting more time into fixing up my grandparents' old place that they'd left to me. It isn't livable at the moment, though. I throw the last bag of my belongings into the back of my truck and head to my first appointment of the day.

I'm waiting in Lacey's driveway when she gets home from work. We haven't talked much today, and I assume she's been just as busy as I have. I have a surprise for her, though, and I need to discuss a proposition with her. She ogles at the large item in the bed of my truck that's currently concealed by the blue tarp. I give her a hug and place a kiss on her lips, fisting her gorgeous hair, and gently pull her against me with an arm around her waist, staking a claim on her mouth again.

"Hello to you, too," Lacey says after we finally break apart.

"I have a surprise for you," I say.

"What did you do?" She eyes me suspiciously.

I grab the side of the tarp and give it a yank, exposing a plush mattress underneath.

"You didn't . . ." Lacey shakes her head at me. "How much do I owe you?"

"Nothing. Just my way of showing that I was thinking about you."

"Jacob, this is too much. I can't accept this. Seriously. My grammy will be rolling over in her grave. How much do I owe you?"

"Nothing. It's not a big deal. And I'm about to ask a really big favor of you."

"So you're trying to bribe me . . ."

"No, it's not like that, either. The two events just happened to coincide."

Lacey watches me expectantly. I take a deep breath, feeling uneasy about asking this of her. No point in prolonging it.

"I'll happily explain the whole story to you, but the short version is Ashley got me kicked out of my house. It was a rent to own through her dad, and she got him to renege on our contract. I own my grandparents' house, and have slowly been renovating it, but it's not livable yet. I was wondering if you'd be okay with me crashing here with you until I get my grandparents' place livable."

"You're kidding me! I swear that girl thinks the sun comes up just to hear her crow. Yeah, of course you can stay here. Stay as long as you need but on one condition."

"Yeah?"

"You can't give me any more flak about my camper," Lacey says, wagging a finger at me.

"I promise," I say with a grin. I hook a finger through Lacey's belt loop and pull her to me again, wrapping her up in a brief hug. "Now, let's get this mattress inside."

I lower my tailgate and grab hold of the edge of the mattress. With a yank, the other end is now resting on the tailgate for Lacey to grab. She takes hold of it and walks with me to the camper. Once on the deck, I reach back with one hand to open the camper door, and we start inside. The top of the mattress catches on the top of the doorframe, causing it to come to an abrupt stop and sending me flying backward onto my ass. Lacey laughs hysterically at me from the other end of the mattress.

"Don't worry about me. Not like that hurt or anything," I call through the door. This sets off a fresh round of giggles.

I stand and curse under my breath as I realize just how tight of a squeeze it's going to be to get the mattress inside. Finally, we find the right angle to slide the mattress through, and we position it on the platform bed in the back of the camper.

"You want to do the honors?" I ask, stepping back against the wall so Lacey can get by me.

"It's so high up now compared to what it was," Lacey says. I offer a hand as she prepares to hoist herself up on the bed. "I feel like an idiot now. This is so much more comfortable. I should have done this a long time ago."

I hop up on the bed beside her. I roll over onto my side to face her, propping my head up on my hand.

"So you're not mad at me for buying it?"

"No, I'm not mad. Thank you. It was very thoughtful of you."

My breath stills as Lacey reaches a hand over, rests it on the side of my face, and slowly leans toward me. I meet her halfway and kiss her deeply. Without breaking the kiss, Lacey pushes me onto my back and climbs on top of me, straddling me and running her hands down my chest. My hands creep down to her hips, and she nips my lip, sending electricity through my body.

It's then that she breaks away from my lips and trails kisses down my cheek and to my ear, nipping at my earlobe. In a sultry voice she whispers into my ear, "But you're still not getting inside my pants. What do you take me for? Some kind of floozy?"

Lacey laughs as she crawls backward down my body and off the bed. She's still laughing as she walks out of the camper. I groan and sit up, adjusting myself, then follow Lacey back out to the truck and help her carry in the groceries she picked up on her way home.

CHAPTER THIRTY-ONE

If I said I wasn't enjoying playing house with Jacob, I'd be lying. After just a week of "letting him crash" at my place, I've come to realize how far off the mark my experience with Ben was. I look forward to the end of my workday, to going home and spending my evening with Jacob. I know this arrangement is only temporary, but it feels right. Everything with him feels right.

After a simple dinner for the two of us, prepared by Jacob of course, we settle on the deck to enjoy the cool breeze and the evening chirping of nature.

Jacob pulls out his guitar, which has become one of my favorite pastimes, and begins playing an original that I enjoy. His fingers dance over the strings, and he sings softly, picking the soothing melody that almost instantly melts away the stress of the day from my body.

I shift in my seat, resting my legs over Jacob's lap and soaking in the sight of this incredibly handsome man serenading me on my deck. It's moments like these that I wish would go on forever. Jacob looks up from his guitar and locks eyes with me. He knows what he's doing to me. I've been doing the same to him. We've both been taking cold showers on the daily per my insistence that we move slowly with the physical side of our relationship.

Unable to resist any longer, I slowly lean into him and kiss him. His fingers pause on the strings, too distracted to play. Heat pools inside me, and I know I don't want to fight it anymore. I take the guitar from his hands and gently set it to the side. Taking the guitar's place on Jacob's lap, I press my lips to his. My fingers run through the hair at the nape of his neck, and I give myself over to him.

Jacob's hands slowly roam over my body, tentatively at first, but as I urge him on his hesitation fades away. His fingers nimbly work across my skin, shooting shivers through my body and heat to my core. Slowly, piece by piece, our clothing falls away, discarded on the deck floor.

He takes his time roaming my body with his mouth and filling me with desire. His warm breath sweeps over my chilled skin, and my breath hitches. This isn't my first time, but it's my first time like *this*. My first time with respect and gentle touches. My first time being cherished. And just when I think I can't take it anymore, Jacob claims me.

I CUDDLE UP TO JACOB, now inside the camper and lying on our bed. I'm blissfully soaking up the warmth of his arms around me. This is how it's supposed to be. My phone buzzes on the bed next to us, pulling me from my reverie.

Ben: You can't avoid me forever.

The blood rushes from my head, leaving me lightheaded. I close out of the text and toss my phone aside, not wanting to touch it. I know it's silly, but even touching a phone holding a message from him is more of a connection than I want to have, but I still can't bring myself to block his number.

"What's that about?" Jacob asks next to my ear. He must have seen the text.

"It's nothing. Really. Just ignore it. That's what I do." I try to sound nonchalant, but I'm confident Jacob can hear the edge in my voice.

"I'll talk to him if you want," he offers.

Yeah. That's just what I need.

"No, really. It's best to just ignore it."

I turn my head to meet his lips over my shoulder, hoping to distract both of us from the unwelcomed message. It works for now, at least, as I melt back into him, inviting him to take me all over again before falling into a blissful slumber in his arms.

I stopped pacing the floor to peer out the window at the sound of a car pulling into the driveway. Ben was finally home. He was supposed to be home from work a couple of hours ago. I watched as he stumbled out of his car, turned back to get something, and pulled a case of beer out, slamming the truck door shut.

"Hey, Ben," I said as he came in the door, then I hesitated, feeling out his mood. "How was work?"

"Same shit show, different day," Ben said and collapsed into his recliner, setting the case of beer on the floor next to him.

"We need to talk," I said my hesitancy replaced with anxiety. Ben scowled at me.

"About what?"

"About us," I said, barely above a whisper. "This isn't working for me."

Ben put a fresh cigarette in his mouth and lit it. He took a couple of puffs and cracked open a can of beer.

"I'm not in the mood for your bullshit today, Lacey." Ben grabbed the TV remote and flipped through the channels.

"And I'm over your bullshit, Ben!" Fear spread through me. Who knew what consequences I could expect from my outburst, but I didn't let the fear stop me. "All you do is drink and bitch and treat me like trash. You need to get yourself some help, Ben. I

can't go on like this any longer. You haven't been sober since Brian died!"

Ben stood from his recliner and moved toward to me. I stumbled back a couple of steps, then found the thread of courage I needed to hold my ground against him. His hot, smoky breath swept over my face, and I braced myself for what was to come.

"Don't. Ever. Speak. His. Name. Again," Ben snapped at me.

I forced myself to look up into his eyes.

"You need help."

"Get the fuck out of my house!" Ben roared, his spit sprinkling my skin. I tried to step toward our bedroom to get my stuff, but he put out his arm and blocked the way. "Now!" he screamed.

When I failed to move, Ben grabbed hold of me and dragged me toward the door. I fought to free myself, desperate to get away from him, but his strong hands were everywhere.

"Lacey, it's okay. It's okay. Wake up. It's just a dream."

I start to come to, thrashing against the hands holding onto me.

"You're safe, baby. You're safe." Jacob's voice gently drifted into my ears. "It was just a dream."

I stop thrashing against him, and he pulls me close to kiss my forehead. Tears soak my cheeks, and I feel sticky with sweat. I push away from Jacob and sit up in bed. Still shaky, I get up and go to the kitchen for a bottle of water from the fridge. I breathe in deeply and take a drink. Jacob comes up behind me and reaches for me, but I hold out a hand that tells him to stop.

"I just need a minute," I say. Hurt and worry fill his eyes. "I'm okay. I just need a minute."

I flip on the light even though it makes us both squint with the sudden brightness.

"What can I do?" Jacob asks.

"Go back to bed. I'll join you in a minute. I'm just going to finish my drink first."

Jacob continues to watch me with careful eyes. Several seconds pass. Finally, he turns back to the bed like I told him.

He's doing what I asked him to do, but I know this isn't going to be the end of it.

THE NEXT MORNING, I'm jarred awake by the sound of Jacob carrying his duffel bag of clothes out the door. I'm lying on the bench where I spent the remainder of the night. The light I turned on last night is still on. I sit up slowly, sore all over, and follow him out the door.

"What are you doing?" I ask, my mind still hazy from the lack of rest. Jacob already has his bag in the back of his truck and is walking back up to the deck where I'm standing.

"I think staying here was a bad idea. I'm going to just suck it up and go stay at my parents' house," he says.

I can see that he wants to reach out and touch me, but he's still afraid to. Afraid of how I'll respond.

"What? Why? You don't have to leave." Panic washes over me.

"I kind of think I do, Gypsy. I don't know what happened last night, but it felt like I was the cause of it. I don't want to stay here if it's going to hurt you."

"No. No, it wasn't you. Please don't go." I hold out my hand to him. Jacob slowly moves toward me, taking tentative steps as though he might spook me.

"I don't know what to do," he says, now only inches from me but still not touching me.

"I'm okay. It was just a bad memory." I wrap my arms around him, and he gradually hugs me back.

"Of your ex?" Jacob asks hesitantly.

"Yes."

"Did it happen because I was here in your space?"

I look up at him now, wanting him to see that I'm speaking the truth.

"No. He has a habit of sneaking up on me when I least expect it." Jacob pulls me closer now. "Please stay."

jacob

"I don't know the guy very well," George says. "I only met him a couple of times, back while we were all in college. He gave me a bad feeling, but I couldn't put my finger on it back then. According to Jay, he messed Lacey up pretty badly. You should be talking to Lacey about it though, man."

After a stiff, uneasy morning together, I told Lacey I had some work stuff to take care of. I drove over to see George at his ranch, hoping that he could give me some clarity.

"It's not something she seems too interested in talking about."

I pick up a brush and start brushing down my side of the horse separating me and George. Thinking about someone hurting Lacey makes my stomach churn and my anger flare.

"Honestly, I don't even think she said too much to Jalynn about it, either. Who knows though, dude? Maybe all of the tension was because you're a sorry lay," George suggests, trying to lighten the mood and managing to get a chuckle from me.

"I told you, nothing happened."

"As in truly nothing happened, or as in, she made you promise not to kiss and tell?" George prods.

"Nothing happened," I lie again.

"Yeah . . . you keep saying that. But you're a lousy liar."

SITTING IN LACEY'S DRIVEWAY, I wonder whether I should even be here. The answer that keeps coming back to me is that I need to trust Lacey's answer. If she wants me here, I need to believe it. I see her peer out the window and realize I need to get inside before she comes to the wrong conclusion about my delay.

"Hey, babe," she says as I walk in, "did your work errand go okay?"

"Yeah, it went fine." I close the door behind me and take a seat on the bench to pull off my boots.

"Want something to drink?" Lacey opens the fridge door and inspects our options, not waiting for an answer from me.

"We need to talk, Lacey," I say. She looks over her shoulder at me.

"I know," she says and sits next to me on the bench. "I hardly know where to start."

Lacey tells me about the dream from last night and how Ben wanted her to quit her job. Ben was working nights at the factory outside of town, so her boss agreed to schedule her around Ben's factory schedule. That way, she could continue working without Ben knowing.

"Nearly nine years of my life was spent in a relationship with him. I never saw a future without him in it until somehow our relationship transitioned from me nursing the bruises his dad left on him to Ben leaving bruises on me," Lacey says.

"Do you love him?" I ask in a hushed voice.

"I did, but our bond was different. It wasn't a storybook romance. He didn't make me feel weak at the knees. We were both broken in a way that even Jalynn couldn't understand."

"Did Jalynn not know what was going on?"

"Not really. I hid it as best I could. I knew she wouldn't understand why I stayed with him. She actually tried to get me to break up with him senior year of high school. She said he was manipulating me, and she didn't like the way he treated me. But I didn't listen. I was already in love with him by that point."

Lacey stands and crosses the room into the kitchen where she leans back against the counter to continue. I sit quietly and wait until she's ready to talk. Her hands are trembling, though she tries to still them on the counter behind her, and I just want to wrap her up in my arms and keep her there, safe.

"Jay and I got an apartment together our freshman year of college. Ben was furious. He moved, too, even though he wasn't taking classes. He just didn't want me living two hours away. At the time, I thought it was sweet of him. I didn't realize it was because he didn't trust me.

"We fought constantly. He was so jealous of everyone, even Jalynn. The week before finals of our first semester, he stopped by our apartment unannounced. I was in the kitchen with a guy Jalynn had brought home the previous night. Ben lost his shit."

I watch as Lacey's fingers graze the scar above her eyebrow that I've always been curious about. She comes back to the bench and takes a seat facing me again, her knees pulled up to her chest.

"That's what this scar is from?" I ask, reaching over and running my thumb gently down the scar. I feel sick thinking of some bastard leaving cuts and bruises on my girl.

"Yes."

"And you stayed with him?" I ask.

"No, we broke up. But that summer, Grammy passed away, and Ben was there, being sweet again. When school started again, Jalynn moved in with George, and I moved in with Ben. We were only a little over halfway through the school year when Ben's brother died, though, and I moved home with him. I let a lot of stuff slide for way too long, blaming his behavior on the grief. Things started to change for me after I found out through the gossip mill in town that he'd started sleeping with a girl from his work. It took finding out about him cheating on me to realize how far my life had spiraled.

"Ben came home that night to me sitting in the den with my bags packed and the plane ticket from Jalynn in my hand. I told him I was done. I was leaving him. He yanked the plane ticket out of my hand and tore it to pieces. I stood, mustering up what little courage I had, and went toe-to-toe with him. He threatened me. Told me the only way I'd ever leave him is if I was dead."

"How long ago was that?" I ask through gritted teeth.

"It was about two months before I got here. I knew if I was going to get away, I was going to have to have a better plan. He wasn't going to let me go. I already had some cash hidden away, and I saved up every penny I could and searched the papers for a cheap camper. I didn't know how much I'd have to move around and didn't want to have to worry about rent and deposits for a place to stay. One evening after Ben left for work, I bought the camper and made a run for it."

"Does he know where you are?" I ask.

"No. I don't think so. And I don't think he would come this far after me even if he knew where to look."

"Are you sure about that?"

"He's probably replaced me with his new little toy from work. I just pity the poor girl. She has no idea what she's got herself into, I'm sure."

"But he knows how close you and Jalynn are. He probably knows that would be the most likely place for you to go. If I were looking for you, that's where I'd start."

"If you're trying to make me feel safe, it's not working," Lacey says, her brow creasing with concern. "He wouldn't come all this way," she says again, as though she's trying to convince herself. "I'm not worth all the trouble to him."

"You're worth all the trouble in the world, Gypsy." I kiss her head and pull her tightly against me, wishing I could chase her demons away.

On Sunday, Lacey and I walk into my parents' house for the weekly family dinner. The house is filled with the aroma of a feast, and I know Mom must be trying out recipes in preparation for Thanksgiving dinner. My stomach grumbles as I take in the fancy spread.

When we make it to the start of dinner without Mia giving me a hard time, I should have known something was up. Turns out, she was just waiting for the perfect moment to light the match and watch me burn.

"Tell me," Mia begins, "how's it going living together? Has Jacob overstayed his welcome yet, Lacey?"

I choke on my fucking sweet potato, sucking a chunk down into my lungs. My face heats up, and I'm coughing and gasping for air, unable to speak. Lacey stares back at Mia like a deer in headlights. Our living arrangement isn't exactly a secret, but I definitely haven't filled my parents in yet, it being temporary and all.

"Excuse me?" Mom asks, her eyes wide as saucers as she looks back and forth between me, Lacey, and Mia.

Damn it, Mia.

"You okay there, son?" Dad asks. He reaches over and hands me my glass of water. I take it from him and gulp it down.

"Oh. Did I let the cat out of the bag? Oops," Mia says, pushing the food around on her plate and stifling a laugh.

"You moved in together?" Mom asks.

I finally clear my lungs of the sweet potato, though they're still on fire, and sparing a glance for Mia, I turn my attention back to Mom. Now is as good a time as any to get this out of the way, I guess.

"Ashley got me kicked out of the house," I explain. "I didn't move in with Lacey. I've just been staying with her while I get Nana's house livable."

"Anyone interested in taking bets on how long that's going to take him?" Mia pipes up, earning another glare from me. She might be laughing now, but she won't be laughing when it's her turn.

"You know our door is always open if you need a place to stay, Jacob," Dad points out.

"I know, Dad. And I appreciate that. Lacey was nice enough to allow me to stay with her for a while, though."

"And this way you don't have to find a place to go park when you're feeling extra friendly," Mia adds, wiggling her damn eyebrows at me.

I glance over at Lacey. She's focusing excessively hard on her plate, one hand shielding her reddened face. Damn Mia.

"Thanks for that, Mia," I say. I reach under the table and give Lacey's knee a squeeze, hoping she doesn't break up with me after this.

"Good point," Dad says, now joining in with Mia. "Though maybe it could be fun feeling like a teenager again." He shrugs. "I know your mother and I like to—"

"Nope . . ." I interrupt him. "I've got to stop you there, Dad. I do *not* want to hear you finish that sentence."

Lacey is never going to agree to come back to another family dinner, and I can't say that I blame her.

"Has Jacob taken you over to Nana's house, Lacey?" Mom asks, taking mercy on us and changing the subject. Lacey's gaze shoots up from her plate to Mom.

"No, he hasn't."

"Jacob, you should take her over there before you start your work on the place. I bet Lacey could give you some good tips on the remodel. You might appreciate knowing her preferences later down the road," Mom says.

Great. Now Mom is ready to start planning for grandkids from me and Lacey.

"Can we move the conversation on to something other than mine and Lacey's relationship?" I ask.

"No fun," Mia whines.

I pick up a roll and chuck it across the table at her.

CHAPTER THIRTY-THREE

I feel around under the blankets for my panties Jacob helped me lose. Feeling the lacey material, I slip them on and tuck myself back into Jacob's chest. He runs his fingers through my hair, and I cannot believe that I've missed out on this all these years.

Sex with Jacob is unlike anything I experienced with Ben. With Jacob, I feel cherished and wanted, like I'm all he could ever need. He makes my head spin with pleasure as I give myself over to him, and he gives himself to me, too. I could spend days right here with him, being adored and indulging in his touch.

"I should get up. I'm supposed to be at my first client's ranch in an hour," Jacob says, not making any effort to get out of bed.

"I should get up, too." I groan and plant another kiss on his lips.

"What are your plans for this evening? Do you want to go over to Nana's house with me? I'd love for you to see it."

"Taking your mother's advice?"

"I mean, it wouldn't hurt. You might decide you like having me around so much that you decide to hide in my suitcase when I leave." He pokes at my sides, making me squirm.

"When do you want to head over there?"

"I was thinking I could drop you off at work this morning so we can ride over there together after without having to worry about an extra vehicle."

"That sounds perfect."

Jacob kisses my forehead, then climbs over me to get out of the bed. I admire the view while he searches for his boxers in the covers and struts into the bathroom to shower.

THE HOUSE IS BEAUTIFUL, even if run-down. The exterior of the two-story farmhouse has chipped white paint. The wraparound porch is decorated with ornate trim and has ample space for some rocking chairs. A barn and an outbuilding stand behind the house, and off to one side stands a small building with a crescent moon painted on the door. The picket fence in the front yard is collapsed on one side and barely standing on the other. Patches of tall weeds indicate where flower beds were once tended to in the overgrown yard.

Jacob takes my hand and, with nervous excitement dancing in his eyes, leads me to the front porch. He pulls back the screen door with a loud screech from the rusty hinges and unlocks the doorknob. With a small twist of the knob, he pushes the door open, and without warning, he scoops me into his arms and carries me through the door. I giggle with surprise and wrap my arms around his neck.

Inside the house, Jacob leads me from room to room, giving me the grand tour of the home, memories and stories included. The large living room is where so many family gatherings once took place and holidays were spent. The kitchen and dining area are where the family gathered for holiday meals, and the office is where Jacob would sit and talk with his grandfather, look through his books about veterinary medicine, and where Jacob first decided he wanted to be a vet. Many of the books were still there, packed away in boxes on the desk. We enter a large room that once served as another family room, and Jacob explains how he planned to turn it into a master suite, leaving four bedrooms upstairs for the children he hoped to have one day. It is evident that the house played a significant role in his childhood.

"What do you think?" Jacob asks after we finish the walk-through.

"It's beautiful, Jacob. I can only imagine what it looked like in its old glory days," I say. "It will be a wonderful home to raise a family in."

"That's the plan. It still requires a lot of work to be done, though. I've also thought of closing my office in town and running my business from here like my grandfather did."

"You'll get it all done eventually. It's a big undertaking for someone to do on their own, especially with a full-time job and life to maintain at the same time. It will make someone a very happy home once it's all done."

"Would it make you happy? Could you picture yourself being the one raising a family here?" Jacob asks.

"With you?" I raise an eyebrow at him.

"I mean . . . I wouldn't rightly want to picture you making a family here with anyone else."

I'm quiet for a minute, circling back around the room like I'm having difficulty deciding. I settle back by Jacob again and wrap an arm around his waist.

"I could see it," I say, looking up at him. "I mean, with only four bedrooms for the kids they'll have to double up at least, but sharing a bedroom builds character, right?"

Jacob's eyes bulge.

"How many kids are we talking about?"

"Do we have to put a limit on it?" I hold his gaze as the worry creases in his forehead deepen some more.

"Well, uh . . ." Jacob steps away, rubbing a hand on the back of his neck. He turns back to me. "I mean, it might be worth having a conversation about so we know what we are signing up for."

I burst into a fit of giggles and hug him tightly.

"I'm teasing, babe. Breathe. Four bedrooms is plenty."

Jacob kisses the top of my head and lets out an exaggerated sigh of relief.

WE SPEND most of our evenings at Jacob's Nana's house, working together on the renovations well into the night. Occasionally, George and other friends come spend the weekend with Jacob at the house, helping him with the many projects. We make some significant alterations to the layout of the first floor, taking down the wall separating the front living room from the kitchen and dining room. Jacob builds a large island to provide separation but still allow an open concept perfect for entertaining.

We frame out a large master bathroom and walk-in closet in the large family room in the back of the house, creating a master suite. The house is slowly coming together. Soon, it will be ready for Jacob to move in. There's already talk from his family about him hosting Christmas dinner.

"I have a surprise for you," I tell Jacob, leading him toward his grandfather's old study in the back of the house. During the last three weeks of renovations, I've had my own project I've been working on.

"Does it involve you getting naked?" Jacob asks, grinning from ear to ear.

Admittedly, I've been insatiable, and Jacob has been more than happy to oblige.

"No, dirty boy. Nobody is coming unclothed," I assure him. "Remember when you first brought me over here to see the house and you told me about your grandfather's study? You told me about the talks you had with him in that study and how that's where you decided to follow in his footsteps and become a vet?

"Yes."

We come to a halt in front of the closed study door.

"Well . . ." I swing the door open and flip on the light. "I thought maybe you would like to have a home office, too."

I step to the side and let Jacob take in the cleaned and painted office. The large wooden desk his grandfather used sits in the middle of the room, restored to its former beauty. Large matted pictures of Jacob and his grandfather working together in his grandfather's vet business hang on the walls.

"Gypsy"—Jacob slides his fingers across the desk as he walks by, taking in every detail—"this is remarkable."

"Do you like it?" I ask nervously from the hallway.

"Like it? I love it, Lace. You have no idea how much this means to me. Thank you. Where did you get these photos from?"

"I saw them in your family albums when your momma was showing me your baby pictures. She helped me get them enlarged and framed."

I rise up on my toes, standing next to him now, and kiss Jacob's cheek.

"This doesn't mean you get out of helping me finish painting the upstairs, though," Jacob teases.

"Gosh, you're so bossy," I say, accompanying my exaggerated whiny tone with a dramatic eye roll.

"You didn't complain about that last night, though, did you?" Jacob says with a smirk.

Heat rushes over my body at the mention of our recreational activities from last night.

No, I most certainly didn't complain . . .

"When will the people come to install the kitchen countertops?” I ask, changing the subject to force the unchaste thoughts away, avoiding distraction.

“The week after Thanksgiving,” Jacob says with a smile, and we make our way back upstairs to finish painting. His smiles are a lot more frequent these days. “When they’re done, and the flooring is finished upstairs, it will be ready to live in.”

“That’s not long,” I say, sadness creeping in at the thought of Jacob leaving the camper. “Next week is Thanksgiving.”

Jacob glances up at me, I’m sure because he can hear the disappointment I tried to keep in. He comes over to me, lifting my face to his with a finger under my chin.

“Thinking about sneaking into my suitcase after all?”

“Maybe.” I fold my arms across my chest.

“I don’t want to lose any time together, either, Gypsy. But I want the decision of us living together to be determined by the progression of our relationship, not by convenience.”

“You’re right.”

We turn back to painting. Silence fills the room as we work. We’re close to finishing, as we’re now both working on the same wall. I break the silence with a question.

“What are the holidays like with your family?”

“Crazy. Everyone comes to town, and most everyone stays at my parents’ house. Mom outdoes herself every year with the food and activities. She loves being a grandmother.”

“That sounds nice. I always felt like holidays were for large families, not small ones like I had. Before my parents’ accident, we spent the holidays at my grandparents’ house, but I was the only child. I didn’t have any cousins. I didn’t even have any aunts or uncles. It was just the five of us, and I don’t remember much from back then. After my parents passed, it was just me and my grandparents.”

I go quiet again, and Jacob comes over next to me and wraps me in a hug. It’s not the first time I’ve found myself wishing I came from a large family like Jacob’s. After a few moments, Jacob pulls back and smiles down at me.

"This is the year that changes for you," Jacob says. "From now on, you can spend the holidays with my family."

Jacob reaches over and swipes a finger down my nose. With widened eyes, I touch my nose where his finger has just been.

"You didn't!" I look down at my fingers. Sure enough, gray paint covers them. "Not your brightest idea, mister."

I lunge at him, unwashed paintbrush in hand.

Minutes later, following a performance of shrieks and screams, we are both covered in paint and calling a truce. We work together to clean up the floor and put away our supplies. I give Jacob a look-over, then examine myself.

"We can't get in your truck like this. We'll ruin it," I say.

"I've got an idea," Jacob says with a mischievous grin.

With the water still turned off to the house due to a recently discovered leak, Jacob leads the way to the water spigot in the backyard. Tossing our ruined clothes aside, we stand in our underwear and let the cold water from the hose wash down our now goose-bump-ridden skin.

"You're frozen," Jacob observes, turning off the hose. "Your lips are turning blue. Let me warm you up," he says with a wicked grin.

"I don't know. You don't appear to be up to the task," I tease.

"If I'm not, I'll keep at till I am," Jacob says, pulling my shivering, wet body against his.

"Ahem." A throat-clearing sound comes from a man who stands grinning at the corner of the house. He looks down at his shoes.

I shriek, eyes widening in horror, and hide behind Jacob. Jacob appears unphased by his own role in the exhibition and walks right up to the man to greet him.

"Jesse! When did you make it into town? I thought you weren't coming till Monday," Jacob says.

"We decided at the last minute to hop in the car and come a few days early. Didn't see a reason to wait," Jesse responds.

"Plus, I couldn't believe all of the drama I've been hearing about my baby brother, so I figured I better come see for myself." Jesse motions to me still hiding behind Jacob. "I have to say, I think I've been getting the watered-down version of the happenings around here." Jacob throws his head back and laughs.

"It's all in the name of keeping things interesting," he explains. Jacob grabs the lone flannel he found in his truck before our yard bath and wraps it around me. "Where's the rest of your crew?"

"They're sitting in the driveway."

"Tell you what, if you'd be so kind as to turn around for my girl, I'm going to help her to my truck, and you can follow us to her place. I think she'd prefer to be dressed when I formally introduce the two of you."

"Probably a good idea," Jesse agrees with a chuckle.

"You get in the shower first," I tell Jacob once we are safely inside the camper. "I'm not going out there, anyway."

"What? Why not?" Jacob asks. "You'll love Jesse and Steph and the kids."

"I'd love them more if they didn't know what I look like in my underwear!" I retort.

Jacob rolls his eyes.

"I'll take a quick shower, and you can take your time," Jacob says.

He reaches into the shower and turns the water on to warm up while he takes his boots and boxers off. Mere minutes later he emerges, clean and in fresh clothes. He gives me a chaste kiss as he walks by.

"Please come out and meet them when you are done."

With that, he walks out of the camper and merrily greets his sister-in-law and nieces and nephews. Joyful sounds of reunited family seep into the camper while I strip off my underwear and take my turn in the shower.

Once out of the shower, I comb out my long, wet hair and tie it up in a bun on the top of my head. I pull on a new pair of jeans and one of Jacob's old college sweatshirts. Examining myself one more time, I decide it will have to do. I take in a deep breath to steady my nerves and step out on the deck.

Four kids are running around by the firepit, playing happily together. A fifth child, about a year old, sits on his mother's lap. Jacob stands and pulls a chair over for me.

"Jesse, Steph, this is Gypsy." I smack Jacob's arm. "I mean, Lacey. Lacey, my oldest brother Jesse, and his better half, Steph."

"Nice to meet you," Jesse says. "Sorry about intruding on you earlier. Had I realized the mischief my little brother would be causing, I would have called first. Lesson learned."

"No, I'm the one who should apologize. I'm not sure how he does it, but he always seems to be at the root of my lack of judgment," I say. I give Jesse a friendly hug, then hug Steph. "Be thankful you missed the show," I tell her.

"Sweetie, if there's one thing you'll learn about these Jones boys, it's that every last one of them is full of the most awful ideas. And they all have an astonishing ability to make them sound so good," Steph advises me good-naturedly.

"Now, what's all this 'gypsy' business about?" Jesse asks.

My cheeks instantly light on fire, and I know I must be beet red. I try to gather myself enough to make a reply, but Jacob beats me to it.

"This is Lacey's gypsy wagon," Jacob says, motioning to the camper.

"Gypsy wagon, huh? So that must make Lacey a real live gypsy then?"

"That's right. And a self-made one at that. I caught me a gypsy."

"Don't mind them, Lacey," Steph speaks up. "They're just

jealous they didn't ever come up with the idea of living in a camper. And Jacob, I don't see a ring on that finger of hers. I'm not so sure you've caught her yet."

"You have a point, Steph," Jacob agrees, glancing down at my hands. "But I have every intention of fixing that."

My eyes, ready to pop out of my head, shoot up from my hand to Jacob's face. We've talked about the possibility of our future together, but this is the first time Jacob has made such a blatant remark about it to someone else. He winks at me and reaches over to take my hand in his as he moves the conversation along.

The evening continues with good conversation and lots of laughter. The children make frequent trips onto the porch to talk to Uncle Jacob and convince him to come back and play tag with them again. I watch each interaction he has with them. He's going to be a fantastic dad, following in his own father's footsteps, no doubt. Jesse and Steph are just as lighthearted and friendly as the rest of the Jones family that I've met so far. I feel like I've known them forever. I wonder if the last brother I haven't met yet will break the mold of perfection I've seen run in this family so far.

THE WEEK of Thanksgiving is busy at work. The town believes in supporting the local businesses, and many of the residents ordered arrangements to beautify their homes for their Thanksgiving feasts. This means a lot more orders than we typically receive, plus the influx of orders from Mia's store as well.

On Wednesday evening, I carry in the bags of groceries to make Grammy's chocolate pecan pie per Maddie's request that I bring a dessert to Thanksgiving. Truthfully, I'm terrified to make a pie for Thanksgiving. I've met almost the whole Jones family, and I don't know how I'll ever measure up. I'm walking into this picture-perfect family as the hot mess I am. They treat me like I belong, but I have nothing to offer them.

I spend way too long trying to get the crust made and shaped perfectly in the pan. It doesn't look like Grammy's, but it is as close as I can manage to get it. I mix up the filling, double-checking the ingredient list to make sure I don't forget anything like I did the last time I baked. Maybe if I can just manage to bring a decent pie to dinner, I can believe that I belong.

Finally, I slide the pie into the oven and collapse on the bed next to Jacob where he is watching football on the TV he installed a couple of weeks ago. I yawn and snuggle into him while I wait for the pie to finish baking.

I'm not sure how long I stay like that, but I wake up coughing thanks to the smoke filling the small camper. The pie! Jumping off the bed, I rush over to the oven. When I open the oven door more smoke billows out, sending me into another coughing fit. I pull the pie out and set it on the counter. Jacob is up now, propping open the door and windows, trying to get the air circulating. I shrink down onto the floor, and immediately, tears flood my eyes and race down my cheeks.

"What's wrong, Gypsy? Are you hurt?" Jacob asks and drops down to his knees beside me.

"No, my pie!" I exclaim. "It's ruined. I've single-handedly ruined everything," I say, choking back sobs.

"No, you didn't ruin anything," Jacob assures me. "The pie looks great, babe, but if you don't want to bring it, it'll be okay. There will be plenty of dessert at dinner without yours."

I glare at him through the tears. I know he's trying to be helpful, but I also know he is lying about the state of my pie. Jacob stands back up and looks over the pie, trying to figure out how to salvage the situation, no doubt. I look at my watch. It's one thirty in the morning. We're supposed to be at his family's home first thing for a full day of festivities.

"Look here," he says, pulling me back up to my feet. "The

top is a little well done, but we'll just scrape it off." He grabs a knife and begins to unsuccessfully scrape the top of the pie. "Okay, so that's not working. Here, I'm going to cut out a small piece to show you how good it is. We can just drizzle it with chocolate to hide the burned spots. If anyone asks why some is missing, I'll just tell them I couldn't stay out of your delicious pie and snuck a piece."

Jacob picks the knife back up and begins cutting into it. He is unable to complete his first cut as the blade of the knife breaks apart from the handle. My sobs deepen. Jacob stops trying to fix the situation and wraps me in his arms instead, trying to console me. Jacob finally convinces me to come back to bed, promising he will help me deal with the catastrophe in the morning.

I wake up the next morning exhausted, mentally drained, and my eyes feel heavy and puffy from my crying last night. Jacob is asleep next to me. I look at the clock. We only have two hours to get to Jacob's parents' house. That's hardly enough time to bake a new pie. Maybe if I'm quick I can get it done without making us too late.

I decide to inspect the pie again in daylight to see if it is as bad as I remember. I stumble out of the bed and make my way over to the counter where I left the pie last night, only it's not burnt. No knife blade is sticking out of it. The pie looks perfect. Jacob is behind me now, wrapping his arms around me and resting his head on my shoulder. I look over my shoulder at him, feeling the tears well up again.

"You baked a whole new pie?" I ask. "How late were you up last night?"

"Not too late," he says, but I know it's a lie. "I couldn't sleep, so I figured I might as well do what I could to help out. No sense in lying around if I wasn't going to rest."

I turn in his arms and take in his sleepy, bloodshot eyes. I wrap my arms around his neck and press into him, kissing him as I push him backward toward the bed. When his heels are against the platform, I push him down onto the mattress and take a step back. I give him my best smoldering grin, then slowly shimmy my panties off my hips, letting the purple lace fall freely to the ground. Jacob's eyes meet mine.

"Oh . . ." Jacob says, realizing the reward he is about to collect.

I turn my back to him and slowly lift my oversized T-shirt inch by inch until I pull it over my head. Glancing back over my shoulder at him, I drop the T-shirt to the floor.

jacob

I grab the eye drops from my glovebox and put a few drops in my tired eyes. Seeing a smile light up Lacey's face this morning when she saw the pie was payment enough for the lack of sleep. Her little display of gratitude after the fact was the icing on the cake. I yawn and pat Lacey's leg as we sit in the driveway of my parents' house

"You ready for this?" I ask. She nods and leans in to kiss me. "Or we could just go back home." I give her a drowsy grin.

"Let's get inside," Lacey says. "They're going to start wondering where we are."

I climb out of the truck and take the pie from Lacey, holding her hand while she slides out after me. We walk hand-in-hand up the sidewalk, and as we make it to the front steps, the door swings open. My other brother, Joseph, answers the door. Joseph looks back and forth between the two of us, eyebrows raised.

"Joseph, this is Lacey. Lacey, this is my brother, Joseph," Jacob says.

"You two look awfully cheerful to look so tired. I remember those days, the days before our sleep deprivation was the product of our previous sleepless nights."

"Maybe you're just doing things all wrong," Jacob suggests and gives his brother a hug.

"Maybe. You're just in time. We're getting ready to put our teams together for the football game."

A chorus of greetings echo through the house as Lacey and I walk inside. Mia comes bouncing up to Lacey, wrapping her in a hug. It's a drastic change from the way Mia used to greet Ashley, and I can't help but smile over how much my family loves my girl. I set the pie down on the dessert table Mom is arranging.

"Oh, Lacey, this pie looks incredible," Mom gushes.

"I really can't take credit—" Lacey starts.

"It's her grandmother's chocolate pecan pie recipe," I cut in. "She whipped it up last night while I was watching football."

"I can't wait to try a slice. I hope you at least cleaned up for her," Mom says.

"What are you talking about?" I scoff. "The kitchen is a woman's place."

Mom smacks my arm, but she doesn't smack me hard. She knows I'm joking. Making food has always been a family affair in our house.

The family is divided up into two teams for the football game, small children included. Mom sits out with the two youngest grandkids and referees the game. Lacey ends up on the opposite team from me, and we wind up nose to nose several times. Most of the touchdowns are scored by the grandchildren due to an unspoken rule that they can't be stopped by an adult. Occasionally, one of the kids is tossed over someone's shoulders or carried under an arm into the end zone. In the end, Lacey's team wins the game.

Three of my nieces come running up to me, pulling on my hands and begging me to come play. I make sure Lacey is in good hands, then let them sweep me away to the other side of the room. The girls command me to sit on a little pink stool, and then they attack me with a pink feather boa, a hot pink wig, and costume jewelry galore. I think I've almost appeased them when one of the girls pulls out her makeup bag. Two of them attack my face while the third paints my fingernails. Pink, of course.

I sit there and take it like a man, allowing my nieces to cake the purple eyeshadow on my eyelids, the pasty pink lipstick over my lips and into the scruff I always leave, and way too much blush on both cheeks. I inspect my painted fingernails, pink nail polish covering my fingers from the knuckles down.

I'm rescued when their mothers take mercy on me and collect their children to get them washed up for dinner. Several wolf whistles ring out when I rejoin the adults looking like a French whore. Jesse snaps a fucking picture on his phone.

"For posterity," he says and slides his phone back into his pocket after forwarding it to everyone in the room.

"I think I'm going to try to wash all of this off," I say and excuse myself to the bathroom.

As I leave the room, I hear Mom order everyone to clean up and get ready for our Thanksgiving dinner. Joseph and Jesse follow me into the bathroom.

"Looks like you and Lacey are getting pretty serious," Joseph says while we wash up.

"Yeah, you could say that," I reply.

"I found a little velvet box in the glovebox of your truck the other night when I was getting that deck of cards," Jesse chimes in.

"Well? Is it true?" Joseph asks.

"It might be," I say with a shrug. "Or it might be something else."

"Yeah, because there's so many things that come in little velvet boxes that men hide in their pickup trucks," Jesse says.

I chuckle and slap Jesse on the back.

"She's the one, guys. She's everything."

I'm grinning from ear to ear when I walk into the dining room, Jesse and Joseph on my heels.

Dinner is delicious. As usual, there are more dishes to try than there is space on my plate. Some of the sides were made by Mia and my sisters-in-law, but the bulk of the meal was prepared by Mom. She always goes overboard.

The tables are covered in her favorite silky white tablecloths with elaborate centerpieces of flowers, greenery, and pumpkins. Rather than paper plates, each place is set with her prized china that she saves for special occasions. Crystal goblets with elegant leaves etched around the glass are used for the punch. Each setting is complete with cloth napkins in a festive napkin ring and a place setting card assigning the seats around the table.

The children are seated at a lower table with a large coloring sheet of turkeys, leaves, pumpkins, and such. Paper turkeys and pumpkins line the center of their table and small jars filled with coloring utensils sit near each spot.

Once the meal is finished, the dishes are cleared away, and we all spread out across the plush couches and chairs in the large family room, designed specifically for occasions such as this one. I silently check in on Lacey. She seems to be soaking in every moment of the day, and I wonder if it's living up to her expectations. I'm about to succumb to a turkey coma when I hear her phone buzz. I glance over her shoulder as she pulls it out to check the message. It's Ben texting her again.

Ben: If you continue to ignore me, I will find you.

Lacey erases the message and puts her phone away. I don't know how much longer I can let this fucking guy harass my girl. I'm still concerned about how much she may be downplaying the situation. I check the time on my watch. As good as it is to spend time with my family, I'm ready to have Lacey to myself again. I yawn and stand up to stretch.

"Mom, it's been lovely as usual, but I'm beat. I think Lacey and I are going to head out for the night."

I hold out a hand for Lacey and pull her up from the couch. Following a chorus of goodbyes and a parade of hugs, I finally get my girl out the door. My family might be as wrapped up in her as I am.

"What did you think about today?" I ask her once we are in the truck and headed home.

"It was amazing. Better than I imagined. I felt like I was in the middle of a movie scene all day. That's how picture perfect your family is. It's exactly the type of family I always dreamed of having."

"I'm pretty sure if my family had to choose between us, they'd choose you," I say.

"Hardly. They're all so sweet to me, though."

"I wanted to tell you, the house will officially be ready in two weeks," I say, shifting the conversation.

"Oh." Lacey looks down at her hands in her lap. "I'm sure you're excited to have more space."

"Gypsy," I say, waiting for her to look at me, "I want you to move into the house with me."

"Are you sure?"

I chuckle at her surprise.

"Yes. Absolutely. What do you think? Will you move in with me?"

"Yes! Of course!" Lacey bumps into me, trying to give me a hug, and causes me to swerve on the road.

"Easy," I say and rest my hand on her knee. "Once we get moved in, I'm thinking we should sell the camper. I know some people who would be interested in buying it." Lacey suddenly stiffens beside me.

"We can't sell the camper, Jacob." Lacey looks up at me, alarm written across her face.

"If you're really set on having a camper, let's just buy a new one. It will hold the temperature inside better, and we can get something bigger and fancier."

"No, you're not understanding. I can't get rid of the

camper. What if I have to leave? I have to have my camper." Lacey watches me, her brow furrowed.

"What do you mean?" I turn off the truck and look at her. Now I'm the one who's fucking alarmed. Lacey adjusts in her seat, shifting to face me.

"If Ben finds me, I may have to leave," she says matter-of-factly.

"If Ben finds you, I'll kick his fucking ass, and you'll keep your ass right here in Montana with me," I say. My anger flares at the mere thought of Ben showing up.

"Jacob—" Lacey squeezes my hand still resting on her leg.

"No, Lacey, I'm being serious here. You can't just run. You wouldn't, would you? You wouldn't leave because of him?"

"Jacob, if Ben shows up—"

I shake my head and climb out of the truck.

I can't do this. What is she saying? How did such a perfect day take such a drastic turn? I breathe in the cold night air. Lacey is climbing out of the passenger door, but she stays on the other side of the vehicle and just watches me. I turn back to face her again, trying to hide the pain that is already claiming my chest.

"No, Lace. No. We're in this together. We're finally together."

"I know that, and you mean the world to me." Lacey takes a hesitant step toward me.

"But not enough to stay?"

It's happening. It's actually fucking happening. I'm not enough.

"It doesn't have anything to do with how I feel about you, Jacob."

"It's got everything to do with it. I'd do anything for you, Lacey. Don't you know that?"

"Ben broke me. I'm finally getting the pieces back together. If he finds me, I'm not going to wait around for him to break me all over again," Lacey says, standing next to me now.

"We're both a little broken, Lacey. It's when we're together that the pieces mend."

"Jacob, you're a wonderful man," Lacey says, touching her hand to my cheek. "You're more than I could ever have hoped for. I don't want to ever leave you, but I may not have a choice."

I pull away from her, not wanting her to see the pieces of me slowly, painfully, cracking and breaking apart again.

"You always have a choice, Lacey. Please. Tell me that I'm the choice you'll make if it comes down to it."

"I can't promise you that."

"I love you, Lacey. I've loved you from the start. I didn't know what it was at first, and I fought against it, but I know what it is now. I love you. I would follow you anywhere just to be with you. Would it really be that easy for you to just walk away from me, from what we have, and never look back?"

"Of course it wouldn't be easy."

"But you'd still do it?" I wipe a shaky hand over my face. My chest is ready to burst. "I can't do this again. I can't sit around waiting for the woman I love to throw it all away again." I turn back to my truck without looking at Lacey.

"Jacob, where are you going?" Lacey asks, taking a step toward me but stopping short. The realization of what I'm saying hits her. "Jacob, don't!" Tears break loose from her eyes and roll down her cheeks. I focus my eyes on the ground, unable to watch her cry.

"Lacey, I can't continue doing us knowing that one day you're just going to walk away." I look back up into her watery eyes. "I won't survive it."

I shake my head, out of strength to put it all into words. I climb into my truck and slam the door closed. Wilted is the best word I can come up with to describe her at that moment as I pull out of her driveway. She looks lost and alone, desperate for someone to take her into their arms and keep her safe from the world. And I hate myself for not being able to be that person for her.

lacey

Standing in the driveway, I watch Jacob leave, my arms wrapped tightly around my chest. My throat is tight and tears stream down my cheeks. I am unable to move. I try to make sense of what just happened, but the pain inside me overtakes my senses. I feel like I'm drowning, and the realization sinks in: he left me.

Finding the strength to push forward, I stumble down the driveway and head for Jalynn's house. She'll know what to do. The cold air stings my bare skin, the breeze whipping against my body.

I strike my fist against the door over and over again, barely able to breathe through the feeling of a million needles in my throat. My chest aches, and my sinuses burn from choking on the cold night air. The porch light illuminates the darkness. The door flies open, Jalynn and George standing on the other side.

"Heavens to Betsy, Lacey, what's going on? Are you okay?" Jalynn asks, pulling me inside. I shake my head, and the sobs finally escape my strangled throat as Jalynn wraps her arms around me.

"How's she doing?" George asks Jalynn down the hall.

"I'm worried about her, George," Jalynn replies. "She got up a couple times to use the bathroom, but I've hardly been able to get her to eat a single thing. Did you find Jacob?"

"Yeah. He's hiding out in his office in town. I brought up Lacey, and he told me I could leave. I don't know what happened."

Jalynn barges through the nursery door where I've been hiding away from the world in the bed Jalynn fixed up for me. She sits on the edge of the bed and pulls the covers down from my face. I groan and cover my face with my arms.

"Okay, Lace, I know your heart is broken, and the last thing you want to do is get up and face the world, but I've had about all of this I can take. I'm worried sick about you." Jalynn pulls my arms down from my face. "Look at me. I'm already about to pop, and if you keep stressing me out like this, you will single-handedly be the reason I go into labor. If I go into labor, I'm going to have a newborn and a sore cooch to worry about. I don't have the time or energy to take care of you, too, which means you'll waste away and die. I can't have that on my conscience, so I need you to sit up and talk to me." I groan again and turn away from Jalynn. "Lacey. Come on, girl. Talk to me."

Slowly, I turn and sit upright, scooting back against the bed's headboard. I thought I was out of tears to cry, but sitting up now, I feel my eyes beginning to fill again.

"Now what?" I choke out.

"That's better," Jalynn says. She looks surprised that I actually listened to her. "Now, tell me what happened, sweetie."

"Jacob broke up with me," I whisper.

"Why? Did you two have a fight?"

"He wants to sell the camper."

"Okay," Jalynn says, waiting for the punch line.

"I told him we can't, and he got mad. He doesn't understand."

"Okay," Jalynn says again. "I guess I don't understand, either. What's the problem?"

"Jay, I can't sell the camper. If I sell it, I won't have a way to get away if Ben shows up."

"Honey, on the off chance that Ben shows up, you aren't going anywhere. Ben is the one that will leave. Without you. You understand that, don't you?"

"No, if he shows up, I'll have to leave. He's not just going to let me be."

"Okay, here's what we're going to do," Jalynn says, turning on her motherly voice again. "You remember what you always used to tell me when I had a breakup?"

"Yeah . . . washing the sadness away is the first step to feeling better," I mumble.

"Exactly. So first, you're going to get up, shower, and put on clean clothes. Once you're respectable, you're going to eat, and we'll figure out a solution."

"I can't get up," I say, tears beginning to spill from my eyes again. "I'm too depressed. I just want to curl up under the covers and disappear."

"I know. I promise you, I get it. But I also know whenever you're upset about something, the first thing you do to feel better is clean yourself up. Lacey, your problem is one with a solution. You aren't going to lie in this bed and waste away over a problem we can fix."

I groan, but I know she's right. I pull myself up out of bed and head to the shower.

Feeling slightly more optimistic after a shower and some clean clothes, I slide onto the barstool at the kitchen island. Just as Jalynn said, a plate of food is waiting for me. Jalynn sits on the stool next to me with a mug of hot cocoa.

"Are you ready to figure this out?" she asks.

I respond with an unenthusiastic nod.

"What's the first problem we need to solve?" Jalynn asks, but she already knows.

"Jacob."

"Why'd you break up? Can you tell me about it?"

I scoot the food around on my plate, my chin resting on the hand that I have propped up on the counter.

"I don't want to sell the camper."

"Why does he care whether you keep it or not?"

"I don't know." My fork clatters onto my plate as I hide my face in my hands.

"Where are you going to live if you sell it?"

"He asked me to move in with him," I say through my hands. "Into his nana's house."

"What did you say?"

"I told him yes. And then he said he knows someone interested in buying the camper."

"What if it was you with the house and Jacob was moving out of an apartment to live with you, but he wanted to keep the apartment," Jalynn asks, rubbing my back.

"It's not the same, Jay. I have a legitimate reason to keep the camper. He wouldn't have any reason to keep the apartment."

"I bet he would think his reason for keeping the apartment was legitimate, too. Just something to think about."

Is she right? I push my plate away and pull my knees up to my chest, hugging them tightly against me. I haven't thought about it from Jacob's point of view. I haven't thought about what it might mean to him. To me, it's survival, but to him it's destruction.

Monday morning comes too quickly. I try calling Jacob on my way into work for the first time since our breakup. He doesn't answer, but I didn't really expect him to. Maybe after work I'll try to go by his office and see him.

The bells chime over the door as I walk in. Maddie is at the front counter, already updating the sidewalk sign, so I put my stuff down behind the counter and look over our list for the day.

"I wasn't sure I'd see you today," Maddie says.

"How's Jacob? Have you talked to him?" I ask.

"He's taking it hard, but he'll be okay. He took off early this morning to go fishing," Maddie says. "How about you, dear? How are you doing?"

"I've been better," I admit, forcing a weak smile. "I was hoping to talk to him today."

Maddie reaches over and squeezes my hand.

"I'm confident it will all work out in time," Maddie says. She picks up the sidewalk sign and takes it out front.

It's hard being at work. Instead of being occupied, I'm surrounded by reminders of Jacob: his mom, our mishaps in the greenhouse, our first kiss in the back room of the shop. The day is torturous but eventually comes to an end. I lock up the shop and head out, ready to curl up in bed and escape this day. My blood runs cold, though, when I turn the corner to my truck and find a familiar man leaning against the hood, waiting on me.

"What are you doing here, Ben?" I ask.

I want to turn and run, but I stand my ground, stretching my spine more to make myself look strong and unaffected by him. That's what they say to do when you encounter a bear, right? Make yourself look large?

"You didn't think I'd really just let you go, did you?" Ben asks, pushing off the hood of the truck and walking toward me.

I visibly bristle, despite my intentions to appear unfazed by him. He stops, hesitates for a moment, and seems to decide not to come any closer.

"What do you want?" I ask, straightening myself again.

"I want you, baby. I wanna talk."

"I don't have anything to say to you. How'd you find me?"

"I found you in the background of a picture Jalynn posted online, so I knew you were here. I drove out and been looking around town till I found your truck. Please, just have a conversation with me. Hear me out. I know you don't owe me anything, but I've come all this way. We can go over to the diner. I'll buy you dinner." Ben nods his head down the street toward the diner on the corner. I fold my arms in front of me. "Come on, don't be this way. I won't even touch you. I just want to talk. I've come all this way. Don't make me leave without the chance to talk."

"I can't make you leave. I can't make you do anything. I can't make you stop drinking or smoking or anything else, because I don't have control over what you do. Your choices aren't my problem anymore. And my choices? They're all mine to make," I say, pointing at my chest. "We can go to the diner and talk, but I'm not going back to what we were. It took me a long time when we were together to allow myself to want more than you could give me, and now that I've found it, I'm not letting you take it away from me. I'm worth more than that. I deserve better than you."

"You're right, Lacey. And my problems are mine to worry about. But please, have a conversation with me at least."

"Okay," I say after a beat of silence. "But then I don't want to see you again."

I follow several steps behind Ben as he walks down the block to the diner. My worst fear is manifesting, and I'm ready to get it behind me. I don't want to run anymore. Something is different about him. I can't put my finger on it, but something has changed.

Ben requests a table for two, and the hostess seats us in a booth in the middle of the diner. I recognize the girl who comes over to take our orders. Her name is Kate. She's been the waitress for me and Jacob several of the times we have stopped in to eat. Jacob always asks about her family. Kate looks warily from me to Ben and back again when she comes up to the table, but she takes our orders and goes to put them in without saying whatever must be going through her mind.

"Talk," I say. "What do you want from me?"

"I want you to come back with me," Ben says without hesitation.

"What makes you think I would want to? I left for a reason."

"I don't know. I hope you still love me, though."

I scoff at his comment.

"I've changed, Lace," he insists.

"How am I supposed to believe that?"

"You can ask around if you want. I changed jobs. I'm not at the factory anymore. I'm doing HVAC now, and I've almost finished the training. It's going to be a good change for me, Lacey. And I put the bottle away." Ben reaches in his pocket and tosses a round emerald chip onto the table. "That's my three-month chip."

I hesitantly reach over to pick up the chip and examine it.

"That's good, Ben. I'm happy for you," I say, handing the chip back to him.

"I know I've been really lousy to you. I didn't handle Brian's death the way I should have. I've said and done a lot of things to you I wish I could take back. But my therapist says I'm making good progress."

"You're in therapy now?" I ask, surprised.

"I go twice a week. It's really helped me escape the demons, you know? I wish I'd listened to you and gone when you suggested it. Maybe if I had, I wouldn't have screwed things up so bad."

"That's great, Ben."

"I know all of this is sudden. It's a lot to take in. But I'm actually doing it, Lace. And I'm doing it for you, baby." Ben reaches over and takes my hand in his, causing me to flinch on instinct, but I don't pull away. "When you left, my world didn't just fall apart, my world was gone. You are my world, Lace, my everything. I realized this life isn't worth living without you. I knew there was no way you would come back to me if I didn't change. You leaving made me realize how bad I'd become. In a sense, you leaving saved me. But I'm doing better now, and you're the only person I want to share it with. I know I still have amends I need to make with you. I don't expect you just to automatically trust me again, but do you think there is any chance you could forgive me? Is there any chance for us, Lace?"

"Ben, I don't know—"

"If you're open to it, I'll tell you what I was thinking. I have just over a week before I have to go back to work. Let me prove myself to you. If things are going okay, I'd like you to think about coming home with me and giving me another chance. You can stay at the house, and I'll stay at the motel until I earn your trust back. If it takes a month, fine. If it's six months, yeah, I probably deserve it. As long as it takes, Lace. I just want you to give me a chance. Let me prove myself to you, show you how I've changed."

This is it. This is what's different about him. The misery and malice are gone from his countenance. Instead, he carries a peace and hope that I don't know I've ever seen in him. For the first time in years, I'm looking into the innocent eyes of the first boy to steal my heart. All of the good memories flood my mind, melting my heart for him all over again. Unable to fight the urge, I reach across the table and stroke Ben's cheek. It's as though we're sixteen again and the center of each other's world.

"You've really changed, haven't you?" I ask. "I feel like I'm looking at the old Ben again."

"You are, baby. You are!"

I take Ben's hands in mine and give them a squeeze. Tears begin to fill my eyes, and despite all that's happened, I'm happy. The Ben I fell in love with is back.

jacob

My stomach growls as I pull back into town. I'm fucking starving. I stayed the night in Bozeman at Mia's. It felt good to have a bed to sleep in again. I pull my truck up in front of the diner and walk my tired, sore body inside. The hike into the canyon and back was harder on me than usual. Probably because of the lack of sleep and spending my nights on the damn couch in the office. I'm not as young as I once was.

The hostess seats me immediately. It's late morning, and there aren't many people here. Kate comes over to get my order and disappears again behind the counter to put it in. I still haven't found much reprieve from my breakup with Lacey, but the trip out into nature helped ground me a bit. When I made it back to my truck, I had a couple of missed calls from Lacey. I almost called her back but caught myself with my finger over the button. Talking isn't going to change anything. It would only prolong the pain for both of us. I don't have the strength to listen to her cry.

Kate sets down a plate of bacon, eggs, and pancakes in front of me along with the Coke I ordered. I give her an appreciative nod and dig in. It's the first warm meal I've had since Thanksgiving. I still need to call my brothers and apologize for not being around the rest of the weekend. I also need to call back a couple of clients and get back to work. I had my time to pity myself, but now it's time to get back to life and move on—if that's even possible.

I glance up. Kate is watching me. That's strange. I give her a nod and go back to eating, focusing on my plate. Moments later, she's standing at my table.

"Hey, Kate," I say. "Your mom doing okay?"

"Yeah, she's doing good," she says. "Can I stick my nose where it doesn't belong for a minute?"

"Um . . . sure," I say.

Kate slides into the other side of the booth.

"Are you and Lacey still together?" she asks.

I harden to her question.

"I'm not sure that's anyone's business," I reply and shove another bite of pancakes into my mouth.

"I know, but here's the thing," Kate says. "She was in here last night, and she was with another guy."

I bristle.

"She's free to do what she wants," I say in barely more than a growl.

"Well, I just thought it was odd. I've never seen him around here, but he definitely talked like he knew her well. I didn't hear everything . . ."

"I don't need to know what they were talking about, Kate."

"He just kept asking her to come home with him."

"What do you mean?" I ask, jealousy winning out.

"I don't know. He just kept saying he'd changed and asking her to give him another chance. Do you think it was an ex-boyfriend or something? Do you think she's going to move back to North Carolina?"

"Did you catch his name?" I ask, dread filling my chest.

"Oh, gosh . . ." Kate says. "Tim or Ken or Ben, maybe? One of those one-syllable names, I think."

I pull two twenties out of my wallet and hand them to Kate.

"Here, I need to get going," I say.

"Oh, this is too much."

"Keep the change." I slide out of the booth.

Jumping into my truck, I drive down the block to the flower shop. Lacey's truck is nowhere to be seen. Without wasting time, I hurry inside. Mom is standing at the counter when I walk in.

"Is Lacey here?" I ask.

"No, she called me last night saying she needed some time to work some things out," Mom says.

"What things? What does she need to work out?"

"I don't know, dear. She didn't say."

"Did she say when she would be back?" I ask, tapping my fist on the counter.

"She said she would let me know."

"Gotta go, Mom. Love you."

I turn and rush out the door. Back in my truck, I head straight for Lacey's. What happened while I was in the canyon? Was it Ben? Did he convince her to give him another chance? The thought of Lacey actually leaving makes me sick. I shouldn't have been so quick to run when we disagreed about the camper. That was weak of me.

I don't want to be without Lacey. Hopefully I haven't realized too late how much I need her. I never should have left like I did. Why didn't I stay and try to understand her reasoning? She has her own past, too. She's just as entitled to her insecurities as I am to mine. I was only thinking of myself. Reaching over and opening the glove box, I pull out the little black velvet box and stuff it into my pocket. I've got to make this right before I lose my chance and lose Lacey for good.

I pull into Lacey's driveway in a panic, hoping she's home and hoping she's alone. But her truck and camper are both gone. My heart drops. She's not here. All that remains is the deck George built her. I'm too late.

Fuck.

She's gone.

I climb out of my truck and pull out my phone to dial Lacey's number. It goes straight to voicemail. I hang up the phone and walk over to the hammock. My body collapses into the frozen threads of the hammock, swinging gently back and forth, as the reality of what I lost and the finality of Lacey being gone sinks in. Pulling the velvet box out of my pocket, I flip it open to look at the ring. Days ago, this ring represented a hope I thought I'd lost. It represented the love I hadn't expected to find and the future I was euphoric to begin with her.

Snapping the box closed, I stand from the hammock and pitch the little velvet box across the empty lot. I yell in frustration and kick over the bench by the firepit, storm back to my truck, and drive away.

Back in town, I stop by my office to grab my camping gear. I need my small insulated tent and other cold gear for this time of year. I load my hiking pack with the necessities and toss the pack in the back of my truck. I make quick work of packing and climb back into my truck. I pull my phone back out, this time to text Mia.

> Me: Headed to the canyon. Be gone a few days. Let mom know for me.

> Mia: You know how pissed mom gets when you stay out overnight this time of year. That why you want me to break it to her?

> Me: Mia, please.

> Mia: Everything okay?

> Me: no

> Me: see you in a few days

I put my phone up and drive out of town. This is the last

place I want to be. Lacey is all over my memories of this town. I won't find any peace here. I need to go somewhere I can forget. Determined not to break, I press my foot down on the accelerator and hightail it down the road.

I CLIMB out of my sleeping bag after the sun has risen and layer my clothing on. I've been in the canyon for three nights now. Between the small insulated tent, a mylar blanket laid on the floor of the tent for extra insulation, and a liner in my hot core sleeping bag, I've survived through the cold nights easily enough. The thermometer outside my tent reads seventeen degrees when I step out into the crisp morning air. I rub my hands together, trying to create enough friction to give them extra warmth.

Putting my gloves back on and taking my pot with me, I walk down to the river's edge to fish out some water. I carry the water back up to my camp, setting it aside in the snow while I get my fire going again. I pull out a bag of cotton balls. Taking a couple out, I cover them in petroleum jelly, position them under my tinder, and light them. Once the tinder catches, I slowly add some of the wood I kept dry by wrapping it in a tarp.

I boil my pot of water, killing any possibility of bacteria, and give myself something hot to warm myself with from the inside. I watch the water flowing down the river and sip on my hot water. I know Mom is probably furious with me and stricken with worry. I'd hoped being out here in nature would wipe my thoughts of the things that are lying so heavy on me, but that hasn't worked this time. Instead, I've had ample time and freedom to sulk and wallow in my misery. No, escaping isn't possible. Today, I'll pack up and hike back out of the canyon. Maybe I'll get Mia to come and drown my sorrows with me, but I know the best thing for me at this point is to get back to work.

Nana's house should be ready to move in to. That's another thing I'll have to face with Lacey gone. The house will be a constant reminder of my loneliness and the loss of the future I thought I was going to have with Lacey. Every thought of myself in that house had Lacey right beside me. The hurt may never go away. I toss the rest of my water and pull my pack out of the tent. Putting away the sleeping bag and blankets, I disassemble the tent and pack it.

The snow crunches under my boots as I hike back out of the canyon, my pack on my back. I have four miles to hike out to my truck. Four miles of walking to contemplate my poor choices that landed me here.

As I hike, I start making a plan of action for once I get home, trying to keep my mind occupied. I'll get moved into Nana's house first thing. I'm not interested in sleeping on the couch at the office any longer. I need to visit the McAllen ranch for a herd health visit. That will take a good amount of my time.

I'll start moving my office to Nana's, too, like my grandfather had it. Lacey fixed it up better than I could've imagined. I didn't think my grandfather's desk was going to be salvageable, but somehow, she managed to restore it to its former glory.

Lacey.

The hole in my chest gapes with the thought of her. This isn't going to be easy, and if the way she keeps coming to mind is any indication, it isn't going to be quick, either. I wonder if she's made it back to North Carolina yet. Is she safe? Has she thought about me?

I toss my backpack into the back of my truck and climb inside to start the engine, warming it up for a minute. My phone is waiting in the glove box for my return. I didn't take it into the canyon because I don't have service out there anyway. Pulling it out, I find the battery is dead, so I plug it in to charge on my way into town. Hopefully the heat will start blowing soon. I climb out of the truck again to scrape my windshield and mirrors, then start my drive home.

The closer to town I get, the worse the gnawing in my chest becomes. Maybe being out in the canyon was helping more than I realized. I wish I could see her just one more time. I need her to know how I feel about her, and I want her to come back to me.

Maybe I should go there. Maybe if I show up in North Carolina and pummel Ben's fucking ass I can convince her to come back to Montana with me. Or will she send me away without a second thought?

Lost in my thoughts, I drive out to where Lacey's camper used to sit. I pull into the driveway, hoping that her camper has magically reappeared. Maybe I'll wake up and discover this was all a horrible dream. The lot still sits empty. The deck is still isolated. There aren't any tracks in the snow. Even the bench I kicked over a few days ago remains lying on its back, covered in fresh snow. I back out of the driveway. Noticing George's truck at home as I'm passing by, I make a quick decision to pull in. Maybe George at least knows if she's okay.

I stretch and walk up to the front door, taking a minute to gather myself, feeling more emotions than I want to share with my friend right now. Once I feel like I'm in control, I knock on the door. The door swings open, and my breath departs from my body. I freeze, eyes locked on the figure in front of me.

Lacey.

Coming to again, I step through the doorway and plow into her, enfolding her in my arms, knocking her backward a few steps. I nuzzle my nose into her hair and inhale her scent. If I'm hallucinating, I hope the mirage never disappears. Lacey wraps her arms around my neck, hugging me back. After several minutes, I pull away, holding her at arms-length and looking her over.

"Are you okay?" I ask in a choked voice.

"I'm fine. Are you okay?" Lacey asks, confusion in her eyes.

"No. Yes. No. I don't know," I say. "I thought you'd left.

Kate said you were in the diner with Ben. Your camper's gone. I thought I'd never see you again."

"No, I'm here. I've been right here."

I pull Lacey back into me and hold her tight. Moments pass and I let her loose again.

"You're not leaving?" I ask.

"No, Jacob. I'm not going anywhere."

"And Ben?"

"He's gone," Lacey says.

I hug her tightly again, my mind spinning so fucking fast I can barely keep up with myself. It's no wonder Lacey stares at me, her look startled and confused.

"I've got to go," I say urgently and turn back out the door. Barely stepping out onto the porch, I turn back around and smash my lips into Lacey's. My hand goes to her hair, holding her close. Her warmth spreads back through my body as our mouths touch, and I remember how easily I can lose myself in her. Pulling away again, I jog out to my truck, hop in, and tear out of the driveway, catching a glimpse of Lacey in the doorway, her hand to her lips. George is now standing behind her.

I pull back into the empty, snow-covered lot and jump out of my truck. Rushing over to the hammock, I turn to face the lot again, thinking. I'm momentarily pulled from my thoughts when George pulls in behind my truck. Snapping back to the task at hand, I stride several feet forward and drop to my knees in the snow, feeling around and digging with my hands.

"What are you doing?" George asks, bewildered.

I glance up at him briefly and continue my search, crawling toward the deck.

"I'm looking for something."

"What are you looking for?"

"A ring. I'm looking for Lacey's ring."

"What ring?" George asks. "Jacob, are you sure you're okay? You look like you might have been out in the elements for too long."

"I need the ring!" I say, desperation overtaking me.

Just then, my fingers grasp something hard and square. Pulling it up out of the snow, I see the black velvet box in my hand. I pry open the frozen box and pull the ring out, inspecting it for damage. It appears to be fine. I hold it up to George, a grin filling my face.

"I'm flattered, really," George says. "But you're not my type."

I stand and brush the snow off my knees.

"I've got to go see Lacey," I say, rushing for my truck.

George puts a hand on my chest, stopping me.

"Hold your horses, Romeo," George says, "What in the hell do you think you're about to go do?"

"I'm going to get my girl. Back off, man."

"No, you're not," George says, shaking his head.

I stumble backward.

"Why the hell not?"

"Correct me if I'm wrong, but you two aren't even a couple right now, are you?"

"That doesn't matter."

"Listen to me," George says. "I'm not saying you shouldn't go back there and get your girl. All I'm saying is save the ring for another day. Plan it out. At the very least, make sure she's still your girl before you pull a ring out."

Huffing, I pace in the snow for a few seconds and mull over George's advice. "No, you're right. I need to do this right."

CHAPTER THIRTY-SEVEN

lacey

I pace back and forth across the living room floor. What just happened? I haven't heard from Jacob since Thanksgiving Day when we had our fight about the camper. I'd called him, hoping for a chance to talk, but he hadn't answered. I heard through the grapevine he'd gone camping, but I didn't know he was back in town and definitely didn't expect it to be him on the other side of the door when I opened it.

Jacob came and went in such a rush I didn't even have time to process. George took off after him, and now I'm anxiously awaiting news. Of course this would all happen while Jalynn is gone. George's mom took her out for a relaxing spa day before the baby comes.

The grumble of an engine outside catches my attention. George must be back. I rush over to the window to see what I can figure out from his expression, only it isn't George. It's Jacob. I hurry over to the mirror hanging by the door to check myself over. My hair is a mess, and I don't have any makeup on. I'm wearing sweats and an oversized T-shirt. I realize there's no hope for improving the situation, and only a small part of me cares. Jacob didn't seem to mind when he stopped by a few minutes ago.

The knock on the door scrambles my thoughts. I take a deep breath to hopefully calm my nerves and pull the door open.

"Hi," Jacob says.

"Hi." I lean against the open door for support, my hand still resting on the doorknob.

"Can we talk?"

"I'd like that," I say. "Where's George?"

"He said he'd give us some time to talk before he comes home," Jacob says and closes the door behind him.

He follows me over to the couch. I take a seat in the center and pull a throw pillow onto my lap, hugging it to my chest for moral support. Jacob sits on the ottoman in front of me, his hands resting on my knees.

"I'm sorry," Jacob says. "I'm so sorry. I screwed up, and I don't know what I'll do if I can't fix this. I love you, Lacey. You're all that I want and the only thing that I need."

"Then why did you leave me?" I fight against the tears I can feel surfacing in my eyes.

"I was a coward. You were talking about leaving me, and I was afraid to get in any deeper with us if I was going to lose you. What I went through with Ashley was bad, but I survived. With you, though, you are so much more to me. If you left me—"

"Then what did it change by you being the one to walk away?"

"In the end? Nothing. I thought it wouldn't hurt as bad if I quit you right then. That's the thing, though, Lace. I was already fully in. I don't know why I thought it would be better to end things like that. It didn't make a difference. I was still alone and still without you. I was . . . I am miserable without you. I thought I could beat the aching in my chest, but I can't. Every breath I take is just one more breath without the hope of holding you again."

"You're not the only one it hurt, Jacob." A tear spills over my lashes and runs down my cheek. I turn my face away from him, trying to hide the emotions brimming over.

"I'm sorry. I never wanted to hurt you—" Jacob reaches for me, but I stand and walk away.

"But you did anyway," I say over my shoulder.

"Lacey, I love you." Jacob is standing behind me now. I spin around to face him, but I keep my distance.

"So you keep saying, but what does that change? You love me, but you still walked away." I wrap my arms around myself, hugging myself tightly.

"You were telling me you were going to leave me."

"I told you I might have to leave, yes, but only if I had to. Only if I were left with no other choice. You did have a choice, and you made that choice so quickly. You put the blame on me, but you were the one who walked away, Jacob. I didn't want you to go."

"Please forgive me. I was stupid. I was being rash. I thought I knew what I was doing, but I was wrong." Jacob steps closer.

"And just like that I'm supposed to trust you again? You say those two little words, and I'm supposed to accept it?"

"No. Your trust I'll earn back. You don't have to give that freely," Jacob says, shaking his head. "I'm asking for forgiveness. I'm asking for another chance. I will work for your trust. I will do anything for the chance to fix this between us."

I turn away again, silently debating which choice to make. Do I follow my head, or do I follow my heart?

"Do you love me, Lace?"

"Of course I do," I say, blinking back more tears.

Jacob steps up behind me, lightly resting his hands on my shoulders. His touch sends shivers down my body.

"Then don't make us both suffer any more than we already have. Please."

I turn back to face him. I can see the pain he feels. It's the same pain I feel without him. Slowly, I raise my hand to his cheek and stroke my thumb across his stubble. He grabs my hand in his, pulls it over to his lips, and kisses my palm.

"Please . . ." Jacob begs, holding my hand in his still.

I let myself go and fall into his arms, pulling him tightly against me.

"I love you. Please don't ever leave me again," I sob into his neck.

"Never, Gypsy. I'll never make that mistake again. I promise."

Jacob runs his fingers through my hair, grabbing a handful, and pulls my mouth to his, consuming me. I wrap my arms tightly around his neck as he lifts me off the ground. My legs instinctively wrap around his waist, and he carries me back over to the couch where he gently lowers me down, never breaking contact. It's only been days, but it's felt like months without him. His touch sets off fireworks across my skin and into my core. His lips are now on my neck and flitting across my collarbone. My fingers grasp at him, needing him closer. Needing more. Needing all of him.

"What made you decide to come back to me?" I ask, my naked body still tangled with Jacob's as we lie on the couch together. I study our intertwined fingers.

"Kate, at the diner, told me about your dinner with Ben. She said you might be going back to North Carolina. That's when it hit me. I went to your place to try to stop you, but your truck and camper were already gone. I thought you'd left. I've been camping in the canyon since."

"How did you figure out I was here?" I ask.

"I didn't know. I unintentionally went back to your place. I just missed you and needed to be close to you somehow. When I was headed back to town, I noticed George was home, so I stopped to ask him if he'd heard from you. I never dreamed you'd be the one to answer the door."

"I never left," I say. "I tried calling you to tell you I sold the camper. George helped me find a buyer. Jalynn insisted I stay here with them until I can get a more permanent place in town."

"What about Ben?"

"He'd figured out where I was and was waiting for me outside after work. I agreed to go to the diner with him to talk. He swore up and down he'd changed and wanted me to go home with him, but I'm never going back to that. I've already told you that. Whether he's changed or not, too many lines were crossed. I could never go back now, and I don't want him. I want you. I'm done running. This is where I want to be. With you."

"And after everything, he just accepted that?" Jacob asks, bewildered.

"Not exactly," I say, turning my head to look up at him lying next to me. "He acted like he was accepting it. He showed up here later that night, and things got a little dicey."

"What do you mean dicey?"

"He'd been drinking, despite the three months sober he'd claimed just hours earlier. He said he wasn't leaving here without me and pulled a knife on me."

"What the fuck?" Jacob props himself up on his elbow to get a better look at me, his expression stern with anger.

"Yeah. It was just his little pocketknife but still. He had hold of my arm and was trying to pull me toward the door. He didn't even notice Jalynn come around the corner and clobber him right in the face with a frying pan." I chuckle, remembering the scene. "That left him stunned. George showed up and handled Ben while Jalynn got the police out here to fetch him. I had to call out of work so I could go give the police my statement. Also, I hired an attorney and filed a restraining order. I've decided to press charges against him. I didn't deserve the things he did to me, and it's time for him to face some consequences. The lawyer thinks I have a good case."

"But you're not hurt? He didn't hurt you?"

"No, I'm fine."

"I wish I'd been here to handle him. That would have made my fucking day," Jacob says. He settles back down on the couch and wraps me in his arms. I raise my chin up and kiss him, holding him close.

"It all turned out okay," I say. "I don't think we'll have to worry about him anymore."

MONDAY MORNING I'm back at work with Maddie. It's starting off to be a pretty quiet morning, but I don't mind. I write up the special on the chalkboard sign and set it out on the sidewalk. After watering the greenhouses, I look over the orders that we have for the week, then go to the back of the shop to help Maddie with some bouquets and arrangements that she's busy preparing for a wedding.

"I'm so glad you and Jacob were able to work things out," Maddie says.

"I am, too. You've built a beautiful family, Maddie. I love getting to witness it."

"I'm personally hoping you get to do more than just witness it," Maddie says with a sideways glance while she works. "I'm hoping sooner than later you will get to become part of it officially."

"I can't pretend that I don't like the thought of that, too." I smile to myself, imagining what it would be like being part of their family and starting one of my own with Jacob. "He really is amazing. And he's going to be such a fantastic dad. Is he always as playful with the kids as he was at Thanksgiving?"

"Oh, yes. Jacob loves children. He has always been good

with kids, even since he was still a kid himself. You should know he has always promised me a houseful of grandchildren in exchange for extra-large servings of desserts."

"He has mentioned kids a time or two," I confess.

I love the thought of raising a family with Jacob.

jacob

I take a seat on the edge of the bed next to Lacey's sleeping body. We've been living in the house for two weeks now. I watch her for a moment as she sleeps. She looks so peaceful. I hate to wake her, but everyone will be showing up soon. I lean over her and begin kissing lightly down her face and over to her ear. I nip gently at her earlobe. She stirs under me, her eyes spring open, and a lazy smile spreads across her face.

"Merry Christmas, my love," I say.

"Mmmm. What time is it?" she asks as her eyes start drifting closed again.

"Time to get up, sleepyhead. Everyone will be here soon. Jesse and Steph are feeding their kids breakfast right now."

Jesse and Steph decided to stay with us for Christmas this year and arrived a few days ago.

"What? Why'd you let me sleep so long?" Lacey asks, shooting up in bed. "I've got to get myself cleaned up and ready."

"You're perfect just as you are, morning breath and all."

Lacey smacks my arm and pushes me out of the way so she can climb out of bed.

Mom and Dad arrive before Lacey emerges from our

bedroom. Christmas dinner is planned for noon, so Mom starts preparing the kitchen for the baking she and Lacey have left to do. Soon, Lacey joins her, giving her a hug and pulling on an apron. Steph hands the baby over to Jesse and joins them in the kitchen. The kids run around the house playing while Jesse, Dad, and I make sure the fresh pastries Lacey ordered from the bakery don't go to waste.

Lacey sure has this place looking nice. A large leather sofa she picked out faces the broad stone fireplace with our Christmas tree decorated in what she calls a classic, rustic style dominating the corner next to it. The mantle is adorned with garland, candles, and stockings. The living room stands open to the kitchen, only separated by the large island with barstools around it. The island is decorated with a forest of miniature silver and gold Christmas trees of varying heights and more garland around their bases.

Joseph and Liz show up with their kids about an hour later, and Mia and her boyfriend show up shortly after. I think Mia said her boyfriend's name is Neil, but I'm too stuck on the fact that he's too old for my sister to remember what the fuck she said. He's got some nerve showing up here in his khaki slacks and button-up shirt and cardigan. He's practically a pair of house slippers away from Mr. Roger's Neighborhood.

My eyes are glued to him as Mia introduces him to Mom and Dad first, and she slowly works through the rest of the family. His hand on her lower back is about three inches away from winning him a knuckle sandwich. They make their way over to where I'm sitting, and Mia introduces us. Neil holds out a hand to shake mine, but I have no interest in making friends with this pervert. I stand but fold my arms across my chest, not saying a word.

Lacey's by my side now. I'm not sure where she came from, but she takes his extended hand and shakes it, then not so gently nudges her elbow into my side. I scowl but do as I know she is telling me to do, and I give his hand a single, firm shake. Possibly more firm than necessary.

It's not until we all sit around the table for lunch that my nerves start to slowly unravel. I have big plans for today that only Jesse knows about. As our Christmas meal begins to wrap up, my hands are so sweaty I have to wipe them on my napkin. Jesse sends me a wink that I think is intended in solidarity.

We move back into the living room for our gift exchange. Jesse's oldest child volunteers to hand out the gifts. One by one, we watch the gifts being opened. My chest is getting tight, and I shift in my seat, feeling restless.

"Are you okay?" Lacey whispers next to my ear.

"Yeah. I think I ate too much," I say.

By the end of the gift exchange the kids are covered in paper and toys, and the adults are lounging around the room in conversation. Jesse catches my eye from across the room, and I give him a nod. Might as well get this over with before I chicken out.

"Jacob, did you get everything you wanted for Christmas?" Jesse asks me over the chatter, catching everyone's attention.

"For the most part, but Lacey did miss one thing on my list," I say.

I look over at Lacey who looks stunned to be called out like that in front of my whole family. She sits up straighter, a blush covering her cheeks.

Shit. I hope I didn't just screw this up.

"What do you mean?" she asks me.

I push myself up off the couch and walk over to the mantle by the Christmas tree. I pull a little box from behind the garland and candles, then go back across the living room to where Lacey is sitting. I drop down onto my knee in front of Lacey, holding her hands in mine.

"Lacey Anne Givens," I say, "I love you more than anything else in this world. You inspire me, and you strengthen me. While I was working on this house, it was always with you in mind. I was building a house that we could raise our family in and grow old in together. When I see the future, I see you. You are the missing piece of the dream come true for me, and I can no longer imagine a life worth living that doesn't include you in it.

"We were both lost and broken when we met, but with each other's help, we put the pieces back together and found something that was so much more beautiful than either of us could have imagined. I've already given you all of me. The only thing I want for Christmas this year is you, your heart and your promise." I open the black velvet box and offer it to Lacey. "Lacey, will you marry me?"

Lacey glances around the room, her face full of shock. Steph shoots her a wink, and Mia is nodding her head like a fool. My mom is wiping the happy tears off her cheeks and smiling at us. Lacey looks back at me, her own eyes watery.

"Yes. Of course, I will. Yes! I love you, too." She leans into me, hugging me tightly, and relief spills through my body. "Now, where's my ring?" Lacey laughs and fumbles to take the ring from the box and slide it on her finger.

I stand and take Lacey into my arms, kissing her deeply, and I know she's the happily-ever-after I've always been looking for.

LACEY

Six Years Later

The earth crunches below our feet as Jacob pulls me to him. My swollen belly has reached the point that it's beginning to get in the way when we embrace. I wrap my arms around his neck and stretch up to press a soft kiss against his lips while we shuffle back and forth to the slow beat of the music filling the night air around us from the speakers of Jacob's pickup truck. The low beams of his headlights provide the only illumination in that dark empty field beyond the full moon overhead. His hands rest on my hips, and even after all these years, his touch still spreads a tingling warmth through my body.

"This is the perfect night out," I say and rest my cheek against his firm chest. "I needed this."

"I'm sorry the boys have been such a handful," Jacob says and kisses the top of my head.

Our son Oliver is five years old. That boy can find trouble in an empty five-gallon bucket. His four-year-old brother, Noah, is nearly as fluent in troublemaking and just as willing to get his hands dirty.

"Your mom says they're like you and your brothers reincarnated," I say, earning a chuckle from Jacob.

"We might've given our parents a run for their money, too."

Jacob leans down, pressing his lips to mine. His warmth spreads into me as he deepens his kiss and our dancing stills. My hands climb up into his hair, pulling him closer to me.

My phone buzzes loudly, vibrating on the metal tailgate of the truck and reminding us of the outside world. Jacob releases me, and I go for my phone to see if it's a call that needs to be answered or if it can be put off till after our date. When I see our teenage babysitter's name on the screen, I know it's urgent.

"Hey, Emma, is everything okay?" I ask after putting the phone on speaker so Jacob can hear, too.

"Sorry to bother you"—Emma's voice is quivering, and I can tell she's on the verge of tears—"but I've found myself in a predicament."

"What's wrong? Is everyone okay?" I ask.

"I think so. We were looking for Noah's stuffy, and Oliver said it was left down in the basement from earlier today. I went down to look for it, and . . . well . . . I think the boys locked the door behind me." A quick sob escapes from Emma, barely more than a hiccup. I sigh and look up at Jacob who is clearly amused by our boys' mischievousness.

"We'll be right there, Emma," I say and hang up the phone.

We don't waste any time gathering our things and rushing home to rescue the babysitter. Jacob catches me chewing my bottom lip and rests a reassuring hand on my thigh. He presses harder on the accelerator, and I know he's speeding up for my benefit.

"The boys are fine," he says.

"They're unsupervised, Jacob. Who knows what could happen."

Jacob looks over at me. His eyebrow is cocked, and he wears a smirk on his lips.

"We both know that supervision never kept them from

getting into a scrape. They're good kids. They're not going to be into anything too treacherous."

"I'd rather not test your theory."

I don't wait for the truck to come to a complete stop in our driveway. Sliding out of the cab, I rush to the front door. Despite my head start, Jacob is on my heels in no time. The tension riding on my shoulders begins to dissipate when we walk through the door and instantly hear happy giggles coming from the kitchen.

The boys are sitting on the island counter in their superhero undies, covered from head to toe in a brown sauce, which I assume is chocolate syrup from the smooshed bottle lying on its side next to them. Noah licks the sauce off the palm of his hand, then scoops out a handful of the pie meant for tomorrow's Thanksgiving feast and shoves it into his mouth, while his other hand holds a spoon. Oliver throws his head back and laughs at his brother.

"Use your spoon, Noah," he says. "Here. Like this."

Oliver puts his dirty hand over Noah's and leads the spoon to the pie, helping Noah scoop up another big bite onto the spoon before bringing it to his own mouth.

"Hey, that's my spoon!" Noah protests.

"Okay, boys. Time for a bath," Jacob interrupts them and captures one under each of his arms.

He bumps the fridge door closed as he heads for the stairs. The boys giggle and kick their legs behind them, enjoying the ride. Oliver stretches his arms forward and holds his legs straight behind them.

"Look, Momma, I'm Superman!" Oliver yells back to me.

I can't help but smile back at my little troublemaker. I watch them disappear up the stairs, overcome by the love I feel for my wild boys. A tapping pulls me back, and I remember I still need to rescue Emma from the basement.

"I'm coming, Emma!" I call out and head to the basement door.

When I open the door, Emma rises from the top step with a tear-stained face. She's no longer crying, but she's still sniffling and trembling, her arms wrapped tightly around herself.

"I'm so sorry," Emma says, either unable or unwilling to make eye contact with me. The mess on the kitchen island catches her attention, and I get a front row view of the terror that creeps over her face. "I'll stay and clean up the mess. I'm so sorry," she says again as more tears begin to well up in her eyes.

"No, that's not necessary, Emma," I say.

"I'm sorry I ruined your evening. I never dreamed—"

"Emma, honey, it's okay. It's not your fault. I'm not upset with you."

"You're not mad?"

"No, I'm not mad. I know better than anyone what a handful they can be. I'm sorry they locked you in the basement. That had to be terrifying for you." I reach out and gently squeeze her arm.

"I'm okay. I suppose there are worse basements to be locked in," Emma says with a sniffle.

I give her a smile and pull cash out of my pocket.

"Here." I hand the wad of cash over to her. "There's extra there for your trouble. I hope you'll still consider babysitting for us again in the future."

"I'll think about it," Emma answers. "I'm going to head out now."

"Okay, be careful," I say.

Once Emma is out the door, I wipe up the mess in the kitchen and get everything put away. Jalynn and George will get a kick out of this story. They have two boys and a baby girl. Our boys are the best of friends, and they adore Jalynn's little girl. She has quite the crew watching out for her.

I head up the stairs to check on the boys. Jacob already has them bathed and dressed in their jammies, the "missing" stuffy found and wrapped tightly in Noah's arms. I lean against the doorframe of Noah's bedroom and rub at the spot on my stomach our newest little one has taken to kicking at this evening. Jacob is lying on the bed, flanked by Noah and Oliver, and is reading their favorite bedtime story.

"Momma, come here," Noah says, noticing me in the doorway.

He reaches out and waves me to them with the fingers on his precious little hand. I push off the doorframe and walk over to him. I sit on the floor next to where he's lying on the bed and place a kiss on his soft little hand and another kiss to his round cheek.

It doesn't take long for both of our boys to fall asleep. Jacob climbs off the bed, careful not to wake them. He scoops Oliver into his arms and carries him down the hall to his own bedroom while I get Noah securely tucked into his bed.

I make it back downstairs before Jacob and take a seat on the couch to watch the crackling fire burn. Within minutes, Jacob walks into the room. With one look at his roguish grin, I know what he's up to.

Without a word, Jacob rests one knee on the couch next to me and presses his lips to mine. He leans further into me, pushing my back down onto the couch, and bites at my lip, which sends tingles directly to my core. He pulls back briefly, staring down at me with his dark eyes, and I'm reminded that this is the type of love I've spent my life looking for.

acknowledgments

Just as some kids dream about being a rock star or an astronaut when they grow up, I dreamed of becoming an author. As a kid, I thought it just might happen. I shared stories with friends and surprised teachers with manuscripts. Then I met a lovely friend named Reality. Reality told me I wasn't good enough or special enough. My chances were about as close as you can get on the sliding scale to zero. The dream drifted away, only to be remembered when friends announced their own publication, and I remembered I wasn't as special as them.

It took a traumatic experience and a journey of healing to get me writing again. I decided I didn't like what Reality had to say, and for the first time in a long time, I didn't care if I was special enough. I was going to do it anyway.

Thank you to my readers for choosing to spend your time getting to know these characters that I have fallen in love with. Thank you for taking a part in me realizing my dream.

Thank you to my husband, who never questions my ridiculous ideas and who put up with so many take-out dinners after I shirked my responsibilities to write. You support me no matter what, and you are my biggest cheerleader. I don't know what I did to deserve you.

Thank you to my kids, for sharing me with my computer when you are used to having me to yourselves. I hope you always believe in yourselves, chase after your dreams, and never forget how capable you are.

To the kind soul who has read so many of my struggling

sentences along the way, has lifted my spirits when others forgot to include the constructive aspect of their criticism, and doesn't judge me for my "mom brain." I couldn't have done it without you, Jana!

My editor, Sarah Fraps, deserves a huge thank-you. You've patiently walked me through the process with the baby steps I needed to make it through my debut novel. Your kindness and patience are exactly what I needed.

Even though you aren't here to witness it, a special thank you to my grandpa. You never doubted me. You led by your quiet example and always encouraged me along whichever path I chose. The time spent on your lap, reading poetry together, holds a special place in my heart.

To my besties, cheering me on in the background, you've put up with my randomness for 20+ years and never throw down on my ideas, even when—let's face it—you probably should have . . . Thank you for being my people.

Born in the summer of 1988, Amora was one of many generations of her family born and raised among the rich history of the Appalachian Mountains. Growing up on two hundred acres of farmland, shoes and propriety were optional, and exploration and imagination were plentiful.

After several years of unschooling on the family farm, Amora and her siblings graced the local public school system with their presence. It was during her stint at the local middle school that she found her first audience. Notebook after spiral-bound notebook, filled with her smudged graphite scrawl, was passed around her friend group.

In high school, Amora found herself obsessed with reading classics such as *Pride and Prejudice* by Jane Austin, *Rebecca* by Daphne du Maurier, *The Scarlet Pimpernel* by Baroness Orczy, and the *Anne of Green Gables* series by Lucy Maud Montgomery.

Amora's college years led her westward to the Rocky Mountains and beyond. She spent several years exploring the new landscapes of the West. She often found herself seeking inspiration from the deserts, mountains, and canyons for her writing. Amora's free time was spent scouting out caves, hiking through the local canyons, and rotating between genres of romance, mystery, and thrillers.

After many memories were made, Amora returned home to the Appalachians, where she met the man brave enough to take on her gypsy soul and who would months later become her husband. With over a decade of marriage and eight kids, they're still living their happily-ever-after.

Aside from creating bedtime stories, Amora's need to write was finally rekindled in the fall of 2019 when *Falling for Gypsy* poured from her fingertips, only to be tucked away and forgotten until four years later when it was rediscovered and rewritten beyond recognition to become her debut novel.

When Amora isn't writing, she's homeschooling her kids, hauling said kids to their extracurriculars, reading a good book, gardening, or coming up with yet another insane idea for her husband to roll his eyes at and lovingly support her in it anyway.

Connect with Amora through her website or on social media:

www.amorablake.com

Instagram

Facebook

TikTok